RAVE REVIEWS FOR KATHLEEN MORGAN'S ROMANCES:

"Kathleen Morgan's *Demon Prince* will delight and captivate medieval fans everywhere...an absolute joy to read!"

—*The Medieval Chronicle*

"Every futuristic romance reader should have Kathleen Morgan's books on their shelves."

—*Romantic Times*

"*Firestar* is another winner from a very talented, innovative writer."

—*Affaire de Coeur*

"Filled with exciting adventures and memorable characters, *Crystal Fire* is a not to be missed read!"

—*Romantic Times*

Demon Prince
KATHLEEN MORGAN

LOVE SPELL ◆ **NEW YORK CITY**

LOVE SPELL®

April 1994

Published by

Dorchester Publishing Co., Inc.
276 Fifth Avenue
New York, NY 10001

The name "Love Spell" and its logo are trademarks of Dorchester
Publishing Co., Inc.

Printed in the United States of America.

Prologue

He stood there, swathed in shadow, the workings of his magic shielding him from human eyes. His amber gaze swept the room, noting the crackling hearth fire, its spark-scattered light throwing the chamber's occupants alternately into brightness then flickering shade.

A lady-in-waiting bustled past. The flurry of her kirtle ruffled the hem of his long, black robe. Wood smoke mingled with the delicate scent of perfume, wafting to his nostrils on the lingering eddy of the woman's passing.

For a fleeting instant he inhaled deeply of the hypnotic, sense-stirring fragrance, savoring it. Then, with a refocusing of power, he fixed his regard on the auburn-haired woman sitting before the mirror, another of her ladies brushing out her long, flowing tresses. Hungrily he watched as the brush slid through the silken, shimmering mass. The air crackled about her head until it glowed like some unearthly nimbus.

Feminine laughter floated through the room. The low, seductive sounds quickened the fires of his passion. His fists clenched as he fought for control, the moisture of long-repressed desire glistening on his brow.

"Tonight, my fair Eislin," the wizard whispered hoarsely, his voice hidden beneath the cloak of his illusions. "Tonight I will have you though you belong to another. You are mine, have always been. The child we conceive will at last seal that union, unholy though it must now be."

The child.

His lips lifted in a sneer. His thoughts traveled through the dark mists of time. "Yes, he, too, is part of the bargain. Though I'll never be father to him, I'll twist his life as well to suit my needs. In the end, his aid will gain me the ultimate revenge—total power.

"Aye, sweet Eislin," the wizard murmured, his features softening. "This night will gain me much. Yet what will it grant you, my dearest love, save endless sorrow? Though our child will be your firstborn and heir to the crown of Anacreon, the people will never accept the spawn of our coupling."

As if reminded of a bitter memory, he hardened his face once more. "Romantic little fool," he spat. "If only your choice had been for me, rather than that preening second son of the House Laena. If only . . ."

The wizard's voice faded, dispersed on the

fluttering breeze that stirred the heavy window hangings. Overbright eyes followed the queen as her ladies led her toward the bed. As she walked, her white linen dressing gown, trimmed lavishly with lace, floated about her, swirling to outline, then hide the soft curves of her body.

He swallowed a savage curse. To distract himself, he directed his attention to maintaining the force of his illusion.

The single bedside candle was snuffed. The furs were pulled up to cover her. Then, one by one, the queen's ladies slipped away.

Silence settled over the room. He waited, savoring the moment to come. The anticipation rose like some spiraling flame.

At last the wizard drew the vial from the folds of his robe and held it to the firelight. He swirled its crimson contents. It had cost him dearly, this gift of the Demon. This gift, bought by a soul-wrenching betrayal. This gift that he'd repay for the rest of his existence—on this plane and beyond.

Yet necessary it was, this last chance to procure Eislin's ardent compliance, to be the first to possess her as it had always been meant to be. To her it would all seem a dream, but for him it was poignant, bittersweet reality.

Aye, he smiled to himself, his firm, sensual mouth twisting in a wry grimace as hot desire again flooded him. To assume the form of her husband-to-be was indeed the only way. On the morrow she would be wed and it would be too late.

He uncorked the vial and raised it to his lips,

then lowered it, hesitation lancing through him. Once begun there was no turning back. The enormity of the act—the fear, the uncertainty—struck him with the force of a blow.

The wizard cringed. Doubts assailed him, wailing at the portals of his soul like the mournful wind through winter-stripped trees.

It shouldn't have happened like this. He was equal in lineage, in bearing, and more than equal in love, for Eislin's hand. Yet still she had chosen another.

Had his obsession with magic turned her from him? If he'd thought for a moment, if he'd realized in time . . .

But it no longer mattered. She'd made her choice. Now, the magic was all he had.

Aye, the wizard reminded himself grimly. At least he still had his magic. With that thought he lifted the vial to his lips—and swallowed the heart-searing liquid.

Chapter One

Sun-fire crowned the oaks and beeches as evening enveloped the land. In the distance a falcon soared over the pastoral view, swooping low across a lazily undulating valley, past a quiet river glinting like molten gold, before gliding on across heavy woods.

Steeped in lavender-velvet silence, the bird floated on a gentle breeze, sole observer to the summer-sleepy land—and a muscled, black-clad man on a powerful war-horse. Through the shadowed forest the pair moved, the shimmering light that pierced the foliage dappling their taut, battle-hardened forms.

The falcon dipped low. Its shrill cry rent the heavy silence. Then, in a blur of rapid wing beats, the bird whirled about and headed toward the distant mountains.

Drawn by the falcon's flight, the warrior

reined in his mount. His massive war-horse reared to paw the air, impatient at the delay.

Enough of this melancholy excursion! the steed mentally grumbled. *'Tis long past suppertime. I'm starving!*

The warrior grinned. "Soon, Lucifer, soon. I'm as tired and hungry as you. But have a care. We've been away a long while, and this land has never been friendly to us."

His muscled thighs tightened about the animal's sides, expertly urging the horse back to the ground. His black-gauntleted hands signaled the high-strung animal forward, as his one eye not covered by a black leather patch swept the terrain with practiced vigilance.

They reached the forest's edge. The man's smile faded and his tautly drawn profile twisted into a bitter grimace. There, perched on the jagged edge of the mountain, was the fortress.

Anacreon . . . Home . . . he thought, his heart as hard and ice-rimed as his features. For long minutes he stared at the scene, awash in a sea of turbulent memories.

Thin spirals of smoke from the village a few leagues from the castle drew his gaze. The warrior's expression darkened. It had been in that nearby wooded glen that, as a callow youth of 15, he had fought Rangor—and killed him.

Even now, after all these years, he wondered if the deed was truly the result of two hot-headed youths who had lost control and turned to battle with tragic results or, the Mother forbid, one of evil intent. Whatever the motive, he realized grimly, 15 years of self-imposed exile had done little to heal the pain of that act. His vow notwithstanding, it was better he left this place as soon as possible.

A faint, anguished cry drifted to him on the breeze. Instantly alert, the warrior reined his charger in the direction of the sound. Had it been his imagination, mayhap the falcon's call? No, there it was again, accompanied now by the cracking and splintering of shrubbery. Someone was fleeing and, by the sound of it, closely pursued.

He exhaled an exasperated breath. "Come on, old friend." The warrior paused to readjust the long sword slung across his back, then nudged his horse forward. "I know I promised you supper and my own throat's parched for a cool swallow of ale, but there's someone ahead who may need our help. A brief detour, no more, then back toward home."

Lucifer snorted, tossing his thick, ebony head in disgust at human foibles. Yet, for a change, he offered no comment. Springing forward, his powerful body quickly settled into a bounding gallop.

The forest loomed again to swallow them. They crashed through the woods. Unerringly, the warrior drove his steed forward, drawing near the frantic sounds of struggle.

The woods thinned. He urged his horse to a faster pace. The cries, now joined by the clang of steel against steel, intensified. With a final surge, they cleared the last of the trees.

There, just below in a small clearing, a slender lad struggled to hold off three burly men with the aid of only a short broadsword. Finally, a stave wielded by one of his attackers caught the boy unawares.

13

With a choking cry he tumbled to the ground. Before he could regain his feet his opponents were upon him. His hands were tied. A rag was bound roughly over his eyes.

Lucifer leaped out in response to his rider's signal. Down the hill they came yet, for what seemed an eternity, the ruffians failed to notice their approach. As the pair thundered ever closer, the three attackers jerked their victim to his feet and began tearing at his tunic. With a bloodcurdling war cry the warrior reached behind to draw his sword—a terrible sound that mingled, at that instant, with a feminine scream.

The assailants turned as one. A terrifying black horse, nostrils flaring red, bore down upon them. Astride him was a dark-visaged rider, his cloak billowing around him like the huge, black wings of some night predator. With a strangled cry the outlaws fled, the last man flinging his bound, bare-breasted prisoner to the ground.

The warrior reined in Lucifer just short of the girl. Silently, he watched her struggle awkwardly to her feet.

Her hair had fallen loose from her brown leather cap, cascading in golden disarray around her shoulders and down her back. Though the filthy rag about her eyes covered half her face, it couldn't hide the promise of great beauty in the delicate curve of her cheek, the generously parted, rosy lips, the smooth complexion with its pale gold undertones. She held herself with a proud grace, defiant though blindfolded, hands tied and bosom exposed through her torn, threadbare tunic.

The wispy haze of hair falling across her chest did little to camouflage the ivory, pink-tipped breasts jutting from the homespun fabric. A peasant lass, the man surmised, but as fair as any fine lady. His gaze caressed the lovely flesh exposed so freely to him. A warm heat spread through his body.

It would be so easy to finish what the others had begun—the girl bound, helpless and unseeing as she was. No one would ever know it had been him. And it had been such a long, long time. . . .

"Who's there?" the girl asked, unable to bear the silence a moment longer.

Though her rescuer had yet to speak she knew he was near, watching . . . waiting. When no answer was forthcoming she wet her lips in apprehension and tried again.

"P-please, won't you free me? My . . . my brothers are sure to be searching for me even now."

At her words, spoken in a tremulous yet surprisingly husky voice, the man wrenched himself from his lusty thoughts. Something inside him twisted at her fear and uncertainty, her sweet entreaty. He banished further contemplation of ravishment as unworthy.

With a self-mocking shake of his head the warrior slid from his horse. He pulled off his gauntlets, then paused to shove them into his belt before bending toward his right boot. As he rose, he clenched a small, lethal-looking dagger in his hand.

"Turn around."

His deep, resonant voice filled her with a curious comfort. She hesitated but an instant, then did as he asked. A warm, heavily callused hand grasped both of hers. Cold metal slid between the thongs and her skin. A second later, she was free.

"My thanks," the girl murmured as she turned to face him. With trembling hands, she loosened the blindfold. "I am eternally in your . . ."

Her voice faded as her gaze met his. The patch over his left eye that hid the fearsome weapon that could smite a person dead with just a glance, the black garb, the eerie tales about the man none dared forget struck her with the force of a blow. Her throat tightened. The blood drained from her face.

In the evening shadows his form assumed the appearance of some evil, otherworldly being. A warm, nauseating dizziness washed over her. Sparkling lights danced before eyes already beginning to dim. Her knees buckled.

Blackness yawned to engulf her. The girl fought against it—and the realization of the full extent of her misfortune. It was too late, however. She fainted.

Something cool and wet trickled down the side of Breanne's face, followed closely by a rough-textured yet surprisingly gentle touch. She moaned softly and raised her fingers to the sensation's source. The feel of a hard, masculine hand jerked her back to full consciousness. Heavy-lashed lids fluttered open in surprise.

There, bending over her in the dimming light, was the dark outline of a powerfully built man.

Breanne forced her eyes to focus more clearly on his face. It hadn't been a nightmare. It was indeed he, the Prince of the Evil Eye.

A tremor ran through her as all the old superstitions flashed across her mind. What would he do to her, alone, with night drawing on? How would she escape?

The man felt her shudder. Imagining it the shock of her recent ordeal, he laid down the water flask and unclasped his cloak. Lifting the girl, he wrapped the heavy fabric around her.

"Are you all right, lass?"

She nodded. "A-aye, m'lord."

Breanne forced herself to answer. There was no other choice. She had to face him. No matter what he might be, no matter what his purported powers, there was no one else who could save her.

The slightest glimmer of a frown marred his brow. "Then why so anxious? The danger is past." He paused, and the light of realization dawned in his eyes. " 'Tis me, isn't it? That's why you swooned. You're afraid of me."

She struggled to sit, clutching his cloak to her. Had she angered him? Panic rippled through her. "Nay! Nay, m'lord. 'Twasn't you. I swear!"

The warrior rose, drawing Breanne to her feet. "Well, no matter. I'll not harm you."

"A-aye, m'lord."

Though still weak from her waning terror, she made herself look up at him. Oddly, he didn't appear quite so formidable . . . so evil anymore. Deep lines of fatigue etched his face, the dark shadow of a beard further evidence of several days' hard travel with little rest. And the unpatched eye staring back at her from under thick, black brows appeared almost gentle, its amber depths meltingly warm, beckoning. . . .

A spell! He was casting a spell! Her heart pounding in her breast, Breanne jerked her fascinated gaze away. Holy Mother, she must escape—but how? As she glanced wildly about her, a hand firmly clasped her arm. Startled, her breath caught in her throat, Breanne turned back.

". . . your name, lass," he repeated, as if aware her attention hadn't been with him. "What's your name?"

"My . . . my name?"

Her thoughts raced. Was that what he needed to complete his ensorcelment—her name? It wasn't what she'd heard to be the usual requirements for a spell, but then he was said to possess powers beyond that of most mages. Nay, she dared not give him her name. Yet wouldn't he know if she lied?

A shaky breath escaped her. "Bree, m'lord," she replied, using her childhood nickname. "I am called Bree."

"Bree, is it?" He arched a dark brow. "Well then, Bree, where is your village? It grows late. I wish to see you safely home."

"Oh, 'tisn't necessary, m'lord. My people live but a few leagues from here, in the wooded dell near the castle of the queen and her—" A sheepish smile flitted across her face. "But you know whose castle 'tis, don't you, m'lord?"

He shot her a black look. "Aye, lass. Every day of my life, whether I care to or not, I remember.

But enough of that. 'Tis time we were on our way."

At her expression of protest, he raised a silencing hand. "I've no desire to waste time rescuing you again. I *will* see you home."

Her sapphire blue eyes clouded in dismay, but Breanne ceased to argue. There was no point. He could do with her whatever he wished—and they both knew it. Ah, if only she'd her sword, but it was lost to her now, lying somewhere in the tall grass, blanketed by the deepening twilight.

She sighed. "As you wish, m'lord."

He grasped her about the waist and lifted her, cloak and all, to sit atop his horse. The beast sidestepped nervously and snorted, as if displeased with his unfamiliar burden. A strong hand quickly grabbed the reins.

"Easy, Lucifer, easy bcy," his master crooned. " 'Tis but a lass. She won't harm you."

Lucifer.

The name sent a chill rippling down Breanne's spine. Wasn't it bad enough to be in the clutches of this dreaded prince, without now sitting atop an animal with such a title? If indeed he were truly an animal!

She'd heard tales, whispered about the communal fire pit at night, of demons who assumed beastlike forms. What if he were such? Together, where might they carry her off to?

The agile movement of Lucifer's master, swinging up behind her, abruptly changed the direction of Breanne's horrified musings. She froze as his arms snaked about her, moving her to sit before him as he settled more comfortably in place.

Her eyes glanced off his face with a rapid, frightened flicker. He wasn't even looking at her. His stern gaze was riveted far ahead toward the mountains.

Lucifer sprang into a smooth, rocking canter. The sudden movement threw Breanne backward into the prince. As her shoulder struck his chest she heard the faint clink of chain mail beneath his high-collared tunic.

So, she thought with no small amount of relief, the tales of his invulnerability were untrue, as were the legends that he was little more than a sinister phantom. That he was mortal man, as much of flesh and blood as she, was brought home quite forcefully as the movement of the horse repeatedly threw their bodies together.

Breanne swallowed hard. Fear warred with a growing anger at his high-handed manner. Yet, at the same time, there was a strange security in the hard-muscled clasp of his arms.

Confusion swelled within. But how could that be? He was the devil's own. Even now her soul hung on the verge of damnation. Was it but a spell he wove to soothe her fears and make her more pliable for his evil purposes?

She dared a covert glance. He was a striking man, to be sure, his hair thick, black and, if not for his tight warrior's topknot, hinting at a carefree unruliness. The stark effect, however, only accentuated the strong, square lines of his jaw, the aquiline nose and firm, sensual mouth.

A powerful, compelling face, Breanne decided. And one that did little to assuage her fears. If anything, she suspected her strange attraction was yet another spell he worked upon her.

"And you, lass. Why were you so far afield, dressed in the garb of a lad and carrying a short sword?" The object of her contemplation glanced down at her, his countenance guarded, unsmiling. "Strange behavior for one of peaceful Anacreon."

Breanne shot him a quizzical look, relieved at the interruption of her unsettling thoughts. "Peaceful Anacreon? Surely you jest, m'lord! I dress in this manner for my protection whenever it falls my task to tend the village cattle. And as to why I was so far from the dell, I was chasing a renegade cow. I'd almost caught her when those cursed outlaws fell upon me."

"You say Anacreon is no longer peaceful?" her dark companion prodded. "Pray, what's amiss in the land?"

" 'Tisn't my place to speak of such things, m'lord." Nervously, Breanne tore her gaze from his intently searching one. "Better you query your father or your brother, Prince Dragan."

He turned her face back to his. The look in his eye flashed cold and brilliant. "But, sweet lass, *'tis* your place if I ask it. Are you so heartless you'd refuse the request of a man so long separated from his beloved land? 'Tis a poor recompense for your rescue."

"I meant no offense, m'lord," Breanne hastened to interject. "But my words, though spoken in truth, might cause you pain, even anger."

"And you fear the outcome of my wrath?"

"A-aye, m'lord."

The reluctant admission was dragged from the depths of her being. She struggled to free herself from the intensity of his gaze, fearing that very anger in her blunt if truthful answer to his question. Yet still he held her, even as his hand fell from her face, impaling Breanne in the bejeweled depths of his single, unpatched eye.

She found herself falling, plummeting into a whirling maelstrom of flashing, mesmerizing lights. A cry rose to her lips. Holy Mother, she was lost, her soul—

With a low oath, he tore his gaze away. "I-I . . . Forgive me. I didn't mean to . . ." Exasperation clouded his features. "By the Mother, I *must* learn to control this cursed power!"

The prince swung to face her, lines of remorse and frustration deepening the furrowed fatigue in his striking countenance. He expelled a weary breath. "Tell me what I ask, lass. You'll suffer no harm. I wish only to know what has become of my home and family, for good or bad. You spare me no pain in the omission."

Breanne smiled hesitantly. " 'Twill be as you ask, m'lord—for good or bad. Yet where to begin, for so much has transpired, the evil, the destruction, the chaos, since you left those many years ago. I was but a young child myself when it all began, barely three and still on my mother's knee, when the House of Laena fell. When the necromancer Morloch began his rise to power—"

The black war-horse slid to a halt.

"Uncle Arlen is dead?"

"The Lord Arlen of the House Laena? Aye, m'lord."

Breanne forced herself to return his gaze, though the effort set her heart hammering beneath her breast. Holy Mother, but the hard brilliance of that single eye was enough to chill the bravest of souls! What must the infamous other eye, the one he kept so carefully covered, be capable of?

"Well, lass, speak!" Impatience frosted his voice. "My father is prince consort, co-ruler with the queen. Are you telling me he lacked the power to aid his brother?"

"Can any man possess sufficient power where a necromancer is concerned?" She glanced at him apprehensively. She trod on shaky ground in discussing those of his kind. His countenance, however, remained impassive.

Breanne forced herself to continue. "For reasons uncertain, though 'tis whispered Morloch destroyed Laena out of revenge, your uncle and his family are no more."

"The entire family? My young cousins who I played with as a boy? How?" The request was husky and strained. "How did they die?"

For a fleeting moment Breanne was filled with an inexplicable urge to offer comfort. Stern and foreboding as his presence was, unsmiling, harsh when the occasion arose, in that instant her woman's insight slipped past his shield. She saw, for the first time, the human heart beating there, scarred and battle-torn though it was.

The realization startled her. How could it be? He bore the mark of the Evil Eye and was surely damned. Yet still she felt compassion and a strange unity with him.

Breanne inhaled a deep breath. "No one knows for certain what happened, m'lord. The duke was discovered clawed to death, the duchess and all but one of their children strangled. The other was never found. 'Twas said Morloch summoned a phantom to destroy the family—they are capable of such acts, you know, and the murders did occur at night when they prowl. No one realized what had happened until the fire awoke the servants, but by then 'twas too late."

"So, my uncle and his family are dead," he said, his tone flat, emotionless, "and you say 'twas only the beginning. Pray, what other happy news have you?"

Breanne paled but somehow found the strength to go on. "'Tis said the curse of your blood has tainted even the innocent. Your mother the queen took to bed and hasn't risen from it since. The prince consort has never been the same, either. Over the years he has abdicated more and more of his power to your brother."

She shot him an agonized glance. There was no change, no flicker of feeling in his hardened features.

"Go on."

Breanne swallowed hard. "Forgive me, m'lord, but 'tis said Prince Dragan isn't fit to rule. He squanders his time and the royal monies on feasts, hunts, and exotic women.

The royal army has deteriorated to little more than the castle guard, with robbers and outlaws raiding the land unpunished. And . . . and all the while the power of Morloch grows."

A shudder tore through her but she forced herself to continue, suddenly determined he should hear the full tale, even if his subsequent wrath cost her life. "Women bear deformed children," Breanne whispered. "Demons and other unnatural beings roam the forests. Anyone out after hours risks a gruesome fate. A strange sense of impending doom, of terrible evil, lies heavy on the land. We are powerless, m'lord, frustrated, frightened, but helpless all the same. . . ."

Silence settled as Breanne's emotion-laden tale faded to its end. She began to tremble as the last of the past years' pent-up terrors escaped to find an eerie reality in the speaking. As she struggled to blink back the tears, a black-clad arm pulled her to him and a gauntleted hand drew her head to his chest.

"A terrible fate indeed, lass," a low, soothing voice rumbled in her ear. "And one I regret forcing from you."

As he waited for her to calm, the prince surveyed the tendrils of darkness spreading across the valley, inching inexorably toward the mountain fortress. Already its stone windows glowed brightly as the castle set about its evening preparations. Somewhere, among the warm yellow slits, was the queen's bedchamber. At the memory of Breanne's words about his mother, his grim mouth twitched in pain.

25

Then, remembering himself, he straightened.
"Let us speak no more of such things," he said gruffly, the now familiar coolness slipping back into his voice. " 'Tis time you were home, safe and snug in your cottage."

He signaled Lucifer forward and the steed's rocking gait soon carried them to the river. After the high emotions of a few moments ago, Breanne was grateful for the silence while her dark companion concentrated on fording the treacherous current. As the horse carefully stepped out into the swirling water, she found herself pulled even more closely to the prince. Once again, her head came to lie upon the wide expanse of his chest. Through his tunic and mail, battle-honed muscles moved with rippling precision as he guided Lucifer across the river.

Muscles that could crush me with but the smallest of efforts, Breanne thought in wonderment. *Yet he wouldn't, just as he won't ensorcel me nor steal my soul. I know this now, though from whence the surety rises is beyond my comprehension. But certain I am, just as I now know the tales about him are false, that his fierceness is but the mask he lives behind . . . to keep others from him.*

The steed's strokes lengthened, once more becoming surefooted as they reached the other side and he gained footing on the rocky bottom again. They climbed the river's bank. A few moments later the horse was bounding across the land, the twinkling lights of Bree's village rapidly growing closer in the approaching darkness.

A short while longer and I must part from him.

The realization filled Breanne with an inexplicable pang. She knew she would never see him again. And why, she asked herself, should it matter? But a time ago he seemed some fearful being. Though her perceptions of him might have changed, what difference did it really make?

Breanne brushed the question aside, exasperated at herself. Of course she would never see him again. He was a royal prince. She was naught but a peasant maid. There was no reason for their paths ever to cross again.

Yet even as Breanne struggled with her swirling emotions the dark prince battled with his. The feel of her soft, slender body pressed close insinuated itself into the very core of his being. Once more a dizzying desire raced through his veins, the hot blood filling his groin. He gritted his teeth to stave off his burgeoning excitement. The futile attempt only increased his frustration.

If 'tis a woman you want, a few gold coins can easily procure one. Lucifer's casual observation intruded into his master's feverish thoughts. *You humans are too quick to complicate a simple physical need satisfied elsewhere. Don't let this female divert you. Lust is no reason to tarry in an unfriendly land.*

A wry grin twisted the prince's mouth. *Always the pragmatist, aren't you, Lucifer?* He inwardly laughed. *But no matter. Once again you speak true.* With a nudge, he signaled the horse to a faster pace.

The sun had shuttered itself behind the jagged peaks by the time they arrived in the village center. The inhabitants had noted their approach. A crowd quickly gathered.

Torches, held high by several of the peasants, cast an eerie red-gold light on the faces of Breanne and her one-eyed companion. Gradually, as the villagers recognized the black-garbed rider, a gasp of horror spread among them. A murmur of frightened voices rose. Hands flicked in warding signs.

"The Holy Ones forgive us, 'tis the Demon Prince!" "Holy Mother, we are doomed. He will kill us all!" "Poor Bree. See, already he has stolen her soul. . . ."

As they spoke among themselves the crowd edged away, until a wide expanse separated horse and riders from those on foot. The prince eyed them impassively, then swung down from Lucifer. Turning his back to the others, he lifted his arms to Breanne.

"Come, lass. 'Tis best I'm gone before your people swoon in fear."

She came to him without the slightest hesitation. "A moment, m'lord," Breanne pleaded as she handed him back his cloak. "Let me but explain, and all will be well."

"Nay, lass." He released her and stepped away. " 'Twould take more than the likes of you to change what is, and what will always be. It matters not what these people think of me. I'm content you're safe."

He vaulted back into the saddle. For a lingering instant the prince stared down at her. In the flickering firelight Bree's long hair cast a shining halo about her. His throat tightened in an uncharacteristic surge of longing.

She lightly touched his leg. "If ever I can repay—"

"And how is that possible?" he interrupted her, his voice gruff, brusque, angry at feelings he'd thought long buried. "You're a mere slip of a girl. Don't trouble yourself over some imagined obligation you can never hope to meet. 'Tis already forgotten."

"Then 'tis farewell, m'lord?" Her sapphire blue eyes gazed up at him with a misty compassion.

A jaw muscle twitched at the pity he read there instead. "Aye. Farewell."

With an abrupt tug he wheeled his black charger around. The pair galloped off into the night, toward the ragged outcropping where the fortress lay. As he rode along, the prince swept further thought of the lovely peasant girl from his mind, concentrating all his efforts on the ordeal to come—his arrival at the castle. Even in the deepening shadows he could make out that the drawbridge was yet down, the castle's huge wooden doors still thrown open from the day's business, beckoning all into the warmth and safety of its stone walls.

A welcome sight for the road-weary traveler. Or rather, he corrected himself quickly, *welcome for any traveler but me. Well, no matter. I'll live as I choose, roam the land where I will, and they can all be damned.*

The thought brought a twist to his mouth. Damned. 'Twas a fate all suspected was already his. All, save the golden-haired Bree.

The memory of her slipped, unbidden, into his mind. Anger swelled within. *You're a fool if you believe that for a moment!* the logical, experience-hardened part of him countered. *She's no different from the others, fair and gentle though she may be. And you've learned long ago to not purposely court pain and rejection. Forget her. Let the recollections die in the past where they belong, for you'll never see her again.*

Aye, a fair lass to be sure, his steed offered, his thoughts rising out of the blackness as they journeyed on. *'Tis well you drive her from your mind while you can—or beware, for she will surely break your heart.*

"Who goes there?" an aged sentry guarding the drawbridge demanded.

"Prince Aidan of Anacreon."

"And sure, I'm the devil himself," the guard grumbled as he limped over to the man and horse shrouded in darkness. He raised his torch for a closer look, then lurched back, nearly dropping the flaming brand. "M-m'lord," the sentry stammered. "Fergive me. I-I had no idea. Please. Enter."

Aidan nudged his mount forward. The *clip-clop* of Lucifer's hooves on the wooden drawbridge reverberated loudly in the night air, echoing off the fortress's thick stone walls. He glanced up at the crenelated battlements. Another sentry passed by on his watch.

Strange that he'd never recalled the castle so heavily guarded. Mayhap the peasant girl's observations weren't so far from the truth.

His jaw clenched as the memory of Bree's impassioned tale returned to haunt him. Mother gravely ill, Father apparently a shadow of the bold, powerful man of former years, and his younger brother completely transformed from the shy, earnest boy of their youth. Bree had said it was all Morloch's work. Yet mayhap her words about his own curse more closely shot the mark. Mayhap the evil of his blood had finally destroyed all who had ever been close to him. . . .

Aidan dismounted in the outer bailey. Glancing around, he settled his gaze upon a stableboy half hidden in the courtyard shadows. He beckoned him over.

"Come along, lad. My horse doesn't bite and I'm too tired to harm you, even if I were so inclined."

The youngster inched forward until he reached Lucifer's head. Aidan tossed him the reins.

"Rub him down well and give him an extra portion of grain. He's more than earned it." He flipped the boy a gold coin, then headed toward the brightly lit Great Hall that lay beyond the gates of the inner bailey.

Sounds of boisterous merrymaking floated from the hall's open windows. Aidan scanned the area, noting that little had changed in the years of his absence. The outdoor kitchen shed and nearby ovens were still nestled along the wall next to the grain tower. The fruit trees, laden with ripening apples and pears, still flourished in the eastern end of the courtyard.

Aye, Aidan thought grimly. From all outward appearances everything was as it should be.

31

Yet like a rotting fruit the true putrefaction lay hidden beneath an exterior semblance of normalcy.

Singing and raucous laughter mixed with amused feminine shrieks grew louder as he neared the hall's entrance. Aidan paused in the doorway, steeling himself for the confrontation that lay ahead. For a moment he stood there, surveying the room.

Long tables—little more than planks perched on trestles, filled to overflowing with noisy, inebriated revelers—flanked the sides of the large, sparsely decorated chamber. Gaily garbed serving maids, their trays crowded with foaming pitchers of ale, nimbly wove through the milling mass of bodies attempting, at the same time, to refill empty tankards and evade the outstretched hands of the men. Their sporadic, laughing squeals were ample evidence of their lack of success in both tasks.

Curses and muffled blows from a corner brawl exploded suddenly into a heated battle as two combatants fought their way across the room, cheered on by those seated at the tables. Others eagerly joined in the fray, scattering ale and platters of roasted meat as they lunged at any likely opponent.

The hall was soon in an uproar. The din of coarse male voices overpowered the melodies emanating from a small band of musicians near the main dining platform.

Irritation, and a rising concern, filled Aidan. Where was the prince consort that he allowed such excess? Never, in all the years of his youth, had he seen such pandemonium!

With an angry growl, he stalked into the hall, his long, pantherlike strides carrying him down the center of the room.

At first the fighting continued around him. A flying tankard barely missed his head. But, as he advanced on the main table, the bedlam gradually stilled. Warding signs were furtively made as the all too familiar whispers carried to Aidan's ears.

" 'Tis 'im—the one with the Evil Eye—the Evil Eye 'e used to kill poor Rangor!" "What's 'e doing 'ere?" "Quiet, you fool, or he'll hear you!" "Holy Mother, save—"

"Welcome, dear brother."

The sardonic voice came from a man rising from beneath the main table, a bare-bosomed serving wench still clasped in his arms. Dressed in a doublet of ale-stained red velvet lavishly embellished with gold bullion, a bearded, slightly florid-faced man came into view. Fifteen years, however, hadn't lessened the instant recognition. It was Dragan.

"And to what do we owe the honor of this visit after all this time?" Dragan wrinkled a nose as aquiline as Aidan's in slightly besotted thought, a malicious grin lighting his features. "Can it be? Is it already the eve of your thirtieth birthing day? Mother said you'd come, but until this moment I had my doubts. So nice to know that, in spite of all your other failings, you're a man of your word."

"I've no time for your drunken mutterings, Dragan," his brother snapped, ignoring the ineffectual attempt at humor. "Where's Mother?"

"Abed, seriously ill. But first, the prince consort awaits you."

Dragan shoved the woman aside. After swilling the dregs of his tankard, he left the table and walked toward the nearest door, motioning for Aidan to follow. "Come with me, *dearest* brother. I'll take you to him."

Aidan hesitated, loath to accompany his brother anywhere. All he wanted was to find the queen and ascertain how ill she really was. But Dragan had said their father awaited. Protocol demanded he first honor that obligation.

With a frustrated sigh Aidan forced himself to step out. Behind him the room maintained its deadly hush, the eerie silence dogging him even as he followed Dragan's retreating form. Up a narrow, winding staircase they went until they reached the main hallway of the royal sleeping chambers.

Familiar sights greeted Aidan as he traversed the corridor, but he steeled himself to look straight ahead. None of it mattered anymore; none of it belonged to him. He'd only to struggle through tomorrow and then forget it all, mayhap this time forever.

Dragan paused before a carved oaken door. "Your room—temporarily, of course," he said with a mocking smile. "I'll fetch Father. An unusual breach of lawful protocol, his coming to you, but under the circumstances an unfortunate necessity." Without further ado, he turned and sauntered down the hall.

Aidan's hands clenched at his sides. The deep-seated anguish and the old, frustrated rage seethed within him threatening, at any moment, to erupt. If not for the strange vow he'd made his mother to return on his thirtieth birthing day, an oath he'd rather die than forswear, he'd have never returned to this miserable place.

Yet he'd given his oath. It was little enough to grant his mother, the only woman alive who still found it in her heart to love him after all he'd become and done.

He pulled down the bronze door handle and entered his room. Without closing the door, Aidan strode over to the high-backed wooden chair set before a crackling fire and flung himself into it.

By the Holy Ones, how I hate this place, he cursed silently. *The memories, the pain! Yet here I am like some dumb, faithful dog, allowing all to heap more abuse, more scorn upon me. Ah, Mother, if I didn't love you so . . .*

Footsteps echoed in the hallway. Aidan leaped to his feet, his big, hard-muscled frame tensing for battle. And battle of a sorts it would truly be, with his father and brother pitted against him.

Marus, the prince consort, was the first to enter. Dragan followed close behind. Despite his advancing years and all that was said to have occurred, the prince consort remained a commanding presence, tall, his bearing regal, with eyes the piercing brilliance of black onyx. Dark brown hair streaked with gray rose like a lion's mane from a face of craggy haughtiness. But it was the more subtle intimations—the careworn lines, the slight slump to the broad shoulders, the hesitation in Marus's step—that stoked the fires of his son's uneasiness.

Aidan stepped forward. "Mother. Dragan said that Mother is ill—"

A royal hand silenced him. "Have you forgotten yourself, that you fail to first render the proper courtesy to your prince?"

Aidan froze. *So*, he thought, *despite the years the rift between us remains*. The old rebellion and wordless conflict flashed hotly in his one eye, before he bowed low in required obeisance to the man who was both his father and lord. After a long moment he straightened, when no request to do so was forthcoming.

His sire glared back at him, a strangely intent expression on his face. "So, you've returned as promised. Your 'faithfulness' is quite commendable."

"Mother—" Aidan persisted.

"You haven't deemed it necessary to inquire after your mother in all these years," Marus interrupted coldly. "The queen's condition won't change in the course of a few hours. For the moment, we have business of more pressing import."

He paused, his gaze moving to the sword Aidan wore harnessed to his back. "And when has it become necessary to enter your home girded for battle? Disarm yourself immediately!"

For an instant amber fire blazed in the depths of his son's one eye. The prince quailed. If Aidan should ever again unleash the power, the fury of the eye he kept so carefully veiled . . .

With a small shudder Marus flung the thought aside and steeled himself for the unpleasant task ahead. Drawing a mask of regal calm over his features, he watched as Aidan slowly withdrew the weapon from its sheath and laid it on the small table standing between him and his brother.

Aidan's unshaven jaw tightened as Dragan's covetous hands moved to stroke the highly polished metal blade and lovingly run his fingers over its bejeweled hilt. It was all he could do not to wrench the weapon from his brother's greedy touch. Even now, when Dragan possessed it all—the right of succession thanks to Aidan's voluntary self-exile, the father's love Aidan had never had, the soft, safe life of a favored prince of Anacreon—he still lusted after the last thing left. The last thing, Aidan's sword, the sword of Baldor the Conqueror.

A hand grasped Aidan's arm.

"There is much for us to talk of," Marus began, "but most importantly of all, have you taken a wife?"

Aidan turned back to his father, a stunned expression on his face. "What did you say, m'lord?"

As the meaning of his father's words filtered through to his brain, he gave a mocking laugh. "A wife? Surely you jest. There's no woman alive who'd have me as husband—and well you know it."

"Then your loss is my fortune." Dragan lifted the sword and clutched it to him. "At long last this, too, shall be mine."

"And the gates of Hell will freeze solid before you possess Baldor's sword!" Aidan took a menacing step toward Dragan.

Once more, his father restrained him. "The issue isn't your brother or the sword." His expression turned bleak and his next words were hollow, emotionless, as if spoken by rote. " 'Tis the law and its fulfillment. Though you be a prince of the realm, it applies as fully to you as to any of our subjects. I ask you again, have you taken a wife?"

"And I say again," Aidan replied, barely able to restrain his growing rage as he continued to eye his sword, "nay!"

His father expelled a deep breath. "Then it befalls me to compel your adherence to this most ancient of laws. On the morrow 'tis your thirtieth birthing day. You will then be granted one final chance to take a wife. If you fail, you will suffer the consequences of disobedience to Anacreon law."

Disbelief spread across Aidan's dark features. He riveted his single eye on his father. "Are you mad? With all the problems this kingdom faces, with Morloch and his minions almost on your doorstep, are you telling me your only concern is some archaic law requiring I wed?"

Marus went ashen. A spasm of gut-racking coughs shook his lean frame. Slowly he doubled over, then, debilitated by the relentless wheezing that followed the coughing spell, sought out a nearby chair. Leaning back, the prince consort signaled weakly for Dragan to continue.

" 'Tis out of our hands, dearest brother," his brother said, stepping into his father's recently vacated spot. A triumphant look gleamed in his eyes. "The choice is now yours or, rather, the women of Anacreon's. The choice *and* the consequences."

"And what might such consequences be?" Aidan demanded, anger flaring in his unpatched eye.

The threat in his brother's demeanor caused Dragan to pause. He glanced toward the prince for reassurance, then forced himself to reply, his confidence returning even as he spoke. "If you, or any male subject of the realm, fail to wed by his thirtieth birthing day, 'tis deemed a failure in the sacred duty of procreation. 'Tis a crime against the people, a blight upon our race."

"A crime is it?" Aidan gave a snort of disbelief. "This law *must* be old. I've never even heard of it. And, pray, what is the penalty for such a heinous offense?"

Dragan's smile slowly widened. "The penalty, *dearest brother,* is death."

Chapter Two

"Hurry, daughter, or we'll not finish before midday prayers."

Breanne brushed aside an errant strand of hair and raised her eyes to the sun's bright glare. "Aye, Mother."

She tossed another fat, tasseled ear of corn into the rickety cart standing between them. "There's time enough, though, with just one more row to pick. We'll be washed and donning our clean aprons before the castle's church tower sounds its first notes."

"That may be," Kyna sighed, "but for a time I wondered if the late start this morning would be our undoing. I shouldn't have let you stay abed so long, but you looked so exhausted after last eve's terror. . . ."

Breanne's thoughts slipped back to a dark warrior with a black-patched eye. "He didn't frighten me, at least not after a time. 'Twas the villagers who exhausted me so, with their endless questions, and then old Sora with all her wise woman's incantations and blessings. . . ."

She paused to twist free another plump ear of corn. "They meant well, I know, but there was no need, no need at all."

"And how can that be?" her mother demanded, her voice edged with concern. " 'Twas no less than the Demon Prince who had you! He is damned, has killed with that eye of his! You are fortunate you escaped unscathed. And as if times were not bad enough without his return . . ."

"What happened to him? He is a royal prince. How can he possess such horrible powers?"

Kyna shook her head as she began to drag the cart further down the row. "A birthing curse, bestowed by no less than the necromancer Morloch. Of course, in those days Morloch was little more than a minor sorcerer—one of the finest students of the great mage Caerlin, mind you—but still adept enough even then to destroy the life of a wee babe and his family with but a few well-chosen words. 'Tis said the prince's father never accepted him after that, the laying on of the curse, I mean."

"But why would Morloch hate the royal family?"

Her mother shrugged. "No one knows why his hatred led him to such fearful acts. Mayhap the strange and sudden disappearance of his old teacher about that time twisted him in some way. Or mayhap the rumors were indeed

41

true that he was once a serious rival for Queen Eislin's hand—"

Bells, clamorous, insistent, pealed an unexpected succession of tones. The two women's gazes met in perplexed inquiry as they listened to the clanging message.

An uneasy light flared in Kyna's eyes. "Most unusual. Instead of a call to midday prayer we women are bidden to the castle. Most unusual indeed."

"Only the women?" Breanne frowned. "What can it mean?"

"No doubt we will discover that answer at the castle." Her mother began to pull the corn-laden cart up the garden path to the cottage. "Come, daughter. 'Tis a half hour's walk and we dare not be late."

Breanne joined her in the task and they covered the short distance to the back door in silence. As her mother waited, Breanne moved the cart into the shade of a nearby apple tree.

Kyna's face was a study in concentration by the time her daughter returned. "I know not what awaits us at the castle, but whatever happens, you are to remain at my side. *He* may yet be there. I've no wish for him to have another chance at you."

"He isn't what you think, Mother. I'm in no danger—"

Kyna raised a silencing hand. "Enough, daughter. I have my reasons."

Breanne sighed. " 'Twill be as you wish."

Breanne's gaze swept the castle's spacious inner bailey. She was amazed at the amount of people who had managed to assemble in the course of an hour's time. Peasant women mingled with wellborn ladies, all gathered for what promised to be some unexpected but eagerly anticipated entertainment. Exactly what that might prove to be was of little import. If it provided a respite from the backbreaking labor of harvest or the boredom of a fading court, it was excuse enough.

The keep's stone doors swung open, drawing the crowd's attention. All eyes riveted on the inner buildings housing the royal family. The imperial seneschal, ceremonial staff in hand, stepped out, followed by the prince consort, Prince Dragan, and several royal guards. Across the broad stone porch they walked, halting only when they were a few feet from the steps leading down to the courtyard. The crowd edged closer in silent anticipation.

The imperial seneschal, his cloak of gold-trimmed blue cloth snapping in the brisk breeze, clapped his staff on the cobblestoned porch three times. "Let it be known to all," he began in strident, self-important tones, "that the thirtieth birthing day has arrived for one of Anacreon and he is yet unwed."

Kyna leaned over and whispered in her daughter's ear. "I cannot believe this! They plan to present some poor man for one of our marriageable women to take as husband. I've heard of this ancient law, but 'tis over a hundred years since 'twas last used!"

"And what could happen?" Breanne whispered back. "If no one chose him, I mean?"

43

"Why, he'd die, of course. Anacreon law demands all subjects, highborn as well as low, wed and bear children. There are no exceptions, save that of the holy sages like your former tutor, old Olenus."

"And the sorcerers," Breanne muttered bitterly, recalling Morloch's terrible curse laid years ago on a royal heir. "No one dares dictate to them, no matter how cruel they become."

". . . and now Anacreon law demands his death," the seneschal was saying, cutting short further speculation, "unless an unwed woman can be found to take him as mate. Consider well, consider long, for a man's life hangs in the balance."

Stone grating upon stone once more drew the gathering's attention. The dungeon door swung open. A black-hooded man, a curved executioner's ax cradled in his beefy arms, was the first to step forth, followed a short distance later by two guards leading a black-cloaked man between them. As recognition of the prisoner spread through the crowd, a collective gasp rose on the shuddering winds.

"The Prince!" "The Demon Prince!" "By the Holy Ones, is it he who must take a wife this day?" "Holy Mother, save us!"

Warding signs spread among the women. They glanced at each other, shuffling uneasily about.

Breanne stared at her friends and neighbors. Horror and revulsion wreathed their faces. This was one time there'd be no pity for the man offered as husband.

The guards led him closer, to the very edge of the porch. His arms were bound and beneath his cloak he was bare-chested. His face was haggard, the exhaustion hovering almost palpably about him. Yet never once did his gaze waver as he stared impassively over and beyond the crowd. Even the removal of his cloak, wrenched roughly from him by one of the guards, elicited no reaction. He stood there, tall and imposing, his stance proud even in the midst of his humiliation.

And he'll die that way, too, Breanne thought, her eyes traveling over his hair-roughened chest and muscled form. *He'll never shame himself by begging for his life. 'Twould do no good at any rate. He knows how all fear and despise him. Yet if they only knew of his kindness, his gentleness . . .*

"Look upon him, women of Anacreon," the seneschal began again, pounding his staff once as he did. "Consider well the consequences as I ask for the first time. Will any of you take this man as husband?"

Breanne turned anxious eyes to her mother. "What will happen? Will they truly kill him if no one steps forward? I can't believe they would do such a thing. He is a royal prince!"

"Hush, daughter. Hush!" Kyna hissed, her glance careening off the raised brows and inquisitive looks of several women. " 'Tis none of our concern. Anacreon law applies to all, royal or no. Let it happen as fate decrees; 'tis for the best anyway. He's an unfortunate, doomed man. 'Tis a mercy his life end now."

"But he saved me, Mother!" Breanne cried, her voice muted in the grumbling, restless murmurings of the crowd. "How can I stand by?"

The seneschal stamped his staff twice. The women calmed once more. "I ask again. Will no one take this man as husband?"

"And who would 'ave that monster as 'usband?" a strident feminine voice cried from somewhere in the milling crowd.

"Aye," another woman chimed in, emboldened by the rising mood of her neighbors. "How dare you call us here for the likes of him? Better you'd severed his head from his shoulders years ago, than waste our time now. You knew our answer before you called us!"

Thrice more the seneschal stamped his staff. "The law applies to all. I ask you again. For the third and last time, will no one take this man as husband?"

"Nay! Never! Kill the demon!" the women shrieked, surging forward as one. "Slay him and let us begone!"

Horror, bitter as gall, rose in Breanne's throat. The closeness of the tight-packed bodies smothered her in its common hatred. Her gaze once more sought out his face, a face as emotionless as carved stone. Tears stung her eyes. Holy Mother, but it was so unfair. He deserved better.

The thought of offering herself as wife flashed through her mind, but the idea chilled her very soul. Though he'd been kind to her, rescued her from certain rape and worse, the consequences of such an act gripped Breanne's heart in a prison of ice. Was there no other way?

As if sensing the turmoil within her daughter, Kyna moved closer. "Don't, child," she whispered.

Her arm encircled Breanne's shoulders. "The sacrifice is too great, even to repay an honorable debt. You risk not only your life but your very soul, if you take him in this unholy alliance. The Mother will understand and forgive this one omission. I beg you. Don't do it!"

The seneschal's gaze swept the mass of angry, hostile women, unsure of his next step. His mouth opened, moved silently. He turned toward the prince consort.

"Your Majesty?"

"Come, come, my good man," Dragan interjected before his father could reply. He motioned toward his brother. "The law is clear in these matters. As loath as my father is to see his beloved son meet such a fate, even the royal family isn't above the law. Do your duty."

Hesitation flickered in the seneschal's eyes. His glance skittered questioningly back to the prince consort. Marus shook his head in a slow, rhythmic cadence—almost as if he regretted more than just his passive acquiescence to his eldest son's death.

The seneschal sighed, then turned toward Aidan and his guards. "Prepare the prince."

The executioner hefted his ax and moved forward.

As the crowd watched in breathless anticipation, the two guards attempted to force Aidan to his knees. The intent, however, proved easier than the doing. Though he refused to beg or grovel, the prince would not so easily go to his death.

In a swift move he swung a broad shoulder into one guard's chest. Caught off balance, the man loosened his grip on the prisoner's arm. Aidan spun around to knee the other man in the groin.

Down fell the second guard, gasping in agony. The women screamed in rising panic. In that instant, Aidan's attention was momentarily diverted.

A blow caught him on his blind side, slamming into his head with a sickening thud. Dazed, blackness clouding his vision, he lurched around. A flash of white shot through the fog. The massive fist of the executioner crashed into his jaw.

Pain shot through his skull—hot, bright, and breath-grabbing. He fell, his bound arms helpless to cushion his descent. His face struck the pavement but an instant after his chest, then bounced off to smash downward again.

Summoning all his strength, Aidan struggled to rise. A hobnailed boot roughly shoved his head down, grinding his cheek into the gritty cobbles.

"N-nay!"

The cry was wrenched from the depths of Breanne's soul. She glanced wildly around her, her plea drowned in the malevolent howl of the crowd. They had tasted first blood, she realized. Nothing would satisfy them now but the spilling of more—to the very death of the man lying up there before them. Dizzy, sick with loathing, she lurched forward, only to find herself still restrained in the clasp of her mother's arms.

"Don't! I beg you child, don't!" Kyna screamed, pulling her around to bury Breanne's head in her bosom. " 'Twill be over in but a few moments more. Be brave. Fight his ensorcelment! Please, child! But a few moments more—"

Ah, to hide forever in the comforting safety of her mother's arms, to forget the harsh world around her! Breanne thought. Life wasn't meant to be so hard, so horrible, so beyond one's powers to change. . . . If only she could shut out the sounds, the hateful cries, the bloodthirsty shrieks! It was like a tempest of wailing, snapping demons, threatening to devour her very soul—

"*Nay!*" she cried, wrenching free of the prison of her mother's arms. "I fear no unholy alliance! There is but one misfortune facing me—the one I'll live with the rest of my days if I shirk my duty to him who saved me!"

She whirled around. The glare of sunlight on an unraised blade momentarily blinded her. The executioner, the strength of his oxlike leg still pinning Aidan's head as the two guards fought to hold down his struggling form, was even now rearing back to deal the death blow.

For an instant slowed in time Breanne saw it all. Her gaze swept from the scene of impending doom to the prince consort, his countenance waxy pale, his lips moving in prayer, and onto the triumphant, exhilarated expression on the face of Prince Dragan. She saw it all and knew, with a certainty welling from deep within that—for her sake and the sake of all Anacreon—she must not let this happen!

The crowd surged about her like waves upon a storm-tossed sea, yet Breanne's desperation drove her onward. A strength beyond her wildest imaginings saw her through the mass of bodies. It steeled her to her mother's screams, blocking out everything save the form of a man lying on the cobbles, an ax poised above him.

Limbs she neither felt nor realized she was moving carried her toward the porch. Suddenly, Breanne found herself free, climbing the steps.

As if seeing her for the first time the crowd fell silent. Silent, save for Kyna's now futile sobs.

"Stop! Halt this senseless murder!" Breanne's clear young voice rang across the courtyard, reverberating off the high stone walls. "Do not slay this man, for I take him as husband!"

Dragan faced her at the head of the steps, his eyes scalding pits of fury. "You're too late, wench," he sneered, his voice pitched low for her ears only. "Think again, for your life as well as your immortal soul. Renounce your offer. Not only will you condemn yourself to eternal damnation as his wife, but you and yours will earn my undying enmity."

She stared up at him, quailing at the implied threat to her family. Then a renewed resolve flowed through her. "And I say, step aside, m'lord. My choice is made. I condemn myself to naught but dishonor if I turn from your brother in his hour of need."

Dragan's hand moved to the elegant sword that hung at his side, its bejeweled hilt flashing brilliantly in the sun. *Mayhap I have been too subtle,* he thought. *Mayhap this haughty wench requires a more overt warning.*

He leaned yet closer. "And what if I were to slay you where you stand? What would you say then?"

"You'd cut me down before all these people? I hardly think—"

"Enough, Dragan," a deep voice rumbled from behind him. "Let the girl pass. The law has been fulfilled. I've no stomach to watch your brother suffer more this day."

Dragan turned, a sly, ingratiating smile on his face. He bowed low. "As you wish, m'lord. I was but ascertaining the maid's true motives for marrying into the royal family."

He sighed dramatically. "Most unfortunately, I fear her offer is tinged with the desire for personal gain, rather than for my dear brother's welfare."

"Then that is Aidan's dilemma, one I'm certain he'll prefer to an imminent death."

Marus eyed Breanne with a coldly assessing eye, taking in the unbound golden hair and poor, homespun dress that covered a small, delicately feminine form. He shook his head, a sad smile touching his lips, then offered his dagger.

"Go to him, lass. Free his bonds and claim him as yours."

She accepted the knife and climbed the last of the steps. As if in a dream Breanne strode across the broad stone porch, passing before the sullen, silent crowd. Try as she might, however, she couldn't shut out the sound of her mother's sobs.

Nerveless legs carried her to where he lay, his knees drawn up beneath him, his head down, bleeding onto the cobbles. Breanne knelt and touched him gently. "M'lord?"

He struggled to rise but the effort proved too much. With a groan, Aidan sank back down. The blood streamed into his right eye from a gash on his forehead, blinding him. Yet even without his sight he recognized her.

"Bree? Is it really you, lass?"

"Aye, m'lord," she whispered, her voice taut with unshed tears. "Lie still but a moment more and I'll have you free."

With a quick movement, Breanne sliced through the ropes. Taking his head, she cradled it in her lap, cleansing the blood from his eye with the edge of her white apron. He moved, his arms falling to his sides. His head lifted.

A single amber eye stared up at her from a bruised and bloodied face. "So, the debt is repaid after all."

Breanne smiled. "Aye, m'lord. So it seems."

She moved back and assisted him to stand. One arm about his naked waist, the other grasping his arm over her shoulder, Breanne looked up at him. Her smile deepened. A joyous light kindled in her sapphire blue eyes.

"Come, let us depart this place. Your wounds need better tending than I can offer here."

He scanned the disgruntled crowd, his gaze moving to where his father and brother still stood. "Aye," Aidan rasped, each word a painful effort, "let us depart this place. I leave no friends here."

"How may I serve you, m'lady?" the elderly maidservant asked with a deep curtsy.

Breanne glanced up from her task of assisting Aidan into a high-backed wooden chair, momentarily nonplussed at her new title. "Ah . . . bring me, if you will, water and bandages for cleansing the prince's wounds—and some healing ointment."

"And have a bath drawn, too, Mara," Aidan shouted after the woman's retreating figure.

He turned back to Breanne, shrugging his broad shoulders in apology. "Thanks to my long journey here and a night in the dungeons, I haven't had a bath in four days. Since I'm to live after all, 'twould be poor appreciation to drive away the only person not afraid to stand close enough to smell me."

Dark lashes fluttered down onto Breanne's cheeks and she colored in embarrassment. "As you wish, m'lord."

A large, callused hand settled on her arm. "And if *you* wish, you may call me Aidan."

Her lashes flew up in astonishment. "But, m'lord, that wouldn't be proper."

He released her arm and leaned back in the chair with a sigh. "And why not, lass? As my soon-to-be wife, are you not an equal and more to every lady in this court? Any that dare snub you risk my wrath, and you must realize how they fear that. Call me what you find comfort in, but be assured I take no offense in my given name."

"As you wish, m'lor—I mean, Aidan." An impish grin stole across her face. "And I must confess my given name is not Bree, but Breanne."

His dark brows knit in puzzlement. "Then why—?"

"I was afraid to tell you the full truth yestereve in the meadow," she hastened to interject, her cheeks flaming with shame. "I-I thought you could use it to cast a spell upon me. Please forgive my foolish fears."

Aidan stared back at her, unsmiling. "And do you still fear me?"

Breanne inhaled a deep breath. " 'Twould be a falsehood if I said nay, but 'tis less a fear now than an uncertainty."

"And do I disgust you?"

"Oh, nay—never that!"

A movement of skirts in the doorway distracted them. It was Mara, returning with a basin of water and a box of bandages and ointments. Aidan turned back to Breanne.

"Well, you're truly one of the most lovely liars I've ever had the fortune to meet." He signaled to Mara. "Pull over that table and set everything on it. Do you wish Mara to tend me," Aidan asked Breanne, "or can you manage it?"

"I think I can manage," she replied, her tone stiff with outrage at being called a liar.

"Then I will continue with arrangements for your bath, m'lord." Mara hurried out of the room.

Breanne sighed and turned to the box of rags and bandages. She rummaged through the contents until she found a soft cloth. Moistening it, she confronted Aidan.

"If you'll allow me, *m'lord.*"

His left brow rose a fraction but he made no comment.

The minutes passed as Breanne set herself to the task of cleansing his wounds, her former annoyance at him softening as she tended the myriad of cuts and abrasions on his face. Holy Mother, she thought, but he'd be black and blue for days. And the gash over his right brow would surely form a scar he'd carry for the rest of his life.

Not that scars were foreign to him, she mused as she glanced covertly at his body. Iron-thewed arms were tracked in spots with the white of old wounds, and his hair-whorled chest, broad and hard-muscled, was owner to several puckered sites of life-threatening injuries. What had he done, how had he lived these many years past, to now carry such marks?

"What are you thinking, Breanne?"

The sound of his deep-timbered voice jerked her attention back to him. He stared up at her, the sight of his splendid features settling over her like some strange spell. By all the Holy Ones, but he was magnificent. . . .

"Well, lass?"

"I . . . I was but wondering what you've done, where you've been these years since leaving Anacreon. Not that 'tis any of my concern," Breanne hastened to add, suddenly embarrassed at her temerity, "if you've no wish to speak of it. 'Tis but your scars," she added, gesturing toward his chest with the cloth in her hand, "that made me wonder."

He leaned forward, his glance sharply assessing. "Do you realize you're the only person who has asked me that since my return to Anacreon? No one else cares how I spent the past fifteen years, or even wonders if I still possess my fabled powers."

A slow, sweet movement of delicately molded lips lit Breanne's features. "I care, m'lord, and would gladly hear it all."

"Would you, lass? Then I'll tell you, though I fear the tale will disappoint your expectations."

Aidan paused to settle more comfortably in his chair, stretching his long legs out before him. "I've learned the trade and survived these many years as a soldier of fortune. My loyalty can be bought for the price of a few gold coins, and I call no man, save one, friend, and no place home."

"But Anacreon . . . this castle . . . is your home."

His head snapped around, and he gave a withering laugh. "This castle of all places has never been a home to me! A lonely death on the battlefield offers more comfort than to remain even one night in these cold, unfriendly walls. I am cursed, as well you know, and capable only of giving and receiving pain. So speak to me not of home!"

"But m'lord, 'tisn't so. You're a good man and—"

The door swung open. Mara swept in, followed by a covered, large wooden tub rolled in carefully by three servants. They pushed it over to a sunlit window, then stopped. The top was removed to reveal half a tubful of steaming, gently undulating water.

"Your bath, m'lord," Mara announced with a curtsy.

Aidan turned back to Breanne. "Though I'd much prefer your assistance, sweet lass, you've preparations of your own to attend to." He motioned Mara over.

"Aye, m'lord?" The over-plump little servant bobbed nervously before him. "What is your wish?"

"Is there some lady in this castle kind enough to assist in properly attiring the Lady Breanne for presentation to the queen?"

"The Lady Sirilla, my lord," Mara offered, "though she be your brother's wife, is quite kind and good. I feel certain she would help your lady."

"But why, m'lord?" Breanne rose to her feet. "What is wrong with the dress I now wear? 'Tis my best."

His glance skimmed her slender form and, for an instant, he almost weakened. By the Holy Ones, but she was lovely. Then reason returned, that and the need to protect his mother from the truth of their loveless, forced marriage. If that were still possible, he thought grimly, well aware of the wagging tongues of the castle servants.

"You are my betrothed and must dress yourself as befits your new rank," Aidan explained, the coolness of his voice masking more passionate desires. "But, more to the point, I desire

57

an audience with my mother, the queen. Her servants have surely told her of you by now. 'Twould be a breach of protocol not to present you."

"But, m'lord—"

He held up a silencing hand. "You chose the life just as surely as you chose me, lady. Abide by it, or leave me now—and forever."

" 'Twill be as you wish, m'lord." Breanne turned to Mara. "Take me to the Lady Sirilla."

She followed the chubby, suddenly gregarious servant out of Aidan's bedchamber and down a long stone corridor. Her eyes swept the hallway, amazed at the wealth of woven hangings and weapons lining its walls. Strange, Breanne mused, that the countryside was so impoverished and yet the royal castle possessed such luxury. Strange, and very unfair.

" 'Tis a dear girl you are, to save our prince from such an untimely death," Mara began, interrupting Breanne's thoughts. "I helped the queen rear him from a wee babe, and I have never found him to be other than good and kind. I thank the Holy Ones he has finally found a woman to love. Mayhap 'tis the end of his horrible curse."

"But you don't understand." As they walked along, Breanne shot Mara a pained glance. "He doesn't love me. Why, we hardly know each other. And how can wedding me have any effect on his Evil Eye? I've no powers, no knowledge of spells and their removal."

The old woman chuckled. "No powers, you say? And what of the power of love? 'Tis said it surpasses all things and heals hearts long thought dead or sorely wounded. Nay, lady, you are his last chance, for the prophecy—"

Her attention diverted, Breanne slammed into a hard, unyielding body. Blue eyes lifted and met Dragan's coldly triumphant glare.

His hands captured Breanne's arms, drawing her to him. "Well, my haughty little wench, it seems we meet again."

Chapter Three

Breanne stared up into Dragan's wickedly leering face. Her surprise, however, quickly transformed into revulsion—and a need to escape his vile grasp. She squirmed in his arms as, from the corner of her eye, she noted Mara quietly slipping away.

"Let me go, sir," Breanne cried. "If you've a wish to speak with me, let us do so at a proper distance!"

"Oh ho, the little whore has suddenly become a decent lady!" His head lowered until his sweaty face, bloated with drink, hovered just inches from hers. "But you and I know the real truth, don't we? To insinuate yourself into wealth and power, you'd lie with the devil himself, which," he chuckled bemusedly, "in a sense you soon will."

Breanne paled. "What I've done I'll not

explain nor apologize for, and especially not to you! You call me a whore for saving a man's life. What does that make you, a man who desired his own brother's death?"

Dragan's lips twisted into an evil sneer. "Think twice before you anger me, little whore. Though you ride high now as my brother's soon-to-be bride, your safety isn't long assured. Aye, for a time Aidan may remain at your side, savoring the pleasures of the marriage bed, but mark well my words. He is hated and reviled here. He'll not long tarry where he knows he's not wanted. Sooner or later he'll set out once again on his stupid, futile self-exile. And where will you be then, when Aidan is no longer here to protect you? Who'll shield you then from the taunts and jeers, the ridicule as the Demon Prince's wife?"

Words, spoken with tortured conviction, with a pain that was soul-deep, stirred in the back of Breanne's mind. Had it been but a brief time ago that Aidan had revealed his need to leave Anacreon, confessed to the fact that he would rather die in foreign lands than live like the cursed being he was in his own home? The fire had burned golden in his one eye, flaring brightly with the single-mindedness of his resolve. Nay, there was no doubt Dragan's words were true.

"He'll never return once he sets out again," her captor's cruel voice intruded, smoothly, confidently leading Breanne back to reality. "You'd be wise to build your allies now, while you've still something of value to bargain with."

She turned anger-dark eyes to his. "And what could a lowly peasant have that would be of any value to you, Prince Dragan?"

Impudent hands glided appreciatively down her arms. "You're an impertinent little wench, but I'm willing to forgive and forget. I've yet to bed a peasant maid as soft-skinned as you, and the fact you're now Aidan's will only sweeten the coupling. Come to me tonight, before my brother has had you, and I swear I'll protect you when he's gone."

"And who'll then protect her from you?"

At the sound of Aidan's deep voice, Dragan released Breanne and whirled around. "I-I was but welcoming your sweet bride-to-be into the family, dear brother," he stammered.

Aidan ignored the suddenly pallid Dragan and motioned to Breanne. "Come here, lass."

She ran to his side and was immediately encompassed by a comfortingly virile arm. He had evidently not even had opportunity to begin his bath for he still wore his black breeches and boots. The scent of his warm skin, masculine and bracing, wafted to her nostrils, plucking at a memory of another time in his arms. Bewildered by the surge of pleasure the recollection stirred, Breanne forced her attention back to the problem at hand.

Her glance swept from Dragan's face back to Aidan. For an instant, she thought Aidan completely unmoved by the incident. But then, on closer inspection, she noted the muscle jumping in his jaw.

The realization of his anger stirred something deep within her, kindling a gladness wholly separate from the relief of her rescue. He felt something for her, if only a fierce need to guard what was his. For the moment, it was enough.

"I tell you this once, and only once, Dragan," Aidan's voice, low-pitched and deadly, rumbled. "I've powers beyond your wildest imaginings, powers forged in the furnace of pain and exile. Powers, all, in their own way, potentially as lethal as that of my eye. Though I be near or far from Breanne, because she is mine I'll know if ever she is harmed. I sensed her danger even now, before Mara came to warn me. If you doubt, test again—and suffer the consequences!"

Dragan gave a shaky laugh. "You mistake my intentions. She was in no danger; we were but making friendly conversation. I meant no harm, no disrespect to you, lady."

"Please, m'lord." Breanne moved to stand before Aidan. It was time to put an end to the highly charged atmosphere. "Truly, 'twas of no import. He didn't frighten me."

An amber eye turned to study her. "Nay, I'd imagine he didn't. 'Twould take more than the likes of Dragan to frighten you." He glanced back at his brother. "Leave us, but remember well my words."

His brother made a hasty move to depart, when he was once again halted by Aidan's parting words. "One thing more, Dragan." The tone was calm but edged in steel. "My sword, the one you appropriated when they led me away last night. Return it to me before the day is out. Thanks to this lady I live still. While I do, as the queen's firstborn, Baldor's sword is mine."

Taking Breanne by the arm, Aidan motioned

for Mara to lead the way. They walked off without awaiting Dragan's reply. Down several corridors the trio went, until they finally reached a door that appeared, to Breanne, like all the rest. Mara paused there.

"This is the Lady Sirilla's chamber," the maid explained. "When shall we have your lady ready for you, m'lord?"

He eyed Breanne with a hooded, enigmatic expression. She waited, her heart beating a wild, staccato rhythm beneath her breast. Why was he looking at her like that, when Mara had asked but a simple question? Had the little servant offended him in some way, mayhap when she'd called her "his lady"? Did he suddenly feel trapped into a marriage he'd no desire—

"An hour's time should be sufficient," Aidan replied, interrupting Breanne's painful self-doubts. "Lady." He bowed his farewell, then turned on his heel and strode away.

By all the Holy Ones, Aidan thought as he headed back to his room, how was it possible to go from total feminine revulsion, save for an occasional highly paid whore, to a woman as fine and beautiful as Breanne in the space of two days' time? His lady . . . Mara had called her his lady. The word and its implications tugged at his heart, eliciting a twinge of longing, of—

Fool! he silently cursed. *She isn't for one such as you. Would you destroy her, drag her down to the depths of your own degradation—and eventual damnation? Is that how you plan to repay her sweet sacrifice?*

One day more. Aidan ground the reminder

into his head. *Bear the pain but one day more and then both of you can be free—her of your loathsome presence, and you of the foolish dreaming of a life you can never have.* He shrugged his shoulders as he stalked away, the gesture as much a symbolic throwing off of futile desires as a physical hardening of a body long accustomed to rejection and self-denial. *Aye,* Aidan repeated grimly in his mind. *But one day more . . .*

The two women stared after him. As the tension melted, they began to giggle.

"Did you see the color Prince Dragan's face turned when Prince Aidan surprised him?" Mara asked between chuckles. "It was the most vile shade of green I've ever seen."

"Oh, aye," Breanne laughed, "and especially when Aidan told him he could sense when I was in danger. I thought Dragan would swoon on the spot. . . ."

Her voice faded as the old woman's laughter suddenly ceased. "What is it, Mara?"

"Our prince spoke true, m'lady. He was halfway here when I met him in the hall. And the look on his face . . ." She stopped, shuddering. "The look on his face was enough to chill the heart of a saint. He knew, lady, and was indeed coming to your rescue."

"But how?" Breanne paused, the realization that Aidan possessed abilities beyond those of his fearsome eye slicing through her. How deep did those powers run, and was their source good or . . .

She flung the horrible thought aside. She would not doubt him; she would not allow the

65

gentleness, the kindness he had shown her thus far amount to naught because of superstitious fears and groundless rumors. If he deserved nothing else from her as his wife, he deserved her loyalty and trust.

Yet sometimes it was so hard. Despite her best efforts, the horrible tales about him slipped past the logical barriers of her mind. What must it be like for those who didn't know him even as well as she?

A sense of overwhelming hopelessness struck her; then renewed resolution surged over and past the negative emotions. Somehow, some way, they would overcome it. He deserved far better, deserved the same measure of happiness as any other man.

With a determined straightening of her slender shoulders Breanne turned to Mara. "And I am thankful that he did. Now, no more of this. There is much to be done if I'm to appear the fine lady in but an hour's time."

Her hand grasped the door pull. "Come, let us seek out the Lady Sirilla."

"Is she ready?" Aidan's massive frame dwarfed the doorway of Lady Sirilla's room.

Mara swung the door open and motioned him to enter. "Aye, m'lord," she replied with a mysterious smile. "Your lady is ready."

He hesitated, his glance scanning the large bedchamber for Breanne. He found only the slim form of a dark-haired lady. By her dress and bearing, Aidan surmised it was his brother's wife.

Sirilla noted his uncertainty. With a warm

welcome in her rich brown eyes, she waved him in. "Please, m'lord. Enter. 'Tis quite all right."

Aidan stalked into the room, his long, lithe strides quickly carrying him to Sirilla. "Lady." He tipped his head in acknowledgment.

"M'lord." She curtsied in reply. "At long last I meet my husband's brother." She studied him closely. "Strange, but you don't look very fearsome. In fact, I find you quite handsome."

"And you, I think, deserve far better than my brother."

Sirilla paled but her smile never faltered. "You are painfully direct, m'lord. But I like that. Mayhap we can be friends."

He accepted her hand and bent to kiss it. " 'Tis Breanne who'll need your friendship in the days to come." The words were low, meant only for Sirilla's ears.

Their eyes met and locked, an understanding honed by separate years of private pain flowing between them.

"She has it already, m'lord." Sirilla paused. "But come, 'tis past time you see your lady. I do hope you approve of how we've prepared her." She turned to the old servingwoman. "Mara, please fetch the Lady Breanne."

Mara bustled over to a door at the far end of the chamber. There was a murmur of feminine voices, then a flurry of skirts, a flash of color, and Breanne was walking toward him.

Though he masked his emotions beneath a cool facade, Aidan's heart lurched madly in his chest. She was lovely, ethereal, more elegant than any fine lady he'd ever seen. Even Sirilla, gentle beauty that she was, paled before the radiant Breanne.

Her gown, molding snugly over breasts, waist, and hips before softly flaring to the floor, was of a deep, shimmering blue that set off her eyes to perfection. Her hair had been carefully dressed into a multitude of tiny braids and then caught up into a netted caul of blue silk threads. It framed her delicate profile like a golden halo, simultaneously creating an illusion of sweet innocence and glorious, ripe womanhood.

Yet it was the handsome flush to her pale-gold skin, a luxuriant bloom that stained not only her cheeks but her neck and the modestly exposed rise of her bosom, that caused something to twist deep in Aidan's gut. Hunger, sharp and gnawing, lanced through him. A fire sprang to life in his loins.

He swallowed a savage curse and forced his blood-heavy legs to move. The walk over to Breanne seemed endless. Offering her a stiff, formal bow required a superhuman effort. And he surprised even himself at the calm tone of his voice when he finally spoke.

"You look lovely, lass. The queen will be pleased."

A shy, hesitant smile touched her piquant face. "And you, m'lord. Are *you* pleased?"

"Aye, Breanne." Try as he might, Aidan couldn't disguise the husky note that crept into his voice. "What man wouldn't find you pleasing?"

But I don't care about other men. Breanne's smile slipped away. *Only you, only you . . .*

A nameless yearning rose within. Forcing a

smile, she attempted a small curtsy. "Then 'twas well worth it, m'lord, though I can scarcely breathe as tightly laced as I am."

Sirilla glided to her side. "Hush, Breanne. Let him think that tiny waist is natural. It drives them wild."

The corner of Aidan's mouth lifted. "Drives us wild, does it? I never thought Breanne thick-waisted to begin with, and she weighs no more than a bit of fluff."

"Aye." Sirilla laughed, the sound gay and tinkling. "And you've had ample opportunity to know, haven't you, m'lord? Breanne told me how you met yestereve. A clear case of fate if ever there were one."

"Fate, mayhap," he admitted, "but I fear not a kind one for Breanne. But enough of this. 'Tis past time for us to visit my mother. Lass?" He extended his arm to Breanne.

The two women exchanged a troubled glance, then moved to hug each other. "Go, Bree," Sirilla urged. "Have hope. All will be well."

Breanne accepted Aidan's arm. "My thanks for everything, Sirilla. I hope we can see each other again soon."

"Ah, fear not, my friend. I intend to deeply involve myself in preparations for your wedding. We'll be spending much of the next several weeks in each other's company."

A dark frown spread across Aidan's face as he led her away. Breanne noticed. "Is something amiss, m'lord? Did I somehow offend you in the Lady Sirilla's presence?"

He shook his head. "Nay, 'twas nothing you did, lass. 'Tis but a misconception that must be cleared. Our marriage is but one of convenience, more mine than yours. I see no reason for an elaborate wedding. All that's required is a priest and spoken vows. There's no purpose in dragging it out. We'll wed on the morrow."

Breanne's throat went dry. *So,* she thought, *now the truth is revealed. He finds the whole thing but a distasteful, if necessary evil. And, though he has never treated me less than courteously, he has no desire for me.*

And what did you think? a bitter little voice countered inside her head. *You are a peasant, he, no matter how reviled, of royal birth. What were you hoping for—his love?*

A tiny tremor racked her body. Breanne hurried to hide it with what she hoped was a carefree toss of her head.

"As you wish, m'lord. As you say, there's no need to drag out a wedding such as ours."

He shot her a sharp glance, his steps faltering for an instant. *'Tis as I imagined,* Aidan thought. *She bears me no feelings save those of pity—and mayhap a desire for the soft life of a royal princess.*

Well, no matter. Whatever her motives, she has well earned all my position can give her. In a day more it won't matter. She'll be free of me forever.

The form of the prince consort, standing beside a bedchamber door, caught Aidan's eye. He tensed, all thought of Breanne taking flight, and girded himself for the confrontation to come. If, after all that had transpired, his father thought to keep him from the queen . . .

He halted before Marus. For a long instant

both men eyed each other impassively. Breanne's nervous glance flickered from one to the other, wondering who would break or be the first to speak. It was the father.

"Will you tell the queen of today?" he demanded.

Aidan's head cocked slightly, lending it a sardonic cast. "After all that's transpired, doesn't she already know?"

"Nay." His father shook his head. "I took pains to keep her from finding out. The servants have their instructions."

"Yet you fear I'll tell her?"

The prince consort's gaze moved briefly to Breanne, then back to his son. "In your anger at me, mayhap your judgment—"

"So you are here," Aidan interjected tersely, "to ascertain I make no errors in judgment. Does that extend to preventing me from even seeing the queen?"

The hand grasping Breanne's arm unconsciously clenched, sending a sharp spasm of pain through her. Biting back an impulse to cry out, she forced herself to turn to Aidan.

"By your leave, m'lord. Mayhap this is a discussion best conducted in private." Her gaze sought out the old servant. "Mara and I can await you elsewhere."

"Nay, lady," he growled, his single eye never leaving his father. "This will be ended as it began—before us all. 'Twasn't my wish to cause problems. My father has made his choice; now he must see it through."

Breanne shot the prince consort a helpless

look, then lapsed into silence. An uneasy realization nudged the fringes of her consciousness as she found her place, once more, at her betrothed's side. Aidan and his father strongly disliked, mayhap even hated, each other.

The knowledge filled her with rising apprehension. Though his life had been spared this day, was Aidan truly safe in the castle? Yea, was he safe while he remained in the kingdom of Anacreon? His desire to marry quickly was not without wisdom. But then what?

"I've no wish to keep you from your mother, as much for her sake as anything else."

Breanne jerked her gaze back to the prince consort. Though she searched for sign of emotion, the steely, black-eyed glance he gave his son was inscrutable.

"Then let me pass," Aidan growled. "She is the only reason I came back to this miserable land. Your welcome last eve most eloquently revealed your feelings about my return. There's no need to play the host any further."

A fleeting look of pain flashed through the prince consort's eyes. Then, with a shrug, he walked away.

Breanne wanted to speak to Aidan of his cruelty, to tell him he was wrong about his father, but couldn't. Though they were soon to wed she shared nothing with him—no affection, no warmth—only a polite consideration. She had no right to admonish him, and no expectation of being heard if she did.

The realization sent a cold shiver down her spine. *Holy Mother, what have I done? In but another day's time I'll be his property. Despite my lofty dreams for him, I still have no idea what being his wife will mean. In the impulse of a moment I have repaid a debt, and will continue to repay it each day for the rest of my life.*

"Come, lass."

Aidan's voice, soft as rough velvet, made Breanne jump. Startled blue eyes turned to him. She swallowed hard.

"Aye, m'lord."

He swung open the door. Captured in the relentless clasp of Aidan's hand, Breanne walked into a large, sunlit chamber.

Her heart thudded in her chest. Holy Mother, was this all truly happening to her—Aidan, their wedding, and now an audience with the queen, her future mother-in-law? All the doubts, all the uncertainty of the day, rose to engulf her in one panic-stricken, smothering instant.

I know naught about how to act, what to say, she inwardly cried. *I'll make a fool of myself and shame Aidan in the bargain. I cannot do it. I cannot!*

"You can do it with my help, lass. Don't be afraid. Trust me."

Breanne half-turned toward her dark companion, a wary, questioning expression on her face. "What did you say, m'lord?"

A spark of deviltry danced in Aidan's unpatched eye. "I said, don't be afraid. I'll help you. And no"—he intercepted her sudden look of anxiety—"I didn't read your mind. That particular talent is yet beyond my powers. I but saw your fear and felt it in your actions."

"Am I so transparent then?"

"Hardly." His lips curled in a wry grimace. "Now, come. The queen awaits."

Together they strode across a fur-strewn floor, the hem of Breanne's gown brushing the soft white hair of countless ermines and snow rabbits. Aidan led her over to a huge, ornately carved canopy bed. As a lady-in-waiting stepped away, he froze.

"A-Aidan? Son?" a sweet, tremulous voice cried. "Is it really you?"

His hand dropped from Breanne's arm, and he inhaled a shuddering breath. Breanne's gaze swung to him. Her own breath caught in her throat.

A dark flush suffused his striking features, the beginnings of a beautiful smile curving his mouth. Once more she saw the man beneath the mask, saw the depth of love he was capable of. All her fears about him died, whisked away by the sure knowledge of a woman's heart.

He took a hesitant step forward. "Mother?"

A pair of thin, wavering arms lifted.

Aidan gathered his mother to him with such passion he half-pulled her out of bed. Breanne watched from afar, her eyes misting at the sight of the dark head bent over the frail form of a woman with silver-streaked auburn hair, wondering at the ineffable tenderness in the touch that pressed his mother to him. How could any doubt the depth of his humanity, the goodness in him, seeing the love he had for his mother?

At last they parted, Aidan pulling back to sit by the queen's side. They talked for a time, in voices pitched too low for other ears. Eislin stroked his face frequently as her eyes hungrily, lovingly, roamed his strong frame.

"You have grown into a fine, handsome man, my son," she murmured. "All these years I wondered, hoped, dreamed of the day you promised to return. Yet never in my wildest imaginings did I see you as such a powerful warrior. The years have made you strong, prepared you well—"

"Prepared me for what, Mother?" Aidan demanded. "And why did you request I specifically return on my thirtieth birthing day? Didn't you know . . ."

His voice faded as he realized where that statement would lead. "Well, no matter. I'm here as you bid, and have brought with me an even more pleasant surprise."

"A surprise?" Eislin's honey-brown eyes brightened with curiosity. "As if your dear presence were not enough, and yet you say it is even more pleasant than that? What could it possibly be?"

Aidan rose. He motioned Breanne forward. When she reached him, he took her hand and drew her to his side.

"The Lady Breanne," he said by way of introduction. "My bride-to-be."

The queen straightened in bed, a happy, heartfelt smile lighting her face. "Your bride?" She extended a slender hand. "Come closer, child."

Breanne knelt by the bed to take the queen's hand. "M'lady," she murmured shyly, bowing low. " 'Tis an honor to meet you."

She raised her head and met the piercing gaze of the other woman. At the searching intensity of the queen's appraisal, Breanne quailed momentarily. But only for a moment.

Though she sensed instinctively that the queen's approval was somehow vital, in spite of the cruel necessity of their marriage she refused to be intimidated. Aidan had said to trust him, that he would help her. It was pointless to pretend to be what she wasn't at any rate. Pointless, and far too late.

The queen stared at her for a long while, memories of beloved scenes and long-dead faces stirring. *There is something about this girl, but what?* she mused. Then, recalling herself, she covered Breanne's hand with her other delicate, blue-veined one.

"Welcome, Breanne." Eislin paused, a smile tilting her mouth. "Tell me, child. How did you and my son meet? And did you love him from the very beginning?"

The questions, couched in gentle tones, surprised Breanne. She'd expected a demand for her lineage, mayhap even for the size of the dowry she knew noble marriages required, but certainly not such eager, purely feminine queries. She smiled and opened her mouth to reply, when a masculine hand settled on her shoulder.

"There's no need to tire yourself dwelling on the past, Mother," Aidan said. "Besides, if the truth be told, at first meeting I terrified Breanne so badly she fainted."

Breanne laughed at the queen's look of surprise. "Aye, m'lady. Aidan speaks true, but I cannot attribute my swoon solely to him. He had just rescued me from some brigands and 'twas the culmination of it all that upset me so."

She glanced over her shoulder at Aidan, her hand covering his. "And as to your question if I loved him from the beginning, I must, in all truth, answer nay. I quickly grew to trust and respect him, though. And each passing moment only increases my affections, but nay, I didn't love your son."

"A young woman with a solid head on her shoulders," chuckled the queen. "I like that. If you had brought me one of those giggling, head-in-the-clouds girls," she said, smiling up at her son, "I don't know what I would have done. But I see you had no need of your mother's advice. You have chosen well."

"Aye, Mother," Aidan agreed, his rich voice rising from behind Breanne. " 'Twould appear so."

The tones caressed Breanne's ears, sending a frisson of pleasure through her. Did she imagine it, or was there a hint of sincere acknowledgment in Aidan's reply? Her lips curved into a soft, unconscious smile.

The queen noted the smile. A radiant glow lit her eyes. As she studied Breanne's face, something about it again gave her pause. She peered at the girl more intently, her fair brow wrinkling in thought.

"Your mother, child." Eislin gently grasped Breanne's chin. With a considering movement, she turned her face to study her profile. "You look familiar. Do I know your parents?"

Here it comes, Breanne thought in sudden apprehension, *for I cannot lie to her!* She shook her head. "Nay, m'lady. I—"

"You've never met Breanne's parents, Mother," Aidan cut in smoothly. "When I relinquished the right to the throne those many years ago, I also cast aside the need to marry one of royal birth. Breanne comes of simple stock."

"Does she now?"

The queen's brow arched as her hand fell from Breanne's face. Was it possible? Had it at last happened as old Olenus had promised? Was the girl indeed the one tied to the prophecy? Had Morloch's attempt to thwart the holy man truly failed? By the Mother, she fervently hoped so!

Eislin smiled. "Mayhap. But mayhap not. I think you misjudge her breeding."

"And I say you search too hard to make her a worthy wife for me," Aidan replied. "Truly, there's no need. I'm content with Breanne."

"As am I." She shot Breanne a conspiratorial grin. "So, let us talk of more pressing things. When is the wedding planned?"

Aidan's grip on Breanne's shoulder tightened. "There's no need for an elaborate ceremony, considering the people's current humor. I hadn't planned on tarrying in Anacreon. Tomorrow suits me."

"Well, it doesn't suit me!"

His mother pulled herself up in bed to a more commanding position. "I care not for the people's temper in this. Breanne deserves a proper ceremony and she shall have it. My own wedding gown should do quite nicely with but a few alterations, but it, along with the other preparations, will take at least a week's time. Surely you can wait but seven days more for a wife."

Aidan exhaled a pained breath. "I swear, Mother, I cannot. Even now, the need to be on my way pulls at me. I'd never have returned to Anacreon if not for the promise I made you. As much as I love and honor you, I cannot stay. I mean you no disrespect but—"

Olenus is yet at the Abbey, a full three days' journey each way, the queen thought. *They cannot be allowed to leave until he has met with them. This moment cannot be lost. The welfare of Anacreon, the hearts and souls of the people, now lie in their hands.*

"A week, Aidan." Eislin's eyes flashed with a regal resolve. "I *must* have a week. All will be revealed in time, but either as your mother or as your queen, I must be obeyed in this. Your marriage to Breanne will occur in seven days' time—and not a moment sooner!"

Chapter Four

A fine mess. 'Tis a fine mess you've landed us in!

Aidan paused in his vigorous grooming. He glanced up and cocked a dark brow. "What did you say, Lucifer?"

The huge war-horse shifted restlessly, swishing his tail back and forth. *The little female,* he grumbled irritably. *The one you're now to wed. What are we to do with her?*

His master shrugged and resumed his sweeping brush strokes. The dust rose from Lucifer's ebony coat with each flick of Aidan's wrist. With a flurry, the descending motes caught and reflected in the setting sun that pierced a grimy pane in the stable window.

"Nothing's changed," Aidan muttered. "We'll be leaving here soon. But a short delay—"

You call seven days a short delay? Are you

daft? Have your loins already taken over from your brain? Lucifer's nostrils flared with a disgusted snort. *And after the wedding? What then? Do you plan to claim your husbandly rights and settle down to producing offspring to enrich the kingdom? Mayhap you now foster some illusion that all is forgiven and—*

"I foster no such thing!" Aidan snapped. He threw the grooming brush into the tack box and picked up a soft polishing cloth, which he applied to his mount's coat with something less than a gentle hand. "I had no choice in accepting Breanne's offer to wed—unless you'd rather have become the property of my brother, along with my sword—and I had no choice but to obey when my mother demanded the wedding be held seven days from now. But that is the last compromise I make. Just as soon as the castle clock tolls midnight on the seventh night . . ."

And the female? This Breanne. What will you do with her then?

"She's certainly not coming along with us, if that's what you're asking. I told you before, nothing has changed!"

In that you are mistaken, my friend. Much has changed in the span of a day. There is a strong feeling of danger, of evil about, even more so since the little female took you for husband.

Aidan halted his grooming. "What do you mean?"

She is in grave danger.

"From whom? Dragan?"

From him, aye. And from someone—or thing— far more perilous. Beware.

81

Lucifer's ears pricked forward. Honed by years of unrelenting danger, Aidan immediately tensed, ready for whatever threatened. His hand snaked to the dagger in his boot.

What is it, Lucifer? Who goes about?

The horse snorted again. *The newest and mayhap greatest threat to your peace of mind,* he replied with a sarcastic curl of his upper lip. *'Tis your betrothed.*

Aidan shot him a narrowed look and slid his dagger back in his boot. An instant later the swish of long skirts on the hard-packed earth of the stable walkway heralded Breanne's approach. Her step was as hesitant as her searching gaze as she at last moved into view.

She still wore the shimmering blue gown, the slight lift of her skirts the only concession she made to the filth of the stable. Aidan smiled. Breanne would never allow the trappings of a fine lady's life to sway her from her predetermined purpose. Though that aspect of her behavior was sure to cause the court ladies considerable consternation, he found he admired it. Admired it as much as he did the woman herself.

Have a care, my friend, Lucifer intruded snidely. *Your loins are stirring.*

"Enough, Lucifer," Aidan growled, then moved into view.

His sudden movement caught Breanne's eye. She started, then smiled in relief. "Ah, there you are, m'lord. In your dark garb you blended into the shadows."

"As intended, lass," he said as he strode over

to stand before her. " 'Tis a decided advantage against one's enemies."

"And what advantage is it against your friends?" she asked with an impish grin.

"I have no friends."

"None, m'lord? None at all?"

Aidan frowned. "What is your point? I tire of a game that accomplishes naught but to taunt me with a cruel reality."

Breanne's smile faded. "I beg pardon. My intent was never to wound you further. I only wished for you to name me as your friend." Her eyes lowered. "I'd hoped . . ."

A strong finger crooked beneath her chin as Aidan lifted her glance back up to his. An amused tolerance warmed his single amber eye. "If it pleases you to be such, so be it. But truly, I cannot fathom any value in taking me as friend."

She stared up at him for a long moment. "Then I must show you where your value lies, until you finally accept it for yourself."

"Lass," Aidan's deep voice rumbled its warning, " 'tis a hopeless quest, this desire of yours—"

"I sought you out to ask a boon," Breanne interrupted before he could continue. "I've a wish to visit my family and gather my belongings. There was no time in the rush of things earlier today. . . ."

Aidan wrenched himself from his growing fascination with her sweet features. "Ah, yes, your belongings. I'll have a man sent for them."

"Nay," she said, smiling once more. "I need time to speak with my mother, to reassure her that all is well. I must go myself."

"As you wish. It draws late for such a journey today. On the morrow a guard may accompany you—"

"Can't you go with me, Aidan?" The surprising request was uttered softly, accompanied by a shy, hopeful light gleaming in Breanne's striking eyes.

Aidan's heart lurched in his chest. By the Holy Ones, how easily the wench could stir him with but a huskily couched question and a pair of beguiling blue eyes! Lucifer was right. He had most definitely landed them into a fine mess.

He wrenched his gaze from hers, suddenly fascinated with the fine weaving of a large spider's web spun between the rafters directly overhead. A fly had entrapped itself in the silken, clinging strands and was struggling to break free. The insect's actions reminded him of his own futile battle against Breanne. Inexplicably, that realization angered him.

"Go with you? And what purpose would that serve," he demanded, "save to stir your village to a fearful frenzy again?"

" 'Twould reassure them I am safe and you aren't the ogre the rumors have you be!"

He met her defiant gaze. A mocking smile curled the corner of his sensual mouth, lending it a sardonic cast. "I see you for what you truly are now, lass—a rescuer of the downtrodden and misunderstood. Have you taken on my salvation as your newest cause?"

At his tone of amused patronization, Breanne

shot him a withering look. Her slender shoulders squared. Her hands fisted to a position of defiance on her hips. "What if I have? Someone has to. You've certainly made a fearsome muddle of it so far!"

Aidan chuckled. "And what makes you think I care what others think of me? Or that I want some slip of a lass championing my cause?" His expression grew solemn. "I thank you for your concern, but I don't need your help. I am content—"

Breanne sighed in exasperation. "And I don't believe that for a moment. But, be that as it may, I still want you to accompany me to my village. 'Tis only fitting that you, as my betrothed, meet my family. Would you shame me by shirking your duty?"

"My duty?" Aidan contained his flare of irritation with the greatest of efforts. "Allow me to make one thing clear, m'lady. I owe no one anything, save if I deign to make the choice. And I certainly don't owe your family—"

Careful, my friend. The lass did save your life. You owe her the boon.

Aidan wheeled around in surprise. "After all your protests, do you defend her, too? Truly, Lucifer, whose side are you on?"

Yours, of course. But fair is fair.

With a flurry of skirt and petticoats, Breanne moved to stand beside him. She glanced around. "Who are you talking to?" A wary anxiety threaded her voice. "Surely not to your horse?"

He turned to face her, a hard glitter in his eyes. "And what if I am? Did you not hear me warn my brother that I possessed powers beyond his wildest imaginings? Does my ability to communicate with Lucifer frighten you?"

She took a step back from him. "I-I don't know. I didn't realize—"

Aidan grasped her by the arms and pulled her to him. Anger clenched his jaw and smoldered in his unpatched eye. "Realize what? That I truly do have unnatural powers? I'd have thought you'd have perceived that after the first time I nearly ensorceled you!"

He gave her a small shake. "Best you face the truth now, once and for all. I am cursed. There is no hope for me. And nothing, absolutely nothing you can do will change that."

"Nay." Breanne shook her head, clenching her eyes shut against a sudden surge of tears. "I will not believe that. And I won't let you go on believing that, either!"

She forced back the tears, her chin lifting in stubborn defiance. "I still want you to take me home to see my mother on the morrow. Will you, Aidan? Please?"

She's won this round, my friend.

"Lucifer," Aidan warned, even as he knew his horse spoke true. He'd seen the tears sparkling in Breanne's eyes and cursed himself for being the one who put them there. She asked so little of him. He'd suffered the fear and revulsion of villagers many times before. Once more mattered little.

He exhaled a deep breath. "As you wish, lass. I'll take you to your village on the morrow."

Joy blazed in her luminous eyes. Tentatively,

she touched him on the arm. "My thanks. Have faith. You won't regret it."

His mouth quirked wryly. "Won't regret the warding signs, the looks of fear, the murmurs of disgust? You must think me made of stone."

Her grip on his arm tightened. "Nay, m'lord. You've a heart as tender as any man. But sometimes the road back is as difficult as the road taken away. At least for a time, that is. Now, however, you'll no longer face it alone."

He regarded her dispassionately. "I never asked for that, Breanne."

Faint color flushed her high cheekbones, but Breanne faced him with a fierce resolve. "Nay, you didn't, m'lord. But you have it, nonetheless."

"Nay." Breanne vehemently shook her head. "It cannot be. 'Tisn't fitting that I share the same bedchamber with you before we're wed."

Aidan halted in his journey through the castle to his bedchamber and pulled Breanne aside into a small alcove. The sun had set hours ago and exhaustion now dogged his every waking action. Yet the decision made, as a result of his growing concerns over her safety, could no longer be avoided.

"Fitting? And what, pray tell, is fitting about anything that has occurred in the past day?" he asked wearily. "If 'tis a fear I'll force myself upon you before we're wed, you've naught to worry about. I've never forced a woman to lie with me and never will. Even one such as I possesses some vestiges of honor."

"I never imagined that you wouldn't," Breanne replied, flushing hotly. "But 'twould seem so, to all who knew. Why is it necessary—"

"You're all that stands between me and death, lass. If something should happen to you between now and our wedding day, do you think another would willingly take me as husband? My fate would be the same as before. I must still wed or die."

"But who would harm me? Surely no one hates you that much to see me dead."

"Breanne, Breanne." Aidan sighed in exasperation. "You are singularly naive if you haven't considered Dragan, or even my father. There's no love lost between us—and never will be."

"Why?" She searched his face for some answer to her question. "What happened between you?"

" 'Tisn't a proper time or spot to speak of such things. Mayhap later, in my room." He studied her intently. "There is more, lass. The danger to you 'tisn't just from my kin. Will you trust me in this, accept that 'tis vital we remain close to each other, especially at night?"

"But who—?" Breanne bit the query off in midsentence, suddenly terrified to ask more. If Aidan felt her to be in danger, it didn't matter from where the conviction arose. He had asked her to trust him, and trust him she would.

She nodded her acquiescence. "As you wish, m'lord." Breanne glanced up at him. "The sleeping arrangements. Must we share the same bed?"

His mouth quirked. "And if we did, would

that be so repugnant to you?"

"Repugnant? Nay." Her lashes fluttered down onto her cheeks. " 'Tis just that I've never slept with a man before, and never thought to, save with my husband."

"Indeed?"

Blue eyes snapped open at the amusement in Aidan's voice. "Indeed. And what's so strange about that? Did you imagine I wasn't a maiden, because I came of peasant stock?"

"Nay, I imagined no such thing, lass." Aidan chuckled. "I was but teasing you to ease your discomfort in speaking of such things. Obviously, I failed."

He took her by the arm. "Come, the night draws on and I find myself bone-tired. I can easily fall asleep on the floor, which is what I intend to do. You may have my bed."

"Ah, nay!" Breanne dug in her heels as he began to pull her forward. " 'Twouldn't be right to take your bed. 'Tis your room. I'll sleep on the floor."

Aidan tugged on her arm, leading her firmly along. " 'Tis hardly a subject to discuss out here in the hall. Come, let us first retire to my bedchamber."

She followed him obediently enough after that and they soon entered his room. The chamber was quite large, lit by several candle-laden wall sconces and furnished with opulently upholstered, heavy wooden furniture. The huge bed, encompassed by thick, blue velvet bed hangings, was already turned down, a woman's bed robe and white lawn gown laid out on the spread. Breanne's eyes were riveted there.

"I told only Mara," Aidan explained, noting her discomfiture. "The queen has appointed her your serving maid. She'll keep your shameful secret."

Breanne whirled around. " 'Tisn't shameful. I was wrong to fret so before over what others might say. You are what matters, you and your feelings."

Something warm flared in his eyes. Then, as if remembering himself, Aidan scowled. "Well, my feelings on this are that I desperately need to rest."

He gathered up an extra pillow and the fur throw folded at the foot of the bed, then turned toward the balcony door. "I plan to sleep outside. You can take whatever suits you—"

A knock sounded at the door. Aidan eyed the door with irritation, then put his bedding down and strode across the room. He jerked open the door to find a servant standing there, the sword of Baldor in his hands.

"I see my brother heeded my words after all," Aidan growled. He reached out and took the sword. The servant remained, rooted to the spot.

Aidan eyed him. "Well, man, speak. Is there something else?"

"N-nay, m'lord."

"Then begone with you!"

With a strangled cry, the servant turned and fled.

His sword clasped to his chest, Aidan shut and bolted the bedchamber door, then strode back to Breanne.

She glanced at the sword. Its bejeweled hilt

gleamed faintly in the candlelit room. " 'Tis magnificent." She touched the large, oval, milky-white stone at the juncture of hilt and handle. As her fingers caressed its contours, for a fleeting moment the stone's consistency seemed to change, to swirl, then clear. Within the stone's suddenly lucid depths appeared the face of an old man, mouthing words Breanne couldn't understand.

With a gasp, she dropped her hand and leaped back. "By the Mother!"

Aidan looked down at his sword, then back up at Breanne. "What is it, lass? What's wrong?"

"Y-your sword!" She shot the bewitched jewel a wary glance. It was again but a milky-white stone.

Breanne swallowed hard. Mayhap the strange scene in the stone had been an illusion brought on by the flickering light and shadows and her own weariness. She felt suddenly foolish.

"Naught." She shook her head to emphasize the word. " 'Twas naught but an overactive imagination." Breanne gestured toward the weapon. "Tell me more of your sword. You appear to prize it highly, and 'tis evident your brother covets it as well."

He smiled thinly. " 'Tis the last vestige of the position that was once mine. Tradition dictates the sword of Baldor be passed on to the firstborn male of the royal house of Anacreon. The first born and heir. Dragan's possession of the sword would seal his succession to the throne."

"But you gave the throne up when you left those many years ago. Why keep a symbol of

91

your continuing position as crown prince?"

Aidan shrugged. "I don't know. Mayhap 'tis a perverse need to anger my father and brother. Mayhap 'tis a reluctance to give up the only thing left that binds me to my birthright. Whatever 'tis, I cannot seem to relinquish Baldor's sword. I'll die first."

"Dragan wants the sword badly." A glimpse of the fetid morass of greedy ambition, broken dreams, and something darker and even more sinister fleetingly assailed Breanne. Dread rippled through her.

"I'm afraid for you, Aidan," she murmured, meeting his gaze squarely. "It could well mean your death if you continue to withhold the sword from Dragan. I fear your father wouldn't—or couldn't—stop him."

The expression in his unpatched eye sharpened to glittering awareness. "Neither of us is safe within these walls. But, be that as it may, I'm far better prepared to defend myself. Remember that, lass, and stay near me. Once I'm gone, the danger to you should pass."

"Gone? When will you leave? Where will you go?"

" 'Tis better that you don't know. My leaving will be for the best, though."

Breanne regarded him thoughtfully. A question burgeoned within her, even as she feared the reply. Still, she gathered her courage, knowing it, like everything else about their fledgling relationship, must be faced. "Will you take me with you when you leave?"

Regret flared in his eye, then was mastered and gone. "Nay, lass."

A multitude of responses bubbled to Breanne's lips—that as his wife her place was at his side, that he needed her if there was ever to be hope of winning the people back to him, that she *needed* to be with him. But his look of iron-clad resolve brooked no argument. And, more than anything, she never wanted to be a source of pain or distress to him.

Her head lowered. "As you wish, m'lord."

He stepped closer and lifted her chin with his free hand. " 'Twill be better for you when I'm gone. I'll leave you virgin on our wedding night and, if you wish, you can have the marriage annulled after I've departed. I'll never return to this land, so the law won't touch me again."

Breanne opened her mouth to protest, but he cut her off. "If you instead prefer the life of a royal princess, keep silent about our marriage bed and all will accept you as my wife."

"And what if I wish a child to comfort me in your absence, to carry on your blood?"

His expression went hard, glacial. "That I'll never give you. 'Twould only propagate the curse and doom the child to a living hell."

"You don't know that, Aidan," Breanne hurried to say, wanting more than anything she'd ever wanted to ease the anguish she knew that admission had cost him. "You can't be certain—"

"Can you be any more certain that 'twouldn't? Would you risk having that laid upon an innocent child?"

"You were innocent as well, when the curse was laid upon you!" Her eyes filled with angry, unshed tears. "The only difference would be

93

that I'd see to it our child developed the courage to fight against it and never give up. Our child would learn to love—and give love—and would eventually find some way to defeat its curse!"

His mouth drew into a ruthless, forbidding line. "Not as his cowardly father has failed to do, is that what you mean, Breanne?"

She glared back at him, her own lips set in a mutinous line, and her silence was his answer.

At the realization, Aidan's anger drained from him in one debilitating rush, leaving only an empty, aching void. He sighed and shook his head. " 'Tis past time that we were abed, and I haven't the strength to fight you on this, at any rate. Those are my terms, lass. Choose which one suits you. 'Twill matter not to me."

He turned then, forcing himself back to the bed to gather up the fur coverlet and pillow. With long, quick strides Aidan headed out onto the balcony, tossed down his bedding, and proceeded to strip off his belt, black tunic, chain mail, and under tunic. His tall black boots soon followed.

Then he glanced back into the room to find Breanne still standing where he'd left her. "Well, lass? Is there something more that prevents you from taking your rest?"

She stared at him, bathed in the moonlight that streamed onto the balcony, broad of shoulder and chest, powerful of body. At the sight of the eye patch he seemed determined constantly to wear, something twisted inside Breanne.

He doesn't dare trust himself even in sleep. He fears his powers even more than others do.

Breanne shook her head, guilt at her former harsh words flooding her. "Nay, m'lord. There's naught but my remorse at my needlessly cruel tongue a few moments ago. That and the explanation you said you'd give me about your father. I can wait till the morrow, though," she hastened to add. " 'Tisn't reason to keep you from your rest."

His gaze narrowed and he went tense once more. "And why would you care what there is between my father and me? I'll soon be out of your life and mind. How will knowing aid you in any way?"

"You will always be my husband, for I'll never dishonor your memory by renouncing my vows to you. And, as your wife, I'd like to know as much as I can of you, to understand."

Aidan inhaled a shuddering breath. "As you wish. 'Twill take little time to tell the tale, at any rate." He motioned her forward. "Come out here, lass. Take a seat on this bench."

Breanne complied as Aidan moved to the balcony's railing. She watched him lean on the stone support, his gaze fanning out across the land, a land black and featureless save for the hazy red glow of the fires blazing in the distance. Blazing in her village, her home.

A home that was no more, Breanne corrected herself quickly. Her home was now here, with this dark, tormented man. A man of many secrets and terrifying powers, yet a man who drew her like no other.

The first time she'd met Aidan she had known there was something different, something special about him. Something that drew her just as strongly, as movingly as the dizzying heights of a mountain peak, or the grandeur of a silent sunrise or dazzling sunset. Her fate, her heart, had been bound to his in that instant he had first ensorceled her, then withdrawn, cursing himself for his weakness. Now, there was nothing left but to follow where he wished to lead—and pray neither of them lost their souls in the journey.

"For the longest time," Aidan began, his deep voice suddenly piercing the darkness, "I imagined my father hated me for the birthing curse Morloch set upon me. For the longest time, I strove, with every fiber of my being, to make amends, to find some way to regain my father's love. But that day I killed Rangor, in an anger stirred by the fires of my youthful passion far out of proportion to the perceived insult, I finally comprehended the truth."

Apprehension, unexpected in its intensity and advent, rose in Breanne like some heated cloud, choking and smothering her. "Aidan, mayhap 'tisn't proper I should hear this after all." Breanne rose from the bench. "I really haven't the right—"

He wheeled about, his features shadowed, but every hard-muscled inch of him emanating a taut message of how much this revelation cost him. "Is this another game you play with me, first to lower my defenses with your soft words, then to pull back like you're afraid the tale will offend you?" Aidan demanded hoarsely.

"Nay!" Breanne took a step toward him. "Ah, nay, Aidan! 'Tis just that I fear I won't be able to bear the pain of hearing what your father did to you. That I have no right to ask you to relive it, either."

"And who else has more right than the woman who'll be my wife? Who else than the one person who possessed the courage to stand up to the people of Anacreon and save my life?"

A swift movement, that ears couldn't hear and eyes barely perceived, brought him to her side. "Do you truly lack the heart to know the truth?" he whispered. "Or do you fear what 'twill further reveal of my sordid, evil nature?"

"Can there be anything more about you that would shock me?"

She saw him start, pause to eye her with a puzzled wonderment, then smile. A bittersweet pang filled her, knowing the gentling it would bring to Aidan's features would forever be hidden in shadow.

Breanne stepped closer. The warmth of his body, his naked chest, touched her like some mantle, encompassing her with a sensation of trusting acceptance. He needed to share his tale and, worthy or not, she was the one he wished to tell.

"Tell me," she forced herself to say. "Tell me, for I'd know everything."

"And what is there to understand about a father who never accepted his firstborn? Whose unreasoning hatred colored every interaction, until that day he finally revealed the full extent of his revulsion for me."

Aidan reached out for Breanne in the moonlight, in a night drenched in shadows and silken summer breezes, and touched her arm. She trembled as his hand stroked her, tentatively at first, the pads of his fingers caressing the length of her limb from shoulder to wrist. Bursts of fire ignited in the wake of his searing path. Her heart commenced a wild beat.

"A-Aidan," she whispered.

"He told me, as we stood alone over Rangor's body in that wooded glen," he continued, his words a sharp contrast to his gentle fascination with her body, "that I wasn't his son, had never been. That what I had wrought that day was indeed the work of a demon's spawn. That 'twould be best for all if I left Anacreon and never returned to challenge Dragan's rightful claim to the throne."

"And your mother, the queen. What did she say to that?"

"Nothing, save to extract my promise to return to Anacreon on my thirtieth birthing day."

"But that was so cruel, so unfair of them!" Breanne cried. "You were untutored in the use of your eye. No one had ever taught you of its power, its control!"

His hand encircled her arm, caressing the silken garment and the flesh that lay beneath. "Indeed? And how would you know that? How old are you, Breanne? Seventeen, eighteen? Far too young to have known what happened fifteen years ago, much less understood."

"I was three years old when you killed Rangor!" she retorted hotly. "But later, when I was of an age to learn, a holy man came to our village as teacher to the children. He taught me many things, including the events of that day. 'Twas he who explained the truth behind it all."

Aidan's grip tightened. "This holy man, how would he know 'the truth behind it all'? And, even more importantly, why would he care?"

"I don't know, Aidan."

He scowled. "Then where can he be found? I'll seek him out and discover my own answers."

Breanne's hand covered his and she squeezed it in a gesture of regret. "He disappeared two years ago, as mysteriously as he had first arrived. I no longer know where he is."

"And why should that surprise me?" Aidan muttered, half to himself. He released Breanne's arm and took a step back. " 'Tis the same fate that has dogged me all these years of my exile. Searching and never finding, until I ceased to hope for any answer to my curse, be it good or evil."

"You must never lose hope, Aidan."

His bitter laugh cut through the night air. "You are truly the most amazingly naive woman I've ever ventured upon. You know naught of me, of the horrors I've seen and even worse that I've wrought, and yet you still stand here and counsel hope. Instead, my beauteous little wife-to-be, you should be running as far and fast as you can from me."

"I'm not afraid of what's in your heart."

His shoulders slumped in what could as easily have been a gesture of defeat as one of weariness. "Well, you should be. I am."

Aidan gestured to the balcony doorway. "Now, no more of this. Enough has been said, and far too much revealed for one night. Get you to your bed, as I intend to go to mine."

"As you wish." Breanne turned to leave, then hesitated. "One thing more."

"Aye, lass," came the weary reply.

"Know this, Aidan, rightful prince of Anacreon. Our fates are joined. In my heart I will never leave you, no matter how far you go from me, how desperate the battle or dark the times become."

"Then beware your immortal soul, sweet lady," he rasped in a voice that broke for a fleeting instant, "for I cannot even promise where my own soul is bound."

Chapter Five

A knock sounded insistently at the door. Breanne groaned, rolled over, and pulled a pillow over her head. She was so tired and Mother surely had some onerous chore for her to do. Ah, if she could only sleep just a little while longer . . .

The knocking continued, a steady pounding now that grated on Breanne's nerves. It effectively dispelled the lingering mists of her drowsiness. Guilt intruded into her sleepy self-indulgence. Her mother needed her help. She must rise.

Breanne threw off the pillow and sat up. She blinked, clearing her sleep-clouded eyes. A large room, opulently furnished, came into view. Breanne gasped as remembrance flooded her. She wasn't home in her family's snug little cottage. She was in the royal palace, betrothed to the crown prince, a prince—her gaze strayed to the balcony—who had slept nearby all night.

Grabbing the satin bed robe that still lay spread out upon the coverlet, Breanne sprang out of bed. She slipped into the garment and, clutching it to her, hurried over to the door.

Mara stood there. She was damp-faced with the exertion of trying to juggle a large covered tray and, at the same time, pound on the thick oaken portal. When Breanne jerked open the door, the little woman nearly toppled over backward in surprise.

"M-m'lady!" she stammered. "You took so long to answer, I feared some evil had befallen you last night." She eyed Breanne's open bed robe and dainty gown beneath, the tousled mane of golden hair, and smiled. "But I see instead that you were quite safe in our prince's presence."

Breanne flushed and motioned her in, shutting the door firmly behind her. "I am quite safe, as you say. As for the prince, I haven't had time to check on him where he sleeps on the balcony." She motioned toward the covered tray. "What do you have there, Mara?"

"Breakfast for you and the prince, m'lady." The servant lifted several lids and inhaled deeply. "There's fresh baked bread, eggs and ham, goat's cheese, apples and plums, and a flask of watered wine to ease your thirst. Unless you prefer ale?"

The maid replaced the lids and cocked her head, awaiting Breanne's decision. Breanne inhaled a deep breath.

"Wine will be acceptable, Mara. Place it on the

table near the hearth while I fetch the prince."

Uneasiness lanced through Breanne as she made her way across the room toward the balcony, effectively dispelling further thoughts of the meal. A half-naked man lay sleeping outside, a man about whom she truly knew little. Who was she to presume to wake him, or know how or when he preferred to break his fast? 'Twas the prerogative of a wife, Breanne admitted, but a wife willingly chosen, not some woman thrust upon a man at the point of death.

'Twas the intimacy of the actions that disturbed her so, that she well knew. An act she had envisioned many times, of tenderly waking her sleeping husband with a gentle kiss, of having him smile and pull her down to lie in his arms, of the ensuing moments spent talking of warm, loving things. But they were the stuff of girlish dreams. And she had ceased to be a girl when she'd cast her lot with a man others named the Demon Prince.

Breanne paused at the balcony door, squared her shoulders, and stepped through. Aidan slept a few feet away, one arm shoved beneath his head and pillow, the fur flung aside in the rising heat of the early morn; he was naked save for his black breeches. From the slow, even rhythm of his breathing it was evident he was still fast asleep, the strain and exhaustion of the past few days holding him in the heavy grip of slumber.

"Aidan?" Breanne whispered, suddenly loath to wake him. She squatted beside him and lightly touched his shoulder. "Aidan? Wake up."

He jerked upright at that, halfway to his knees

in the space of a gasp, grabbing Breanne by the arms. His single eye blazed amber fire. Then he recognized her.

"By the Mother, Breanne," he groaned, wrenching his gaze away. "Don't ever touch me like that when I sleep! It could well mean your death."

She drew back. "I-I am sorry. I meant no harm."

"I know that, lass." Aidan released her and climbed to his feet. "And normally I'd have wakened before you could have drawn so near." He shoved an unruly lock of hair that had fallen free from his warrior's topknot out of his eye. "I failed us both in my carelessness."

"We are still alive, m'lord."

"Mayhap," he admitted glumly, "but thanks to no effort on my part."

Breanne gestured back toward the bedchamber. "Mara has brought us breakfast. Are you hungry?"

Her questioning gaze sought out his, only to find Aidan's attention riveted on the opening of her bed robe. The fabric had fallen free when he'd grabbed her and, in the ensuing confrontation, she had forgotten to recover herself.

Breanne glanced down. The thin lawn gown hid little, from the swell of her breasts jutting impudently against the cloth, to the slight curve of her belly and shadowed valley blatantly obvious at the juncture of her thighs.

But what disturbed Breanne most of all was the look of yearning, of acute, almost palpable physical hunger, that glittered in Aidan's eyes. His expression reminded her of something feral, desperate, and dangerous. Fear shuddered through her—an emotion equally disturbing and strangely primal.

She gripped the edges of her bed gown and drew them closed. Aidan's gaze slowly lifted. A dark brow arched over an eye that considered her with a wary intensity. An intensity that bespoke of many things—his need, his silent question, and a guarded waiting.

Suddenly, Breanne couldn't deal with it, not him, nor his surprising desire for her, nor her own confusing mix of emotions. She backed away.

"I-I will join you at breakfast once Mara has helped me to dress," she hastened to explain, then turned and fled.

He was fully garbed as well when she returned from the adjoining dressing room, his face clean-shaven and his hair once more smoothly pulled back in his warrior's topknot. Mara followed closely behind her mistress. Aidan glanced from Breanne to the maidservant, seeing the old woman as the quite evident chaperon she was. He rose and came around the little table to seat Breanne.

As she took her chair, he leaned over and whispered in her ear. "You don't need Mara, lass. You're quite safe from my unwelcome advances."

His warm breath caressed her ear and neck, sending a wild excitement quivering through her. Breanne shot him a flushed, anguished glance, then cast her eyes down at her lap. "You may leave us, Mara."

"As you wish, m'lady."

The door closed before Breanne dared lift her gaze back to Aidan's. He regarded her with a searching scrutiny, then returned to his meal.

"I beg pardon if I caused offense earlier," he said as he sliced a generous chunk from the pale yellow round of cheese and placed it on a slice of warm bread. " 'Twas only a look. 'Twon't happen again. I told you before that I'll ease my lust elsewhere."

Breanne's knife clattered to her plate.

Aidan glanced up. Her face had gone white, her eyes huge, her lips trembling. By the Holy Ones, he thought, what have I said now to offend her?

"Breanne," Aidan began; then words failed. He was suddenly at a loss as to what to say to reassure her.

She forced a small, wan smile. "I-I beg pardon, m'lord. Truly, 'twasn't offensive, what you did. I-I just didn't know how to respond, what to say. I am innocent in such things and . . . and I still hardly know you."

And there is no good served in the knowing, he thought, bitterly harking back to last eve when he'd revealed far too much of the source of the conflict between him and his father. Mayhap it had been an over-generous amount of ale imbibed at supper, or his exhaustion, but he'd warmed far too quickly for good sense to the beguiling little peasant lass. He must take care in the future. She was as skilled a sorceress with her woman's ways as he was with his darker powers.

"It matters not. The customary wedded life

will never be ours at any rate. You realize that now, don't you?"

He doesn't really want me. I am beneath him, Breanne thought with a shattering pain, then silently cursed herself. She had known it would be this way from the beginning, but his continued kindness to her, and the looks . . .

Breanne nodded, steeling herself to the reality of their situation. "Aye, m'lord. 'Twill be as you wish."

"Good. 'Tis better that there be no misunderstandings." He took a bite of his bread and cheese and swallowed it before continuing. "About last night. About the rift between my father and me."

Breanne glanced up from the slice of bread she'd forced herself to butter. "Aye, m'lord?"

"What I told you is best forgotten. It accomplished naught save mayhap stir pity for me in your heart. And I loathe—"

"You loathe pity," she finished for him with a gentle smile. "I know that, and assure you that you aren't the kind of man who could ever stir my pity. Compassion—concern, mayhap—but never pity."

"I see little difference."

She considered him briefly. "Nay, I suppose you don't, after all those years of rejection and loneliness. I only wish to help you."

A fierce burning fire sprang in his eye. "I never asked for your help!"

"Nor can you yet trust me enough to accept it," she countered softly.

Aidan willed himself to relax. 'Twas pointless to vent his anger at Breanne's well-meant kindness. "This marriage grows more complicated by the moment. Truly, lass, you owe me naught more than what you've already given in saving my life. Mayhap if you assure your mother of that, 'twill ease her concerns."

At the mention of her mother, Breanne's eyes brightened. The thought of today's visit to her village effectively banished the somber effects of their previous discussion. "Oh, aye, 'twill indeed," she agreed happily, "especially when she has a chance to meet and talk with you. And my brothers, Cavell and Perkin. They are very protective of me, so you must not take offense if they're not initially over-warm with you. But give them time as well to get to know you. . . ."

Aidan reached across the little table and laid a hand upon her arm. "Lass, I tell you true. I haven't the interest or inclination to make social talk or garner your family's friendship. 'Tis a hopeless quest, not to mention beyond my skills. I'm a warrior, and no longer possess the verbal talents of a diplomat or royal personage."

"But you *are* a human being, aren't you?" Breanne demanded, barely containing her rising aggravation. "Truly, Aidan, but you put up as many barriers against others as they do against you!"

He leaned back in his chair, wry amusement curling his lips. "Mayhap I do, but 'tis my choice. If your 'compassion' for me extends that far, I ask that you respect that."

Breanne threw her napkin in her plate and rose with a regal grace. "As you wish, *m'lord*."

She smiled archly. "At least for the time being, at any rate."

Breanne could barely contain her excitement as they headed down the castle road that led to her village. Clasped securely before Aidan on Lucifer's huge back, she felt surprisingly content, curiously happy.

As the horse cantered along, she glanced about her. The late-morning sun burned warmly overhead, the land glinting green and gold in the orb's celestial radiance.

To Breanne's right spread the queen's deer park, hunting and wood gathering there forbidden to any but the royal family. To her left lay wheat and rye fields interspersed with plots spread with manure to lie fallow for a year to replenish the soil's fertility. Soon, she knew, the grain would be ripe for harvest, a harvest this year she could only watch from afar.

Briefly, Breanne wondered what kept a noble lady occupied from day to day. There was more than enough to do as a peasant, laboring from dawn to dusk in an endless round of cooking, cleaning, spinning and weaving, then sewing the clothes, not to mention the candle making, meat curing, gardening and communal grain planting in spring, and harvesting of the village fields in late summer. Mayhap as a noblewoman there'd be more opportunity to read the books she dearly loved, like the ones borrowed from the parish priest so oft in the past. Mayhap there'd be more time for lessons for the children.

The children. A sweet pain plucked at her

heart at the memory of the village children. Marta, Shamus, Gwynn, Oona, Clarine, and all the others.

As a prince's wife, would she be permitted to mingle with the villagers? If not, who would teach the children to read and write when she was gone? Who would regale them with tales of glorious exploits, of heroes and ladies, of courage, self-sacrifice, and love?

She shot Aidan a fleeting glance. His stern profile was riveted straight ahead, his body straight and strong, his countenance unsmiling and proud.

His words of earlier that morning returned with an aching clarity. *Truly, Breanne, you owe me naught more than what you've already given in saving my life.*

It was kind of him to attempt to reassure her, to assuage the fears and uncertainties of what a life as his lady might be like, but it was unnecessary. He didn't understand that she had sacrificed everything in that moment she'd claimed him for hers. There was nothing left to relinquish.

But would he value her total self-offering? Somehow, Breanne sensed he viewed it instead as yet another burden to be borne, in a life already laden with more cares and hardship than any one man should bear. No, the only path left her was to carry her own sacrifices silently, and find some way to win his trust. Yet there was so little time left—and so much still to accomplish.

They passed the wooded pasture wherein grazed the village goats, then the water mill and far sheep pasture, before turning east on the well-worn road that led into the village. The house of Daron Godman, the freeman who owned the largest farm, signaled the perimeter of the village proper. Past his imposing house, the smithy's cottage and carpenter's shed, a small, straw-thatched cotter's hut with its long, backyard croft came into Breanne's view.

She moved restlessly before Aidan. "There." She pointed with an excited motion of her hand. "The tan house with the three barrels and bench by the front door, and the corn rows and apple trees in the rear garden. That's my home."

Aidan nodded and guided Lucifer in the direction of the little cottage. As they made their way, villagers paused in their tasks, started in surprise, then backed away. Breanne chose not to acknowledge their looks of fear and revulsion, knowing full well they were directed at her companion. Instead, she waved and called out to each.

"Good morning, Jastow!" she cried to the brawny smithy. "How goes your house building, Martin?" she inquired of the aging village carpenter. Their only reply to her was a curt nod and a furtive warding sign against Aidan.

Then they were halting before Breanne's house. Before she could even climb down from the great war-horse, Cavell, her oldest brother, strode from the cottage. Deep-set brown eyes squinted up at Aidan; then, as recognition filled him, he blanched beneath his dark tan. His hand lifted in the beginnings of a warding sign.

Breanne jumped down and rushed over to him. She caught his hand in hers. "Don't,

Cavell," she pleaded. " 'Tis cruel to treat Aidan so. He's but a man, as much of flesh and blood as you."

Her brother hesitated, shot Aidan another narrow-eyed glance, then lowered his hand. His gaze turned to his sister.

"You're yet unharmed, I see. Mother will be relieved at that."

Breanne smiled. "Where is she? And Perkin? Where is he as well?"

"Perkin has taken the oxen to be fitted for a new yoke. And Mother is inside, baking bread." He paused. "Shall I call her for you?"

"Nay." Breanne shook her head. "I'd rather surprise her." She turned to Aidan, who had dismounted. "M'lord, I wish to introduce my eldest brother, Cavell. He works at the fish ponds when he's not assisting my younger brother, Perkin, with our farm plot."

Cavell schooled his features into an inscrutable mask and bowed stiffly. "M'lord."

Aidan returned the salutation with an equally stiff nod.

Nothing more was said as the two men continued to eye each other. The silence grew until Breanne felt compelled to intercede. She indicated the front door.

"If you please, m'lord, would you care to enter our home and meet my mother?"

He glanced at the cottage, then shook his head. "I'm content to await you here. Surely you've a need for some private words with your mother."

"Aye," Breanne nodded slowly. "I suppose you're right." She pulled over the well-worn wooden bench. "If you've a wish to sit," she explained. Then, with an uncertain little smile, she turned and entered the house.

Movements from behind a small partition that separated the oven from the rest of the large, one-room cottage alerted Breanne to her mother's presence. The scent of baking bread wafted to her nostrils. Breanne's mouth watered, as she imagined biting into a slice of one of the crisp, brown loaves that would soon emerge.

She paused to scan the cottage's interior with a loving glance. Sides of meat and whole fish hung from the rafters where the cook fire's smoke would draw past before exiting one of the smoke holes at either end of the roof. Her gaze lowered to the packed dirt floor, swept to spotless tidiness each day by her mother, passing over the rough-hewn dining table and benches, to the sleeping pallets lined along the wall. Beyond a wall on the opposite end of the cottage from the bake oven lay a small store-room, filled with clothes chests and the family's other meager possessions and, past that, the stalls for their prized oxen.

'Twas a simple, threadbare existence, Breanne mused, but one that had contented her until now. Strange how meeting one man could change everything in such a short span of time—and in every way.

She tiptoed over to where her mother worked and tapped her on the back. "Mother? 'Tis I, Breanne."

With a small cry, Kyna wheeled around. Flour dusted her silver-threaded brown hair, and her face and hands. She quickly wiped her palms clean on her apron, then pulled her daughter into her arms. For long minutes Kyna held Breanne close, the only sound the muffled sobs of both women.

Finally, Breanne pushed back to gaze into her mother's moisture-filled eyes. "I hope those tears are of joy for me," she teased in a choking voice.

"That you are still alive and untouched, aye," Kyna whispered. "But for how much longer, daughter?"

"I am quite safe with Aidan, Mother." Breanne took her by the arm and pulled her around the partition and over to the dining table. "Come, sit and we'll talk."

She glanced at her mother's face and damply clinging hair. "A cool cup of water would be most welcome as well, would it not?"

Kyna nodded and wiped her face with the edge of her apron. "Aye, that 'twould."

Breanne poured out two cups from the ancient earthenware pitcher of water that sat on the table and shoved one over to her mother. Both women sipped briefly in silence; then their gazes met.

"You call him Aidan now," Kyna began. "Does that familiarity mean he's already bedded you?"

"Nay, Mother." Breanne set down her cup. "He but asked me to call him that, considering I'm soon to be his wife."

"When? When will you wed?"

"In six days. The queen wished for time to make adequate preparations for our wedding."

"She doesn't know then, even seeing you," Kyna murmured. "Ah, by the Mother, what am I to do? What am I to do?"

A small frown formed between Breanne's slender brows. "What do you mean, 'she doesn't know'? Are you speaking of Queen Eislin?"

Kyna downed the contents of her cup with one gulp, then set it down. She considered her daughter for a long moment, then exhaled a deep breath. "Aye, I mean the queen. One would think an aunt would have recognized her niece."

"Aunt?" Breanne's eyes went wide as she struggled to fathom the implications of her mother's words. Nausea coiled in the pit of her stomach. "How can that be? You are my mother, and no kin to Queen Eislin that I know of!"

Kyna reached across the table to take Breanne's hand. A sad, loving light gleamed in her eyes. "I'm not your natural mother, Breanne."

Panic surged through her. For a long, terrifying moment, Breanne couldn't take in a breath. "N-nay!" she finally cried. "It cannot be! You are my mother, Cavell and Perkin my brothers! I want no others!"

"And would your wanting change the truth?" Kyna softly demanded. "You are my foster child, brought to me by Olenus after the death of your real parents."

"M-my real parents?" Breanne blanched.

"You are the daughter of Lord Arlen and the Lady Tessa. You are the only survivor of the murder of their family, these nearly fifteen years ago. You are related to the royal house through the prince consort, and through him, to your betrothed. He, sweet daughter, is your first cousin."

Breanne stared back at her, speechless.

"Do you begin to understand?" Kyna prodded. " 'Twas of vital importance that no one knew you survived, even the queen, for fear Morloch might discover your presence and kill you as well. For whatever reason he meant to destroy the House Laena, we must make certain that he fails. The prophecy . . ."

"What prophecy?" Breanne demanded when her mother's voice faded. "Mara mentioned it once as well, but I know of no prophecy. What is it? Tell me, Mother!"

Kyna smiled grimly. " 'Tis an ancient one that no one could fathom all these hundreds of years, foretelling a horrible curse laid upon the land. Yet, when the Demon Prince was born with his Evil Eye, and then the family of the heir of the House Laena was destroyed . . ."

She paused, drawing her hand from Breanne's and fixing her with a piercing stare. "The Evil One and his servant will fall," she solemnly proclaimed the words of the prophecy, "when the House of Laena rises from its ashes to free the heart of the one-eyed son."

Utter silence descended upon the little cottage. Blood pounded through Breanne's skull, growing louder with each pulsing beat of her heart. The room shifted, swam before her eyes and, for a dizzying moment, she thought she might faint. Then she inhaled a deep breath, squared her shoulders, and met her mother's gaze once more.

"If what you say about me is true, that I'm truly the queen's niece and . . . and Aidan's cousin, it still doesn't necessarily mean I'm integral to the prophecy."

Kyna arched a speculative brow. "Do you think not, daughter? Then you are the only one. Olenus was convinced enough to come here, risk Morloch discovering his true identity, and teach you what someone of your breeding should know. Didn't you ever wonder why you received such a fine education, unsuited for a peasant?"

"But Olenus taught all the village children, not just me!"

" 'Twas but a diversion from his true student, you." She rose and came to sit beside Breanne on the bench. " 'Tis all falling into place now, isn't it, daughter? The tales Olenus told you of Prince Aidan, so different from those whispered over the communal fire pit at night—did they not set the tone for your rapid acceptance of him? Did you think instead 'twas your usual headstrong, impulsive nature that compelled you to step forward to save his life?"

Confusion clouded Breanne's eyes. "I-I don't know. I thought I but saw the man beneath the facade, sensed his true humanity and goodness beating within his well-guarded heart."

"I know not of that, nor do I care what he is truly like." Kyna moved closer, her voice dropping. "I care only for you, daughter. And I now see more danger to you if you wed the prince, than if you don't. Mayhap we should tell the queen and her consort—"

"Nay!" Breanne cut her mother off with a vehemence that shocked even herself. "He has no one else but me. If I refuse to wed him, cousin though he may be, he will die."

"But you cannot wed your first cousin! 'Tis forbidden, by law and religion. The children that would come of such a union—"

"Fear not, Mother," Breanne hurried to explain. "Aidan has no plans to bed me. For his own reasons, he wants no children, either. He will leave Anacreon immediately after we are wed, and never return."

"And you. What will he do with you?"

She sighed. "He will leave me here."

Kyna considered that bit of information. "So, the marriage will be in name only? And when he is gone, what then?"

"I can remain as his wife, or have the marriage annulled."

"Olenus must be consulted," Kyna murmured. "He must decide what is the safest course for you."

"And what of Aidan?" Rising anger threaded Breanne's voice. "Shouldn't we consult Olenus on *his* fate as well? Or has that never been a concern?"

Exasperation tightened Kyna's mouth. "Now, daughter, don't let your emotions get the better of you. 'Tisn't my decision to make. My only task all these years has been to love you and keep you safe. The rest is beyond me or my meager powers."

As much as she hated to admit it, much less accept it, Breanne knew her mother spoke true.

She had risked much when she'd taken her into the family, hidden her away all these years from Morloch's evil notice.

But whatever had happened, 'twas all in the past. What mattered now was the present, and the need to assume the terrible burden of responsibility herself. And a large part of that responsibility, it seemed, was to support Aidan, whether as cousin or wife.

His cousin. The admission of their heretofore unknown relationship stirred unbidden emotions. Emotions as tumultuous and unsettling as regret for what now could never be. For guilt at the need for her deception of Aidan, for she didn't dare tell him, not knowing what his reaction might be. It didn't matter anyway. He'd soon be gone and need never know.

She rose from the table, suddenly remembering he still awaited her outside. "Come, Mother. Aidan brought me to visit, and I'd like you to meet him." She smiled. "See for yourself he's not half so fearsome as others think."

Kyna stood, a dubious look in her eyes. "Cousin or no, daughter, he still possesses the Evil Eye and fearsome abilities. No matter what Olenus hopes for him, can anyone be certain which way he'll turn with those powers? Can even you, in your heart, truly know?"

Her mother's question stabbed at Breanne, piercing deeper with each word that fell from her lips. How, indeed, could she be certain if Aidan's powers would eventually lead him to good or evil? He himself wasn't even certain, she thought, harking back to his warning last night before they retired.

" . . . *beware your immortal soul, sweet lady, for I cannot even promise where my own soul is bound.*"

She forced back the doubts that had no hope of answer now, and mayhap never. "What does it matter, Mother? Can anyone truly know another's deepest stirrings? But whatever sort of man Aidan becomes, it seems my destiny has always been to aid him in the battle against Morloch and the Evil One.

"And mayhap, just mayhap," Breanne added with a small, secret smile, "the battle to regain his heart as well."

Chapter Six

The ride home was quiet, Breanne immersed in contemplation of all her mother had revealed, Aidan maintaining his usual stoic silence unless prodded otherwise. Lucifer, however, was unusually gregarious, which caused his master no end of exasperation.

What say you, my friend? the big war-horse inquired mildly as he galloped along. *Was it a worthwhile visit, meeting your future mother-in-law?*

Aidan scowled. *Enough, Lucifer. I'm in no mood for your snide gibes.*

But did they not welcome you into the family with open arms? I thought you did quite well with the older brother. By the time we departed, he seemed almost relaxed around you.

A monumental achievement, Aidan agreed dryly.

A start, my friend. And you have the little female to thank for that.

His master shook his head. *Another five days and 'twon't matter.*

Are you so certain she'll be safe, once we're gone?

A muscle began to twitch in Aidan's jaw. *What are you getting at, Lucifer?*

Didn't you see the change in her, once she returned from talking with her mother?

Aidan shrugged. *Breanne seemed quieter, more preoccupied, and a little sad. I but attributed that to the pain of leaving her family—and all that has transpired in the past few days.*

She looked at you differently, too. There was something akin to regret, and a certain wistfulness, in her eyes. I don't like it.

Do you think she means to betray me?

Nay. But she bears watching—for her sake as well as yours.

Well, I rarely let her out of my sight as 'tis. Aidan grinned. *Unless you think I should now be present at her robing and disrobing, and her bathing as well?*

A most pleasant consideration, to be sure, Lucifer snorted. *As if you haven't enough trouble without bringing your loins back into this.*

Aidan's smile faded. *She doesn't want me, so put your mind at rest in regards to my loins.*

The big war-horse tossed his head. *Doesn't she now? You humans are all alike. You can't see the truth unless it walks up and slams itself right into your face!*

"Enough, Lucifer," Aidan gritted, finally los-

Demon Prince

ing his patience. "I see what I want and need to, and that's sufficient to me!"

Breanne glanced over her shoulder. "Talking to your horse again, are you?"

"More like he lectures and I listen," her dark companion growled.

She turned back to face the road. "Does it do any good?"

"What?" Aidan demanded, suddenly at a loss as to her meaning.

"Do his lectures help you? Give you guidance, comfort, companionship?"

Aidan sighed. First Lucifer's prodding, and now Breanne's! "Sometimes. He's been a trustworthy friend for many a year. I can depend on him."

"And no one else, Aidan? You haven't made any other friends in all those years of your exile? There's no place you can call haven?"

"Breanne!" he exploded in exasperation. "What does it matter?"

Her back straightened and she went stiff in his arms. "I just wanted to think there was someone else out there besides your horse, when you leave Anacreon once more. Someone you could go to if you needed succor, or you became lonely."

"I don't get lonely!" he snapped.

Come, come, my friend. You and I both know the truth of that.

Aidan rolled his eyes. "There is one man," he finally conceded. "His name is Dane. He's the lord of Castle Haversin. I fought for him one year as his mercenary captain. He saved my life."

123

"And now you owe him a boon of friendship?"

He nodded. "For my life, but even more so for his acceptance of me as a man."

Breanne smiled. "So, there *are* people out there who see you as something more than a demon prince."

"One man's friendship doesn't constitute total acceptance or forgiveness. The people haven't changed in their perception of me. Your village today was a prime example."

" 'Twill take time, Aidan. 'Twas a start. Did you see any warding signs by the time we left?"

"They were in their eyes, and thoughts, nonetheless."

"Ah, Aidan, why do you persist in being so pigheaded?"

Aye, Lucifer added, *why* are *you so pigheaded?"*

"Lucifer," his master warned.

"Is he on my side, then?" Breanne inquired. "Your horse, I mean?"

"He's on no one's side but his own!" Aidan shot her a narrow glance. "And that's the end of this topic!"

Her mouth curved into a slow, unconsciously provocative smile. "As you wish, m'lord."

He noted the smile and felt the frustration rise. "Breanne, don't bait me!"

"Aye, Aidan," came the meek reply.

"You look beautiful!" Sirilla exclaimed from her chair beside the queen's bed as Breanne stepped out from behind the dressing screen.

"Aye, that she does," Eislin agreed smilingly. She motioned to Breanne. "Come closer, child."

Breanne did as asked, drawing to a halt beside the bed of the woman she now knew to be her aunt. Four days had passed since the visit to her village and the shocking revelation of her true heritage, but she still marveled—and struggled to accept it. Long hours in the queen's presence or working with Sirilla on wedding gifts to give to Aidan, as was the usual bridal custom, had done little to ease her startling transition from peasant to noble lady.

Self-consciously, she smoothed the crimson silk tunic dress, trimmed with bits of white ermine, and straightened the wine-colored surcoat embroidered with silver thread. Like Sirilla's blue dress that day she'd first met the queen, the effect on Breanne was startlingly regal and beguilingly seductive.

Eislin nodded in satisfaction. " 'Twill be a fitting wedding gown, once we've added your veil and silver coronet. Aidan will be pleased."

Breanne smiled softly. "I pray so, m'lady. He deserves his share of happiness, after all he's been through in these many years."

A shadow passed across the queen's face. "Aye, that he has, poor lad. But there was no other way. . . ."

As if catching herself, Eislin straightened, pulling herself up to her full, most commanding height. "We can all use some new life in this gloomy castle."

She glanced toward Sirilla, who was busily at work embroidering Aidan's personal coat of arms onto a pair of leather gloves Sirilla planned to give him as her own wedding gift. "I know for a fact Sirilla is delighted to call you friend. Aren't you, dear?"

Dragan's wife looked up and smiled. "Aye, m'lady. That I am."

"Mayhap 'twill be for the good of all, Aidan's return and marriage to you," Eislin continued. "If Aidan can successfully reclaim his birthright, mayhap Dragan will finally accept that he was never meant to rule and devote himself to what he does do well."

" 'Twould be wonderful, m'lady," Sirilla replied, though her look was anything but hopeful.

The queen smothered a yawn behind a delicate little pat of the hand and lay back against her pillows. "Have Mara help Breanne out of the gown, will you, Sirilla? I feel in need of a short nap before my evening meal is served."

Her glance strayed to the large, stone-cut window. The sun had just sunk below the horizon and long fingers of purpling twilight stretched across the land. She smiled over at Breanne and Sirilla. "You two young ladies should dress for supper, shouldn't you?"

"Aye, m'lady," Sirilla said, rising from her chair and laying aside the gloves. "All is in preparation for the wedding on the morrow. The gown is ready, the chapel decorated, and the holy man arrived."

The holy man has indeed arrived, Eislin thought as her lids lowered in drowsy satisfaction. *And tomorrow night, when the castle's abed, he will call Aidan and Breanne to a quest that will finally end Morloch's reign. At long last my son will be free of his curse.*

A bittersweet pain filled her. 'Twas most likely too late for her and Marus, and Morloch had decided his own fate long ago. But the kingdom, and her two sons—there was still hope for them.

A rustle of skirts and low murmur of voices caught her attention. She opened her eyes for a final glimpse of Breanne and Sirilla as they departed the room.

Eislin smiled. Vibrant, courageous Breanne and gentle, loyal Sirilla. She'd been doubly blessed, first with a wife for Dragan who loved him despite his weaknesses and indiscretions, and now with Breanne, who bore within her the long-awaited fulfillment of the prophecy. Eislin sighed and snuggled beneath her down comforter.

Aye, there was now hope for all, each to his own needs. 'Twas enough, Eislin thought as the heavy veil of slumber settled over her.

It had to be.

Breanne and Sirilla passed the torch lighter as they hurried down the corridor that led to Aidan's bedchamber. The servant paused to nod and smile before continuing along at his appointed task. Bursts of red-gold flame illuminated the long, darkened hall in his wake, throwing the area into alternating shadow and light.

Sirilla glanced at Breanne as they walked along. "Is he kind to you? The prince, I mean?"

Breanne's mouth quirked. "Aidan? Aye. Most kind."

"I pray the queen's words come to pass."

"Indeed? And which ones were those?"

"That Dragan accepts his true fate," Sirilla replied. "He has changed so very much in the past eight years since I wed him. He was once a kind, gentle, and sensitive man. But then he began to visit a witch who lives in the forest of Raven Woods."

She shot Breanne an anguished look. "I-I think she uses her powers to seduce him, and bend him to her will."

"But for what purpose?" Breanne pulled Sirilla to a halt. "What need would a witch have with Dragan?"

"To undermine the kingdom, mayhap?" The dark-haired woman shook her head, her eyes shimmering pools of agony. "The hand of Morloch seems to touch everything these days. He is slowly killing the queen and Marus wastes away watching it. Why not destroy Dragan as well?"

She gripped Breanne's arm. "The prince has powers. Will he help us? Oh, say that he will!"

"I-I don't know, Sirilla." At the torment and fear she heard in her friend's voice, Breanne's heart went out to her. "After all that has happened, Aidan bears no love for Anacreon. . . ."

"Ask him for us, Breanne," Sirilla implored. "There must have been some reason he was gifted with his powers, that he came back to us when we needed help most!"

Aye, Breanne thought, but was the purpose to aid Anacreon—or destroy Aidan? She had to hope it was for the good of all. For Anacreon *and* Aidan.

"I will ask him," she said, "though understand that he is his own man and—"

"M'lady?" The plump form of Mara stepped from the shadows, backlit by the flickering light of the wall torches.

Breanne turned. "Aye?"

"The prince wishes me to bring you to him."

"We were going to his chamber this very moment." Breanne extracted her arm from Sirilla's clasp with a gentle movement. She gathered her skirts.

"A moment, m'lady." Mara hastily stepped into her path. "He isn't in his chambers. He awaits you in the garden."

"The garden?"

"Aye, m'lady. He mentioned something about a walk before supper. The roses are especially fine this year, and 'tis the eve of your marriage. . . ."

"Is it possible?" Sirilla laughed. "Is our prince suddenly becoming the lover? 'Tis past time, I'd say, and none too soon."

Breanne flushed. "Hush, Sirilla. I'm certain 'tisn't any such thing. He most likely wants to talk over his plans for the morrow." She motioned to Mara. "Lead on. We mustn't keep the prince waiting."

The old servant curtsied her farewell to Sirilla, then turned and hurried away. Breanne followed, mildly surprised at the elderly woman's sudden burst of energy. Mara led her down several corridors, taking unexpected turns at several junctures, until Breanne began to lose track of where she was in the castle.

Then Mara was pushing open a thick oaken

door and gesturing down a flight of stairs. "There's a door that opens to the garden at the first landing," she said, indicating to Breanne that she should go ahead of her. "Hurry now, m'lady. Your prince awaits."

Damp, musty air rose from the depths of the darkened passage. A premonition encompassed Breanne, rank with warning, laden with evil. She hesitated, uncertain of what to do.

"Surely this doesn't lead to the garden, Mara," Breanne protested. "Though I'll admit I haven't your knowledge of the castle, it seems you've taken me in quite the opposite direction."

She backed away. "I think it better I return to Aidan's chamber and await him there."

"And miss your assignation with your demon lover?" the maidservant snarled. Her hand snaked out, clenched about Breanne's arm in an iron clasp.

Breanne gasped in surprise, for the woman's strength was astonishing. She stared down into Mara's eyes, and saw something there that chilled her to the marrow of her bones.

The woman wasn't Mara!

"By the Mother!" Breanne cried, and jerked back against the strength of the other woman's hand. "Let me go. Unhand me at once!"

"And fail the one who sent me?" demanded a voice that was no longer Mara's. The woman's cackling laughter reverberated in the stone-silent halls. "Come along, little one. I promise 'twon't hurt for long. 'Tis better this way, at any rate," she said as she began to drag Breanne toward the open doorway. "Better to die still unsullied than face a living death with a follower of the Evil One."

"Nay!" Breanne screamed, even as her futile struggles failed to stay her progress back to the door. "Nay, let me be!"

With one final, superhuman jerk, the witch pulled her over and shoved. For a heart-stopping moment, Breanne clutched wildly at empty air. Then she fell headlong into blackness—and a terrifying bottomless void.

Breanne!

Aidan wheeled around in his chair, struck by a sudden sense of overwhelming urgency. Breanne was in danger!

He leaped up, grabbed his sheathed sword, and ran to the door. Flinging it open, Aidan glanced down one end of the corridor, then the other. Though he'd sensed her approach but a few minutes ago, she was now nowhere to be seen.

Something was wrong. Very wrong.

Closing his eyes, he summoned his powers, envisioning Breanne, calling her location to mind. Then he saw her and the witch who was cloaked in the form of Mara. Malevolence emanated from the enchantress, rising in a black mist to swirl higher and higher about Breanne.

With a savage oath, Aidan sprinted down the corridor at a dead run, fear that he'd not reach her in time entwining about his heart, squeezing tighter with each surging beat. By the Holy Ones, he cursed himself, how could he have been such a fool, to leave Breanne unattended

131

even a moment, on this the last night before they were to wed?

It had been the relative peace, the easing of all sense of threat and danger in the past days, that had lulled him into thinking she'd be safe for a short while with his mother and Sirilla. Now, his carelessness might well mean her life!

Powerful legs pounded down stone halls, unerringly yet unthinkingly carrying him closer and closer. He heard a cry, then evil laughter, another cry, then silence. His breath caught in his throat.

One turn more, then Aidan caught a glimpse of a single form, female in shape, standing at an open doorway. His sword's unsheathing rasped loud and metallic in the sudden quiet.

The woman turned. Lips curled from a perfect set of teeth, transforming the sensuous mouth set in a flawlessly beautiful face into an evil sneer. Her long black hair floated up around her in an eerie halo, as if suddenly lifted by some hidden breeze. She raised her arms to halt him, her black robes swirling about her.

" 'Twill do no good, demon spawn!" the witch cried. "You have lost her. I have won!"

Aidan's pace never faltered as he raised his sword above his head. "Die, devil's whore!" he shouted. "Die, and return to your master!"

His sword sliced downward, even as he knew she was gone, dissolving into thin air. Aidan passed through the spot upon which she had stood, pausing only when he teetered on the brink of tumbling down the stairs himself. His single eye stared into the darkness, piercing it, delving ever deeper until he found Breanne, sprawled limply at the bottom of a long flight of stairs.

"Breanne!" Aidan whispered. He quickly resheathed his sword and fastened it about his waist, then scrambled down the stairs.

Kneeling beside Breanne in the darkness, he brushed a lock of hair from her face. "Ah, lass, what have I done to you?" Aidan groaned. "What have I done?"

She whimpered, tried to lift herself, then fell back. "A-Aidan?"

"Aye, lass. 'Tis I."

Her eyes opened and found only blackness. "'Tis so dark," she moaned. "Where are you, Aidan? Am I blinded?"

"Nay, lass," rumbled a deep voice, hoarse with relief, from beside her. "'Tis but dark in here. Are you hurt in any way? Any limbs broken?"

Gingerly, Breanne moved her arms and legs. Everything seemed in working order. She managed a shaky little smile. "Nothing seems broken, only badly bruised."

She reached out to where she thought him to be. "Take my hand and help me. I-I think I can stand."

"Nay." He scooted nearer and slid his arms beneath her. "I think it better that I carry you," he said, pulling her to him and rising to his feet.

Breanne gasped, as much at the sudden change in position as at the surprising contact with Aidan's hardened body. She winced as he pressed her close, belatedly realizing she was more bruised than she'd first imagined.

In an effort to assist him, she entwined her arms about his neck. With a gathering and bunching of powerful muscles, Aidan turned and ascended the stairs.

The faint light above grew brighter as he climbed, until they finally reached the doorway. He stepped into the corridor and carried Breanne over to the nearest wall torch. Concern tightened his sternly chiseled features. At his look of ravaged worry something poignant and bittersweet twisted within Breanne.

Her hand lifted to tenderly stroke the side of his face. "I'm all right. Truly I am. You can put me down now."

"Nay," was his hoarse reply. He pulled her closer to him, burying his face in the tumble of her hair. "I nearly failed you, lass! By the Mother, will you ever be safe, even when I'm gone?"

"Hush, hush," she murmured. " 'Twill be all right. You'll see."

He lifted his head, his unpatched eye anguish-bright. "Will it, lass? I wonder."

Hefting her more securely in his arms, Aidan turned on his heel and strode down the corridor. As they moved along, Breanne studied his face in the torchlight. A question came to mind, though one she was loath to ask.

"The woman who took Mara's form. Who was she, and why did she want to see me dead?"

"She was a witch, a shape-changer," Aidan ground out the terse reply. "I cannot say why she wished you dead, whether 'twas to suit her own purposes or someone else's."

A memory assailed Breanne. "She said something just before she shoved me down the stairs . . . about not wishing to fail the one who sent her. Is it possible?" Her grip tightened about Aidan's neck. "Could someone want me dead so badly he'd stoop to enlisting the aid of a witch woman?"

"Evidently."

"But still you vanquished her! Truly, Aidan, your powers must be awesome to frighten one such as she!"

"She never stayed to fight," he muttered. "As soon as I attacked, she disappeared."

"Well, no matter," Breanne murmured, snuggling closer and laying her head on his shoulder. " 'Tis over and done. We must just be more careful in the future."

Aye, Aidan thought, *and will that future encompass but tomorrow, or the rest of our lives?* He suddenly didn't know, and that realization unsettled him. He had planned on riding off tomorrow night, never to return. Breanne could go back to whatever life she chose, and he could return to his. But now—now he wasn't so certain it would all be as simple as that.

He paused before his bedchamber door, reached for the door latch, then kicked the portal open. Striding over to the bed, he laid Breanne down, removed her shoes, and pulled the fur coverlet over her.

She made a small sound of protest. "Aidan, 'tisn't necessary you coddle me so. I've suffered far worse mishaps in my life. I wasn't raised a noblewoman, you know."

"Lie down anyway," he commanded, gently shoving her back onto the pillows when she

135

made a move to rise. "I want you where I can see you at all times."

Aidan pulled a chair over to the bed, then sat down. He laid the sword of Baldor across his lap.

He glanced over at her. "Are you hungry, lass? I could send for something for you to eat."

"The supper meal is soon served," Breanne offered. "We could just as easily go down to the hall and—"

"Nay!"

Aidan's unexpected vehemence startled her. Puzzlement wrinkled her brow. "But why, m'lord? I feel quite up to maintaining appearances and unless I have some horrible bruise marring my face, no one will be the wiser."

"You've no outward bruising that I can see," Aidan growled, "but that is not the issue. I've no taste for a meal among people that might well wish you dead, and I'll not pretend that something hasn't happened this night. I tell you true, if Dragan said one thing that could be misconstrued—"

"I understand," Breanne hastened to interject. " 'Tis of no import. I've little appetite. 'Tis better we both take an early rest. The morrow will be difficult enough."

She glanced at him. "You needn't sit here as my guard dog, m'lord. No one would dare attack me with you nearby."

Aidan's mouth twitched wryly, the first sign he was beginning to relax. "You've a high opinion of my prowess, lass. For all my powers, I'm not invincible."

"But who's to know that, aside from me?" she demanded with an impish little smile. "*I* certainly won't reveal your secret."

"Nay, I suppose you wouldn't," he admitted, a sudden realization flooding him that Breanne would always support and defend him, no matter how the tide of public opinion turned. The admission unsettled Aidan, stirring emotions he rarely allowed himself to feel anymore. Emotions like caring, concern, and a burgeoning desire. Emotions that, combined with the growing fear she'd remain in danger of her life even after he left, complicated everything.

He glanced over at Breanne, ensconced among the pillows, her fur pulled up to her chin, her eyes half-lidded with drowsy contentment. She'd never have been so relaxed, so completely at ease after what had recently transpired, if he hadn't been near. She trusted him completely—that he well knew. Trusted him with her life.

With a soft sigh, Aidan shifted in his chair to gaze out the window. Night blanketed the land. It was the eve of his wedding day, he mused. On the morrow he'd be married.

With that event would come an additional burden—the responsibility for another's life and welfare. The fact was inescapable. Since Breanne would be his wife, her fate would be inextricably tied to his. So inextricably that he didn't dare risk leaving her behind.

Frustration spiraled within him, a dark despair snaking about his heart. Whether he wished it or not, he must take Breanne with him. Their destinies had met and joined that eve he'd rescued her. For good or bad, their lives were now entwined forever. Entwined so quickly and deeply, he realized with a sudden, breath-grabbing insight, as almost to have an element of outside interference in it.

Aidan straightened, every muscle going taut as the memories of the past few days rushed through his mind. True, there was no way anyone could have arranged his chance meeting with Breanne, unless that someone had magical powers, but his arrival back in Anacreon had definitely been arranged, in his mother's request 15 years ago to return on his thirtieth birthing day. She would've known as well that Breanne, as one of her loyal subjects, would be called to the gathering of women to decide his fate, if Breanne had been the one intended to wed him all along.

With a low groan, Aidan bent over and shoved his face into his hands. By the Holy Ones, was it possible his mother was enmeshed in some plot that involved him? And Breanne, was she entangled, too? If so, for what reason?

Aidan's head began to throb. His mind roiled with unanswered questions and a rising uncertainty as to everyone's true motives that included, most of all, his mother's. Surely she, of all people, would never wish him harm. Yet he had almost died, and was now forced to take a wife against his will, risking her life as well.

What did it all mean?

With a deep, bone-weary sigh, he slumped back in his chair. 'Twas too late to go to the queen tonight, but on the morrow . . . On the morrow, Aidan vowed, his anger banking to a fiery, smoldering resolve, he'd seek out his mother and demand answers. Answers, he prayed with all the strength of his tormented heart, that would ease his painful questions—and spare him the agony of finally learning that his mother, like all the others, had conspired against him.

Chapter Seven

Aidan stalked into the queen's bedchamber the next morning, scowling blackly. "Get out," he snarled at the servingwomen, indicating the door with a curt motion of his head.

The maidservants glanced apprehensively at Eislin. She nodded. With a rustle of petticoats and murmur of frightened voices, the women scurried from the room.

"'Twas all planned long ago—your request that I should return on my thirtieth birthing day—knowing full well I'd be put up before the women for choice as husband," Aidan growled without preliminary as he strode over to his mother's bed.

Eislin eyed him calmly, delaying her reply as she straightened her bed cap and smoothed the wrinkles from her ivory silk bed robe. "And, pray, what led you to such a conclusion?"

She lifted rich brown eyes to his, a slender brow arched in inquiry, and met his gaze.

With great effort, Aidan controlled his rage. " 'Tis past time for games, Mother. Too much has fallen all too conveniently into place for me to ignore it any longer."

"Indeed? And what exactly might that be?"

His fists clenched at his sides, but Aidan smothered his anger beneath an expressionless mask. "You knew of the ancient law—that was why you requested my return on my thirtieth birthing day. If not, why didn't you have me return at twenty, or twenty-five, or even every year? A devoted mother would surely wish to see her son more often than once every fifteen years."

Eislin shrugged. "Mayhap I wished sufficient time to pass to ease the people's fear."

"Oh, aye." Aidan snorted his disbelief. "And what of your immediate acceptance of Breanne, without concern for her lineage?"

"Why should that concern me, if it doesn't you? I wish only for your happiness."

"Is Breanne in league with you?"

His mother's eyes widened. "Oh, nay, Aidan. The lass knows naught of my plans. I swear it."

His jaw went taut. "Then you knew naught of how I was forced to take her as my betrothed? Tell me the truth, Mother, for once and for all!"

Eislin went pale and averted her gaze. "Aye, I knew. It sickened me to permit such a thing to happen, but there was no other choice. Olenus told me that if you didn't come back on your own before your thirtieth birthing day, we had to have some way of bringing you back. The prophecy foretold the necessity of you somehow joining with one of the House Laena to defeat Morloch. And that wasn't possible if you remained far from Anacreon."

"The House Laena? And what has that to do with Breanne?"

His mother shook her head. "Everything or nothing. I cannot yet be sure. Olenus, I'm certain, still withholds some of the pieces."

"But what was the point of risking my life in the process of piecing all this together? Do you know how close I came to losing my head, before Breanne stepped forward?"

Wide, anguish-dark eyes turned to him. "I trusted in Olenus. He promised me 'twould all work out for the best, that Breanne's and your paths were destined to merge."

"Then tell me where this Olenus is," Aidan demanded, "and I'll bring him to you. Let's get to the bottom of this mystery here and now."

"Nay." Eislin drew herself up, becoming queen once more. "Though 'tis past time you met him and learned what must finally be set into motion, the danger is too great for him to show himself in daylight. Morloch might find out. Tonight is soon enough to speak with him."

Excitement coursed through Aidan and he controlled it with the greatest of effort. "He is here, then? In the castle?"

A smile twitched at the corner of his mother's mouth. "Nay, so 'twon't do you any good to attempt to search him out with that all-seeing eye of yours. Have patience, my son. You've waited all these years. Surely a few more hours can be tolerated."

She paused to study him intently. "Your wedding draws near. Are you prepared?"

"For an event I and Breanne both seem manipulated into?" he silkily drawled. "Oh, aye. And what are your and this Olenus's plans for us afterward? Shall you and Olenus stand as witness to my bedding of Breanne, to assure the ceremony's consummation?"

His mother flushed. "Aidan, you are being crude. What is between Breanne and you is a private thing. We can only bring you together."

"You mean force us together," her son snapped. "Have you even considered Breanne's desires in this? How do you think she must feel, wedding one such as I?"

"She hardly seems awed by you, or in any way frightened."

Aidan opened his mouth to refute his mother's comment, then paused. She was right. Breanne was far from intimidated by him, or his reputation.

"Nonetheless," he persisted stubbornly, "I'm certain she'd prefer not to wed me, if she could be assured I wouldn't die in the process."

Eislin smiled. "Indeed? And are you so certain of that, my son?" She paused. "Well, no more of this. I must prepare for your wedding. Say nothing about Olenus to anyone and be patient. All will be revealed soon."

"Mother, after all these years, after all this plotting and subterfuge, I won't be dismissed so easily—"

143

"Away with you." Eislin's lips tightened and she gave a dismissing motion of her hand. "No more, I said."

Aidan's anger surged anew. He made a move to protest, then thought better of it. He knew his mother well enough to realize that, once her mind was made, 'twas made. He shot her a narrow-eyed glance, then bowed and turned toward the door.

His thoughts whirled, however, as he made his way back to his bedchamber to prepare for the wedding. It was just as he'd surmised. He was indeed being used to some purpose, by his mother and a mysterious old man named Olenus. But who was Olenus? And what were his true motives?

The queen seemed convinced he worked for their good, and appeared to trust him implicitly. But what if she were wrong, or misled? What if this Olenus were a sorcerer as evil as Morloch? What if he intentionally misled the queen for his own purposes?

Well, there was nothing to be done until tonight, Aidan thought with rising frustration. But tonight he would finally discover, by any means necessary, all he wished to know. The mystery would remain a mystery no longer.

Aidan met her at the door to the castle chapel, together with a wan-faced prince consort, a smolderingly angry Dragan, and the parish priest. Led by Sirilla as her matron of honor, Breanne came, her journey heralded by a little troupe of musicians playing on flute, harp, and bagpipe, then the queen, carried in a sedan chair, and her ladies. Breanne was garbed in the stunning crimson-and-wine gown, her golden hair unbound beneath a long, sheer veil that fell to below her hips, and with a finely wrought silver circlet about her brow. Aidan thought her the most beautiful woman he'd ever seen.

As Breanne drew to a halt before the men, the priest stepped forward with open prayer book and the wedding ring. He bowed to the queen and her consort, who'd moved to stand beside his wife; then he turned to Aidan. "Take your place at your lady's side," the thin, little man in white satin robes said.

Aidan—dressed as always in black tunic, breeches, and boots—complied, taking Breanne's hand in his. It felt cold and he squeezed it gently. Her eyes met his. In their deep blue depths he saw her fear and uncertainty.

Regret surged through Aidan that he must subject her to this. But there was no other choice. Despite past events, he was still of royal blood. The formalities must be adhered to.

His mouth twisted briefly in an attempt to reassure her. It must have worked, for Breanne managed a wan little smile. Aidan turned back to the priest.

The man glanced at the couple, then cleared his throat. "The bride's dower, if you please."

Aidan scowled, then shot his father an angry glance.

"The bride brings no dower," Marus began. "Under the circumstances—"

"She brings all I require," Aidan cut him off. "Her devotion to me is riches enough. Now, get on with the ceremony."

The priest's eyes widened, but at a nod from the prince consort, he continued. "Then I ask you both, are you of age?"

Aidan and Breanne both nodded.

"Do your parents consent?"

Again, the couple nodded.

"Do you both consent to this marriage?"

Aidan glanced down at Breanne. "This is your last chance, lass. If you wish to be free of me, say so now."

Her smile this time was open and joyous. Though the ceremony and assembled personages intimidated her, there was no doubt, no hesitation in her decision to wed Aidan. "Nay, I've no wish to be free of you, m'lord. I gladly consent to this marriage."

Something flared in the beautiful, measureless depths of his unpatched eye, but it passed so quickly, Breanne was uncertain what it had meant. The husky catch in his voice, however, as he turned back to give the priest his own consent, didn't go unnoticed.

She saw Dragan scowl blackly, and Sirilla's radiant smile. The warm, happy little flare that Aidan's words stirred within Breanne's own heart was unexpectedly disturbing. As disturbing as the words that next fell from the priest's lips.

"Do you swear then, that you are not within the forbidden degree of consanguinity?"

Breanne felt the blood rush from her face. As Aidan's answer in the affirmative reverberated in the corridor, she glanced from first the queen, to the prince consort, to Dragan and Sirilla. All appeared unaffected by the question, as if it were but one in a necessary line of ceremonial queries.

Her gaze lifted to Aidan's. He, too, evidenced no emotion, no flicker of hesitation or guilt in his reply. She, Breanne realized, seemed the only one present who knew differently. Knew differently and must swear a falsehood.

Forgive me, Holy Mother, she silently implored. *For his sake and the sake of Anacreon, I must commit this sacrilege.*

Her glance met the priest's. "I swear that we are not within the forbidden degree of consanguinity."

The priest smiled. "Then I see no obstacle to this marriage." He blessed the wedding ring, then handed it to Aidan. "Place it upon your bride's hand."

Aidan took the ring and did as requested, slipping it in turn on each of the first three fingers of Breanne's left hand. When he reached her third finger, he slid the ring down in place. Glancing up to lock eyes with her, he uttered the final words.

"With this ring I thee wed."

The wedding party entered the church then for the nuptial mass. At the end of the ceremony, the priest gave Aidan the Kiss of Peace. "Go, pass it to your bride," he urged smilingly. " 'Twon't be over until you do."

Aidan turned to Breanne. Taking her by the shoulders, he leaned toward her, until his mouth was but a warm breath away. " 'Tis as he says, lass. 'Twon't be over until I kiss you."

She heard the hesitation in his voice, saw the uncertainty glittering in his eyes. "And are you asking my permission, husband?"

"Aye."

Breanne smiled with a shy tenderness. "Then you most assuredly have it."

He took her then, pulling her into his arms, his mouth slanting over hers. The kiss, though Breanne had imagined it would be both brief and chaste, was anything but that. Though she only half-sensed, barely understood the kiss, it seared her to the depths of her soul—as if all the pent-up longing, loneliness, and unrequited desire had finally broken past the floodgates of Aidan's embattled heart.

The overwhelming evidence of the intensity of his need, of the extent of the wound that laid open his soul, frightened her as the tales about him never had. She hadn't the strength, the courage necessary to heal a man such as he, Breanne thought in rising panic. The task was beyond her, both emotionally and intellectually. In the end, she would surely fail him.

The realization stabbed through her, piercing her heart, spilling her life's blood with each throbbing, agonized beat. By the Holy Ones, more than anything she'd ever wanted, she wanted never to fail Aidan, but she was so inadequate to the task! Yet she was all he had. Ah, curse the cruel fate that sent her to him, rather than a better woman!

Then the memory returned, of her mother's words, of the prophecy. *The Evil One and his servant will fall, when the House of Laena rises from the ashes to free the heart of the one-eyed son."*

There was no one else of the House Laena still alive but she, and the prince consort. And there was little hope that the prophecy spoke of Prince Marus, aware as Breanne now was of the enmity between father and son. She choked back a tiny sob. There seemed no one who could help Aidan but her.

Aidan felt as well as heard the soft sound. Guilt flooded him. He'd frightened, and probably repulsed her with the sudden, savage expression of his passion. Aidan shoved Breanne back from him, cursing himself for his brutish behavior.

It mattered not that she looked so delectably lovely, that he desperately needed the physical solace of a woman's body after weeks on the road without one, that she was now his in every legal and religious way. His needs, quite simply, didn't matter. Breanne's did.

Her lips were moist, swollen, almost bruised from his crude and vicious assault. Self-loathing filled him. By the Mother, he must learn to master himself when he was with her. Yet, in light of his decision last night to take her with him, the task before him seemed crushingly, despairingly hopeless. And now pointless as well.

"Come, lady," Aidan said, extending his hand. " 'Tis over now. The wedding party and people await us at the feast. But a short time more, bear with this."

Breanne gazed up at him and smiled. "For your sake, m'lord, I'll bear with that and all else that is asked of me. I am your wife now. 'Tis my sacred duty."

Glancing down into her eyes, at the fierce devotion and trust gleaming there, Aidan knew she spoke true. The realization didn't ease his pain. It only made it worse.

The feast—replete with wine by the barrel, beef, mutton, veal and venison, capons and ducklings, rabbits and fish, followed by breads and a multitude of vegetable dishes, and then dessert of glazed fruit and pastries—lasted hours. The queen retired after the first course was served and cleared away; she pleaded exhaustion.

Aidan wanted to follow, but Breanne implored him to stay a while longer, whispering it was her wedding feast as well as his. He complied to please her, but couldn't relax or keep his mind long from wandering to a contemplation of the meeting to come. Finally, Aidan could stand it no longer.

He leaned over to Breanne. "I wish to retire."

She turned slowly to look at him. For a moment, Aidan thought she'd again protest. Then Breanne nodded.

"As you wish, m'lord."

He stood and pulled out her chair. With a rustle of stiff satin and silk, Breanne rose. At her movement, Dragan pulled his attention from a buxom serving maid he'd been ogling all night and glanced up at Aidan.

"So soon to bed, brother dear? But then, how can I blame you," he said, his leering gaze traveling down the length of Breanne's body, "when you've such a fetching lass to ease your lust. Of course, if the castle tales be true, you've already sampled her fair charms, sharing the same bed-chamber as you have these past nights."

" 'Tis none of your affair," Aidan growled, forcing an expression of distaste and cold boredom onto his face. He was determined not to let his brother's needling affect him. Too much was at stake this evening to distract himself with such petty concerns as Dragan.

The younger man shrugged, a sly, ingratiating smile curling his lips. "Mayhap. I'd only thought, as brothers, you'd wish to share your joys as well as sorrows with me. At any rate," he said, lifting his goblet of wine to his mouth, "let me assure you that bedding a hot-blooded peasant maid is certain to be a far more pleasurable experience than lying with one of our cold, passionless noblewomen."

Sirilla, sitting beside him, blanched, then quickly looked away. Anger flared in Breanne. How dare he publicly insult his wife, a woman who had long borne with his infidelities and still professed to love him?

She took a step forward, intending on delivering a stinging retort, when Aidan's hand clamped down on her arm. He squeezed it in warning. Breanne halted.

"You may be right, brother," Aidan agreed amiably, "but then, surely even one such as Sirilla or Breanne would pale when compared to the love of a witch, with powers to do one's wildest bidding? One who's strikingly beautiful, with long, black hair?"

Dragan eyed him narrowly, his mouth tightening. "Indeed? And have you mayhap bedded one such as she? If you did, truly, you risk great harm."

"Nay." Aidan sighed in mock regret. "I tried, but she'd already promised her heart to another. I may well have to kill him, if ever I discover who that lover is."

The barest flicker betrayed Dragan's fear, then was gone, hidden beneath a mask of scornful derision. "Have a care, brother dear. You may find even your abilities aren't strong enough to face a witch. They aren't without friends of similar or greater powers, you know."

"And *you've* yet to fully fathom the depth of *my* powers, either, brother," came the gritted warning, muttered low so no one but Dragan and Breanne could hear. "I warn you one last time. Don't try to harm m'lady again!"

With that Aidan pulled Breanne around, nodded a terse farewell to his father, who, engaged in a heated discussion with his chamberlain, had missed his sons' entire interchange; then they strode from the Great Hall. They walked through the long, cold corridors in silence for a while. Finally, Breanne shot him a quick glance.

"Do you think it worked, your warning to Dragan?"

He shrugged. "For his sake, I hope so. I bear him no love, brother though he be. He wants me dead and will stop at nothing, even killing you, to accomplish that. I can tolerate no further threats on either of our lives."

"I'd not be a source of discord between you and your family."

Aidan's mouth quirked in bitter irony. "Discord, lass? I only wish that were the extent of it. The only discord you caused was saving my life and wreaking havoc with all my brother's—and father's—finely laid plans."

"If that be true," Breanne muttered grimly, "they have only begun to suffer the problems I will cause them."

He glanced her way, a dark brow arching in amusement. "You're a loyal little vixen, aren't you? I'm not sure I deserve such devotion, though."

"By the Mother!" Breanne dug in her heels, dragging Aidan to a halt. "I am your wife and I will not hear such words from you again! I may not be able to change your beliefs in what others think of you, but I most certainly intend to make clear my feelings!"

"Indeed?" Laughter glinted in Aidan's single eye. "And what might those be?"

"For one thing," Breanne began, after inhaling a steadying breath, "stop patronizing me! Am I of such little worth to you, that what I think and feel elicits only amusement from you? If that is so, you're hardly better than your brother!"

Aidan's mouth went grim. "I beg pardon, Breanne. I didn't mean to disparage your opinions." He glanced away. "Mayhap I'm just uncomfortable with kindness and find it hard to accept, after all these years, that a woman can see something of value in me."

"Well, 'tis never too late to change your views!" she retorted, even as her ire slowly ebbed away. "Aidan, won't you please give me a chance? I know there's still room in your heart for friendship and trust. Why, there's that friend of yours, the Lord Dane, and . . . and your horse!"

He grinned then, and the change it brought to his features was devastating. She had thought Aidan handsome before, but the sudden boyish animation, the unguarded joyfulness, cast a special, almost unearthly beauty about him.

Breanne's breath caught in her throat. Her heart commenced a rapid pounding. A naked, wanting heat coursed through her body.

In that moment, she knew she loved him—and would until the day she died. Knew that his pain had become her pain, and her happiness would always be diminished if he were unhappy. Forbidden though he now was as cousin, she would nonetheless willingly—and unreservedly—give her heart to him, and stand by him in whatever capacity he might need her.

"Truly, lass," Aidan said, chuckling, the rich tones of his voice skittering pleasantly down Breanne's spine, "your perception of the scope of my friendships is most gratifying. One man, from an entire kingdom, and my horse!"

She glared up at him in indignation. "Well, mayhap if you begin to take a more positive approach, things will change. You count how little you possess. I see how much you have. You have good friends in Dane and Lucifer, your mother loves you, and now you even have a wife, who also wishes to be your friend."

He sobered. "Aye, you're right, lass. And all are greatly valued." He smiled and tenderly stroked her cheek. "I thank you for pointing that out to me. I won't forget again."

His hand moved to her hair. Picking up a lock, he examined it, rolling the silken strands between his fingers. "You have such lovely, lovely hair."

At his touch, Breanne felt a warmth flush her cheeks. Longing filled her, but she quickly tamped it down. Disengaging her hair from his clasp, she stepped away.

"See that you don't forget, m'lord." Breanne gestured down the hall. "Shouldn't we be making our way to your bedchamber? The night draws on, and I know you've plans for the morrow—"

The reminder of his earlier intention to depart this eve without Breanne jolted Aidan back to reality. For a moment, as he'd gazed into her sapphire blue eyes, he'd imagined some spark of affection gleaming there. The realization had thrilled him, stirring his blood, filling him with a heated desire. Then, when he'd touched her, she'd stepped back and the warmth had faded. The chasm between them yawned wide again.

"Aye, plans I have aplenty," he muttered, "but best not spoken of here." He offered her his arm, which she promptly accepted. "Come, let us go to our bedchamber."

The slight change in his reference to his bedchamber, now altered to "our", sent a tremor through Breanne. What if Aidan had changed his mind and now wished to consummate their marriage by bedding her? What would she do? Mayhap 'twould be best to reveal their close relationship, now that the wedding was over and Aidan safe. He still planned to leave her, at any rate. That determination had been evident in the resolute gleam in his eye as he agreed with her earlier reminder.

She followed him without protest and was soon standing in their bedchamber. He shut and bolted the door behind them, then turned to face her. His gaze, gleaming in the flickering candlelight, seemed suddenly eerie, penetrating. Breanne shivered. A premonition prickled down her spine.

"Aidan," she whispered in the stone-muffled room, "what are you doing? Are you trying to ensorcel me, or . . . or pierce the privacy of my mind?"

"Would you care, Breanne?" his voice resonated from the shadows. "You are mine now. Doesn't your offer of trust extend to what I might wish to do to you?"

"My offer will never extend to my soul, Aidan."

His lips twitched. "And did I ask for it, lass?"

Frustration filled her. "Truly, I don't know what you're asking, save that when you looked at me a moment ago, you wanted something."

"You are now my wife." He regarded her with an unnerving directness. "Mayhap I wish to claim my rights as your husband."

Breanne felt the blood drain from her face. She averted her gaze. "B-but you said you'd leave me virgin, that you'd depart this night and never return! What has happened—"

"The attempt on your life," Aidan immediately offered. "I'm not so certain you'd be safe even if I left Anacreon. There's an evil that permeates the land, and it appears to center its greatest virulence on the royal house. You, sweet lass, are now part of that royal house."

"Aye," Breanne agreed slowly. "But how does that impact on your former decision?"

"Isn't that obvious?"

Aidan stepped from the shadows, a dark, vital presence. Before Breanne could gather her scattered wits and move away, his hands closed over her upper arms, imprisoning her. Breanne swallowed hard, then forced herself to meet his gaze.

"Nay, m'lord," she choked out. " 'Tisn't obvious at all."

Regret flared in his unpatched eye. "As loath as I am to interfere further in your life, I must. You aren't safe here, Breanne. I must take you with me when I leave Anacreon."

"T-take me with you?" She wasn't sure she'd heard him correctly. "But surely, m'lord, you don't mean you wish me to accompany you?"

"Aye, that I do, lass."

She quashed the surge of joy his admission stirred. By the Mother, to be with him, to remain at his side no matter where their destinies led, was her dearest wish! Yet her desires in this were ultimately as self-serving as his. "But where would we go? What would we do?"

"Does it matter?" His jaw tightened, and a wary look transformed his features. "You're my wife now. Isn't it enough that we'll be together?"

"It indeed means a lot that you wish for us to be together, Aidan," Breanne admitted, choosing her words with care, "but what purpose would it serve if we left Anacreon? Your home is here; your people need you."

He stared down at her for a long moment. Then anger surged through him, anger, and a sharply intense pain that she persisted in refusing to understand. "Are you daft, Breanne? What will it take to convince you I'm not wanted here? No one will ever need me, no matter how desperate Anacreon becomes!"

"And what, in the end," Breanne countered softly, "does it matter what others think or want in regards to your life? What matters is what you want, what is right—and that you follow the call of your heart."

"My heart?" His grip on her tightened, until Breanne was forced to bite back a gasp of pain. "What does that have to do with anything?"

" 'Twill color all you do, Aidan, and the satisfaction you ultimately derive from life." Breanne dragged in a deep breath and forged on. "What have you to say for your life so far? What have you accomplished of value, or given to others?"

"Not every life has to be lived in the service of others!"

"Nay, I suppose not," Breanne admitted, "but if you divorce people from your life, something must fill the void. Something of lesser value, that might ultimately corrupt you." She glanced up at him archly. "Like magic, mayhap? 'Twas what happened to Morloch, was it not? Is that the kind of man you wish to become?"

"Ah, so now I stand accused of becoming a necromancer if I turn my back on Anacreon?" Aidan shook his head and sighed. "Truly,

Breanne, your constant needling grows wearying. You are my wife. 'Tis past time you cease your harping and learn to obey."

"Obey?" Breanne nearly choked on the word. "By the Mother, Aidan, but your view of marriage is as sorry as your resolve to desert Anacreon in its hour of need! I may be younger and less worldly than you, but I was raised to believe there should be more between a husband and wife than obedience. What of your respect for my thoughts, my opinions?"

Before he could reply, a tentative knock sounded on the door. Aidan held Breanne a moment more, stunned into silence by her open rebellion. Then, gathering his wits about him, he released her and strode back to the door.

He wrenched it open. Mara stood there.

"Aye," Aidan demanded gruffly. "What do you want?"

The old maidservant gazed up at him in apprehension. "Th-the queen, m'lord. She wishes your presence in her bedchamber. And she said to bring the sword of Baldor."

Remembrance of this evening's meeting rushed back to banish the frustrating argument with Breanne. Excitement coursed through Aidan. At last, he thought. He shot Breanne an icy glance over his shoulder. "My mother wishes to speak with me. I'll return—"

He paused, realizing he didn't dare leave her alone. With a sigh, he turned back to Mara. "For her safety, I must bring m'lady with me. You and she can await me in my mother's antechamber."

"Twon't be necessary, m'lord."

Kathleen Morgan

Aidan shot her a quelling look. "Indeed? And why is that, Mara?"

She squared her shoulders as if to gird herself for the confrontation that lay ahead. "The queen expressly commanded that the Princess Breanne come as well. What must be said this night, she told me to tell you, must be said to the both of you."

Chapter Eight

The queen was in her bed when Breanne and Aidan arrived. Eislin smiled and motioned them over. "Come, come. The night draws on, and we've much to talk about."

As Mara securely locked the door behind them, Aidan paused to readjust the sword he'd slung across his back. Then, taking Breanne by the arm, he joined the queen. She indicated the two chairs pulled up at her bedside. "Sit; be at ease."

Aidan frowned and shook his head. "I'd prefer to stand, thank you." He glanced about the room. "Where is this Olenus you spoke of?"

Breanne started and glanced up from the chair she'd just taken. "Olenus? My old teacher? Is he here, returned from his abbey?"

She made a motion to rise, when the queen waved her back down. "Aye, 'tis he. Have

161

patience. He'll arrive shortly."

Eislin quirked an inquiring brow. "So, you, too, know of Olenus, child? He never told me of your presence here until just recently, but I suppose it shouldn't have surprised me. The less any of us knew of the others, the better. And Olenus, for all he tries to hide it from Morloch, is a very clever man."

"For many years, he was my and the other village children's teacher. We'd meet him every day in the old oak grove and he'd give us our lessons. He didn't call himself Olenus in those days," Breanne hastened to explain, "and I only came to learn his true name shortly before he left us."

"So, you can read, can you, my child?"

Breanne smiled. "Oh, aye, m'lady. And cipher, as well. 'Twas my calling, once Olenus left us, to carry on his education of the children. I love it so!"

Eislin reached over to pat the hand that Breanne had laid upon her coverlet. "Then you shall again, child. Once all is done, and the kingdom—"

A gust of wind whirled into the room through the open balcony door, ruffling the heavy window hangings and causing the flames in the candle wall sconces to flicker wildly. Then the wind was gone, and the figure of a middle-aged man, garbed in long gray robes, appeared. He was of medium height, with a tendency toward fleshiness, and his long brown hair was streaked heavily with silver. His nose was large and hooked, his mouth spare, but the light that twinkled in his dark eyes was gentle and warm.

He stepped forward, holding out his arms. "Breanne, lass. 'Tis been so long. Come, give your old teacher a hug."

With a joyful cry, Breanne leaped from her chair and ran to him. He engulfed her in an expanse of thick, woolen robes and, for a moment, Breanne nearly disappeared from view. Then Olenus released her and stepped back. His gaze swept over her, critical, measuring.

"You look well," he observed smilingly. "And grown into a beautiful woman in the bargain."

Breanne flushed with pleasure. "I have tried to carry on as you'd have wished."

"And I'm certain that you have." His eyes lifted, scanning the room until they alighted upon Aidan. "And you. You must be the queen's other son."

"Aye," Aidan growled with a sardonic edge to his voice. "I'm the 'other son.' And who are you, aside from a seemingly benevolent old monk— with some very magical powers?"

Olenus shrugged. "Nothing more than that— these days. But before . . . before I was a sorcerer in training to the great mage Caerlin. The same mage who taught Morloch."

"And are you cut of the same cloth as Morloch?" Aidan demanded, slicing right to the heart of the matter. "Were your intentions these past years, when you worked to win my mother's trust and become Breanne's teacher, meant to aid Morloch? I've yet to see proof that I should consider you a friend."

"Mayhap Baldor's sword will help to verify my tale." The monk indicated the weapon slung

163

across Aidan's back. "Unsheathe it and bring it to me." He walked over to the queen's bed and pointed to a spot at her feet. "Lay the sword there."

Then Olenus turned, motioning for Breanne to join him. "Come, child. You've a vital part in this, too."

Aidan removed his sword and strode over to the bed, but refused to relinquish it. "What do you mean to do with my sword? I'm not in the habit of allowing every curious onlooker access to it."

The older man smiled. "Fear not, young prince. My intent is only to teach you more of your sword's powers, not harm it. First, though, I should tell you my tale. 'Twill ease your suspicions, I'd wager."

"Mayhap." Aidan snorted his disbelief. "And then, mayhap not."

"I was very young when I went as apprentice to the mage Caerlin," Olenus began. "I loved him dearly, for his goodness as much as for his great powers. And, though I desired to become a great mage myself someday, I never begrudged my teacher his wondrous skills." A sudden bleakness settled over his well-lined features. "Not so, however, with Morloch."

His glance met that of the queen. "Morloch loved your mother, desired her for his wife. He was of noble heritage, sprung from as fine a lineage as your father. For a time, your mother seriously considered him."

"Aye," Eislin murmured, "that I did. He was so gay and handsome, and so very romantic in those days. But, even then, I saw his obsession

164

with magic, his jealousy of those more skilled than he, and his willingness to do anything, use anyone, to gain what he hadn't. It frightened me."

She paused to inhale a shuddering breath. "As much as I still cared for him, I finally faced the fact that 'twouldn't work between us. Morloch would never possess the compassion, the self-awareness and respect for power, that I needed in my husband."

"And how did he react to that, Mother?" Aidan asked. "He didn't interfere in your marriage to Father, yet I can't believe Morloch would take such an affront lightly."

Eislin shot Olenus an imploring look.

He nodded reassuringly. "To bury his grief over losing the queen"—the monk once more picked up the tale's thread—"he immersed himself in his magic, determined that the only way to become worthy of the woman he still loved was to become a great sorcerer. And the quickest way to accomplish that was to steal someone else's powers."

"Caerlin's?"

"Aye. There was only one way to do that, however. Morloch lacked sufficient skill to overcome Caerlin on his own, so he enlisted the aid of the Demon. For the purchase price of his own soul, Morloch gained the ability to trap Caerlin's life essence within the confines of a soulstone. In exchange, Morloch gained powers he'd never had before—powers that remained his to command as long as he was in possession of the soulstone. Almost overnight, he became as great as Caerlin."

Aidan moved to stand behind Breanne's chair. He clasped her shoulders, noted how stiff they were, then gave her a quick squeeze in a gesture of support and unity. As he did, he locked gazes with the monk. "You speak as if he also lost those same powers."

Olenus smiled, though the movement never quite reached his eyes. "I suspected Morloch was up to something and set out to spy on him. I saw it all from a hiding place in his chambers—that night he summoned the Demon to aid him. I saw his betrayal and imprisonment of Caerlin within the stone. In my anger and pain, I vowed that night to find some way to thwart Morloch and avenge my teacher.

"Finally, the opportunity arrived. One evening, when he was elsewhere engaged, I crept into his chambers and stole the soulstone. Though I lacked the power to loose my teacher from his enchantment, I at least had freed him from Morloch's possession."

"But that was years ago," Breanne protested. "Where has the stone been all this time?"

"Morloch discovered 'twas I who had taken the stone," Olenus said. "For years I moved from place to place, hiding from his notice as best I could. I became a monk, changed my name and identity. 'Twas there, in the abbey library, that I discovered the ancient prophecy, long-hidden and forgotten. 'Twas then I realized I'd at last found the answer to my dilemma. There was only one man who could someday free Caerlin and defeat Morloch. I determined to aid him by giving him the soulstone to use against the necromancer."

Olenus's gaze locked with Aidan's. "I meant to seek you out when you came into your manhood, but then you killed Rangor—and everything suddenly changed. The night before you departed Anacreon those many years ago, I decided on a desperate plan. The sword of Baldor was yours as firstborn and heir. I knew you'd take it with you. Taking care not to reveal the stone's presence to Morloch, I implanted the soulstone in the sword."

"Then that is what I saw in the white stone in the hilt of Aidan's sword!" Breanne cried. If not for Aidan's restraining hands still on her shoulders, she would have leaped from her chair.

All eyes turned to her. "Go on," Olenus prompted. "Tell us what you saw."

"Th-the face of an old man," she replied, forcing some semblance of calm into her voice and expression, though she couldn't still the sudden pounding of her heart. "And it seemed he was trying to tell me something, something I couldn't quite understand."

Olenus glanced at the queen. "Did I not tell you she was integral to the prophecy? But now to find Breanne also possesses special powers . . ." A joyous wonder threaded his voice. "By the Holy Ones, 'tis more than I dared hope for!"

"And what did you dare hope for, old man?" Aidan demanded. "You speak about Breanne and me as if we are pawns in some intricate game you play. But 'twon't work. I answer to no man and now that Breanne's my wife, her welfare is of equal importance as my own."

Olenus smiled sadly and shook his head. "I play no game, save the one Morloch set into motion all those years past, a game he plays with people's lives and destinies. And we are all pawns, until Morloch is finally defeated—if that is still even possible."

"Indeed?" Aidan cocked a dark brow. " 'Twould seem you must think it so, or you wouldn't be here." His hand moved to caress his sword's bejeweled hilt. "I find it hard to believe, however, that a mage resides in Baldor's sword. I've carried it all these years and never found it to be anything more than what it was—a fine killing weapon."

"A weapon that has served you well, kept you undefeated through many a battle."

Aidan's mouth quirked. "I'd prefer to think my warrior's prowess kept me undefeated."

Olenus shrugged. "Mayhap 'twas. But that would mean your magical powers have never extended to the sword. 'Twould also mean you aren't the one to free Caerlin to aid in the fight against Morloch."

"Or mayhap there has never been any mage in the sword to begin with," Aidan countered.

The monk smiled. "Shall we see for ourselves?"

Aidan's eyes narrowed. "How do you propose we do that?"

"Give the sword to Breanne," Olenus said. " 'Tis past time she know how to summon Caerlin. Ultimately, she must find some way to free him. For all your powers, Prince Aidan, you cannot defeat Morloch without him."

Aidan's hand tightened about his sword. "And what makes you think I care one way or another what happens to Morloch? I'll be gone from

168

Anacreon before the sun rises, to the relief of all, I'm quite certain."

"Will you now?" Olenus sighed. "Then it has all been for naught. Anacreon is doomed, as is your family."

"Dragan and Marus can be damned!" Aidan ground out. "They chose their fate long ago. I bear no blame for them!"

"Marus is no longer the man I married," Eislin interjected hotly, straightening in bed, "nor is your brother the same person you left behind fifteen years ago! Morloch has corrupted them. His spells are slowly eating their hearts and souls away. And, unlike you, there was never any choice for them. Never!"

Aidan shot her a pained look. "Mother, I've no wish to hurt you—"

Eislin sighed and shook her head. "I had such hopes for your return, but now I see you've become so hard and embittered that, even knowing the terrible danger to Anacreon, all you wish to do is turn your back and walk away. 'Tis my fault, my failing. And Morloch will surely destroy you as he will the rest of us." She clamped shut her eyes, fighting back the tears. "Ah, Holy Mother, what have I done? What will become of us now?"

Breanne glanced over her shoulder at Aidan.

His gaze met hers and the haunting entreaty he saw glinting there sliced through to his heart. She was pleading with him to listen, to trust and lower his guard once more.

Rage rose, boiling within him like a fiery acid. Curse her! This time, she asked too much. He owed no man anything anymore. He had his own plans, however self-absorbed they might be, his own needs to consider. . . .

What have you to say for your life so far? The memory of Breanne's sweet challenge once more intruded, slipping past his hastily constructed barriers. *What have you accomplished of value, or given to others?*

No one, before Breanne, had ever expected, much less asked for his help. True, his former employers had paid handsomely for his warrior's services, but they had kept their distance. Breanne, he well knew, would ask for his help—and more.

Aiding Anacreon wouldn't be the end of it. Nay, not by a long shot. Yet to refuse her anything was becoming harder and harder. And if there *were* some way to free the land of Morloch's evil influence, mayhap 'twould at last make it safe for her to go on with her life as he'd originally planned. That and whatever solace ridding Anacreon of Morloch would give his mother were strong motivators.

He shrugged in mock resignation. "Have it as you wish, Mother. What do you want me to do?"

Relief flared in Eislin's eyes, then a tender affection. "Ah, Aidan, thank the Holy Ones! I knew you wouldn't fail us. You and Breanne are our last hope!"

"Are we now?" He gave a disparaging laugh. "Then Anacreon must be desperate, to expect a girl barely turned woman and a despised outcast to save them."

Breanne smiled up at him. "Not desperate, m'lord. Fortunate."

He met her gaze, his mouth quirking in amusement. "Ever the little optimist, aren't you, lass?"

"Morloch has met his match in you, m'lord. 'Tis the best reason of all for optimism."

"Aye, you are indeed a formidable foe," Olenus agreed as he rejoined the conversation. "But Breanne is integral to the fulfillment of the prophecy as well. She is light to your darkness," he said, his gaze moving from Breanne to Aidan. "She is hope to your despair. She is the dreamer to your realism. And she possesses the powers that complement yours."

He motioned to Breanne. "Take up the sword, child. Take it up and I will teach you how to summon your powers."

Breanne shot Aidan an uncertain look. He hesitated for a moment, then nodded his agreement. " 'Twill do no harm, lass, whether you succeed or fail. And if the monk speaks true, whatever he can teach you will only aid us in the end."

"As you wish, m'lord." Breanne moved to where the sword of Baldor lay at the queen's feet. She touched it gingerly, paused, then picked it up. "What do I do now?" Breanne asked, turning to Olenus.

"Sit. Close your eyes, child. Focus inward," her old teacher instructed. "Go deep within yourself where eyes cannot see, but the heart will know. Then listen, wait, and Caerlin will come to you."

She resumed her seat with the sword in hand. "What should I do then, when Caerlin comes to me?" Breanne's eyes gleamed with apprehension. "I know naught of what to say to a mage. He will most likely find me silly and foolish."

"He will find you the good, intelligent, courageous woman that you truly are, Breanne. He needs you as much as you need him. He is lonely and tormented, bitterly frustrated after all these years of a limited existence and utter helplessness. You are the key to his eventual freedom—and to his revenge against Morloch."

A warm reassurance shone in Olenus's eyes. "Have no fear, child. Caerlin will welcome you with the greatest joy."

Breanne forced her mouth into a tremulous semblance of a smile. "Then I must go to him. I couldn't bear to be further cause to his suffering when I might hold the power to ease it."

With that, she clasped the sword to her and closed her eyes. She willed herself to relax, concentrating at first on her breathing, until the slow, deep, rhythm lulled her into a state of waking repose. She felt a strange freedom, then saw herself spiraling down into a black void toward a faint glow at the end of the darkness.

A sudden fear coursed through her. She was out of control; she couldn't stop herself now if she tried. Someone else had claim to her mind and Breanne didn't like it.

Caerlin. It had to be he. There was no reason to be afraid, she tried to tell herself. He was good, honorable.

But he was also desperate, tormented, and lonely. What if he refused to let her go? What if he kept her with him within the soulstone to assuage his loneliness? Who really knew what the years trapped there had done to him? Was he truly good anymore?

The doubts rose, burgeoning in her mind until Breanne was caught in the grip of an all-consuming terror. She must turn back before 'twas too late. This power, this joining, was not meant for one such as she!

A cry, silent and choking, rose in her throat. She struggled within herself, clawing frantically upward. Blackness engulfed her, and finally, blessedly, she knew she was climbing away from the dim light. Joy filled her.

Then an image of Aidan flashed through Breanne's mind. What would become of him if she turned from this encounter? He'd still set out to find Morloch, but what little assistance she could offer would be for naught. The power of the soulstone was all she could give him—that, and her love. For his sake, if nothing else, she must face the mage.

Breanne turned then, back to the dim light, and rode the wave of fearful anticipation to its source. Curiously, this time as the light brightened, the terror abated. She heard a voice, deep and soothing, warm with gratitude, beckoning her.

"Come, Breanne. Come, join with me and learn. Learn, for only in your growing knowledge will your own power increase, and you will at last be able to free me."

She went to him willingly, joyously then, her heart suffused with gladness and trust. Caerlin stepped from the light, a radiant aura surrounding him. He was old, his hair snow-white, his beard long and flowing. His eyes were dark, yet glowed with a gentleness like none Breanne had ever seen. She smiled up at him.

"There is much that lies ahead," he began. "Much heartache and pain if you're to redeem Aidan's soul. Morloch wants it as badly as you and will stop at nothing to have it. You must beware, Breanne, beware and never lose hope. Without Aidan, even my powers won't be enough to vanquish Morloch."

"But why?" she asked. "What is Aidan's part in this? Why does Morloch want him?"

"In time you will know the answer, horrible though it may be. In the meanwhile, Aidan needs you. You are now his wife. Bind his heart to you, touch his soul. It is Aidan's only salvation."

"But I cannot. We are—"

"All is not what it seems," Caerlin said, staying her protest with an upraised hand, "but much is still too hard to understand, much less accept. You will see that in time. Have faith until then."

He smiled. " 'Tis wonderful to speak with someone after all the years. You will come and visit me again? We have much to discuss, and you, much to learn."

Breanne nodded. "Aye. Will you teach me how to free you from the stone?"

"In time. In time. Powers such as those cannot be developed overnight, but aye, I'll teach you. There is magic in you, Breanne, of a purer, more benevolent kind than Aidan possesses. He will need your tempering if he is ever to withstand Morloch."

"Then teach me, for I will do anything to help him."

"Aye, that I know. That I know." He made a motion with his hand. "Now go, Breanne. Return to him. To tarry longer with me just now grows harmful to you. I will call you again when the time is right."

"Farewell," she murmured, even as she felt herself drawn to leave the brightness. "Farewell, until then."

Blackness engulfed her once more, then a loud rushing sound of wind, and finally silence. A silence in which, in her heightened awareness, she heard the soft soughing of breaths inhaled, the faint rustle of bedclothes and bodily movements. Breanne opened her eyes.

Olenus smiled down at her. "Caerlin? Was he well?"

She nodded. "Aye."

Aidan stepped into view. "What happened, lass? Did you truly see the mage?"

She turned to him. "Aye, Aidan. I did."

"And what words of wisdom did he impart? Have you the answer how to defeat Morloch?"

Breanne shook her head. "Nay, not yet. But Caerlin will teach me what I need to know." She lifted the sword and handed it back to him. "In the meanwhile, we must carry out the quest as planned."

"So, the great mage had nothing more to offer than what we already know?" Aidan growled. "He promises to be a real help, in that case. If he truly even exists."

"Oh, he does, Aidan. He told me that Morloch wants your soul and will stop at nothing to get it." Breanne's eyes mirrored the horror of her statement. "Caerlin didn't say why, just added that without you even his powers wouldn't be sufficient to vanquish Morloch."

"How comforting," Aidan drawled sarcastically. "The necromancer wants my soul, and Caerlin won't say why. By the Mother, but I tire of all these riddles and cryptic utterances!"

"All will be revealed in time," Olenus said. "Some revelations are too shocking, too difficult to bear just now. 'Tis hard to accept, but truth nonetheless."

Aidan made an impatient motion with his hand. "Then let us get on with it. 'Tis evident nothing more of import will be revealed this night."

"You are right," the monk agreed. " 'Tis enough for one night. But heed me, and heed me well for a few moments more. You must journey to the Improbus Mountains, where Morloch keeps his fortress, and confront him. Only with his death will his ensorcelment of Anacreon and the royal house cease."

"Indeed," Aidan muttered. "And how do you suggest we accomplish this monumental task? A sword with an entrapped mage who chooses to keep his secrets and an Evil Eye whose killing power most likely won't touch a necromancer seem hardly sufficient to the quest. If Morloch can even *be* killed."

"Oh, he can be killed," Olenus assured him. "But 'twill take great magic or he will rise again."

"Indeed? How comforting."

"Mayhap not, but Caerlin can see to it, if you succeed in freeing him. But if Morloch gains possession of the soulstone . . ." Olenus paused, considering his next words. "He needs you and the soulstone," the monk stated flatly. " 'Twill seal his powers once and for all."

"Then what is the point of taking the sword to him?" Breanne asked. "Mayhap 'twould be better to hide it."

"Nay, 'twould only prolong the inevitable."

"So, instead, Breanne and I are to boldly ride up to Morloch's fortress, knock on the door, and when he answers, slay him with Baldor's sword," Aidan snarled, anger harshening his voice. "Presuming, of course, that this necromancer is blind as well as stupid."

Olenus frowned. "I never promised a safe nor easy quest. There is much still to be done before you dare confront Morloch in his lair."

"I haven't the time nor patience for extended lessons, old man," Aidan rasped. "One way or another, I plan to depart this very night."

"And depart you will." The monk glanced at Eislin and smiled. "What must still be learned and forged can just as easily be accomplished on the trail."

Puzzlement furrowed Breanne's brow. "I don't understand. We have a sword that bears the soul of a great mage—a mage whose powers we need—and we don't yet know how to free him. We also have no specific idea as to how to defeat Morloch. This undertaking is quickly becoming too great for just one man and woman. And you want to send us out tonight?"

"It seems hard, child, to accept so much on faith alone," Eislin gently intruded. "Well I know that. I, too, have borne with the doubts, the fears, the endless questions that had no answer for many years. Yet many answers still, only you and Aidan can determine. Each in our own way, Olenus and I have helped to bring you two together and set the prophecy in motion. Our task is over, yours just begun."

"Breanne's task is more than evident. But I," Aidan demanded, "what part do I play in all this?"

Olenus turned, his wise old eyes burning straight to Aidan's soul. "You, too, have your own special battles and lessons to be learned. You are naught without Breanne, nor can she accomplish aught without you. Open your heart, for she will lead you if only you let her. Trust. Believe. And never let her go into danger. You are doomed—just as certainly as Morloch already is—if you lose Breanne."

He motioned to Breanne. "Now, come, child. I, too, have a wedding gift for you."

She smiled and rose. "Truly, there was no need. You gave me all the gift I ever wanted, those years you taught me to read. I will cherish that ability to the end of my days."

"As will I the memories of your eagerness and enthusiasm for learning. You were truly a joy." Olenus reached into his robe and withdrew two beaten copper bracelets. "But now my time as teacher is past, and the only thing I can leave you are these bracelets of protection. They are inscribed with the runes of *eolh* and *doeg*, which allow you to detect evil magic of any sort near you and provide you with some magical resistance."

He took her wrists and clasped the bracelets around them. "Until this quest is over and Morloch destroyed, never remove them. They could well mean your life if Aidan and you are ever separated."

Breanne glanced down at the bracelets. Inscribed with ancient letters, they were surprisingly light, considering their size and thickness, and gleamed softly in the candlelight. She smiled up at Olenus. "If these will aid us, I'll wear them, and gladly."

"Have you anything more, old man?" Aidan demanded. "If not, the night draws on and I'd like a few hours sleep before I set out. As Breanne must surely desire the same," he said, shooting her a piercing glance. "This was a wedding day like none any woman has ever experienced."

"Aye," she agreed with a smile, "most certainly." Breanne gave Olenus a quick hug, then stepped back. "Will we see you again?"

The monk shrugged. "Mayhap. One can never predict when our paths will cross. And you know where I can be found."

"You'll return to the abbey then?"

"Aye. 'Tis best for you if I continue to hide my presence from Morloch. 'Twill, I hope, offer you some element of surprise." He took her hand and squeezed it in farewell. "Well, at least for a time. 'Twill be impossible to hide your intent from Morloch indefinitely."

Breanne managed a small laugh. "Farewell, then, old friend." She turned to the queen. "M'lady."

Eislin motioned her closer. Reaching out, she clasped Breanne's hand. "My heart and thoughts will be with you. Help my son . . . and bring him back to me."

Breanne rendered her a small curtsy. "Aye, m'lady. That I will."

"Aidan." The queen's gaze sought out that of her son. "Come, say your farewells to your mother." Her arms lifted to him.

Breanne moved aside to allow Aidan the opportunity to say his good-byes in his own way. He strode past her and sat on the edge of the queen's bed. Once more, he took his mother into his arms.

"Take care of her," Eislin whispered into his ear. "She is our salvation—and yours as well."

Aidan kissed her tenderly on the cheek, then leaned back. "And do even you think I need saving?"

Eislin's mouth tilted in one of her old, impish smiles. "All men need saving, my son. Why else were women put on this earth?"

He stood, gave her hand one final squeeze, then released it. His mouth twisted wryly. "Why else, indeed?

"Lady?" he said, offering Breanne his arm. " 'Tis past time we took our rest."

She came to him then, her eyes alight with a warm joy. "Aye, m'lord. The morrow calls us to a great undertaking. We must be ready—in every way."

Olenus moved to stand by the queen's bed as Aidan and Breanne departed the room. He waited until Mara followed and closed the door quietly behind her. Then, the monk turned to Eislin.

"There was so much more I wished to tell them," he murmured with a tinge of regret. "But the bonding, if it comes, must arise from their own efforts, not from outside influences. Otherwise, 'twon't be soul-deep and lasting. And 'twon't be powerful enough to withstand what lies ahead."

"What lies ahead . . ." Eislin repeated. "By the Mother, I'm so afraid for them. They've no idea what horror awaits."

"Nor what joy, if they've the courage to face their doubts and fears."

A soft smile lifted the queen's mouth. "Aye."

"I only wish," Olenus sighed, "that I could have revealed Aidan's true parentage. Mayhap 'twould have helped prepare him."

Eislin's expression altered and grew grimly solemn. "Aye, but it could have just as easily destroyed what little hope he still has. Nay," she said, her mouth tightening with a fierce resolve, "he'll learn the truth soon enough. I only pray that, by then, Breanne's influence over him will be strong enough to blunt the shock."

"And that he will love her, and she, him, m'lady?"

"Aye." Eislin lay back on her pillows and expelled a weary sigh. " 'Tis his only hope."

Chapter Nine

Mara finished the last few brush strokes to Breanne's coiffure, then stepped back to admire her handiwork. Her gaze warmed with admiration, taking in her mistress's long hair, brushed to a flow of burnished gold. Beneath the sheer veil of shimmering strands that cascaded down Breanne's arms and back peeked a lace-trimmed bed gown of creamy satin and the matching cream-satin, floral-brocade bed robe.

The old maidservant smiled. "You look so beautiful, m'lady. The prince will be pleased. Shall I call him for you?"

Breanne's glance strayed to the balcony, where Aidan had gone to allow her some privacy in her bedtime preparations. Tonight was their wedding night, and she knew Mara imagined Aidan the eager lover. Breanne sighed. 'Twould do no good even if he had been.

She glanced up at the older woman. "Aye, tell him 'tis safe to return." Her mouth quirked in an attempt at humor. "He needs his rest for the journey ahead."

"Oh, I'd wager he'll not be thinking much of rest," Mara teased, "once he sees you, m'lady."

Breanne smiled thinly. "Please fetch him, Mara."

As the servant hurried across the bedchamber to the balcony, Breanne rose, walked over to the little cherry wood side table set with a crystal flagon of wine and two jewel-encrusted, gold goblets. She poured herself some wine, then turned. Aidan was even then striding into the room, Mara in his wake.

He walked over to her and halted. "Lady," he said, rendering her a cool inclination of his head.

The look in his single eye, however, was anything but cool. As his gaze swept over her, Breanne felt an unsettling heat flush her body. His appraisal was bold, yet languorous, sensual yet guarded. Bemusement filled her.

"I'll be taking my leave now, m'lady," Mara's voice intruded, "if you've no further need of me."

Breanne glanced over at her maid. "I've no further need, Mara," she lied, desperately wishing she could depart instead of the other woman. "Thank you for your assistance this eve, with my bedtime preparations as well as in gathering me clothing and our supplies for the morrow. And, thank you, as well, for the true friend you've been in the past days."

As if suddenly realizing she wouldn't see her mistress again before her departure, the maidservant's eyes filled with tears. " 'Twas my honor, m'lady. I only hope I can serve you again, upon your return."

"Of course you may." Breanne smiled in gentle dismissal. "Good night then, Mara."

"Good night, m'lady." Mara curtsied and backed to the door.

When she heard the door close softly behind her, Breanne turned to Aidan. "Would you like a cup of wine, m'lord?"

He considered her briefly, then nodded. "Aye. 'Twill relax me, after all that has transpired this eve." He accepted the goblet she offered to him. "My thanks."

Both raised the goblets to their lips and drank, their eyes meeting over their drinking vessels. Aidan's single eye burned through Breanne, piercing to the depths of her soul. For a moment, as she stared into its bejeweled depths, Breanne fleetingly imagined Aidan once again was attempting to ensorcel her.

The realization frightened her, but even more so the admission that, this time, she almost wished he would. 'Twould free her of responsibility for the moral considerations of his bedding her, if that was indeed what his smoldering, almost feral look meant. She wrenched her gaze away before she succumbed to the temptation.

Glancing down at her goblet, Breanne feigned a sudden interest in its intricate pattern of ancient scrollwork. "Is all in order for the morrow, m'lord?"

"Aye." The husky catch in his voice belied his outward calm.

"And when shall we depart?"

"In the hour before dawn. 'Tis best to draw as little attention as possible." He paused. "Breanne, though I'll take you with me because I fear the dangers for you here at court, 'twould be better, once we're away, that I place you in some nunnery for safekeeping and go on alone."

"How can you say that?" Breanne felt the blood drain from her face. "After all Olenus and your mother just finished telling us, how can you—"

"I don't believe any of it," he tersely interrupted her. He strode over to set down his cup, then returned to stand before her, his expression hard, remorseless. "At least not about Caerlin and the soulstone."

"But I saw him. Talked with him!"

He arched a dark brow. "Did you now? Or was it mayhap some spell of Olenus, meant to make you think you did?"

She blinked in confusion, suddenly not certain what she had truly seen when she'd communed with Caerlin. Could it have indeed been but a spell of Olenus's? "But what of your words? You told them you'd take me with you."

Aidan smiled thinly. "What I said and what I'll actually do can be two different matters. 'Tis the way of survival."

Frustration mixed with shock, to roil madly in the depths of her hurt and despair. Suddenly, Breanne felt light-headed. She swallowed hard and clenched shut her eyes to ward off the dizzying sense of disembodiment.

Two hands clasped her shoulders, then gave her a small shake. "Breanne, look at me!" Aidan commanded, concern threading his voice. "What's wrong with you?"

"N-naught, m'lord," she stammered, unnerved by his sudden nearness. She twisted away to place her goblet back on the table. "I-I am just weary. I'd like to take my rest."

Aidan's large hand curled around her arm as she stood there, pulling her about to face him. "Breanne, I ask you again. Look at me."

She dragged reluctant eyes up to his. "Aye, m'lord? What is it you wish?"

He gazed down at her, an intent, wary expression sharpening his features. "I'm sorry if my decision is not to your liking. I don't mean to hurt you or disparage your kindness in wishing to aid me, but I believe 'tis for the best."

"I-I . . . nay, you haven't hurt me. Far from it," she replied as, all the while, her mind raced. By the Mother, what was she to do now? Rest, she resolved. She was too tired to think. But on the morrow . . .

Breanne forced herself to smile up at him. "I already told you. I'm weary, m'lord."

"Aidan," he urged in a deep velvet voice. "Call me Aidan."

Breanne twisted in his grip, but was unable to free herself. "I do call you Aidan, from time to time. But you are the crown prince and my husband, and deserve my respect."

He grinned. "Indeed? And am I to assume

that respect will arise only when the mood moves you? And that the rest of the time, you'll continue to devote your efforts to defying me, or informing me of how you'd like things done?"

By the Mother, Breanne thought, but 'twas difficult to distance herself from him when he acted so charming, so . . . so endearing! But she must. 'Twas the only way to keep her head clear, to plan.

"Aye, whatever you say," she agreed distractedly as her fingers covered his and she attempted to pry his hand free. "Now, if you don't mind—"

His gaze moved to her hair. A thick lock had tumbled down over her breast and he quickly captured it. Lifting it, Aidan inhaled deeply. "Ah, but you have such lovely hair, Breanne. And its scent . . . 'tis so fragrant and haunting, like wild violets in the forest's depths."

He twisted the lock around his fingers, drawing her closer and closer with each circling movement of his hand. Breanne's breath caught in her throat. What was he about? Surely he didn't intend to—

"Aidan, please!" she cried. "What are you doing?"

His dark head cocked in quizzical amusement. "And what does it look like, lass? I intend to claim a kiss from my sweet bride, before I carry her off to bed."

"But you told me you'd leave me virgin!"

He smiled. "Did I? Well, that was before I decided to take you with me. Now, 'twon't matter. And I must confess to a certain gladness that I can have you after all." His gaze dipped from her lips to the rounded fullness of her breasts. "You truly are a delectable creature, my lady wife."

Before she could reply or protest, Aidan's head lowered, his mouth capturing hers. Panic swelled within Breanne, then was smothered by the riot of sensations that tumbled through her.

His lips were softest velvet, gently, slowly caressing her, before becoming more aggressive with the added nibbling and nipping of his strong, white teeth. Then his tongue emerged to stroke the swollen, sensitive fullness of her lips. In an almost instinctual response, her mouth opened to him.

At her yielding, Aidan made a soft sound of pleasure, then plunged his tongue into her. He pulled Breanne to him, his hand capturing a lush buttock, his body hard, throbbing with hot, frantic need. His mouth lowered, moved voraciously against her throat, her ear, then back to her mouth, as if he didn't know what spot was the most luscious.

Caught up in a tidal wave of pleasure, Breanne's head arched back and she thrust against Aidan as ardently as he crushed himself into her. He was hard, every inch of him, from his broad, thick-muscled chest and rippling abdomen, to his iron-thewed thighs and straining groin.

"Breanne," he groaned, his voice ragged. "By the Holy Ones, you're now my wife, yet I still can't quite believe it. Not that, nor that you come to me willingly, and aren't repulsed."

His words, combined with the large hand that gently cupped her breast, jerked Breanne back to reality. She trembled wildly, fighting past her own hot, aching need as his fingers found her nipple beneath the sheer gown and teased it to pebble hardness. Desire engulfed her, threatening the last vestiges of her control, and with only the most superhuman of efforts did she fight past it. The Mother forgive her, she thought in an agony of regret, but she had no other choice.

"A-Aidan!" she gasped, pressing, with all her might, against the solid wall of his chest. "Don't! Stop!"

He nuzzled her throat, his hand persisting in its aching exploration of her breast. Panic grew in Breanne. 'Twas her responsibility to prevent this unholy act from finding consummation until she dared tell him the truth. Yet even tonight was not the time, husband and wife though they now were.

Aidan's decision to take her along only so far as the nearest nunnery must still be thwarted. To reveal their common heritage now might seal his resolve once and for all. Though 'twas mayhap a cruel thing to do to him, on this their wedding night when he was so obviously aroused and wanting her, 'twas the only choice she had. Later, once she'd overcome his stubborn intent to exclude her from the quest, she would tell him all. Later, he would mayhap find it in his heart to understand—and forgive.

"I don't want this, Aidan! Not now, not tonight!" she cried, forcing the words past a painfully constricted throat. "Stop. Take your hands from me!"

Every muscle in his big body went rigid. His head lifted, and he impaled her with his single eye. "What did you say, lady? You don't want your husband on your wedding night?"

She shoved away from him, her breath coming in ragged gasps. "Not tonight, Aidan. Please! I thought before you didn't want me, and now . . . now you do. I'm not ready; I haven't had a chance to accept it. Give me more time. Please!"

"And what will more time solve, m'lady?" His mouth went grim. "I don't think time is the problem; I think 'tis fear. Fear, that, in the throes of our lovemaking, I might find some way to steal your soul, or corrupt your heart as I corrupt your body. Surely you've heard tales aplenty of what rutting with a demon's spawn can lead to? But, ah, the exquisite pleasure as well! Wouldn't you'd like to take a chance, risk it just this once?"

Breanne stepped back, her fists clenched at her sides. "You are crude and cruel to speak to me thusly. You don't understand, yet still you dare judge. I only asked for time; I didn't accuse you of being disgusting or some ungodly creature.

"But you"—she made a disparaging motion in his direction—"you choose always to suspect the worst of me. By the Mother, Aidan, but you're the most pigheaded, arrogant man I've ever had the misfortune to know!"

"Or wed?"

"Aye!" she flung back at him, her temper

finally getting the best of her.

His contemptuous gaze raked over her. "Well, *m'lady,*'tis far too late to remedy that situation. But that's your misfortune, for I asked you before if you were certain you wished to marry me. For good or bad, we are now bound to each other."

He strode across to the bed, gathered up the fur throw and a pillow, then wheeled around to face her. "I also told you before that I never force myself on any woman who doesn't want me. That same courtesy extends to you, wife that you be. You asked for more time, Breanne. I give you the rest of your life!"

They rode out in the grayness of dawn, in a damp, heavy mist that shrouded the land. Aidan, mounted on Lucifer, led the way. Breanne, garbed once again in the clothes of a lad, her long hair woven into a single braid and shoved under a soft brown cap, brought up the rear on a gentle bay mare.

She glanced behind her only once, when they skirted her village and turned north. Just one more look to sear into her mind the memory of home, she told herself, twisting in the saddle. A home that, at the very worst, she might never see again. And, at the best, would never be the same.

Aidan said nothing for several hours, his face set in an inscrutable mask, his body rigid. Several times, Breanne was tempted to ride up alongside him and try to explain about last night. But what explanation would he accept, save the one she yet dared not give?

The sun rose behind a heavy cloud cover, its weak rays barely illuminating the day. Thunder rolled in the distance; the air grew heavy and thick. And, finally, the oversaturated sky released its burden. The rain fell, pelting the land in a steady flow until the ground could absorb no more.

Puddles grew, the road became a sucking morass, and rivulets of water coursed wherever the terrain sloped even slightly. Though both Breanne and Aidan had brought along hooded, woolen cloaks, the dense fabric could repel water only so long. A wind began to blow, cooling bodies already soaked to the skin. Waterlogged hair dripped into eyes and down necks, only adding to the general feeling of sodden misery.

Breanne refused to complain or demand they seek shelter, determined not to cause Aidan further trouble. If he meant to ride on all day and night, so be it. She wouldn't be the first to call a halt, no matter how much it cost her.

Aidan, immersed in his own morose, tumultuous thoughts, hardly gave the weather notice. Consumed with frustration and a smoldering anger, he wished only to put as much distance between him and the royal castle as soon as possible. It took well into the afternoon, and Lucifer's prodding, before he gave Breanne's welfare any consideration.

So, do you plan to kill your new wife the first day out then? his war-horse snidely inquired.

What in the world are you babbling about?

Your anger at her blinds you to the condition of the day.

Aidan's legs tightened about his mount's sides in irritation. *My personal feelings about Breanne are not a topic of discussion.*

My intent was not to pry into human matters of the heart, only to assure the female lives long enough to assist you in this crazed quest.

She appeared healthy enough last time I looked!

Lucifer shook his head and neck, sending a spray of water sailing into Aidan's face. *And when was that? This morning before you set out? You've not stopped once all day, save to water me, and certainly not long enough to allow a noonday meal. You treat me, a mere animal, better than you do your new bride!*

Aidan grimaced. *And mayhap that's because my animal treats me better than my new bride!*

Ah, a lovers' spat. You certainly didn't waste any time antagonizing your little wife.

I didn't start it, Aidan replied. *'Twas Breanne.*

The big black horse snorted his disbelief. *Breanne? That sweet, gentle creature? Did you know we are quickly becoming friends? She has discovered my weakness for sugar crystals, and even carries a small supply for me in a pouch she wears at her—*

Enough! Aidan jerked slightly on the reins in warning. *Eat sugar crystals until your teeth rot from your skull, but leave the issue of Breanne be! She is my problem, my responsibility, not yours!*

Then take care of her, you obstinate dolt! Your wife is all but freezing to death and in danger of catching the ague. Even my cousins, the mules, have more sense than you, and that's not saying much!

At Lucifer's words, Aidan wheeled around in his saddle. In the relentless drizzle and slippery mud, Breanne had fallen behind on the trail. She was little more than a small, water-soaked figure hunched over her horse's back, riding about 30 yards back. Yet even from that distance, Aidan could see the pale face, blue-tinged lips, and the shivers that wracked her body.

With a savage curse, he pivoted Lucifer around and galloped back to her. Sliding to a halt beside Breanne, he ground out the first thing that came to mind.

"If this attempt to catch the ague is your way of keeping me from your bed tonight, you needn't have bothered. You look like a drowned rat and would hardly tempt my lust."

Ever so slowly, as if the effort required more energy than she could muster, Breanne lifted her head. She looked half-frozen and exhausted, but a spark of defiance still flickered within her.

"I thank you for your most kind comments on my appearance, m'lord," she whispered. "But as to your first observation as to why I never mentioned the wet and cold, I must confess to imagining you might appreciate a good trail partner, especially on this, the first day of our trip."

At her words, guilt flooded Aidan. He'd been so angry, so hurt by Breanne's rejection of him last night, that he'd purposely chosen to ignore not only his own discomfort with the weather, but hers as well. And she was but a lass, not a battle-hardened warrior like himself.

"And a good partner you've been, too," he admitted softly. " 'Tis I who have been the insensitive boor, keeping you out in such miserable weather. Come, let's head for the forest and see if we can find some kind of shelter there. No purpose is served in continuing on this day." He leaned over and grabbed for her mount's reins.

Breanne jerked her horse's head out of Aidan's reach. "And no purpose is served in treating me like I'm some pampered noble-woman. You and I both know the lie to that." Her blue lips tightened in a thin line. "Fear not, m'lord. I can endure as long as you!"

A confusing surge of irritation, renewed guilt, and amusement at her bedraggled defiance flooded Aidan. The confusion, most of all, stemmed from a reluctant admiration for her courage and perseverance. Breanne might not want him as a lover, but 'twasn't from a fear of his demon's reputation.

"Well, I find my own endurance at an end for this day," he said. He gestured toward the forest that sprawled to the left of the road. "Follow me, if you will, lady."

Without awaiting her reply, Aidan turned Lucifer toward the trees and cantered off. Breanne watched him ride away, still inwardly seething at his insult to her person. By the Mother, would the man sulk over her rejection of him last night for the entire quest?

She sighed and shook her head, then signaled her mare to follow. 'Twas amazing the facets of a man's character that were revealed with every waking moment. And 'twas equally amazing how tiresome they became. One would think one had cut his manhood to the quick.

A sudden realization struck her. Was it his manhood that had been wounded, or his feelings? Surely he knew how physically attractive he was? There was only one reason a woman would reject him—his demon's reputation. Or so Aidan would think, at any rate.

Frustration filled Breanne. Holy Mother, the last thing she wanted Aidan to believe was that she still considered him loathsome, accursed, and evil! What must he think, though, after all her fine words encouraging him to trust again, to offer his heart in friendship, and then have her turn from him on their wedding night?

Mayhap her decision to keep the truth of their close kinship from him had been flawed. She should have told him before they wed, no matter the consequences. In her attempt to help him and ensure he took her along on the quest, mayhap she had done more harm than good.

But there was no calling back what had come to pass. And he *had* brought on some of this with his stubborn refusal to believe Olenus or accept that she was as integral to the quest as he. Breanne heaved an inward sigh. Everything was fast becoming far too complicated.

She glanced up at Aidan, the sight of his big, broad-shouldered form filling her once again with a curious, aching need. Aye, she glumly mused, everything was fast becoming far too complicated. The least of which were her most uncousinly feelings for him.

They found an old forester's hut deep in the woods, deserted, from the look of it, for years. The roof leaked copiously, but a large space before the crumbling hearth was relatively dry. Aidan broke up what remained of two wooden chairs and a table for firewood and soon had a blaze going. Then, while he saw to Lucifer's care and feeding in the shed beside the hut, Breanne stripped off her sodden clothes, rubbed herself dry, and donned another set of tunic and breeches. Her boots she set as close to the fire as she dared to dry them out.

By the time Aidan returned, she had a small pot of soup simmering, thrown together from the rations they'd brought along from the castle. A small loaf of bread was set out on a clean cloth, accompanied by a round of cheese and several apples and pears. Breanne glanced up as Aidan stomped in and threw off his cloak. His gaze met hers for a fleeting instant; then he turned aside.

He peeled off his tunic, chain mail, and under tunic, then sat on the rickety bench shoved against the wall. As he began the difficult task of pulling off his boots, Breanne quickly rose and hurried over.

"Allow me, m'lord," she said, kneeling before him.

His single eye ensnared hers. "You needn't trouble yourself."

The frigid dismissal was like a slap in the

face, but Breanne persevered. " 'Tis no trouble, Aidan. Truly 'tisn't."

Before he could refuse, she picked up the rag she'd left by the door, wiped off what she could of the mud that coated his boots, then grabbed hold of the heel and toe and tugged. With a cynical arch of a dark brow, Aidan permitted her assistance. His tall black boots soon sat beside hers at the fire.

An excuse to stir the soup was Breanne's way of providing Aidan with the privacy to change into a dry pair of breeches. Then, as he sat before the hearth, toweling his hair dry, she dished him up a bowl and placed it in front of him. The meal was a silent one, but Breanne noted with secret satisfaction that Aidan wolfed down two bowls of soup and several slices of bread and cheese.

She shot him covert glances from time to time, admiring how thick and curling his hair, now free of its severe topknot, was as it dried. A wavy lock tumbled down onto his forehead, lending his face a surprisingly boyish look. An impulse to stroke the hair back filled Breanne. With the greatest of efforts, she controlled her sudden, unaccountable desire.

Her gaze lowered to his chest, a bulging mass of whipcord muscle and sinew, of flat male nipples in a tangled sea of dark hair that densely covered his upper torso before tapering to a narrow river that disappeared beneath the top of his breeches. She noted, once again, the thin, white scars on several spots across his arms and chest, reminders, Breanne well knew, of some battles not as successfully fought as others.

He was a magnificent, devilishly handsome, powerfully built man—that much was undeniable. The realization, once admitted, however, only served to stir her anguish to greater heights.

"You really must learn to control those eyes of yours," Aidan's deep voice suddenly intruded. "You have a way of visually stripping the clothes from a man's body and arousing him that would bode poorly for your maidenhead in the wrong company."

Breanne jerked her gaze back up to his face, flushing hotly. "I-I'm sorry," she stammered. "I beg pardon."

Aidan shrugged, then poured himself another cup of watered-down wine. "'Tisn't necessary to apologize. I liked it." His single eye raked over her. "As much as you did, whether you're honest enough to admit it or not."

Apprehension coursed through her. "I did no such thing," Breanne began, then caught herself. Curse the man! How she hated it when he was right!

She glared over at him for a moment more, then, with a sigh, dropped her eyes. "It doesn't matter what I like or don't like about you, Aidan. In the eyes of God, our marriage was never meant to be." She forced herself to look up. "But, for the sake of the quest, to free Caerlin and destroy Morloch, we must try to make some kind of peace between us. 'Twill be our only hope of any success."

Aidan's jaw clenched. "Oh, aye, the quest, with all the rules dictated to us by the monk Olenus. I've given our meeting with him last night a lot of thought." His mouth twisted wryly. "There was little else to do riding in the rain today."

"And what conclusions did you come to? Anything that might make you change your mind?"

"Nay, naught that you'll like, at any rate. I'm still convinced that Olenus tried to manipulate us both into believing what he wished."

Breanne shook her head fiercely. "Nay. Olenus would never lie, nor use magic to another's harm. He is a good, holy man."

"Mayhap he is," Aidan conceded grudgingly. "But if so, his concern must be for the good of the masses, not for two people. And if manipulating you to think you saw a man who may have died long ago—"

"I won't believe it! I know Olenus well, while you met him only last night. You aren't qualified to judge a man on such meager acquaintance."

His mouth went hard, and he set down his cup with enough force to slosh the remaining liquid over the sides. "Nonetheless, I've judged and have come to a decision." Aidan leaned forward, impaling her with his single eye. "Though I don't necessarily agree with the monk on a magical sword, or some ancient prophecy, I do agree that Morloch is a growing danger to Anacreon and must be destroyed."

"Good," Breanne breathed in relief. "In the end, that's all that matters. That, and the fact I'm vital to the eventual success of the—"

Aidan held up a silencing hand. "Without a mage in the sword or a viable prophecy, there is no need for you. And the hope of going against the necromancer and coming out alive is virtually nonexistent, so I doubt there's much chance of success, at any rate. Yet, for my mother's sake and that of whatever good people you insist remain in the land, I still mean to seek him out. I have naught to lose. You, on the other hand," he continued, "have everything. You are young, innocent, with your whole life yet to live. And far too lovely to condemn to a nunnery."

His gaze locked with hers. "There is another, better way."

An uneasy premonition curled within Breanne. "Aidan, what are you saying? I'm your wife. No matter the problems between us, I am vowed to you. I won't leave your side, whatever the danger."

"Ah, but you will, lady wife," Aidan said, a resolute expression settling over his features. "As your husband, I command it. Did you not vow to obey me?"

She glowered back at him.

"Well, did you not, Breanne?"

"Aye," she muttered.

"Then obey me in this. The friend I spoke of before, Dane, the lord of Castle Haversin—his lands lie only three days' ride from here. We will journey there and, once you are settled comfortably, I will ride on."

"To take Morloch on alone?"

"Aye."

"Oh, nay, Aidan!" Tears of frustration and despair filled her eyes.

"You must obey me in this, lass," he said, steeling himself to her distress. "Dane is a good

201

man. In time, you'll come to like him, and mayhap even learn to love him."

Her glistening eyes widened. "L-love him? And why should that ever be a condition of my obedience?"

A look of pained regret crossed his face. "Because, once we've reached Castle Haversin"—Aidan forced himself to answer one of the most difficult questions in his life—"I intend to annul our marriage and give you as wife to Dane."

Chapter Ten

She stared up at him for a long moment, stunned by his totally unexpected pronouncement. "You wish to annul our marriage?" Breanne finally gasped out the words. "And give me to another man?"

"Aye, lass. 'Tis for the best. Trust me in this."

"F-for the best? Trust you?" she repeated, her anger rising. "And who are you, you arrogant, self-serving, flea-bitten son of a kennel man, to make such decisions?"

"You vowed to obey me," Aidan growled. "That gives me the right to make choices that serve your best interests."

"Well, I say, curse your right!" Breanne rose to her feet to stand over him, her fists clenched at her sides. "Vows or not, I will not obey you in this!"

Aidan glanced up and eyed her calmly. "And won't you, wife?"

"Nay, I won't, *husband!*"

An impulse, stirred by his own rising frustration and muddled emotions, rose in Aidan to tell her that, if she didn't care to cooperate, she could just ride out on the morrow and go back home. But he knew, whatever the source, Breanne would remain in danger if he sent her back. That realization, not to mention the distinct possibility that Olenus would manage to find some way still to interfere, stifled Aidan's initial inclinations to send her packing. But, once they were far enough from the royal castle, those who wished Breanne's death might not know what had happened to her or, hopefully, where she was.

"And how will you stop me, if I decide anyway?" Aidan demanded coolly. "You won't leave me if you're so determined to remain on the quest, and I intend to head for Dane's lands on the morrow. If you come along, your fate is sealed."

"Well, I won't stay!" she snapped, grasping at anything to counter his smug self-assurance. "You can ride out without me, but I'll follow. And you can't force me to marry another man, much less keep me from coming after you!"

"Ah, but I can keep you from following me, lady. I'll just have Dane lock you up until I'm long gone."

"And you say he's a good man?" Breanne gave a disparaging laugh. "He sounds, rather, just another copy of you, mindlessly obeying your every whim!"

Aidan's mouth drew into a ruthless, forbidding line. "Your insults against Dane won't change anything. My mind is made, Breanne. 'Tis for the best for you at any rate. You'll come to see that in time."

"And the gates of Hell will freeze solid before that day comes!" She turned on her heel and stomped across the short expanse of the hut to place as much distance between her and Aidan as she could. Flinging herself down, she scooted back against the wall out of one of the many roof leaks, and glowered over at him. "I'm far from beaten in this, m'lord," she bit out. "Caerlin will aid me, and even your powers are as naught against his!"

He looked definitely irked by her comment. "Indeed," Aidan drawled. "Then call to him now. Call to him and prove me wrong."

Breanne went quiet, her eyes growing huge.

Aidan smiled grimly. "Not so certain of Caerlin's presence in my sword anymore, are you?" He climbed to his feet and walked over to where he'd hung Baldor's sword from the edge of the mantel. In one effortless movement, Aidan unsheathed the gleaming length of steel. Striding across the hut to where Breanne sat, he squatted and laid the sword across her lap.

"Go on, lady. Prove me wrong. I'm man enough to accept my error—*if* you can do it."

"Fine," she responded, her hands moving to clasp the sword to her. " 'Twill be an easy enough task."

Clenching shut her eyes, Breanne willed herself to relax, concentrating on her breathing as she had before. Thoughts, questions, however, roiled in her mind, interfering with her inward journey.

What if Aidan was right? What if Olenus *had* bespelled her into thinking she'd seen and communed with Caerlin? If he truly believed the prophecy, he might think he must do whatever it required to coerce Aidan into taking her with him. Or, mayhap, the monk imagined the falsehood of a mage within the sword was justified by the enormity of the undertaking. Whatever worked to encourage Aidan to agree to the quest was fair and reasonable in the end.

It didn't matter, whatever Olenus's true motives. She'd never know for certain unless she tried to seek out Caerlin. His presence within the soulstone—or lack of it—would be answer enough.

Breanne inhaled a deep breath and once more willed herself to relax, until the slow, deep rhythm of her breathing began to lull her into a waking repose. Blackness, deeper and darker than she had ever before experienced, engulfed her. She felt herself spiraling downward into a whirling vortex. But, this time, there was no light at its end.

She willed herself to concentrate harder, determined to find the light. Caerlin was there, at the tunnel's end. She must reach him and prove Aidan wrong. She must, or the quest for her was over before it had barely begun.

Yet, try as she might, Breanne couldn't find her way past the void, nor still the doubts that churned in her mind. And, as the effort grew increasingly difficult, the doubts became louder, distracting her, weakening her attempts to set them aside. A heavy weariness, compounded by the long, stressful day, encompassed her. Suddenly, the strength needed to go on fled her in one debilitating rush.

Dizziness, and a stomach-churning nausea, filled her. Her eyes snapped open, to slam straight into Aidan's. Her breath came in ragged gasps.

Aidan grabbed her by the shoulders as her face went white and she swayed to one side. "Breanne, stop it. Let it go! 'Tisn't working and you're just making yourself ill."

Gently, he lowered her to lie upon the floor. By the Holy Ones, what a fool he'd been to taunt her into this! Aidan cursed himself. Yet it had been necessary, if he were ever to prove his point.

The sooner Breanne accepted the realities of their quest, the better for the both of them. To carry on, expecting some long-dead mage eventually to come to their aid, was not only foolhardy, but most likely fatal. Better they know from the start what weapons they truly had to aid them. And who was necessary—and who wasn't.

"Breathe slowly, deeply, lass," he instructed. "Relax and the sickness will pass."

She shoved his hands away. "N-nay. Let me go. I don't need or want your help!" She rolled away from him to face the wall.

Aidan stared down at her, uncertain what to say to soothe the anguish and confusion he knew she must be feeling. He had won, made his point, but felt no particular triumph in it. Rather, if the truth be told, he wished it had been different. The powers of a great mage, like Caerlin was said to have been, would've been most welcome in the undertaking that lay ahead. But he'd learned long ago not to waste time mourning over what couldn't be. Far better and more productive not to look back, to move on to what could be instead.

He inhaled a fortifying breath and touched her gently on the shoulder. "Breanne. Don't fight what is. Accept there's no sorcerer in the stone. You were manipulated by Olenus. His is the failure, not yours."

"Oh, aye," she choked out. " 'Tis easy for you to say. You're not the one who feels the fool, who is now useless and soon to be cast aside!"

"I don't take you to Dane because you're a fool or useless," Aidan growled, irritation beginning to thread his voice. "I do so to protect you, to give you a chance at a new and better life. Curse you, woman! Why can't you see that?"

"I see only that you regret our meeting!"

A sharp intake of breath, a pause, then a slow, forceful exhalation of air was his reply. "Aye, in some ways I do regret it."

Tears welled in Breanne's eyes and spilled over onto her cheeks. She pushed herself up and crawled over to sit hunched in the farthest corner. Above her, the rain fell in a steady, rhythmic thrum to *plunk* and *plop* on the floor through the myriad of chinks in the rotting roof.

The incessant drumming only intensified Breanne's rising despair and, with it, the anguished realization of the arduous task that lay ahead. Used and lied to by one man to

208

manipulate her onto a danger-fraught quest, and soon to be discarded by the other as a useless burden, she saw little point in going on. Yet turning back seemed just as pointless.

Aidan rose and walked back to sit before the hearth. "Come, Breanne. 'Tis too cold over there, away from the fire's heat. 'Tis past time we took our rest. We've another long ride ahead on the morrow. Come back, Breanne."

Aye, she thought with a sudden, surprisingly intense flare of pain, *another long ride that will only bring us closer to the day you may rid yourself of me once and for all*. But, though Aidan admitted regretting that they ever met, Breanne could never feel that way. Still too recent was the memory of his mouth upon hers, hot and tasting sweetly of passion. Still too fresh was the lingering feel of his body, hard and throbbing with need, pressed into hers. And, though forbidden between them, still she couldn't help but savor the joy of having him as husband, however fleeting it might have to be.

Breanne's earlier resolve to tell him of their close blood ties faded in the agony of his rejection. It no longer mattered, at any rate. The truth, now, would only serve to solidify Aidan's resolve to annul the marriage. Better to keep it from him. 'Twould mayhap buy her time to change his mind.

If all else failed, she'd find some way to escape him and seek out Olenus at his abbey. The monk would need to know what had transpired. Besides, Breanne thought bitterly, she had a few questions of her own to ask of her old teacher. Questions regarding his deception, and why he'd tried to make her believe she was someone special . . . when she never was nor ever would be.

Aidan woke slowly, languorously, to bright sunlight streaming into the ramshackle hut. He yawned, stretched, then glanced over to where Breanne slept, as far away from him and last night's fire as possible. Her bedding was empty.

With a frown, Aidan levered himself to one elbow and looked around. She was nowhere to be found. Irritation flared. She knew better than to leave his side.

A snort and shuffling of hooves outside reminded him of his horse's presence. Aidan smiled. Mayhap Breanne was with Lucifer.

He rose, pulled on his boots, still slightly damp from yesterday's soaking, and took down his sword and sheath from the mantel. The rickety door creaked open at his touch, nearly falling off its rotting leather hinges. Warm air assailed him on a freshened breeze. Aidan paused on the threshold, blinking in the sudden glare of sunlight. Then he stepped out onto the still muddy ground and strode around to the shed where he'd stabled Lucifer.

The big war-horse was calmly chewing a fresh pile of grass. Breanne had indeed been there, but wasn't now.

Looking for your lady?

Aidan glanced up at his horse. "Was I that obvious?" His mouth twisted in annoyance. "She knows better than to leave my sight!"

Well, she never left my sight, so I thought no

210

need to wake you prematurely.

"Where is she?" Aidan looked around. "I certainly don't see her."

With a bob of his head, Lucifer pointed to the left. *There, through the trees. She's bathing. Are you certain you wish to disturb her?*

"Am I certain I wish—?" Aidan scowled. "Of course, I'm certain!"

But your lady wife is bathing—naked—*in the pool,* Lucifer protested. *It might be wiser, for your own peace of mind and body, to await her here—*

"'Tis far too late for any peace where Breanne's concerned," his master snarled. "And I mean to teach her a lesson she won't soon forget!"

I only hope 'tisn't a lesson you *won't soon forget,* were his mount's parting words as Aidan stalked off through the trees.

Aidan didn't really know what he'd meant by the threat, if the truth were told. All he knew, through his rising fury, was that Breanne had defied him one time too many. She seemed determined to risk her life at every turn and someday, if she wasn't careful, he wouldn't be around to rescue her.

The sound of splashing water reached his ears, the glint of sunlight upon water, then the gay sound of feminine laughter. Aidan's steps slowed as, through the last of the trees, he saw the pool—and Breanne. She was indeed naked, and standing in waist-deep water, her upper body bared.

Her hair was loose, the ends honey-dark from their immersion in the pool. As she splashed

Kathleen Morgan

water up onto her chest and scrubbed herself vigorously, Aidan's gaze was drawn to her full, pouting breasts, the nipples taut and puckered from the cool water and her rough actions.

A wave of desire consumed him. He felt himself thicken, grow hard. He bit back a tormented groan. By the Holy Ones, but he'd indeed made a mistake by coming here!

Aidan stepped back into the shadows, intending to leave as silently as he had come, when Breanne suddenly turned and dove into deeper water. A glimpse of lush buttocks and long, shapely legs flashed into view, then was gone. At the sight, Aidan thought he'd go mad.

Then Breanne surfaced, sputtering, flinging her long, sodden mane aside. Her arms lifted, combing back the hair from her face. The movement lifted her breasts, tightening them into delectably pert, white mounds. Unconsciously, Aidan licked his lips, mentally savoring the soft velvet of pink nipples and silk of tender flesh. Through his breeches, he touched the taut swell of his sex.

Once more Breanne dove into the water, swam for a short distance, then broke the surface. She turned then and, with strong, expert strokes, made her way to a nearby pile of sun-warmed boulders. Clambering up on the rocks with all the unabashed innocence of a child, she turned to face in his direction and stretched out on her back. Breanne propped herself on her elbows, flung her head back, and jutted her breasts proudly up toward the sun.

Aidan dropped his sword to fall soundlessly on the dense mat of rain-damp, fallen leaves.

His hand released his breeches, slid beneath the cloth, and tightened about himself. He freed his organ and began a slow, rhythmic stroking. His breathing turned harsh, uneven.

He shouldn't be here, he told himself again and again. He shouldn't be watching her like this. But she was so beautiful, so perfectly formed—and she was his wife.

His wife, curse it all, and, whether as a consequence of her rejection of him or his decision to give her to Dane, he could never have her. Instead, he was relegated to this, covertly watching her bathe naked and finding his release in lonely—and ultimately frustrating—self-gratification. The realization twisted his gut into a tight, painful knot, but never once did the movement of his hand, stroking, squeezing, and kneading himself, falter.

Breanne moved slightly, arched like a cat, her thighs spreading as if to take in each radiant beam of warmth into every orifice of her body. At what her parted legs offered to his view, Aidan nearly lost control. He clenched shut his eyes, visualizing himself crouching over her, naked as she, his huge, thick shaft hovering a hairsbreadth from her sweet, secret sheath. His hand jerked faster, harder now, his release but a moment away.

"Breanne," he whispered, her name an endearment and entreaty, all in the same word. He threw back his head, the thick cords of his neck straining with his efforts to hold back, to savor the experience to its fullest.

She moved and the sound snapped his eyes open. She had turned over on her stomach, and the sight of her buttocks, full and white and woman-rounded, was his undoing.

With a strangled groan, Aidan sank to his knees, spewing his seed onto the ground. Spasms of exquisite, unspeakable delight racked his body, receding in gradual, ecstatic little shudders until he was nothing more than a trembling, sweating mass of muscle and bone.

He couldn't recall how long he knelt there, alone in the damply pungent leaf mulch and mud, before he recovered himself and fastened shut his breeches. Grasping his sword, Aidan rose to his feet. As he watched Breanne finally leave the rocks and begin to dress, a confusing, anguished tumult of emotions roiled in his head—a tumult that soon clarified into two equally savage and disparate emotions. In the aftermath of his humiliating actions, all Aidan knew was shame, that he'd finally stooped to such depravity as pleasuring himself while his wife lay naked but a short distance away, and a grim determination that he must soon rid himself of the source of his torment—or go mad once and for all.

Engrossed in wringing the excess water from her hair as she headed back to the hut, Breanne didn't notice Aidan's presence until she almost walked into him. His hand, reaching out to stay her, was her first indication she wasn't alone.

With a gasp, Breanne stumbled back. "A-Aidan? What are you doing here?"

"I came to fetch you," he gritted out, a startling fury smoldering in his unpatched eye. "You know better than to leave my side."

"But surely the danger is past, now that we're far from the castle." She gave a nervous little laugh, unsettled by his strange anger. "Besides, how was I to bathe with you watching me?"

"The same way you bathe at any other time," he snapped. "And don't, for a moment, lower your guard and think you're safe, far from the castle though we may be."

"You're jesting, I'm sure. I-I couldn't bathe with you watching me."

"Indeed? And why not?"

"Because I just—" Her gaze narrowed. "Exactly how long were you standing here? How much did you see?"

"Does it matter?"

"Aye, it certainly does matter!" A flush warmed her cheeks. "Were you spying on me?"

His face darkened with annoyance. "Nay, I wasn't spying on you! But for what I did see, you have only yourself to blame."

Breanne swallowed and looked away. By the Mother, he'd seen her naked and she hadn't even known. Her thoughts raced, trying to recall how much she might have revealed. And did he think her behavior wanton?

"Then you did see . . ." Her voice faded. Her head lowered.

"You are my wife, Breanne. Console yourself 'twas I and not some other man."

Aidan grasped her by the arm and began to lead her forward. "Come. 'Tis past time we departed. We'll speak no more of this, but next time you decide to bathe, or go anywhere from my presence, we must first work some plan

215

out. Do you understand me, Breanne?"

"Aye, m'lord."

As she allowed him to escort her back to the hut, Breanne struggled through a tumult of emotions. Embarrassment warred with an unsettling curiosity as to Aidan's reactions upon watching her bathe. Had he been repulsed, angry, or just indifferent? Or, though she hardly dared think it, aroused?

Breanne shot him a surreptitious glance. His expression was inscrutable, his handsome jaw taut and hard, as if he were fighting against emotions he didn't care to reveal. But what *were* those emotions? Breanne desperately wanted to know.

Then the remembrance of their close kinship intruded. What purpose would be served in stirring the cauldron of their secret yearnings, whether for or against each other, when nothing could ever come of a relationship between them anyway? 'Twould be pointless and cruel.

With a small, inward sigh, Breanne tamped down further speculation of what her bath in the pool had wrought, and cast her thoughts to the journey ahead.

He watched them in his enchanted mirror, his only link to the outside world from the depths of his mountain fortress. Morloch watched, and realized all his plans lay in the gravest danger. After all these years of careful manipulation and intricate scheming, everything might well be lost.

Everything and, once again, thanks to the wiles of yet another seductive female. Just as

Eislin had enticed him, his futile pursuit of her tempting him onto paths he'd never have taken otherwise, this golden-haired temptress was now leading his son astray. Women, no matter their age or breeding, were all alike—destructive, self-serving, and ultimately soul-rotting.

But this one wouldn't have his son. Aidan was his, to use to *his* needs, and had been since the moment of conception. The female would only complicate things, divert him from his true destiny, stir his heart to hope for what could never be. Men such as they must live on a higher plane. Carnal desires were more than a distraction; they were an insurmountable barrier.

Morloch replaced his mirror of discernment in its carved, ebony wood box and firmly shut the lid. There was only one solution to the problem. The female must die—now, before she insinuated herself further into Aidan's heart.

Before she ruined everything.

By early afternoon the weather turned hot, the late summer heat soothed only by a light breeze, a distinct contrast to the chill deluge of the day before. Aidan, however, despite the impending warmth, had insisted on donning battle dress, complete with chain mail. His hair pulled back once more in the severe warrior's topknot, his eternal eye patch in place, he looked the fearsome, formidable man of legend. He also began to sweat profusely as the day burned on.

They soon left the forest for the more open and well-traveled road through rolling hillside and verdant meadows. As the day faded to early evening, little notice was given them by the occasional passersby, a farmer taking his produce back from market, a herdsman with his flock of black-faced sheep, and a trader with creaky old wagon overloaded with goods. Aidan gave them all a wide berth, stoically ignoring their shouted greetings as if he hadn't heard them.

Breanne noted it all in rising concern. "How do you ever expect to rid yourself of your fearsome reputation if you persist in treating everyone so abominably?" she demanded in exasperation after the third time Aidan slighted a traveler.

He glanced over, his brow arching in feigned amusement. "You forget, lady, that 'tis your idea to improve my lot in life, not mine. Besides, I don't know their motives for such friendly greetings. Mayhap they're not who they seem, but outlaws in disguise or some creature of Morloch's, seeking to take us unawares."

Breanne gave a small snort of disbelief. "Outlaws, mayhap, though I doubt it, but never magical, evil creatures. You have the power to see through such illusions, as supposedly do I while I wear these bracelets, and I've sensed nothing untoward in the people whom we've yet encountered."

"So, you still have faith in Olenus and what he told you, after last night?" Aidan smiled thinly. "Truly, Breanne, you need to curb your overly trusting nature."

She flushed at his patronizing tone. "Mayhap

I do, but you need to temper your overly suspicious nature with a little trust."

His mouth tightened. "It suits me to remain exactly as I am. It has kept us alive so far and 'twill continue to do so, if"—his voice lowered sarcastically—"you can manage to project the possible consequences of your actions before embarking on every deed that enters your head."

"But mayhap, m'lord, it suits me to remain exactly as I am, as well," Breanne countered sweetly.

"Then you're a fool."

She turned to smile at him. "My point exactly, m'lord."

He shot her a thunderous glance, but said nothing.

They rode on in silence, Aidan thereafter limiting his replies to Breanne's queries to clipped monosyllables. She soon gave up and instead turned her attention to the scenery, even as her puzzlement over Aidan's strange change in behavior continued to nag at her.

She had thought they were becoming friends, that he was beginning to trust her. But ever since their wedding night, he seemed to be slowly pulling back, rebuilding the walls between them. And then, after this morning's bath in the forest pool, Aidan seemed positively frigid, hovering on the edge of fury.

True, her needling of him didn't help his temper any, but someone must point out his flaws if he were ever to hope to change them. Breanne smiled wryly. 'Twas mayhap a hopeless quest, this desire to teach Aidan how to make friends. She had never met a more obstinate man. Nor one who needed loving more than he did.

The trail led once again into a forest, one that, according to Aidan's map, sprawled on for miles. He guided Lucifer close as they rode along, leaning near to speak in a low voice. "Outlaws roam here," he informed her tersely. "Keep your dagger ready and, if I am set upon, don't linger to help me. I'll catch up with you down the road."

"And what makes you think, if we are overwhelmed, that you could get away?"

His reply was to unsheathe Baldor's sword from his back. "This may not be a magical sword, nor contain the essence of a mage, but it has always served me well. I spoke true when I said I'd never been beaten."

"Well, there's always a first time," Breanne countered bluntly, "and your continued arrogance will only lead you down the path to your destruction. Have a care, Aidan, or you'll—"

"Quiet!" He drew Lucifer to a halt.

Breanne quickly reined in her horse. "What is it? What did you—"

He held up his hand in a command for silence. His powerful body went still, his eyes narrowed. And still he said nothing.

The tension built as the minutes passed. Breanne strained for any foreign sound, and heard nothing save the rustle of leaves and chirp of birds. She looked to Aidan, who never lowered his position of vigilant tautness.

Do you hear them?

The large band of men, hiding in the trees up ahead? his horse asked. *Aye. I was wondering when you'd finally notice.*

My deepest thanks for your help, Aidan muttered. *A little advance warning would've been greatly appreciated.*

I was distracted with your and Breanne's discussion. You two have some of the most rousing arguments.

Be that as it may, his master snarled, *I suggest we turn back before 'tis too late.*

A wise plan.

Aidan glanced over at Breanne. "Let's get out of here. Now!"

He wheeled his horse around and pointed in the direction they'd just come, then spurred Lucifer forward. An instant later, Breanne urged her mare after him. Behind her, a sudden outcry of rage filled the air, then a pounding of feet and crackling of underbrush as their attackers sprang from hiding.

Rocks and arrows sang past her head, some thudding into trees on either side of her, others falling to the earth ahead. Shrieks, unearthly in their fury and intensity, swallowed Breanne in a fearsome cacophony. Terror filled her. She crouched lower on her horse's back and prayed with all her might. And she rode.

Aidan reined Lucifer in to allow her to take the lead. Fresh terror flooded Breanne then. What if Aidan, in the process of attempting to shield her, took an arrow himself? What if Lucifer stumbled, or Aidan fell, wounded?

On and on they rode. The cries grew weaker. Hope swelled within Breanne's breast. They were getting away. They'd outrun their attackers.

Suddenly, a rock wall appeared, rising from the road they were on to tower far above her head. With a wild cry, Breanne reined in her horse with all her might, trying to stop the animal before they hit the obstacle. The mare reared back, rising to its hind legs, but its forward momentum was still too strong.

The horse slammed into the wall, twisted, then toppled over, its back broken. Breanne flung herself free of the fatally injured animal, striking the ground with breath-grabbing force. For a long moment, she couldn't move as wave after wave of pain washed over her. Then, with a superhuman effort, she shoved awkwardly to her knees.

Through a blur of sparkling lights, she saw Aidan jump down from Lucifer and run to stand before her, his sword poised for battle. As he did, a horde of hideously grotesque creatures burst from the forest.

Chapter Eleven

For a heart-stopping moment, Breanne just gaped in horror. Outlaws were fearsome enough but, with them at least, there was always hope they'd just take valuables from Breanne and Aidan and leave them alive. But *these* creatures!

There were all manner of terrible beings, some a repulsive mix of human and animal with horns and claws, others totally demonlike, their eyes eerie and burning, armed with a lethal assortment of sickles, scourges, spiked clubs, and double-bladed battle-axes. Many also carried capture nets tucked into their belts. They came at them from every side, until Aidan was backed to the stone wall, with Breanne behind him, and Lucifer to her left.

Breanne withdrew her short sword. "Aidan," she whispered, "what shall we do? How can we hope to prevail against such creatures? And who summoned them?"

"One guess," he muttered. " 'Twas either Morloch or that witch who tried to kill you at the castle." He shot her a quick glance over his shoulder. "Are you determined to use that sword?"

She nodded, a resolute set to her features. "Aye. I'll not hide behind you. 'Twouldn't do much good at any rate. Even with the aid of Baldor's sword, you are fearfully outnumbered."

"Then cover my back and right side, and keep to the wall, no matter what happens. If I manage to cut a hole in their numbers at any time, leap onto Lucifer and ride out."

"Nay! I won't leave you to these creatures!"

"Obey me in this, Breanne. There's no sense in both of us perishing!"

"Nay, Aidan. I won't—"

With a spine-tingling outcry, the creatures attacked. Two quick slashes of Aidan's sword cut down the first demon. Three more immediately leaped over their fallen comrade to confront Aidan. Out of the corner of her eye, Breanne noted Lucifer joining the fracas, rearing to strike out with hard, killing hooves.

Then there was no more time to watch anyone else. Simultaneously, two horned, goatlike beasts sprang at Breanne. Their foul stench rose to encompass her, and it was all she could do not to double over and retch. But even that small pause would have been fatal.

A sickle sliced through the air. Leaping aside, she stabbed one beast in the belly.

With an ear-splitting shriek, the creature fell
at her feet.

A spiked club whistled by, barely missing her
head. Breanne lurched back. Slashing wildly,
she forced her other opponent to retreat. A
quick parry, a feint to the side, and then an
agile undercut with her sword soon disposed
of her second attacker.

But, to her horror, as one creature fell, the
one she'd initially disposed of climbed to its
feet, fully recovered. Uttering a crazed howl, he
attacked again. As he did, five other creatures
moved in to join the fray.

Beside her, Aidan fought against twice as
many, delivering fatal blows with nearly each
stroke of his mighty sword. And as quickly as
one assailant fell, another stepped forward to
take its place.

Breanne heard his breath come raggedly
now, mingling with her own, frantic gasps.
Was Aidan's sword arm already growing heavy,
his fingers turning numb from the bone-jolting
impact of parrying numerous weapon thrusts?
Her hand and arm most certainly were.

Panic snaked through Breanne. The battle
was hopeless if their attackers couldn't be
killed. 'Twas only a matter of time before
they both tired. Then 'twas certain death or
even worse, if the unfurling of capture nets
was any indication of their eventual fate. But
what other options were left them, surrounded
on three sides, an impregnable, magical wall at
their back?

Was this where their quest was doomed to
end, slaughtered by someone's evil minions

before they even drew near the necromancer? Anger filled her. Curse Olenus for sending them out to certain death! Curse him for filling her with hope that she and Aidan were equal to such overwhelmingly dismal odds! What purpose did he ever hope to accomplish, save the sacrifice of their lives?

For a time, her impotent fury fueled Breanne's strength. Her sword thrusts quickened. Several bestial creatures fell. But even anger couldn't long prevail against a body's physical limitations.

Breanne stumbled, sank to one knee. A club struck her sword arm, and her weapon flew from her grasp. A capture net sailed toward her.

With a strangled cry, Breanne dove aside. Then they were above her, leaning down to grab at her, their hideous faces contorted in triumph. She lifted her arms to ward them off, her wrists crossing.

The runic bracelets rang together, emitting a piercing, melodious tone. Something bright rose from them, surrounding her in an aura of light.

Shrieking in pain and terror, one beastman leaped back, then turned and galloped off through the trees. Another creature flung itself at Breanne. She turned, wrists crossed. Again the bracelets flashed, the aura engulfed her, and the beast screamed in pain.

Then four creatures sprang at her at once. Breanne managed to fend one off by directing the force of the bracelets toward it, before two grabbed her arms and wrenched her hands apart. Dragging her to her feet, they pulled Breanne away from Aidan. One beast engulfed her in the stinking expanse of his mighty arms and, while he held her, another tied her hands behind her back.

"Aidan!" Breanne cried in frantic desperation, as they began to drag her away.

He wheeled around. As he did, three of his assailants grabbed for him. He threw two off, then, with the hilt of his sword, caught the third squarely in the jaw. The creature refused to let go of Aidan's arm as he fell, however, pulling Aidan down with him. Suddenly, he was engulfed by a horde of bodies, all leaping into the melee.

Despair flooded Breanne. 'Twas over. There was nothing more anyone could do—

With a shrill whinny, Lucifer leaped forward. He knocked two of Aidan's attackers away with well-placed forefeet. Then, with a snake of his head, he grasped another's filthy jerkin between his teeth and flung him aside. From beneath the teeming mass of bodies, Aidan threw off three others. Before the rest could recover from Lucifer's surprise attack, Aidan leaped to his feet and pulled out his boot knife.

It was a brave but futile try, Breanne thought, as she watched him back to the wall, a throng of creatures following him. A knife was a puny weapon against so many. If only Aidan had the magic of Caerlin to aid him, or . . . or his own magic!

"Your eye!" Breanne screamed above the chaos of bloodthirsty cries. "Uncover your eye!"

He shot her a startled glance, hesitated for the span of a sharply inhaled breath, then shook his head.

"By the Mother, Aidan!" Terror for him pounded through her veins. "What have you to lose? We are surely doomed if you don't use it!"

Breanne spoke true, Aidan thought grimly, gazing out at a sea of hostile, horrible faces. But to use his killing eye again after all these years, to break the vow he'd made that day he'd killed Rangor! Even if his own life were forfeit, he'd promised himself he'd never turn those dreadful powers upon another being again.

Breanne's cry jerked him from his moral dilemma. He glanced back, to find she was even then being dragged farther away. Something shattered in him then. A rage, white-hot and searing, exploded in his brain. All he saw was Breanne in danger—and she was his!

With a snarl of pure animal fury, he wrenched the patch from his left eye. Amber fire blazed forth in a wild, uncontrolled conflagration. The creatures immediately surrounding him fell back, screaming in terror, then turned and fled, slamming into the rest of their comrades. In a chaos of bodies, of flailing arms and churning legs, they ran over the other attackers they'd knocked down, never stopping to look back.

Another burst of amber fire aimed in the direction of the fallen beast-men encouraged their hasty departure as well. Then Aidan turned to the creatures who held Breanne. Though the fire was quickly banked to spare Breanne, her captors chose not to linger. They flung her aside and raced off into the trees.

As suddenly as they'd appeared, the magic-summoned assailants were gone. The wall faded, once again to reveal the long expanse of road leading through the forest. Aidan ran over to Breanne, sliced through her bonds, and grasped her by the arms.

"Are you all right, lass?"

Her only reply was to pull him to her and bury her face in the broad expanse of his chest. His arms encircled her and, for a brief, forbidden moment, his head lowered to rest atop hers. Then, with a wrenching of heart and body, Aidan shoved her back from him.

"We must leave this place. They might well regroup, discover some way to shield against my eye, and return."

Breanne looked up at him and smiled. For a fleeting instant, Aidan was struck with the surprising realization that she wasn't at all cowed by his unpatched eye. The revelation, however, was bittersweet. If she only knew how little control he truly had over it . . .

"Aye," she said, dragging him from his morose thoughts, "your killing weapon that all fear and revile. Yet, this time you used it for good, not evil."

He frowned. " 'Tis an evil power, no matter how 'tis used."

"Nay, Aidan. 'Tis the man who controls its use. And if that man is good—"

"It doesn't matter," Aidan cut her off, his expression turning grim. He began to pull her toward Lucifer. "What matters is we're still in the gravest danger."

He paused beside his horse, grasped Breanne by the waist, and placed her atop the big war-horse. Then, in a few quick strides, Aidan retrieved his sword, slid it back into the sheath fastened to his back, and picked up Breanne's.

As she resheathed her sword at her waist, he retrieved her pack of clothes and supplies from her dead mare. In the next moment, Aidan had lithely leaped up before Breanne and secured her pack alongside his. She grasped him about the waist, scooting close to the strong, comforting expanse of his back. Aidan urged Lucifer forward. Then, with a powerful bunching of muscles, Lucifer sprang out.

They rode through the darkness of a dense forest that allowed little of the meager moonlight, once it rose, to pierce the thick canopy of leaves. Breanne sat rigid with apprehension as they galloped along, dreading the possible consequences of unseen obstacles that lay ahead, until Aidan whispered back, "Fear not, lady. My eyes can see in blackness as if it were the light of day."

Breanne relaxed then and, with a small sigh, leaned into him once again. A warm sense of contentment and surety filled her. She was safe with Aidan. He had powers that would see them through this, and anything else that Morloch chose to throw at them. They had only to fight on, and someday they'd prevail. If only they never lost courage, or the conviction of the rightness of their quest . . .

Their quest. Breanne sighed, the full enormity of their precarious situation encompassing her in the aftermath of the vicious assault they'd just endured, dampening her earlier surge of optimism. They had so little power of their own ever to hope to defeat Morloch. Though Aidan's magical abilities were impressive when compared to those of the average person, they lacked the depth or scope of a high-level mage, not to mention a necromancer.

And she, without the presence of Caerlin in the sword, had nothing to contribute. Absolutely nothing.

Despair once more swelled within her breast. Breanne closed her eyes and laid her head against Aidan's back. She was nothing more than a burden to him and, though he was too kind to say it, she knew he felt it as well. Mayhap 'twas best that he did take her to his friend Dane. With her out of the way, he'd at least have a fighting chance.

You are wrong, child, a deep voice rumbled in the silence of her mind. *He has no chance at all without you.*

With a tiny gasp, Breanne jerked back, her eyes snapping open. There, in the sword that hung across Aidan's back, the stone glowed in the blackness. Breanne blinked, thinking to clear her vision, and still the soft light remained. She looked closer, and found the face of Caerlin gleaming there.

Is it really you, she asked, *or just some image conjured from my desperation?*

Caerlin smiled. *I am real.*

Then why didn't you come to me, back there in the hut?

Your doubts had closed your mind to me.

231

And now? Breanne prodded. *What's so different now?*

Your desperation has opened you to other possibilities. Your pride is no longer an obstacle, as it was that night you tried to prove yourself to Aidan. He'd angered you, and you meant to get back at him. My powers can never be used for revenge of any kind.

Breanne frowned in puzzlement. *Yet you wish to help us destroy Morloch. Is that not revenge?*

Nay, child. Morloch was my finest student, my greatest achievement, until he chose to follow the Demon's way. 'Twill break my heart to harm him, but it must be done. Anacreon can't survive unless Morloch is stopped.

Anacreon and *Aidan,* Breanne interjected firmly. *Tell me what to do to help him.*

Keep yourself open to me, child. Never again permit your pride or anger to shut yourself off from your powers. I cannot help you otherwise.

But what are *my powers?* Frustration welled in Breanne. *The ability to talk with you will serve little purpose if we're attacked again. We need* you, *free of the stone, to use* your *powers.*

And free I shall be, with your help, when the proper time comes. But that time cannot happen until I am near Morloch and your powers have ripened.

You speak of my powers, yet I see no special abilities.

Don't you, child? Already you commune with me with far less effort than you did before. And you used your bracelets well today. The next step will be harnessing my powers through the sword.

But how? How will I do that?

In time, child. In time I will reveal that to you. But not now. Not tonight.

Breanne exhaled a deep breath and wearily rested her forehead upon Aidan's back. *You speak true. 'Tis too much to fathom after such a day.*

Aye, 'tis, child, Caerlin agreed. *Until next time, I bid you farewell.*

Wait! Breanne mentally cried, but it was already too late. The mage was gone.

'Twas for the best, she consoled herself. She truly couldn't bear much more this night. And, with that, Breanne scooted closer to Aidan, laid her cheek against his broad back, and promptly fell asleep.

He noted the change in her breathing, the slackening of her tense position against him, and knew that she finally slept. The knowledge that, after all that had happened, Breanne felt safe enough in his company to sleep was the only comfort he found in the endless hours that passed. Despite the distance that widened between them and their magic-summoned attackers, Aidan continued to urge Lucifer on at a wildly reckless pace.

As he rode along, his mind raced as well. His worst fears had come to life in the unexpected and vicious attack. Someone, whoever it was, wished them captured if not dead. Someone, whose powers extended unnervingly far, meant to see them stopped, not just gone from Anacreon.

But was it Morloch, or another? Aidan wasn't sure. All he could be certain of was their situation was rapidly worsening. The sooner he got Breanne to the safety of Dane's castle, the better. Then he'd be free to confront whoever was after them, and not worry about Breanne.

At the memory of her spirited response to the attack, Aidan smiled in the darkness. She'd fought alongside him without complaint or hesitation, a brave, resolute little warrior. Then, just as soon as they were safe, Breanne had once again become the beguilingly feminine woman who so entranced him.

He could feel her soft body pressed against him, the swell of her breasts, the thrust of her woman's hips against his backside with each roll of Lucifer's gait. Desire surged through him. Aidan swallowed a savage curse and forced his thoughts to other, just as troubling paths.

His eye. What would he do, now that he'd once again unleashed its devastating fury? 'Twould be all too easy to use it again, especially in Breanne's defense. Yet the weakness inherent in the act, the release of all those years of tightly controlled restraint, sickened him to the marrow of his bones.

Breanne was wrong when she'd claimed he'd used his eye for good, not evil. She had no way of knowing the wild, uncontrollable joy he'd experienced as he'd released the power of his eye. She had no idea of how good it had felt. Even now, the impulse to use his killing powers again nibbled at the edge of his consciousness, a nagging, aching wanting that festered in the very heart of him.

He feared it. Feared his powers because of their fierce attraction. Feared them, because they symbolized all he'd fought so long and hard to deny. Yet, for Breanne's sake, he'd been forced to confront the terror again.

Aidan only wondered how long he could contain the evil that lurked within him, now that he'd once more unleashed his killing powers. Those powers had returned too easily and far too potently for him to deny the truth any longer. This time, whether he wished it or not, there was no running from the final confrontation with the man that destiny had always called him to be.

Aidan rode all night, coming out upon mist-blanketed meadows a little before dawn. Breanne continued to sleep soundly and he let her until midmorn, when Lucifer finally demanded a stop. She awoke as he drew to a halt beside a merry little stream that gurgled and burbled its meandering way down through a stand of trees. As she swayed groggily atop Lucifer, Aidan dismounted, then pulled her down to stand beside him.

After all night in the saddle, her legs buckled when she touched ground. Aidan steadied Breanne once again, grabbing her arms to lend support. She lifted sleep-weighted eyelids then, an expression of puzzlement gradually replacing her slumberously sensual look.

"What's wrong, lass?" he asked, his lips quirking in amusement. "Lost your bearing?"

She stared up at him a moment longer, then shook her head. "Nay, though I must admit to not knowing where we are. But what really confused me for an instant was the realization that you'd somehow changed, yet I couldn't quite fathom what 'twas." She smiled. "Then I suddenly knew. 'Tis your eye patch. You're not wearing it anymore."

Aidan studied her in thoughtful silence. "Did it frighten you, when you realized what was lacking in me?"

"Oh, nay." Breanne gave a little laugh. "I told you before, the powers themselves aren't inherently evil. 'Tis what the man chooses to do with them. And I know you're a good man, so what is there to fear?"

"More than you'd ever care to know," he muttered uneasily. Releasing her, he stepped back and gestured down to the stream. "Go, see to your ablutions. We depart in fifteen minutes."

Breanne arched a delicate brow, then shrugged. "As you wish, m'lord."

Aidan watched her walk away, then withdrew his eye patch and donned it. Next, he turned to Lucifer. "Don't say a word," he warned his horse when he sensed a snide comment forming. Loosening the cinch, Aidan then walked Lucifer down to the stream.

Exactly 15 minutes later, after freshening up in the chill water and eating a quick trail breakfast of dried, seasoned beef strips and what remained of the bread, they were once again on the trail. As the morning mist burned away in the heat of the rising sun, the world around them became a bedewed wonderland. The rich, pungent scent of damp earth wafted to Breanne's nostrils. She inhaled deeply. Birds chirped and flitted from limb to limb in the groves of oak and alder they occasionally passed. A playful breeze swirled through, its passing gusting at times, and other times gently caressing.

Breanne hugged Aidan close, enjoying, for a brief moment, the forbidden pleasure of feeling his big, hard-muscled body against hers, of inhaling his bracing scent, of just being with him, no matter the place or circumstances. His resumption of his eye patch had temporarily disturbed her, but she refused to allow the disappointment to linger long. She had made progress, if only for a short time, and his stubborn refusal to cease wearing the patch altogether was only a temporary setback. And 'twas too wonderful a day to waste in glum regrets.

A joyous exaltation filled Breanne, that the land was so beautiful, that she was still alive . . . and still with Aidan. 'Twas the simplest things in life that gave the greatest pleasure, she decided, especially when one was with the man one loved.

The admission caught her up short. She had no right to love Aidan, at least not the way she loved him. 'Twas far from a sisterly, or should she say, cousinly, kind of love. Yet 'twas still a secret joy as well as bittersweet pain—and would always remain her secret. Aidan need never know.

She shook the increasingly morose thoughts aside, determined not to let anything unpleasant intrude on the glorious morn. She lifted her chin to rest upon Aidan's shoulder.

"What are the plans for today?" Breanne inquired blithely.

Aidan shot her a quick glance over his shoulder. "A large town called Windermere lies about a half day's ride away. We'll make it that far, then spend the night. There's an inn there—the 'Bed and Brisket'—that's clean and comfortable. A night's slumber in one of its beds would ease my saddle-sore muscles considerably."

"An inn? With beds, and mayhap a bathing tub?"

Aidan's mouth twitched at Breanne's sudden interest. "Aye, and a tavern that serves the best roasted pork and potatoes in the land. Does that plan meet with your approval?"

"Oh, aye. It sounds like heaven!"

And heaven it probably was, Aidan thought, after what she'd been through in the past day. Yet still she carried on, cheerful, optimistic, all brightness and hope.

Olenus's words, that night in his mother's bedchamber, drifted back to Aidan. *She is light to your darkness . . . hope to your despair . . . dreamer to your realism.*

Aye, she would've been all that and more, Aidan thought with a heart-deep pang, if things had been different. The memory of her, gloriously naked at the forest pool, flashed through his mind. Again, a rush of hot blood filled his groin. He cursed silently.

Time to ease your lust, is it, my friend? Lucifer inquired.

Aye, Aidan admitted grudgingly.

You're in luck then. Doesn't that buxom, black-haired maid live in the town we're headed for?

238

The one that has always had a special love for your gold coins?

Aye, what of it?

Lucifer gave a small snort and flung his luxuriously long mane about to frighten off a persistent fly. *I was but wondering what your wife will think of an illicit meeting with the town whore?*

I'd hardly think she'd care where I slept, just as long as it wasn't with her. But her desires—and mine—to the contrary, I won't be leaving her side this night.

The war-horse's lip curled in amusement. *A cozy picture, indeed. I only wonder what your little wife will think of that arrangement?*

Aidan sighed in exasperation. *Enough, Lucifer. I haven't the patience to entertain you at my expense. But rest assured, I can handle Breanne.* With that, Aidan nudged his war-horse into a slow canter.

Can you now? was his mount's parting reply, before he turned his attention back to the road ahead.

Chapter Twelve

By late afternoon, they crested the hill that overlooked Windermere. Aidan had understated the town's size, Breanne thought, as her gaze took in the crowded chaos milling outside Windermere's huge main gate. Her glance lifted, scanning the sand-colored city walls, over twenty feet of rough-cut block limestone. Above the walls rose the town roofs, chimneys, and church spires.

They crossed the drawbridge slung over the dry moat, patiently waited their turn in the teeming mass of wagons, livestock, and people, then passed through the iron gates flanked by twin towers. Shortly, they made their way through the narrow, winding streets, past three- and four-story frame houses and shops shouldering precariously onto the pathways. Though Aidan seemed unmoved by the noise, crowds, and variety of wares on display, Breanne could hardly keep herself from constantly swiveling about on Lucifer's back.

There were shoemakers, weavers, purse makers, woodcarvers, locksmiths, spice merchants, and tanners. There were rug makers, oil merchants, wine sellers, and barbers, besides the usual assortment of carpenters, butchers, tailors, and coopers. The shop fronts were painted red or blue, or faced with tile, and often ornamented with paneling, moldings, and sawtooth. Colorful signboards hung over each shop, decorated with their tradesmen's symbols. And within, shopkeepers and their apprentices could be seen, busily at work.

" 'Tis truly wonderful," she breathed. "I've never seen such wealth of goods, and rarely, so many people massed in such a small area."

Aidan glanced back at her and smiled. "Have you never visited a town then?"

"Nay, never. Do you visit Windermere often?"

"Often enough," he replied dryly. "I tend not to attract as much undue attention in a town this large."

Nor frighten off the women, either, Lucifer silkily offered.

Aidan chose to ignore his mount's comment. Instead, he turned his attention back to Breanne. "Would you like to visit some of the shops, buy a few trinkets?"

Breanne flushed. "Oh, nay. Not today. I know how tired you must be after riding all night, and there'll be no time to do so on the morrow, before we leave. Mayhap, on our return—" She stopped short, realizing the truth of that statement. "I-I thank you for your kindness, though."

"Breanne," Aidan ventured carefully, "I have sufficient coin, if that's the problem."

"Nay. Nay, Aidan." She choked back an uncharacteristic swell of tears. "'Tis of no import. I've no wish for any trinkets."

He frowned, but said nothing more, turning his attention back to the journey through the town.

Breanne, for her part, struggled to fathom her own emotional response. Had it been Aidan's generous offer that had touched her heart, or the knowledge that, one way or another, they'd never travel together again?

It mattered not. Anything she could have bought would have served as nothing more than a painful memory of the short time she'd had with Aidan. Steeling her heart to what lay ahead, Breanne said no more as they made their tedious way across Windermere to the inn.

She was the first to notice the gaily painted sign board heralding the "Bed and Brisket Inn" that hung over the door. Breanne pointed it out to Aidan, who nodded and headed Lucifer down the side alley, which led to a small stable.

He dismounted, helped her down, then handed their packs of clothes and supplies to her. "Await me here while I see to Lucifer's care and feeding." Then Aidan led his horse over to the stableman, gave a few curt directions, and flipped the man a gold coin.

As Lucifer was taken away, Aidan returned to Breanne's side. He shouldered both packs, then motioned her forward. "Come, let's find a room." He glanced up at the midafternoon sun. "By the time we both bathe and don clean clothes, 'twill be time enough for an early supper."

A wide grin split his road-grimed and weary face. "If we hurry, I might well manage to stay awake until I finish my meal."

She managed a wan smile, then followed as Aidan turned toward the inn. Though the furnishings were plain and sparse inside, the inn was indeed clean. The scents emanating from the kitchen were appealing as they passed by it to climb two flights of stairs to the upper floors and bedchambers. In spite of herself, Breanne's mouth began to water.

The room the innkeeper's wife offered them was small but well furnished. A large bed stood in one corner, plump with fluffy down comforter and pillows. The wide window opened onto the noisy street and a panoramic view of the town and surrounding countryside beyond the walls. Sunlight, streaming through the delicate lace curtains, cast the room into a jewellike fairyland. After the past few days, Breanne had never seen anything that looked more beautiful.

The innkeeper's wife indicated the tall, wooden screen that spanned the room's opposite corner. "Yer bathing tub lies beyond the screen. I've a kettle I always keeps steaming over the fire for bathwater. I'll send some of my servants up presently with yer water."

Breanne smiled. "We'd be most grateful."

The woman smiled in return and departed. Aidan flung down the packs, lowered himself onto the nearest chair, and heaved a huge sigh. "Come, lass. Pull off my boots, will you? Then I'll return the favor."

She hurried over and soon had Aidan's tall black boots standing beside his chair. Then she slipped behind him and began to massage his shoulders. He shot her a wary look, but soon relaxed under her soothing ministrations. The tenseness slowly eased from his body. Aidan's eyes lowered in drowsy contentment.

"Truly, lass," he murmured in a rough velvet voice, "you really should have a care. If I weren't so exhausted . . ."

"Hush, Aidan," Breanne chided. "None of your threats. Enjoy it for what 'tis meant to be—one human being easing the aches and pains of another."

And I could name another ache that I need eased far more than this, he thought wryly, but wisely withheld his comment. Her kneading of his neck and shoulders did feel wonderful, and he knew if he dared allude to things of a more physical nature, she'd stop immediately and draw away. So, instead, he turned his conversation to more practical matters.

"You may have the first bath," he offered, "if you promise to take it quickly. Otherwise I'm certain to fall asleep, and once that happens, you'll not waken me before the morrow."

"I can be very fast," Breanne promised. "Unless, of course, you'd prefer to go first?"

"That won't be necessary, lass. I can wait—"

A knock sounded on the door. With a sigh, Aidan relinquished the delicious feel of Breanne's hands and rose. A serving maid—the buxom, black-haired maid Lucifer had needled him about—stood there, a wooden bucket of steaming water in her hands. When she saw Aidan, a slow, provocative smile stole across her face.

"Why, m'lord," she purred. "How pleasant to see ye again. Would ye like me to assist with yer bath, once I've filled the tub to yer liking?"

Aidan stepped aside and motioned her in. "That won't be necessary." He indicated Breanne who still stood beside his chair. "My . . . my squire can help if need be."

The maid eyed Breanne. "He doesn't look too stout fer the job," she muttered sullenly. Then her look brightened. "Well, mayhap later this evening. Ye can send him away for a time, can't ye?"

Aidan smiled thinly. "Mayhap." He took the bucket from the dark-haired woman and carried it over to the tub, where he emptied it. Then he returned the bucket to the serving maid. "Three or four more of hot water, then a few of cold should do."

She accepted the bucket, shot Breanne one final assessing glance, then flounced out of the room. Aidan shut the door quietly behind her.

"Squire? So now I'm your squire?" Breanne demanded.

Aidan shrugged. "It seemed the most prudent course to maintain your disguise. My initial premise hasn't changed. A man and woman traveling alone always attract notice."

"Mayhap." Breanne sniffed. She eyed him with a speculative look. "You've done more

245

than sampled the food and bed here before, haven't you?"

He glanced up at her in surprise. If he didn't wish it so badly that he doubted his usually keen powers of observation, Aidan could have sworn he'd seen a flash of jealousy in Breanne's eyes. But instead, he chose to take her question at face value.

"Aye, I've bedded the lass a few times, if that's what you're asking. Her fear of my powers is well compensated by a few gold coins. And even I have to satisfy my 'baser' needs from time to time. Magic doesn't fulfill everything, you know."

"Nay," Breanne muttered, "I wouldn't know that. Do you intend to bed her tonight?"

The directness of her question left him momentarily speechless. Then his composure returned. "And what if I do?" Aidan challenged tautly. "Why would you care? You've made your lack of interest in me more than apparent. I'd think you'd prefer I fulfill my carnal desires elsewhere. 'Twould lessen the risk of me taking them out on you."

Breanne suddenly realized where the course of this conversation was leading. Cursing herself for her unthinking response to the serving maid's overtures to Aidan, she hastily regrouped. As she opened her mouth to reply, however, another knock rapped at the door.

Thankful for the interruption, Breanne strode past Aidan and wrenched the door open. Another servant, this time a sturdy, tousle-haired boy, held another bucket of steaming water in his hands. Wordlessly, she waved him in.

Both watched the lad deposit his load of water and depart. The dark-haired serving maid soon followed, as did the innkeeper's wife. Aidan shot Breanne a questioning glance when both women had departed, as if challenging her to pick up the thread of their conversation, but she merely shook her head and clamped shut her lips. Within another ten minutes, the tub was filled.

Aidan closed and locked the door after the last servant departed, then turned to Breanne. "Well, what's it to be? Your bath first or mine?"

"Mine," Breanne answered. Grabbing a fresh set of clothes from her pack, she stomped over to the screen and disappeared behind it. Only after she'd stripped and climbed into the tub did her high emotions clear enough to realize the precariousness of her situation. Here she sat, naked, protected from Aidan's gaze by only a thin, wooden screen.

A sudden thought assailed her. Could he mayhap see through objects as well as he saw through darkness? She scooted lower in the tub, her arms lifting to cover her breasts.

"I don't hear any splashing water or body scrubbing going on," a deep voice rose from immediately on the other side of the screen. "My bathwater cools the longer you tarry."

With a small squeak, Breanne sank even lower. "Don't you dare look over!" She grabbed the bar of soap and quickly lathered her arms. "And . . . and I'm washing myself right now."

Aidan's chuckle and retreating footsteps were his only reply.

In but five minutes more, Breanne rose from the tub and toweled herself dry. Wrapping the thick bath sheet about her, she grabbed her clothes and slipped around the screen. "Your bath is ready, m'lord," she snapped, her irate glance slamming into his.

At the sight of Aidan, clad only in breeches in preparation for his bath, Breanne paused. Her gaze traveled from his face to the play of muscle and sinew along his arms and shoulders, then down to the massive swell of his hair-roughened chest and taut, flat belly. For a fleeting, forbidden moment, Breanne lost herself in his virile, masculine beauty, admiring him for the magnificent animal he was. But only for a moment. To linger on such thoughts would only court disaster—for both of them.

Aidan noted the smoldering look in Breanne's eyes. A wild hope surged through him. He tamped it down with the greatest of efforts, refusing to believe what all his instincts screamed was truth. He rose from his chair, intending to walk past Breanne to the bathtub, but as he took in her bare arms and shoulders, water-slick and glistening, his gaze narrowed. With her long hair, honey-dark from its washing, hanging down her back, and the attractive flush to her skin from the water's heat, Breanne looked a seductive little water nymph.

The memory of the last time he'd seen her wet flashed through his mind. From there, it was a simple thing to complete the image of how she'd appear beneath the bath sheet, all beguiling curves and womanly secrets. Aidan's heart began a dull thud beneath his breast.

Blood coursed through him, to pool in his suddenly turgid organ.

An impulse to stride across the few feet separating them and rip the bath sheet from Breanne filled him. Wild emotions, crazed thoughts, roiled in his mind.

She was his, by religion and law. He had the right to take her. And mayhap, just mayhap, once she saw no danger to her in their coupling, she'd lose her fear of the act. Aye, Aidan thought in a rising surge of passion-clouded reason, 'twould never change between them if he didn't make the first move.

Breanne saw his expression alter, his sudden decision that boded poorly for her continued resolve to maintain a chaste relationship between them. She took a step backward. "Aidan, whatever you're thinking," she began, "it cannot be."

A feral look gleamed in his single eye. A wolfish grin twisted his mouth. "And what exactly am I thinking, lass?" he silkily inquired as he advanced on her.

Unsure whether it was wise actually to confront the topic, Breanne continued to back away as she struggled to find some tactful way to change the subject. "I-I wouldn't know. But shouldn't you hurry, before your bathwater grows cold?"

The wall suddenly halted Breanne's further progress. In the next instant Aidan was before her, unnervingly intimidating in his towering presence. Gazing up at him, she was struck with the utter helplessness of her situation. With one sweep of his hand he could strip her and, with another, throw her down on the floor. The realization both terrified and excited her.

He smiled, a ruthless, predatory lifting of lips from strong white teeth. "Don't concern yourself over my bath, lady. I find my interest turned suddenly to far more pleasant considerations. Such as," his smile widened, "what I plan to do to you."

His hand moved to where she'd tucked the bath sheet between her breasts. Breanne's hand shot out to capture his in midair. "Aidan, don't."

"And why not?" His expression had sharpened to glittering awareness. "I think 'tis past time we end this little game."

" 'Tis no game!" she cried, as his fingers slid beneath the bath sheet and clenched in the cloth. "It cannot be, this act between us! 'Tis—'tis a sacrilege!"

At her words, something snapped in Aidan. Too many times had he heard similar words fall from the lips of a woman. Too many times had he turned away in rejection, his unrequited desires a searing pain he was forced to carry endlessly in his heart. And now to have Breanne—who knew him better than he'd permitted any other woman to know him—repulse him once again!

With a snarl, Aidan shoved her against the wall and tore away the bath sheet. She didn't stir, just stood there pressed back in astonishment, her eyes wide, making no attempt to cover herself from him. For the longest moment, the only movement was her ragged breathing, and the erratic rise and fall of her full, white breasts.

He dragged his gaze from her bosom, down
past her trim waist and softly rounded belly to
the tangle of curls at the apex of her thighs. Lust
rose in him, hot and mind-numbing, blocking
out all honor or thought of gentleness. Aidan
reached out, grabbed Breanne, and jerked her
to him.

"A sacrilege, is it?" he rasped. "Fine words
from a woman who willingly, nay, eagerly
stepped forward to take me as husband! Do
you now deny that you knew the consequences
of your act when you saved me from the executioner? That you were ignorant of the duties of
the marriage bed?"

"N-nay," Breanne gasped. "I knew."

His fingers entwined in her hair and, with
a slow but inexorable pressure, he pulled her
face close. Leaning down, Aidan moved until
his lips were but a warm breath from hers.
"Then fight me no more, lady."

His words, harshly spoken, sent a premoni-
tory prickle down her spine. She saw his resolve,
and the first tendril of fear coiled in her stomach. He meant to have her and Breanne suddenly wasn't so sure anything she could say would
sway him. But she had to try, nonetheless.

"Aidan, please," she whispered. "Listen to
me—"

He silenced her with a hard, slanting kiss,
grinding her lips against her teeth. As she tried
to jerk back, uttering a small cry of protest, he
thrust his tongue into her mouth. One hand
moved to imprison her head; the other slid
down to clasp her buttocks and slam her hips
into his.

The swollen, rigid length of his manhood throbbed against her belly, hot, hard, and exciting. An aching heat stirred deep within her. Blood pumped through her wildly beating heart.

As his mouth plundered hers in savage abandon, Breanne fought to regain her reason—and lost. Her arms snaked about Aidan's neck, and she clung to him as if he were the source of all life and comfort. Their tongues met, melded, stroking the other in a fierce mating dance of their own.

Wild, crazed, primitive needs flooded Breanne. She rubbed her breasts against his chest, delighting in the rasp of his coarse body hair across her highly sensitized nipples. One of her hands encircled his waist, then slid lower to grasp a taut male buttock.

At her touch, Aidan groaned. His hand slipped between them to free himself, then moved to grasp Breanne's thigh and pull it up around him, pressing her sweet, moist flesh against his throbbing erection. At the touch of naked flesh against flesh, he flung back his head, his expression one of exquisite agony.

"Do you know how badly I've wanted you . . . since yesterday at the pool?" he demanded, his voice raw, agonized. "There's hardly been a waking moment since then that I haven't fought not to think about you, and how 'twould be to join with you. Do you know what you drove me to, as I watched you swim naked, then flaunt your luscious body in the sunlight?"

"Please, Aidan," she begged. "Don't. I don't want, I don't *dare* know!"

"And why not, little one?" he murmured huskily, as he moved to nuzzle her throat. "Are you afraid to hear how deeply, how passionately, you affect me?"

"A-aye!" She jerked aside as he lifted his head to recapture her mouth. " 'T-'tisn't decent!"

"Decent?" Aidan expelled the word on a soft, almost sorrowful, breath of sound. "Mayhap not, but what I did to relieve my lust was far more decent than joining you in the pool and raping you. And rape 'twould have been then, and most likely is now, as well, knowing how much the thought of coupling with me disgusts you."

"Nay!" Breanne's head snapped around, and the sudden heat of her anger dispelled the last of her reluctance to tell him the truth about them. "You have never disgusted me! Never! I've wanted you from almost the first moment I realized what kind of man you truly were. But"—she paused to inhale a deep breath—"it cannot be. We are cousins, Aidan. Your father and mine were brothers."

A frown of puzzlement furrowed his brow. "What are you talking about? The prince consort's only brother died almost fifteen years ago, as did his entire family. And your family is of peasant birth. How could you possibly be related to the House Laena?"

His voice faded and a wary, speculative look flared in his eye. Aidan released her leg and pushed away from her. "The prophecy. Somehow, Olenus convinced you that you're of the House Laena so that, too, would fulfill the prophecy." He shook his head and sighed.

"First he leads you to believe you can speak to a nonexistent mage in my sword, and then he builds upon your dreams of being of noble birth. Truly, Breanne, can't you see what he's trying to do?"

"I never aspired to the nobility!" Breanne said, bristling at his inaccurate assessment of the situation. "Until I met you, I was quite content with my life, simple though it may have been. And you are wrong about Olenus. He spoke true of Caerlin. I've communed with him again."

She lifted her hand to silence his disbelieving interjection. "It doesn't matter if you doubt it or not. In time, I'll prove you wrong. And as far as the issue of my lineage, 'twasn't Olenus who told me, 'twas my foster mother, Kyna."

"Your foster mother?" Aidan's mouth twitched mockingly. "And have you ever thought her motives might have been to keep you safe from me?"

"I don't know what you mean."

"How could we wed, much less even bed, if we were truly cousins?" He cocked a dark brow. "In fact, if you knew we were blood relations, why did you even consent to marry me? Our marriage was invalid."

"Aye, that 'twas," Breanne hotly agreed, "and I knew it, even as I made my vows. But what else was I to do, Aidan? If I'd revealed the truth, you would've once more been in danger of your life. And who else would've stepped forward to claim you for husband?"

He eyed her closely and an expression of incredulity spread across his face. "You truly believe this ridiculous tale, don't you? You really think we're cousins."

"Aye," was her simple reply.

Something hardened in him. "Then there's naught more to be said—or done. I don't see you as cousin, but what I think matters not, if you do. It also seals my decision about what to do with you."

Breanne's heart began a wild beat. "And that is?"

"When we arrive at Dane's, our marriage will be annulled. One way or another, you entered into it believing 'twas invalid. That belief, in itself, makes it so."

She moved to grasp his arm. "Nay, Aidan. Invalid though our marriage may be, our partnership remains of the greatest import. I am the one of the prophecy, don't you see? When I survived the murder of my family and the fire that destroyed my home, I rose from the ashes, just as the prophecy foretold. It is I who must somehow free your heart so that Morloch will fall. And I cannot do so if you give me over to Dane and ride off to fight the necromancer alone!"

"Lies," Aidan growled. "Lies, all spread by that devious, manipulative monk! Am I the only one who can see through his schemes?"

"I think, rather, you're the only one who lacks the faith to believe and trust," Breanne countered, her frustration growing. "And your stubborn blindness to the truth could well be the end of us all!"

He grabbed his towel and strode around the back of the screen. "Then mayhap you'd be wise to separate yourself from me while you can! 'Twould be a tragedy to be dragged down with me."

"Aye, that 'twould," Breanne shot back. She stomped over to the bed, then paused, glancing back at the screen. "Enjoy your bath, *m'lord!*"

Aidan stripped off his breeches and flung them aside. "Aye, that I will," he snapped savagely back. As he climbed in the tub, however, he bit back a gasp of distress. The water was already cold.

Chapter Thirteen

'Tis time. Time to call Aidan home before the woman wins his heart.

Morloch turned from his enchanted mirror, back to a somber chamber of shadows and flickering mage light. He strode over to a tall chest, opened the door, and extracted a cloth-wrapped parcel. Carefully he unfolded the black velvet to expose an oblong, irregularly shaped crystal. Stalking back to his chair, he sat, then placed the stone on the small table that stood before him.

With a rustle of richly brocaded, black robes, the necromancer leaned back, all his powers of concentration focusing on the crystal shard. Through it he would marshal additional energy for spell casting and weave a web of enchantment that would draw his son to him. A spell that would beckon Aidan day and night, growing in intensity with each passing hour, until his only surcease lay in reaching his summoned destination as quickly as possible.

Aye, Morloch thought grimly, 'twas indeed time to bring his son to him. The attempt to kill the woman had failed and more deadly spells, cast with great difficulty and inaccuracy at such a distance, might just as easily harm Aidan as her. And complicating everything was his son's surprising increase in powers, powers he seemed determined to use to protect the woman. She had indeed woven her spell around his son's vulnerable heart and was even now strengthening the bonds.

Time was of the essence if he were to win Aidan back. Time, and enchantments that could best be intensified and utilized within his magical fortress. Enchantments neither his son nor the woman had any hope of withstanding.

Strange dreams assailed Aidan, rife with whispered words he couldn't quite fathom, lurking shadows that loomed over him, stirring an odd, aching need to follow. He tossed and turned all night, his rest fitful, exhausting. Finally, just before dawn, he rose from the pallet he'd made on the floor and strode over to gaze out the window.

From the vantage point of the upstairs bedchamber he could see over the town and beyond. In the mist that rose from the land, the faint glow of the rising sun illuminated the distant horizon—and the Improbus Mountains. As he stared out at their faint outline, the ache within him grew. They called to him, Aidan realized, mass of towering earth and rock though they were, filling him with an unsettling longing, a rising need to go to them.

He turned from the sight of the mountains, unnerved by the intensity of his yearning. He would reach them sooner or later, but first he must attend to one bit of unfinished business to see to its completion. Castle Haversin lay but another three days' journey away. If they rode fast and hard, he could likely cut the time to but two days and a half. Breanne would need her own horse, though, and they'd have to set out soon.

With that resolve, Aidan strode over to the bed and shook Breanne awake. She rose in a drowsy mumble of slumber-driven words, her golden hair a riotous tumble about her shoulders, and rubbed the sleep from her eyes. As she climbed from the bed, Aidan choked back an anguished curse.

By the Holy Ones, but would the sight of her never cease to stir him? She wore the sleeping shift she'd packed along with the rest of her clothes and, in her early morning grogginess, seemed unaware of the seductive image she presented. Sleeveless and simple, her garment revealed a tantalizing swell of pert young breasts before loosely falling to follow the flaring curves and undulations of her slender body. Though the fabric was opaque to his piercing gaze, her chill-hardened nipples thrust impudently against the cloth.

Aidan clamped down on his rising frustration and turned before she could see the arousal that was once again straining against his breeches. Two days and a half, he reminded himself grimly. He'd suffered far worst torments in his life. He could bear another two days and a half.

A gray gelding was bought from a nearby livery and, an hour later, they were once more making their way through Windermere. Already the town was beginning to stir, housewives hanging bedding out the windows to air, the town crier bellowing the time, the milkman slowly pulling his cart, laden with jugs of fresh, foaming milk, through the streets to sell door-to-door.

The baker was equally industrious, busily turning out fresh loaves of bread from his huge clay ovens; Aidan paused to buy two loaves for their breakfast. As they rode out the town gates, Breanne eagerly tore off a chunk of her loaf. She inhaled deeply of the bread's tantalizing aroma before biting into its delicious mix of crisp crust and soft, warm interior.

Once again a heavy, late-summer mist lingered overlong on the land. Occasionally, birds chirped from trees that were little more than great, looming shadows somewhere off the road, but for the most part, the morning vapors seemed to mute sounds as well as sights. At times, they'd ride through an especially dense patch of mist, and Breanne would find herself surrounded by an eerie whiteness that seemed to transport them into another world.

She'd glance around nervously then, fearing every shadow or swirl of vapor, imagining all sorts of creatures leaping out at them with no warning. Aidan, however, leading the way, appeared calm and unperturbed. Each time, Breanne would swallow a small giggle and force her mind to other matters.

As the sun rose, its light and warmth pierced the haze. The moisture dissipated, leaving behind only a bedewed reminder twinkling on the grass. Breanne relaxed then, chiding herself for her earlier apprehension. How was she ever to brave Morloch in his den, she asked herself, if she couldn't even ride through a morning mist without fear?

Once the way was clear, Aidan nudged Lucifer to pick up the pace. They rode all morning without pause, halting only for a half hour at midday to rest the horses and eat a quick lunch. Then Aidan resumed the punishing pace, pushing them until twilight fingered the land with its deepening shadows. All the while he rarely spoke, save to give some terse command.

Uneasiness snaked through Breanne. There was something different about Aidan since last night, something more than what prompted his usual gruff, taut response to her. He had a strained, haunted look in his eye, and a sense of urgency seemed to consume him. Was it just his need to be rid of her, before the tension between them came to a head?

After last night, she wouldn't blame him. Every time she remembered those moments in Aidan's arms, naked, his sex pressed to hers, she was overcome with a heated desire. Then, as Breanne reminded herself that such feelings were forbidden, an unexpectedly savage pain slashed through her. The extreme swings in her emotions were pure torture. If Aidan was feeling anything similar, she could well understand his urgency to be free of her.

Finally, well past nightfall, Aidan drew Lucifer to a halt. Breanne reined in beside him, paused to lean back in the saddle to ease the soreness from her aching legs and back, then glanced around.

A full moon shone overhead, illuminating the night in silver elegance for leagues in every direction. They'd stopped above a large river that twisted sinuously through forest and open country. Stands of towering oaks dotted the land—great, monstrous shadows whose leaves made gentle, rustling sounds in the night breeze. At long intervals, the flickering lights of small farming villages could be seen.

It was a peaceful, idyllic eve, the breeze a warm, velvet caress against Breanne's cheek. Scents assailed her, of pungent horseflesh, of rich, dark earth, of wood smoke from a distant village. Life and its mysteries seemed so deep, so poignant at moments such as these. Moments that should be savored and cherished—and shared.

She exhaled a blissful breath. " 'Tis so beautiful, isn't it, Aidan?"

Distracted, he turned toward her, his scowl casting his face into sudden, shadowed ferocity. "What are you talking about, Breanne?"

"The night. The land, the breeze, the smells. 'Tis all so beautiful. Can't you see it, sense it?"

Irritation filled him. By the Holy Ones, here he was, exhausted after a long day's ride and little sleep the night before, driven half-mad not only by her seductive presence but by the gnawing compulsion to travel on until he reached the Improbus Mountains, and all she could do was comment on the night as if she were on some romantic moonlit ride!

He choked back an angry retort with the greatest of difficulty. "Nay. I haven't the leisure for such things," he gritted instead. " 'Tis past time we find camp and get some rest."

With that, Aidan nudged Lucifer down the hill. Breanne hesitated but a moment, then, with an exasperated sigh, followed. After a sparse, cold supper, Aidan set Lucifer to the first watch, he to the second, and Breanne to the third.

His sleep that night was no better than the eve before. Aidan tossed and turned, his frustration growing with each passing hour of tension-fraught wakefulness. Curse it all, he thought. Danger was still all around them, he must rise in two more hours for his turn at watch, and, despite his utter weariness, he couldn't seem to rest.

Finally, in desperation, Aidan rose and took over early from his horse.

What ails you? Lucifer inquired. *Surely not the little female? You've borne with unrequited desire before.*

Aidan shook his head. *'Tis that and more. I've just a need to get this over with. She eats at me, the quest to destroy Morloch eats at me, and my frustration at being manipulated by that wily monk eats at me. My life, as lonely and dangerous as it may have been, was far simpler before I returned to Anacreon!*

And empty as well, with little hope for anything more.

A fresh surge of irritation flooded Aidan. *So, 'tis better to trade madness for emptiness? I think not!*

Nay, his horse replied. *Rather the hope of a better life, with a woman who loves you, for what little you now have.*

Irritation flared into anger. *Enough, Lucifer! She doesn't love me. She doesn't dare let herself. We are cousins!*

Cousins? Lucifer gave a snort of disbelief. *And do you truly believe that?*

It doesn't matter what I believe, so long as she believes it.

Then, 'tis simple. You must convince her otherwise.

And call her beloved Olenus a liar, not to mention her mother? Truly, Lucifer, you're sometimes as naive as Breanne!

Mayhap, his horse grumbled, *but 'tis, nonetheless, the only way.*

Go, get your rest. Aidan motioned him away. *My problems are my own.* "And, one way or another," he added privately to himself, "I'll soon see them solved."

Once he'd deposited Breanne at Dane's, the physical torment being with her constantly wrought on his body would be over. His mind would clear; his full attention could be turned to the problem of Morloch. The necromancer was a formidable foe, mayhap the worst he'd ever encountered, but Aidan knew how to do battle, how to confront fear, pain, and danger, and fight past it to victory. Soon, everything would once again be simple, straightforward.

But, even after he'd left Breanne behind, he was no longer so certain he could as easily expunge her memory from his mind. She wasn't like any other woman he'd ever known. With her flawless, golden beauty, her exuberant love of life, her dauntless courage, and her surprising, and most unsettling, devotion to him, Breanne was everything he could have ever hoped for—yet didn't dare—in a woman. Nay, he wasn't so certain he could ever forget her.

As he gazed off into the night, Aidan wondered if he wasn't just trading one painful dilemma for another.

Breanne woke to a hazy sunrise and the sounds of Aidan breaking camp. Throwing back her bedding, she climbed hastily to her feet. Her glance found him in the process of tossing the saddle onto her gelding.

"Aidan." She strode over to stand at his side. She eyed him intently, a small, worried frown furrowing her brow. "Why didn't you wake me for my watch?"

"I couldn't sleep," he muttered tersely. "There seemed no purpose served in waking you to share a watch I would've taken as well."

Breanne touched his arm in concern. "Did you get *any* sleep?"

He jerked away, leaned down to grasp the saddle's girth, then straightened. "Don't worry about me. I need no nursemaid."

With a tug, he tightened the girth and fastened it. Then he turned.

Breanne gasped in shock.

His unshaven jaw was clenched tightly, the shadowed growth there a stark contrast to his strange pallor. A dark circle smudged beneath his unpatched eye. But it was the look in his eye that disturbed her most of all.

A fever burned there, a wild, haunted expression that Breanne had never seen before. Was he ill, or had he taken some injury that now festered, filling his body with fever? Surely nothing else could account for his appearance.

"Aidan," she whispered. "What is wrong? How can I help?"

He grasped the hand she extended before it could touch him and make matters even worse. By the Mother, did she have any inkling how close he teetered on the brink of losing control? If she touched him now, if she lingered an instant longer standing so close, her sweet woman's scent filling his nostrils, he feared for her safety. And for her maidenhead.

"There's naught wrong with me that a few hours' sleep and the confines of Castle Haversin won't cure." Aidan flung her hand away and stepped aside. "See to your needs, then mount up. If we hurry, we can be at Dane's by tomorrow afternoon."

They rode hard all morning, taking breaks only when absolutely necessary to rest the horses in the rising elevation that led to Dane's more mountainous lands. Finally, about midafternoon, Lucifer demanded a stop, refusing to go on until *the little female has a time to get down, walk a while and stretch her legs.*

Not to mention, he added, *have her dinner meal.* And, despite Aidan's threats, the big war-horse then refused to budge until his master complied.

The forced stop did little to improve Aidan's mood. Not only did he feel that his horse was now siding with Breanne over him, but the uneasy sense of urgency had steadily increased as the day burned on, roiling inside him until it had finally lodged in his chest, a hollow, tautly strung, sickening sensation like nothing Aidan had ever experienced before. Something was definitely wrong with him, but what, he didn't know, save that he *must* get to the Improbus Mountains and Morloch.

By late afternoon, they passed the turnoff that would have taken them straight to that distant mountain range, another two days' travel away. For a fleeting instant, Aidan considered sending Breanne down the road that led to Dane's lands and heading off to the mountains alone. But only for an instant. Not only did he seriously doubt that Lucifer, who had developed a surprising affection for Breanne, would have allowed him to leave her, but Aidan himself knew he couldn't dare risk her in such a manner.

Whether he liked it or not, he'd have to endure the insistent call for another day or two. He owed Breanne that much. If only he wasn't so exhausted, so distracted, so constantly on edge.

By the time the afternoon faded into early evening, Aidan's endurance was at an end. He could barely stay awake on his horse. Breanne took the lead, knowing Lucifer would look out for his master's welfare, and searched for a safe spot to camp for the night.

She found it in a forested area not far from a waterfall that emptied into a large lake. Nearby, thrusting from the forest floor, was an outcropping of volcanic rock that contained a small cave. Breanne eyed the stony shelter with satisfaction. The cave would both provide cover and protect their back, there was adequate water available from the lake, and the location was a good distance from the main road so smoke from a fire wouldn't alert any unwanted guests.

"Get down, Aidan," she said, glancing over to where he was dozing on Lucifer's back. "We stay here tonight."

At her words, he jerked awake. He glanced around, then shook his head. " 'Tis still light. We can travel a few hours more."

"Nay," she countered firmly. With a determined motion, she dismounted. "I'm tired. Get down from there. We go no further this day."

Do as she says, my friend, Lucifer prodded. *Unless you're determined to walk on alone.*

Aidan knew when he was beaten. He swung down from his horse. Unfastening his sword from his back, he paused to hang it from a nearby tree limb, then began to unload the packs and bedrolls.

Breanne stepped up to help him, but he shrugged her aside. "I can manage," he growled. "I'm tired, not helpless."

He turned then, the gear in his hands. "Take the horses down and water them while I make camp. Afterward, we'll cook supper together."

She nodded her acquiescence, biting back a small sound of compassion at the sight of him. He was utterly exhausted, forcing himself to function on sheer willpower alone. The sooner she carried out Aidan's instructions and got a hot meal into him, the sooner he could take his rest. If she and Lucifer had to stand guard all night, Aidan would get all the sleep he so desperately needed.

As Aidan laid out the bedding, then began to gather firewood, Breanne led the horses down the hill to the lake. The falls cascaded into the water but 50 feet away, enveloping them in a thick mist. Breanne threw back her head, reveling in the invigorating coolness of the fine spray caressing her face. She felt encompassed by the beauty and noise, swallowed up in another world as the roar of the water plummeting from high above drowned out all other sound.

She stood there for a time, allowing the horses to drink their fill, savoring the majesty and power of the falls. Then she remembered Aidan— and their supper. Breanne tugged on the horses' reins. "Come along, you two. I've a hungry man who—"

Lucifer's ears pricking forward and his angry snort were the first warning Breanne had of the danger. She tensed, glancing around. Her hand snaked to the hilt of her short sword.

"What is it, Lucifer?" she whispered, knowing, without any sign to indicate that it was so, that threat permeated the area. The scent of wood smoke wafted to her nostrils. Aidan, she thought. He'd started a fire. A fire that would bring whoever was lurking out there straight to them.

She dropped the horses' reins and stepped forward, intending to climb the hill to warn Aidan. As she did, a pair of strong teeth sank into the shoulder of her tunic. With a jerk, Lucifer pulled her back.

Breanne glanced over her shoulder. "What? What are you trying to tell me?"

The horse released her, then nudged her over to the left. A small path wound up the hill and into the trees, leading around the side of the volcanic rocks that ended at the edge of the hill overlooking the lake. The realization that Lucifer was warning her not to return directly to camp sent an icy chill prickling down Breanne's spine.

Her heart pounding beneath her breast, Breanne swiftly but stealthily made her way up the path that Lucifer had indicated, slipping through the dense foliage and past the outcropping of rocks that blocked her view of camp. If attackers, whether human or not, watched Aidan from the trees, how was she to warn him? Various plans raced through Breanne's mind, but none could be acted upon until she had the opportunity to assess the situation.

As the roar of the falls began to fade, other noises rose in volume. Men's shouts. Sounds of struggle. Then silence.

Breanne quickened her pace, knowing her chance to warn Aidan had passed. Whoever had found him had already attacked. An urge to throw all caution away and rush through the forest to fight at Aidan's side surged through

her. She forced it back with only the greatest
of efforts. She was of more help to him now by
keeping her presence secret—or at least until
she'd the chance to take them by surprise.

A cry, anguished and quickly cut short,
pierced the air. An instant later, Breanne
reached the edge of the small clearing where
they'd made camp. She choked back a gasp.

There, staked down hand and foot, a gag
shoved into his mouth, lay Aidan. Around him
stood roughly clad men, clubs and swords
gripped in their hands.

Outlaws, she thought. Breanne counted them.
Eight. Eight big, well-armed outlaws. But
human, she quickly consoled herself. They
could at least be killed.

But how had they managed to take a seasoned
warrior like Aidan unawares? Even exhausted
and distracted as he was, once he'd had the
sword of Baldor in his hands, the outlaws
wouldn't have been able to overcome him.
Her glance scanned the area and soon found
the answer. Aidan's weapon still hung from the
tree where he'd left it. He'd never had a chance
to reach his sword.

As Breanne frantically considered her
options, one outlaw, a torch in his hand,
stepped forward and lowered the flaming
brand to Aidan's midsection. As she watched
in horror, Aidan's face contorted in pain and
he writhed on the ground, helpless to escape
the fire.

The outlaw with the torch laughed. "Burn,
demon spawn! Burn, and return to the depths
of Hell from whence you came!"

The bottom dropped out of Breanne's stomach. The blood rushed from her head and she thought she might faint. Then a fierce resolve filled her. Aidan needed her. She must think of something to do. But what? Holy Mother, what?

Caerlin's words flashed suddenly through Breanne's mind. . . . *The next step will be harnessing my powers through the sword . . . to use the sword to your own needs . . .*

A wild hope flooded her. Was it possible? Could she indeed harness the mage's powers in Baldor's sword to her own needs? There was a chance for Aidan if she could. And if she couldn't? If she was yet too untutored, too weak in her abilities to summon Caerlin and utilize his wondrous abilities? What then?

Then Aidan's fate and hers would be the same. She could do no less for him, even if it required the sacrifice of her life. Breanne eyed Baldor's sword, gauging how to approach it without notice. As she did, the outlaw's torch lowered once more to Aidan.

The scent of scorched clothing and flesh filled the air. Aidan twisted futilely in his bonds, his tormented groans muffled by the gag. The outlaws' laughter, however, was gleeful and loud. Breanne began her stealthy way around the clearing to the sword.

Once again, the torch-bearing outlaw temporarily paused in his cruel game. Another man stepped forward to heap handfuls of dried grass and small twigs, then the remaining pile of firewood, onto Aidan's body. The other men quickly joined in. Aidan's torso was soon covered, then the torch lowered once more.

Horror shivered through Breanne. By the Mother, they meant to burn him to death! She discarded all caution and sprinted the last several yards in full view of the outlaws. As she passed by them, a shout of surprise rose. She didn't care. All she saw was the sword.

Then her hands were grasping at it, her fingers closing about its hilt. Footsteps pounded toward her. Voices rose in lustful delight, drowning her in a deafening cacophony. With a frantic wrench, Breanne pulled the weapon free of its sheath.

With a fierce cry, she swung around, Baldor's sword clasped in her hands. Swung around to find Aidan afire and eight brawny men confronting her. Breanne uttered a silent prayer, then summoned forth every bit of strength she possessed, calling on Caerlin to aid her. For a heart-stopping moment, nothing happened. The outlaws fanned out, intent on encircling her.

Then the power surged through her. It began as a flush of warmth that suffused Breanne's body, starting where her hands gripped the sword. A vibration followed in the sword as well as her body, growing in intensity until she shuddered with the force. Baldor's sword began to glow and flash brightly. A sound akin to wind rushing through the treetops filled the air.

Then, with a pounding of hoofbeats, Lucifer joined the fray.

The outlaws halted, confusion in their eyes.

"Go!" Breanne cried. "Go now. Before I can't control the sword's power anymore!"

A few men laughed nervously. "What trick is this?" one demanded.

It was too late for further warning. Light exploded, surging forth from the sword's tip. The outlaw standing closest was pierced through the heart. More beams sprang from the sword, splitting to strike two men at a time.

Cries filled the air, horror gleamed in eyes and twisted faces. Breanne directed the sword's power to yet another outlaw. With a shriek, he, too, fell. That final, most convincing demonstration of magic was enough for the rest. They grabbed up their fallen comrades and, to a man, turned and fled.

Breanne ran over to Aidan. Shoving Baldor's sword into the earth beside her, she knelt to fling the burning tinder off Aidan with her bare hands, then slapped out the flames still searing his flesh. With her dagger, she sliced his bonds free and pulled the gag from his mouth. Then, grabbing a bowl from her pack, she glanced up at Lucifer. "Stand guard while I run down to get water to cool him."

The big horse nodded. Breanne dashed off, flying down the hill to the lake. She scooped up a bowlful of water, then hurried back as fast as she dared to prevent spilling the water. Then, kneeling beside Aidan, she gently poured the water over his burnt torso.

He groaned and made a move to stop her. "By the Mother! Breanne, don't!"

She quickly shoved his hands aside. "I must, Aidan. 'Twill cool your burn and flush away

274

what charred skin as can be easily removed."
Her hands trembled. With an effort, she forced
them to steady.

"Wh-what happened?" He gritted his teeth
against a fresh flow of water across his abdomen. "The f-fire. The p-pain. I didn't see how
you drove the outlaws away."

"The sword of Baldor . . . your sword." She
paused to pour more water through his wounds.
"I summoned Caerlin's power and he aided me.
Your sword flashed brilliant light that killed
several outlaws. The rest deemed it wiser to
depart while they were still able."

"M-my sword?" Confusion clouded his single
eye. "But th-that's impossible!"

"Is it, Aidan? Then how did I frighten off
eight big men?"

He shook his head in frustration. "I don't
know. Ah, by the Mother, Breanne, enough!
There isn't any more you can do for me!"

"In a moment." She rose, dragged over her
pack, and pulled out a clean tunic. Tearing the
bottom of the garment into several long strips,
Breanne proceeded to cover Aidan's abdomen
with the rest of the tunic and bind the bandage
in place.

As she worked, she surveyed him. His most
severe burns were over his torso, where the
flesh was charred and his chain mail shirt
was seared to his skin in several spots. His
upper thighs were also burnt, but thankfully
only superficially.

The injury to his torso was life-threatening
enough, though. She had to get him out of
the forest and to someplace where the proper

healing salves and potions were available. But how to move him in his condition?

"Aidan," she said, cupping his face in her hands to gain his already fading attention. "I need your help. We must get you to some village or farmer's cottage. I-I don't know what else to do for you, nor do I have the proper supplies."

"Dane." He turned his pain-misted gaze to her. "His castle lies but a three- or four-hour ride away. F-fetch him to me."

" 'Tis too far," Breanne protested as she began to untie his feet. "And I cannot leave you so long unprotected."

"L-leave Lucifer here. He'll not allow anyone to approach me."

"Nay, Aidan. I cannot—"

"Aye, you c-can and you must," he cried. "I won't have you out there, r-riding over the land searching for help for me. Go to Dane, or stay here and watch me die. The choice is yours."

"Fine," she muttered. "Have it your way then, you stubborn son of a . . ." She let the insulting invective die. 'Twas cruel and pointless to curse a man in such terrible agony. What he needed was her reassurance of a speedy return and the comfort of knowing she did his bidding, not a strength-sapping argument.

"I'll go to Dane," Breanne said. "But first, let me get you over to the cave. Lucifer can more easily guard you there."

He tried to rise, but the pain of movement was too great. With a moan, Aidan fell back. " 'T-tis no use. I cannot do it, lass. L-leave me here."

"Nay." Breanne moved to grasp him beneath both arms. "I'll drag you there myself if I have to." And drag him she did, bit by agonizing bit, until Aidan finally lay in the shelter of the little cave.

She ran back then to fetch him two blankets and both of their water flasks. Kneeling beside him, Breanne tucked one blanket beneath his head and the other over him, then handed him a flask. "Keep warm and drink often," she instructed. "Until my return."

Breanne made a move to rise, when Aidan halted her. "Take the sword with you, lass. 'Twill keep you safe, if the mage truly dwells within it."

"But what will you have then?"

"My survival depends on your return, not anything I could do with any weapon." He smiled wanly. "I haven't the strength to wield it, even if I were attacked again."

She knew he spoke true. On impulse, Breanne leaned down and kissed Aidan's clammy forehead. "Until my return, then."

"Lass?"

"Aye?" she replied, pausing once more.

"A kiss on the lips would ease my pain far better than the one you just gave me."

Tears filled Breanne's eyes. "Aidan, I . . ." Her voice faded. The issue of their kinship be damned. He might well die before she returned. Love glistening in her eyes, Breanne bent and kissed him, long, deep, and hard.

His mouth twisted wryly when she finally pulled away. "A most *uncousinly* act, if ever there were one."

She shook her head in exasperation, then rose, strode over to her gelding, and mounted. Glancing back at Aidan one last time, Breanne wheeled her mount around and rode away.

Chapter Fourteen

Breanne drove the gelding hard, slowing only when she knew the animal could give no more. At times, she dismounted and ran along with the horse to rest it, but never once did she permit herself to ease the punishing pace. She had to get to Castle Haversin, had to get help and return to Aidan. Every minute wasted was yet another minute he was suffering—and in danger.

Luckily, the road they'd originally been traveling led right to the castle. And, luckily as well, the moon's light was sufficient to illuminate the way once the late summer sun had set. The only blessings, Breanne thought grimly, in a day fraught with terror and a gut-twisting tension.

She arrived at the castle gates just as the guards were closing them for the night. Reining in her lathered mount, Breanne sought out the nearest guard. "The Lord Dane Haversin," she choked out the words past a thirst-parched throat. "I must speak to him at once!"

The guard's gaze roved down her body, taking in her grimy face, the hanks of blond hair that had escaped from her braid, the simple clothes. His mouth quirked in amusement. "And what makes ye think the Lord Dane would care to see ye, considering the time o' day? Come back on the morrow. 'Tis his day to hear the needs o' his people. Mayhap ye can see him then."

The unsheathing of a sword rasped through the quiet night. The tip of a blade was suddenly at the man's throat. "I'll see him tonight," Breanne gritted, "or you'll be a head shorter."

Out of the corner of her eye, she noted the other guard surreptitiously move up. "And your friend will never make it in time, if he entertains hope of rescuing you."

The guard swallowed convulsively, his pale blue eyes widening. "Stay away, Wendell. The lass means what she says." He forced a wan little smile. "What can we do to aid ye, m'lady?"

"Tell Lord Haversin the Crown Prince of Anacreon has need of him. Tell him to come to me immediately."

"As ye wish, m'lady." The man frowned, then motioned to his compatriot. "Ye heard her, Wendell. Fetch the Lord Dane."

"And no tricks!" Breanne flung after the retreating guard.

"A-aye," her captive echoed. "No tricks, Wendell."

As they waited for the lord of the castle's arrival, Breanne stole quick glances at his imposing fortress. It appeared immensely long, its battlemented walls connected by several towers, both square and cylindrical. The stone, varying from gray limestone to yellow and dark red sandstone, bespoke the castle's age and more than one period of construction.

The Haversins must be a very old family, Breanne mused. *And a powerful presence in the land*. Briefly, she wondered what the Lord Dane would be like. She imagined him gray-haired, with kindly eyes, a father figure to Aidan, who had never truly known a real father. Probably widowed, considering Aidan's plans to wed her to him, with several children her age or older.

But, whatever the lord's age and progeny, the only thing that mattered was convincing him of Aidan's need, and the urgency of returning to her husband as fast as possible. If Aidan should die out there, alone and in excrutiating pain, before she could get back to him . . .

The sound of footsteps intruded on her anxious thoughts. Breanne went rigid, her legs clasping tightly about her horse in preparation for the meeting to come. The forms of two men strode from the darkness, one carrying a torch. She recognized the torchbearer as the second guard, Wendell. Beside him walked a tall man, broad of shoulder, with a carriage and vitality suitable to a much younger man than Breanne had earlier imagined would be lord of Castle Haversin.

Confusion flooded her. Was this some trick?

Kathleen Morgan

Had the Lord Dane sent an impostor, or may-hap one of his sons in his stead? The consid-eration angered her. Aidan's life hung in the balance. She had no time for games.

The two men halted several feet away. "And who are you, lady?" the younger man demanded, his deep voice rich and pleasant. "I was told the Crown Prince of Anacreon had need of me. Where is he?"

"I speak only with the Lord Dane Haversin," Breanne snapped, her patience, ground down by the tension of the day, wearing thin. "And I told this Wendell to bring him, not one of his lackeys!"

"L-lackeys!" Wendell sputtered in outrage. "Why you impertinent, ungrateful little wench. I'll have you know—"

The younger man silenced him with a ges-ture of command. "I am the Lord Dane. And I ask again, who are you, lady?"

Breanne's mind raced. Was it possible? Was this man really Dane Haversin? Well, despite her earlier preconceptions, she supposed he *could* be much younger than she'd expected him to be. Breanne leaned forward slightly to study him.

He was as tall as Aidan, and just as heavily muscled. His hair was dark brown and curling, dipping onto a wide, intelligent forehead and down the back of his neck. His eyes were shad-owed, but burned with a fierce, inner intensity. And his face, though not classically handsome, was nonetheless ruggedly attractive, from his straight, dark brows to the arrogant jut of his chin and jaw.

Though his dress was simple—plain, dark breeches and white linen shirt tucked hastily beneath his waistband, completed by a pair of shiny black boots—there was no mistaking the cut or quality. The man, whoever he was, was someone of stature. But how to be certain he was truly who he claimed to be?

Breanne wet her lips. "My name is Breanne, wife of Prince Aidan of Anacreon."

The tall man smiled up at her. "Indeed? I wasn't privy to any wedding plans, and I saw Aidan but two months ago."

"A lot has happened since then." She cocked a brow. "But the circumstances I'll not share with just any man. Prove to me you're who you say you are, that you know Aidan."

His glance shifted to the sword pressed to the guard's throat. "You carry Aidan's sword, the sword of Baldor the Conqueror. I would know it anywhere."

"Many men have had the misfortune of encountering Aidan's sword. That, in itself, doesn't make you his friend."

The man shrugged. "If you'll permit me to draw closer, I'll tell you more."

Breanne's eyes narrowed. "If this is some trick . . ."

"No trick, lady. Just information not pertinent to others' ears."

She withdrew her dagger and, with its tip, motioned him over.

He moved until he stood beside her. Breanne's dagger lowered until it pricked the skin of his neck. "Well, out with it."

"He talks to his horse, Lucifer."

Kathleen Morgan

She controlled a surge of excitement. "Many talk to their horses. What of it?"

"Aidan's horse talks back."

Breanne lowered her dagger from Dane's throat. "Aidan lies in the gravest danger, m'lord. I beg you, bring a litter and men, and follow me back to him."

A strong hand clasped about her wrist. "What happened?"

"We were set upon by outlaws and Aidan was overcome and set afire. Even now, he is in great pain, alone—save for Lucifer—and defenseless."

Breanne leaned down, entreaty gleaming in her sapphire blue eyes, trembling in her husky voice. "Please, m'lord. We must go to him forthwith."

The Lord of Haversin Castle extended a hand. "Come down from there, lady. You look exhausted and in need of a good meal and a brief respite from your journey."

"Nay, m'lord." Breanne firmly shook her head. "I cannot eat or rest until Aidan is safe."

"And what good will you be to him, if you cannot make it back to him?" Dane smiled up in gentle understanding. "Come down. 'Twill take us the good part of an hour to gather the men and equipment. You can at least wash the grime from you and partake of a small meal in the meantime."

She lifted a hand to her face, warmth flooding her cheeks. "Do I look that bad, m'lord? Grime, is it?"

He grinned. "Aye, m'lady, I'm afraid 'tis."

284

With a deep sigh, Breanne swung down off her horse, her legs buckling as her feet touched ground. Strong arms encircled her, pressing her against a hard body for support. Relief that she no longer had to bear the terrible responsibility alone flooded her. Relief, and a warm gratitude that Dane Haversin indeed seemed to be the kind of man Aidan had claimed him to be.

Dane handed the gelding's reins to Wendell. "Walk this horse out until he's cool, then fetch the lady a fresh mount." He turned to the other guard who was still gingerly rubbing his throat where Breanne's sword had not so lately pricked. "Gather me twenty armed knights, two horses to carry back a litter on, and supplies sufficient for a day's travel. Have them ready for departure within the hour."

"M'lord," Breanne hastened to interject. "A physician as well, and salves and potions sufficient to ease Aidan's pain and care for his burns. His chain mail . . ." She paused, blinking back a hot swell of tears. "His chain mail has burnt into his flesh."

Compassion warmed his eyes. "Aye," Dane agreed, his glance never leaving hers as he added that final order. "Call out our physician as well."

Less than an hour later, the rescue party was on the road, riding hard back the way Breanne had come. She took the lead, with Dane Haversin at her side, boldly traversing the terrain in the moonlit night. He glanced over at her from time to time as they galloped along, his expression one of frank curiosity.

"Truly, lady?" his deep voice finally rose on the night air when the party was forced to walk the horses for a time. "You're truly Aidan's wife?"

She nodded.

"Would I be prying if I asked how this came about? No offense to you," he quickly added, "for you are certainly beauteous, and courageous as well. I can understand why any man—Aidan included—would find you attractive. But I know my friend, and his outlook on people and life. And that would have never included a wife."

"He was forced to wed me. 'Twas either death or marriage. 'Twas the ancient law—wed by age thirty or die."

Dane frowned in consideration of this surprising revelation, then nodded. "Ah yes, that old law. Well, Aidan couldn't have picked a better wife if he'd had the choice."

Breanne flushed at the compliment. "My thanks, m'lord."

"Dane. Please, call me Dane. I would hope we, too, could be friends."

"Aye . . . Dane. And you may call me Breanne."

"As you wish, though we are hardly of the same standing—I but a mere lord, you, the crown princess." He shot her another assessing look. "One question more, if you please."

"Ask it." Her gaze returned to the road before them.

"Why were you and Aidan out in such dangerous lands? His choice of life I understand, but to risk a wife to such threats . . ."

"We are on a quest," was her terse reply. "The rest is better explained after Aidan is rescued and recovered."

She could feel his thoughtful gaze on her for a long moment more, then knew he turned aside, focusing his attention on the journey still ahead. And, as the hours dragged on, Breanne's thoughts flew as well, onward, to where Aidan lay, alive and guarded still, she fervently hoped, by Lucifer.

What would she do if he were dead? How would she go on, live without him? In the short span of a few weeks, Aidan had found his way into her heart. Cousin or no, she loved him, and would do anything for him, even to the sacrifice of her life. And that willingness to sacrifice all for Aidan, she knew as well, must carry over to the continuation of their quest, with or without him. Soon, it might be the only thing left she could do for him. . . .

Breanne heard the waterfalls long before they reached the turnoff into the forest. It was dark, the going treacherous with low-lying branches and fallen logs. Finally, she dismounted and continued on foot, leaving Dane and the rest behind.

"Aidan!" Breanne cried, not caring for the personal danger if some outlaws lurked nearby. "Aidan, are you there? Can you hear me?" Her only reply was a loud snort from Lucifer.

Then she was at the cave, kneeling down to grasp at Aidan. He was still warm, thank the Mother, and he breathed, but he lay there, so very still.

Breanne scooted close and lifted his head

and shoulders onto her lap. She stroked his clammy forehead, then bent to kiss him. "Ah, Aidan," she murmured. "I came as fast as I could, truly I did."

He stirred, mumbled something, then sighed. "Bree? Is-is it really you, lass?"

His words, so reminiscent of his response when she'd saved him from the executioner's ax, brought back a bittersweet surge of memories. He'd suffered so much, the scorn and rejection of others, the pain of knowing people wished him dead, the attempts on his life. Yet still Aidan fought on, to the extent that he now risked his life on a quest to save Anacreon, with no real hope that any would care or think better of him for it.

"Aye, m'lord," she whispered. " 'Tis I."

The sounds of men crashing through the forest, and the erratic flicker of torchlight, reached them. Lucifer snorted and pawed the ground.

"They are friends," she called out to him. Then, turning back to Aidan, she blotted the dampness from his face with the edge of her tunic. "Dane comes, my love. You will be safe now."

He smiled weakly. "You found him, did you? I knew you would. . . ." He drifted back into unconsciousness then, a respite from his intense pain that Breanne could only be grateful for.

Dane strode over and knelt at the entrance to the little cave. "How is he, Breanne?"

"Alive, but unconscious."

He reached in and grasped Aidan beneath the arms. "Here, let's get him out of there and into some light so the physician might examine him." With that, Dane lifted Aidan into his arms and carried him from the cave.

A campfire had been relit from the original one Aidan had laid. The physician hurried over as Dane lay his unconscious friend close to the light. He made a cursory examination, then shook his head.

" 'Tis a fearsome burn," the lank-haired man in long, dark blue robes said. "The mail will have to be cut from his flesh, and even then, I doubt 'twill heal."

Breanne leaned over and grasped the physician by the arm. Ice-water-blue eyes swung up to meet hers in surprise.

"Do what must be done, but be quick and gentle."

The physician shot Dane an inquiring glance. His lord nodded. "As you wish, m'lady. 'Twould be wise to bleed him as well. Tonight is a lucky night for it and—"

"Nay!" Breanne cut him short. "You will *not* bleed Aidan. He's weak enough as 'tis. Just treat his burns—and nothing more!"

"But 'tis accepted practice," the man protested. "If you don't allow me to bleed this patient, I cannot speak for his recovery."

"Nay, you cannot, but I can," Breanne stated firmly. " 'Twill be on my head, not yours. But you will not bleed him. Not now, nor ever. Is that understood?"

"Aye, m'lady," the physician muttered. He opened up the satchel he carried, spread out a snowy white cloth, and proceeded to lay out a variety of evil-looking instruments. Next, he extracted a copper pot, several packets of herbs, vials, and a generous supply of clean bandages.

"Here," he said, handing the copper pot to one of the soldiers. "Fetch me water. We must treat these wounds, excise the ruined flesh, and apply healing salves and bandages before we begin the journey. To tarry a moment longer will only hasten the putrefaction, if," he added under his breath, "it hasn't already set in."

Breanne remained at Aidan's side the entire time, not only to assure the physician didn't try some outlandish treatment but to assist as well. By the time the man was finished, Aidan's abdomen was dotted with a myriad of small, gaping wounds where the chain mail had to be forcibly cut from his charred flesh. He'd be horribly scarred for the rest of his life, Breanne thought in sickening realization. And all because some outlaws wanted—

She paused, not certain why the outlaws had attacked them. Had it been for whatever riches they imagined they possessed, or were they sent by the same person who'd summoned the undead creatures to attack them several days ago? It didn't matter. Aidan was now terribly injured because of it.

At last the wounds were cleansed, a healing ointment and clean bandages applied. At last Aidan was lifted, still unconscious, to the litter slung between the two packhorses. As Breanne tucked the blanket snugly around him, Dane walked over.

"Come, lady. There's naught more that can be done until we reach Castle Haversin. For his sake, I hope Aidan sleeps until then."

"As do I," she whispered achingly. Then, Breanne turned and mounted her horse. Silently, somberly, the party set out for Castle Haversin.

Blessedly, Aidan remained unconscious until dawn, when they crested the last hill that separated them from the first view of the castle. At his first moan, Breanne dismounted and hurried over to walk at his side.

"Aidan, 'tis Breanne," she murmured. "How do you feel?"

Pain twisted his features. A hectic flush stained his cheeks. "I've felt better. W-where are we?"

"Nearly at Castle Haversin."

Dane rode over. "How goes it, old friend?"

Aidan managed a weak smile. "I've survived the night. I'd say there's hope." He shot Breanne a piercing glance, then motioned Dane close.

"Aye?" Dane asked, dismounting as well to walk alongside the litter. "What is it, Aidan?"

"Breanne." The name was exhaled on a pain-racked breath. "If-if something happens to me, promise you'll take care of her. Though we are wed, the marriage was never consummated. 'T-tis invalid at any rate." Aidan's hand moved, his fingers entwining in Dane's tunic to pull him even closer. "Marry her. Too long have you been without a wife. You'll never find one finer than Breanne."

Dane frowned. "I thank you for such a wondrous offer, but what of her? Mayhap she'd prefer to choose—"

"Nay!" Aidan gasped. "She'd choose poorly. She'd choose to go back home, where she'd be in the gravest danger. Someone tried to kill her there, and would try again, even as my widow. She must not go home!" His grip tightened in Dane's tunic. "Promise me, Dane! 'Tis the only comfort I'll have, if I should die. . . ."

The other man shot Breanne a questioning glance. She clamped her lips shut and fiercely shook her head. He turned back to Aidan. "I'll do what I can, my friend. I promise you that."

With a deep sigh, Aidan released him. "Good. More than anything I've ever wanted, I want to know Breanne is safe and happy. She deserves it, after what she's sacrificed for me."

"Aye," Dane agreed. "And soon you'll be the one to make her happy once again. I swear it."

If we can stop the fever and keep his wounds from festering, Breanne thought, blinking back a hot rush of tears as she watched the two men. Aidan had good reason to worry about the future, even if he had no right to demand such things of Dane. But that could be dealt with later, whether he lived or died.

He looked so awful, his skin waxy pale beneath his feverish flush, his brow clammy, his breathing ragged. 'Twas partly the pain she knew he must be enduring, but the worst was the result of his wounds. Breanne began to doubt anything short of a miracle—or magic— could save Aidan.

Magic.

A wild hope shot through her. Mayhap Olenus possessed some healing skills along with all the rest of his wondrous abilities. Breanne knew she risked him by doing so, but if there were some way to bring the monk here . . . She moved closer to Dane and motioned him over, away from Aidan.

"Aye, lady?"

"The Abbey. How far does it lie from here?"

"About a day's ride."

Hope flared within Breanne's breast. "There's an old monk at the Abbey with healing abilities we may need. His name is Olenus. Can you send a man for him?"

Dane frowned in puzzlement. "If you wish, but there's no healer more skilled than my physician."

"I'd like Olenus, nonetheless," she reiterated. "Please, Dane."

He grinned. "Well, when you couch your entreaty in such a sweet way . . ." He motioned over one of his soldiers. "Ride to the Abbey forthwith, spare no time in getting there, and bringing the monk Olenus back. Tell him the Lady Breanne has need of him."

"*Desperate* need of him," Breanne added.

The man nodded and, wheeling his horse around, rode off down the road. She turned back to Aidan, who had once again dozed off in a fever-driven sleep. With a sigh, Breanne retrieved her horse from the soldier who led it and remounted.

They carried Aidan into a large room, just down the hall from Dane's chambers. The bed was huge, complete with blue velvet hangings, pillows, and a fluffy comforter. Across the room, a fire blazed in the hearth to cut the chill of the higher altitude of the Haversin lands. With Dane's and the physician's assistance, Breanne quickly stripped Aidan of his boots and what remained of his clothing, then tucked him into bed.

The physician then proceeded to prepare a decoction of willow bark boiled in water. He poured the liquid into a covered jar and carried it over to a small table that sat beside the bed. "When it cools, we can give him a mouthful every three or four hours as needed. 'Twill promote sweating in chills and fevers."

He paused to eye Breanne. "You look on the verge of collapse." He turned to Dane. "Find the lass a bed and send her there."

"Nay," Breanne protested. "I won't leave Aidan's side."

"But you need to rest, lady," Dane said.

"I won't leave Aidan!"

He studied her for a moment, then sighed. "As you wish. We'll set up a pallet beside Aidan's bed. Then will you sleep?"

"He needs watching, his face and body bathed to cool the fever—"

"The physician can do that and, when he tires, there are servants. All will be instructed to wake you if Aidan asks for you, or if his condition worsens." Dane cocked a dark brow. "Is that acceptable?"

"Aye," Breanne admitted reluctantly.

"Good. I'll make arrangements for your bed, clean clothes, a bath, and a hot meal. By the time all is done, I'm certain you'll be ready for sleep."

She smiled. "Aye, I suppose I will."

Dane hesitated a moment longer. "About today . . . Aidan's request."

Breanne's gaze met his. " 'Tisn't proper to speak of it. Aidan still lives, and he is my husband."

"Aye," he admitted. "I'd not wish it to come between us, that's all. I want you to feel safe, comfortable with me."

"I thank you for that." She turned back to Aidan, wet a cloth in a bowl of water, and wiped his brow and face.

Dane lingered a moment longer, gazing at the tender scene of Breanne leaning over his friend, the firelight bathing her in a soft, golden glow. As the memory of Aidan's plea, asking him to care for, even wed Breanne, returned once more, something twisted within Dane. Something painful, filled with a heart-deep longing. Then, with an effort, he pushed aside the forbidden yearnings and left the room.

Aidan's moans woke her late that night. Breanne rose from the pallet and hurried to his side. He tossed and turned, his face contorted in pain, his body bathed in sweat. She glanced over at the servant who attended him.

"How long since he had the willow bark decoction?"

"Only an hour ago, m'lady."

Breanne frowned. The medicine wasn't working to keep Aidan's fever down. She motioned to the large bowl of water. "Bring me another, full of the coolest water you can find. I must bathe him to bring down his fever."

The maidservant nodded and hurried from the room. Breanne grabbed a light cloth, stripped back Aidan's covers and, for her sense of modesty more than his, quickly covered him across the groin. Wetting several cloths in the basin of water, she lightly wrung them out, then spread them across his chest, arms, and legs. The final cloth she used to sponge his brow.

He didn't seem to notice, his movements fitful, restless. From time to time, Aidan would mumble something unintelligible, then lapse back into silence. He was ill, mayhap even dying, and there was naught more they could do. If Olenus didn't come, and if he hadn't some way to rid Aidan of his fever, 'twould soon be over.

That somber consideration renewed Breanne's determination. Aidan couldn't die; she wouldn't let him! She just wouldn't!

A gust of wind whirled into the room, ruffling the heavy bed hangings, causing the flames in the hearth to flicker erratically. Then the wind was gone. Olenus appeared, garbed as always in his long gray robes. He strode over to Breanne.

"You risked much in sending for me," he chided gently. "I had planned on meeting with you soon, but not now. Do you not think Morloch watches, now that you draw close to him?"

"And is not Aidan's life worth the risk?" Breanne flung back. "You, too, bear responsibility for this," she cried, indicating the man lying delirious in the bed. "Why must the gravest risk be just Aidan's?"

A warm light flared in the monk's eyes. Olenus

smiled. "You care for him deeply, don't you, child? 'Tis as it should be. The bond deepens, and 'twill strengthen you both for what lies ahead."

"I care not for your prophecy, or how we shall yet serve your needs in the future!" Breanne hovered on the edge of bursting into tears. "J-just help him, Olenus. Please!"

"And aren't your powers sufficient to the task, child? Isn't your love yet strong enough?"

Confusion darkened her features. "What are you talking about? I have no healing powers!"

The monk took her hand, pried the damp cloth from it, then guided it to Aidan's bandaged abdomen. Her fingers touched him, splayed, and settled. She felt his breathing, a ragged, fever-quickened pace that was slowly draining what little of his strength remained. She felt his heat, searing her even through the bandages. She felt his life, his essence, weak and faltering.

With a small gasp, Breanne jerked her hand away. Startled eyes turned to Olenus.

"Aye, child. You can sense many things, can't you? And that same sensitivity can be turned back to him, to give him strength, to heal. If you've the courage."

"Courage?" Breanne whispered.

"Aye, the courage to face your own fears, your doubts, your reluctance to let yourself love him wholeheartedly and without reserve. Can you cast such burdens aside? Free your powers to soar to their fullest potential?"

"I-I'll do anything for Aidan. Anything."

"Then give him your heart, child, and the

rest will follow." He guided her hand back to Aidan's abdomen. "Do it, child. Now."

Indecision flooded her. Then, with a resolute squaring of her slender shoulders, Breanne glanced down at Aidan. He lay there, naked save for the cloth across his middle, his powerful body struck down in its prime by a cruel turn of fate. He lay there, deathly ill, the once proud and invincible warrior now helpless to do anything to save himself.

Memories flooded her, of his arms about her, pulling her close to his tautly muscled body. Of his mouth, hot and savagely sweet, upon hers. Of his passion, his gentleness, his courage. Of that day he stood in the castle keep, his fierce pride his only shield against a crowd of jeering women who called for his death.

He'd had only her then, to help him, to save him. He had only her now.

Something welled within Breanne, a power that heretofore had been hidden, buried beneath the day-to-day cares, the limitations of the only life she'd ever known. It flared, grew to a white-hot heat, stoked by the fires of her love. It burgeoned, coursing through her body until it reached her fingertips, to flow into Aidan.

On and on it went, feeding him, sustaining him—healing him. She could feel it when the fever began to subside. Feel it when the mutilated flesh began to join and mend. She could see his skin become whole, the redness subside, the scar tissue absorb. And see, as well, the hectic flush leave his cheeks, his color return to normal.

He shuddered beneath her hand. His uncovered lid lifted. A single, amber eye stared up at her.

"Breanne?"

"Aye, Aidan. 'Tis I."

"You did this, didn't you?" He shoved to one elbow. "My healing."

She nodded. "Olenus taught me how."

His glance swung to that of the monk. "Then, for once, you've taught her something of value. Your magic has finally served some good."

" 'Twas the strength of her love that healed you," the old man said. " 'Twas naught I did."

"Love?" Aidan's gaze slammed into Breanne's. "What is he talking about, lass?"

She flushed crimson. " 'Twasn't meant for you to know, Aidan. I'd intended on keeping my feelings for you a secret. 'Twas for the best, considering our close kinship."

"A kinship that has never been," Olenus stated flatly. "You and Aidan have never been cousins."

In the aftermath of his startling revelation, two pairs of eyes swung to the monk.

"I-I don't understand. What of Kyna's tale?" Breanne demanded, apprehension threading her voice. "Was she wrong in claiming I'm the daughter of the Lord of Laena?"

"Nay. Kyna spoke true."

"Then how can you say Aidan and I aren't cousins?" Confusion, and a rising anger, churned her emotions into a roiling tumult. "If his father is the prince consort, and mine the Lord of Laena—"

"Aidan's father has never been the prince

299

consort." Olenus's gaze met that of the younger man. " 'Tis a difficult thing to tell you, now, so soon recovered from your illness."

"Indeed?" Aidan drawled. "And why now? Why not when we last met?"

"When we last met the bond between you wasn't strong enough to bear this." Olenus sighed. "I only hope 'tis now. There's little time left, at any rate. And 'tis better, I think, that you hear it from me, than learn the truth from *him*."

"Go on, then," Aidan prodded, his voice dark and silky, his single eye gleaming ominously. "You were about to tell me who my true father was."

"And have you never suspected?"

Anger flared, tautening Aidan's jaw to granite hardness. "What? That I truly *am* the Demon's spawn? Is that what you mean to tell me? If so, 'tis nothing new."

The monk shook his head. "Nay, you're sprung from the seed of man, as are we all."

"Then who, old man?" Aidan snarled. "Who is my father?"

Olenus paused but a moment more, then spoke the fateful words. "The necromancer, Morloch. *He* is your father."

Chapter Fifteen

A stunned silence momentarily settled over the room. Aidan's glance met Breanne's and the horror he saw there filled him with anger. By the Holy Ones, now, on top of everything else, must she bear this as well?

He forced a mocking laugh. "Morloch? My father? Surely you jest! The man never loved a woman. . . ." His voice faded. His hands fisted at his sides.

A deep compassion flared in the monk's eyes. "Aye, no woman, save the queen, your mother."

"Despite that, there's no reason to believe Morloch ever lay with her," Breanne protested, even as a wild hope spiraled through her. "You have no proof. 'Tis cruel to taunt Aidan so!"

"Cruel it may be," Olenus admitted, "but truth nonetheless. Search your heart, Aidan. From whence do think your own powers arise? Why do you imagine the curse lies on Anacreon? Why do you think the queen wastes away? Why is Marus helpless to save her, or himself, for that matter? And Dragan. Why is he changed to such an evil, arrogant man?"

"Why don't you tell me?" Aidan snarled. "You seem to be the man with all the answers, answers you choose to keep close to yourself!"

" 'Twas necessary, all these years," Olenus said. He moved to stand closer to the bed. "The danger from Morloch was great, and I was the only one with the knowledge of what he had done—and how to stop him. You and Breanne were young. I had to wait until you came into your maturity. That's why 'twas necessary to let you roam all those years, not bringing you back until your thirtieth birthing day. I had to wait until Breanne came of age. You couldn't wed her until she was eighteen, nor she choose you, until then."

"That might explain us," Aidan admitted, "but it doesn't explain the state of the kingdom, nor my family, nor even why I should believe Morloch is my father."

"Morloch decided, when he couldn't have his beloved Eislin, no one else would, either. After he lay with her and fathered you, he put a curse on Marus and Eislin, hoping to prevent further children. I was able to dispel his magic for a time, long enough for the queen and her consort to conceive their first and only child—Dragan. But my powers weren't strong enough to hold the necromancer off for long.

"When Morloch discovered Eislin carried Marus's child, he flew into a rage. He renewed the curse, strengthening it so that 'twould slowly weaken them until they could not only not breed another child, but gradually lost the ability to rule the kingdom."

" 'Tisn't fair," Breanne murmured. She clasped her arms about herself as if to hold the tragedy at bay. "Because Morloch would never know happiness, he refused to allow others to know it, either. A poor token of his love, to my estimation."

"He let rejection and bitterness eat him alive, until nothing remained of his soul." Olenus turned the full force of his gaze upon Aidan. "He wants the same fate for you, my son, wants you as empty as he. Then, if he can turn you to him, regain control of the soulstone, and join powers, he may at last be able to completely subjugate Anacreon. After, of course, he destroys the royal family."

Aidan straightened in bed, anger once more clouding his brow. "And you think me that weak that I can be so easily led?"

Olenus shrugged. "Before Breanne, what else kept you from turning your back on mankind? Most rejected you, reviled you, and wished you dead. Who could blame you if you turned to darker things?"

"My conscience is all the blame I'd need," Aidan snapped. "No man will coerce me into doing what I don't want."

The monk smiled. "No *man* might, but we aren't dealing with a man anymore. Morloch, though still living, has joined the legions of the undead. His powers are no longer those of any man."

"Yet you insist we go on, confront him at his seat of power."

"'Tis your destiny, my son. You cannot be free until you do."

Aidan shook his head. "Nay, 'tis no destiny. 'Tis suicide! And I will not risk Breanne in the attempt."

"Do you think there has ever been a choice for you?" Olenus sadly shook his head. "Since the moment he first laid that birthing curse on you, Morloch has meant to have you. And have you he will. 'Tis better not to fight it, but to go forth bravely and meet him. Meet him with Breanne at your side to keep you joined to humanity, and to a reality that will soon seem but a dream in the hands of the necromancer."

Breanne moved close and took one of Aidan's hands. She gave it a squeeze. "Aye, 'tis meant for us to be together, Aidan, no matter the danger. And now there is naught left to keep us apart. Can't you finally see that? Accept it as truth?"

He turned to study her, the expression in his single eye sharpening to glittering awareness. "Too much has happened, too much has been said this night to know what to accept, and what not. And I'll not be rushed into any decision by you, or some old man. Not tonight or ever!"

She pulled her hand free of his clasp, stung by his words and the withdrawal in his suddenly icy demeanor. She'd thought he'd be happy, especially after what had transpired at the inn, to learn they weren't cousins. But he wasn't.

"So be it, Aidan." Breanne forced the words past tight lips. "Take all the time you need. 'Twill change naught." Breanne turned to Olenus. "You've come a long way. Do you desire some refreshment, or a bed for the night?"

"Nay, child." He smiled down at her. "I've done all I can here, revealed the last of my secrets. The rest is up to you." Olenus stepped forward, took Breanne in his arms, and kissed her gently. "If you need me, I will come, but Caerlin is now the true power in the quest against Morloch. And never forget your own abilities, either. They are a potent force indeed, when used with Aidan's."

"Aye, Olenus." Breanne's smile was tremulous and uncertain. "I only hope 'twill be so."

" 'Twill be, child, as long as you don't lose hope—in yourself or Aidan."

He moved away. Then, with a swirl of long gray robes, he stirred the wind to blow. One moment Olenus was there, and the next, he was gone.

For a long moment, Breanne stared at the spot where the monk had stood; then she turned back to Aidan. He lay there, his mouth grim, his jaw set in implacable resolve.

"Is there anything you wish?" she asked, refusing to engage in further argument with Aidan that night. "Something cool to drink, or a bit of broth? Though the fever is gone and your wounds healed, 'twill take, I think, several days more of rest to regain your full strength."

"I haven't the time for such luxuries."

She smothered a smile. He was so much the grumbling bear, as were most men when they began to recover. 'Twas a good sign, but a challenge as well. "You owe me a boon for healing you, m'lord."

He arched a dark brow. "Do I now? And what would that be?"

"That you obey me in your recovery. That you not leave your bed or push yourself too fast, without my leave."

Aidan scowled. "You ask much. I'll take care not to accept your favors so lightly in the future."

Triumph filled her. She had won at least this battle. "And I, m'lord, will take care to ask your permission from now on—when and if you ever regain consciousness."

His single eye regarded her dispassionately. "You're a devious little wench. I think I may have just met my match in you."

A smile glimmered at the corners of Breanne's mouth. He wasn't as cold to her as he let on. There was indeed still hope. "I pray so, m'lord," she pertly replied. "I aim to save you whether you wish it or not. 'Tis a wife's sacred duty, is it not?"

The next three days were torment for everyone. As Aidan began to recover, the strange call to the Improbus Mountains rose again, clawing at him with ever sharpening intensity. Burdened by the vow he'd made to obey

Breanne in his recovery, there was nothing he could do but try to make her existence just as miserable as he considered his to be.

Between calling incessantly for various and sundry tidbits to eat, or someone to rub his shoulders or smooth his bedclothes, Aidan attempted to make his enforced bed rest a greater burden to all concerned than his being up and around would have ever been. Even being allowed to advance to several hours in a chair by his second day, as well as a short walk in the halls by the third, failed to placate him.

He had erred, however, in taking the full measure of Breanne's determination. She bore his incessant requests and grumbling complaints with a calm equanimity, not wishing to involve Dane or the servants in their personal battle of wills. Dane, however, who visited his friend as often as his castle duties allowed, saw enough finally to stir his ire.

"She's your wife, man, not your servant," he blurted on the evening of the fourth day, after he'd sent Breanne off to fetch Aidan's supper meal. Dane lowered himself into a chair beside Aidan's at the hearth, determined to set his friend straight—once and for all. "After what you've put her through so recently, she deserves your deepest gratitude and respect, not the added burden of your foul mood and unreasonable requests."

"Did you know that we're not cousins after all?" Aidan growled instead. "That we truly can lie together as man and wife?"

"A most pleasant consideration," Dane dryly agreed, momentarily nonplussed at the sudden turn to the conversation. "Most men, with a wife as beauteous as Breanne, would be overjoyed at the thought of taking her to bed."

Aidan shot his friend an assessing glance. "Do you think so? Then does my offer of her as wife gain added value in your mind?"

"Your offer?" Dane's brows lifted in amazement. "Are you daft, man? She is yours. Why would you want to give her away?"

"For her safety, her welfare." A dark, haunted expression settled over Aidan's features. He looked away. "I can't take her with me. 'Tis too dangerous."

"For her or for you?"

Aidan jerked his head around. A barely contained rage smoldered in his single eye. "Stay out of what doesn't concern you!"

Dane settled back in his chair and laughed. "You try to give your wife to me, and then say this doesn't concern me? 'Tis amazing what love can do to a man's sanity!"

"Love isn't the issue here!"

" 'Tisn't? Then mayhap 'tis the *fear* of love, of letting yourself care enough to risk the potential hurt and rejection inherent in the act?"

"It doesn't matter." Aidan sighed and ran a hand raggedly through his unbound hair. "There's no place for her in my life. Though I wed Breanne, naught has changed—and naught will."

"If you defeat the necromancer," Dane offered softly, "end the curse on your family and land, a lot might change."

"I'd still be his son!"

"And the queen's as well. Right of succession is passed down through the ruler, not the consort. You'd still be crown prince."

"And I'd still possess the Evil Eye, and all my other fearsome powers. Do you think the people would ever accept a ruler such as I?"

Dane shrugged. "If they knew those powers were meant for good—"

"*I* don't even know that, Dane!" Anguish twisted Aidan's features. "I can't even trust myself to control them. If you only knew how close I came to going mad with the pleasure of wreaking death and destruction, when I was forced to use my eye to defeat the creatures who attacked us in the forest . . ."

His head lowered. "I'm afraid, Dane. I have such evil lurking within me. I don't want Breanne to be there if I ever lose control of it. I don't want her hurt by it."

He looked up, torment burning in his unpatched eye. "I fear, as well, what the confrontation with Morloch will unleash in me. How else can it be, if I'm to have any hope of defeating him? 'Twill be my powers against his, son against father!

"By the Holy Ones!" Aidan groaned, throwing himself back in his chair. "My father! What if something even worse happens when I meet him? What if I choose to join him? What would then become of Breanne?"

"I'll go with you, bring my men."

"And what good would that do against Morloch's magic?" Aidan shook his head. "If I truly am his son, I at least have a chance of getting into his fortress, getting close to him—something even an army couldn't hope to achieve. Nay, Dane, though I'm deeply grateful for your offer, you serve me better by taking care of Breanne. What must be done against Morloch must be done alone."

He leaned forward, gripping the chair arms for support. "Do you see now why I can't take her with me? Why I want to give her to you, sever our bonds before 'tis too late? Why, even if I survive and return, I'll most likely not be the same?"

" 'Tis already too late," came the gentle, unexpected rejoinder. Two pairs of eyes swung to the doorway. Breanne stood there, a covered tray in her hands.

" 'Twas too late long ago, Aidan," she said, walking across the room and setting the tray on the table next to his chair. " 'Twas too late that day you rescued me from the outlaws, when our fates first became entwined. And now I need you just as much as you need me."

"I don't need you, Breanne," he snarled. "I don't need anyone!"

"And I don't believe you, especially after the way you responded to me at the inn in Windermere."

Dane rose to his feet. "I think this conversation is fast becoming too personal for the likes of me. I'll take my leave of you. We can talk further later."

Aidan glared up at him. "So, leave me, will you, to fight her alone?"

His friend grinned down at him. " 'Twill weigh the odds better, I think. In her favor."

"Will it?" Aidan shouted after him as Dane made his hasty retreat to the door. "Well, I can withstand the both of you! My mind won't be swayed in this!"

Dane's only reply was a quiet shutting of the door.

A giggle wrenched Aidan's attention back to Breanne. "What's so funny?" He glowered up at her.

"Naught, m'lord, save that your behavior reminds me of a trapped bull, bellowing his distress."

"I'm not trapped! And I'm not bellowing!"

"Mayhap not." She shrugged and moved to uncover the tray. "Here's a beef stew, thick with potatoes, onions, and carrots, and a plate of fresh baked bread. And, for dessert, a currant pie." Breanne glanced up, her gaze innocently inquiring. "Do any of those tempt your palate?"

"Nay," Aidan muttered. "We need to talk. About my departure on the morrow, about what happened between us in Windermere." He gestured to the chair Dane had so recently vacated. "Sit. Please."

Breanne took the seat, carefully smoothing down the folds in the emerald green silk gown Dane had so generously given her. Though he hadn't admitted it, she knew the dress had belonged to his late wife. It fit her as if she had been the other woman's twin in height and weight.

The realization sent a twinge of compassion for Dane shooting through her. She glanced up at Aidan. "You spoke of departing on the morrow. 'Tis too soon."

His mouth twisted in exasperation. "Four days, Breanne. I've done your bidding for four days now. I can stay here no longer!"

When she made a move to protest, he held up a silencing hand. "Boon or no, I will leave on the morrow."

Swiftly Breanne considered her options and decided she had few. "Have it your way. I'll make preparations for our journey. Food must be prepared, our horses readied—"

"Lass," Aidan intruded gently, "I meant what I said. You're not going with me."

She smiled. "Ah, but that's where you're wrong. Dane won't keep me here against my will."

"Are you so certain of that? I've explained, quite graphically, what might happen when I confront Morloch. I think he finally understands the grave danger to you."

"And what about the grave danger to you?" she demanded, her ire rising. "Doesn't he care about that?"

"He cares, but knows, as well, that nothing can be done for me."

"Then you are both blind to the truth!" Breanne slipped from her chair and moved to kneel before him. She took both his hands in hers. "Ah, Aidan, we are meant to face this together, have always been! If you accept that you are Morloch's son, and that Caerlin's in your sword, then why can't you accept the rest?"

He couldn't quite meet her gaze. "I-I didn't say I accepted that I'm Morloch's son. The very consideration sickens me!"

"Well, it doesn't sicken me!" Breanne stoutly insisted. "I don't care whose son you are. You could be a peasant by birth and I'd still love you!"

Aidan went very still. "What? What did you say, Breanne?"

She flushed then, embarrassed by her temerity. "You owe me naught, Aidan, especially not protestations of similar emotions you may not share. What I feel for you is something I must deal with myself."

He freed his hands from hers and, leaning down, grasped Breanne by the arms. *"What did you say?"*

At his tortured look of anguish and disbelief, Breanne's breath caught in her throat. Holy Mother, why had her simple statement of love upset him so? "I-I love you," she forced herself to reply.

His fingers dug into her flesh. She bit back a cry of pain. "Please, Aidan. You're hurting me!"

He released her with a jerk.

"Aidan, what's wrong?" Breanne stared up at him, her heart hammering beneath her breast. "Did I offend—?"

"Nay." He gave a fierce shake of his head. "You didn't offend me. I just never thought . . ." He inhaled a shuddering breath. "It doesn't matter. I can't let it."

At last, Breanne knew what he was talking about. Joy surged through her. Somehow, she had touched him with her admission.

She reached up to stroke the side of his face. "Aye, but you *can* let it matter. I am your wife, I love you, and I want to be yours in every way. *In every way.*" A hesitant smile trembled on her lips. "You said you desired me, that day at the pool, and you confirmed that passion most graphically at the inn. Do you want me still, Aidan?"

He captured the hand that had paused to delicately encircle his lips. "Don't." The word was uttered on a hoarse exhalation of sound.

"And why not?" Breanne demanded, emboldened by the excitement she heard in his voice, saw tightening his body.

She had naught to lose in seducing him this night; indeed, 'twould likely be her last chance if he was determined to set out on the morrow. As brazen as it might be, as untutored as she truly was in the feminine arts, there was no other choice. No other choice, if she meant to fight for him in every possible way.

"Why not, Aidan?" She leaned toward him to entwine her arms about his neck. "We are husband and wife. 'Tis past time we consummate our vows in the joining of our bodies."

"You thought our marriage invalid," he rasped. "That made it so."

"Mayhap on one plane," Breanne murmured huskily. "But, on another, though I thought you cousin, I still wished it could be otherwise. And now, 'tis."

"You can't know that for certain. Olenus could be wrong, or lying to manipulate us further."

She smiled, a slow, unconsciously provocative movement of her lips. "Mayhap, but you never believed him in this to begin with, and I no longer do, either." Breanne scooted closer, until she pressed between his splayed thighs and against his groin.

Aidan choked back a tormented groan. The ripe curves of her breasts, where silken cloth met skin, were a tantalizing undulation of tender flesh and shadowed valley. Her scent wafted to him, sweetly fragrant, reminiscent of a field of springtide flowers. And the feel of her soft body, thrust so intimately against his, was but tinder to his long-banked fire.

Almost of its own accord, his hand drifted over her back in a slow, restless caress, moving her even closer to his length. With a small sound of pleasure, Breanne came to him. His powerful thighs straddled her, capturing her in a prison of muscle and sinew. He felt his manhood swell, straining against the taut fabric of his breeches. And, with her small start of recognition, he knew Breanne felt it as well.

" 'Tisn't right, what we do here, lass," Aidan whispered. " 'Twon't solve anything, and 'twill only ruin you for another man."

"And how will lying with my legally wedded husband ruin me?" She pulled his head down to hers. "As if I'd care, at any rate. 'Tis you I want."

"But Dane," Aidan protested halfheartedly, as his resolve shredded before her seductive onslaught. "He'd take you as wife. I know he would, and be a far better husband than I could ever be."

"Dane is a wonderful man," Breanne murmured, then kissed Aidan lightly on the lips, "but he's not the man for me. You are, Aidan. You, and no other."

"You don't know the mistake y-you're making," he warned, shuddering as her mouth fluttered down on his, then retreated, to once more hover a hairbreadth away. "But if you don't get back from me—and quickly—I soon won't care."

"I already don't care," she purred and once again kissed him.

This time Aidan responded, parting her lips in a deep, languorous kiss. The kiss and its intensity grew with each passing moment, until a savage excitement swelled between them. He pulled her up to him, crushing her body to his hardened, straining length, his excitement spiraling like some rising flame.

He could barely function. The nearness, the sweet solace of Breanne's body interfered with coherent thought, with his breathing, with all sense of reality save what he experienced within the haven of her arms. But, ah! how he needed it, needed her! Never had he known such shattering tenderness, such exquisite pleasure, his heart as deeply touched as his body.

To finally be accepted, cherished—loved! To be taken as the living, breathing, vulnerable man he truly was, rather than the monster the tales painted him to be, struck Aidan with such intensity that it brought tears to his eyes.

At the realization he quickly blinked them back, unnerved that Breanne could affect him so strongly. He had never cried, not since that day he'd wept over Rangor's mutilated body. Not once in all those years of his exile, not in the dark nights of utter loneliness and despair, nor with the most life-threatening, agonizing injuries, or when he'd been repeatedly and viciously reviled.

She was the answer to his prayers, even when he refused to admit he'd faith left to pray. Yet, as much as he needed Breanne, his conscience balked at the very real potential of dragging her down with him. If only he could be certain of a life with her—that, together, they could over-come Morloch. But there had never been any guarantees—and never would. That realization, more than anything else, frightened Aidan.

With a desperate, frantic sound, he pulled back from her. "I'm afraid," he groaned. "Not for me, but for you, lass. I want you at my side, but if anything should happen to you because of it . . ."

Breanne went still, all breath suspended. "We are all doomed, one way or another, if Morloch isn't stopped. And I'd rather face the danger with you in the attempt to defeat him, than wait in safety for the death that will come if you go against him alone—and fail. I'd rather die fighting at your side, than remain passively behind and wonder what happened."

Her hands lifted, her fingers threading through his mass of wavy, unruly hair before trailing down to the patch that shielded his eye. " 'Tis past time for you to discard this. 'Tis but another symbol of your self-doubts, the shield you raise before your heart."

"Nay, lass." Aidan frowned. "You don't know what you ask. You can't begin to fathom all that lurks within me."

"A man of evil, with a black, irredeemable soul?"

Aidan's mouth quirked at her earnest appraisal. "Well, when you say it that way, I'm not so certain I'm quite *that* bad."

He stood, pulling her up with him, then exhaled a deep, acquiescing breath. "If you wish it, you may remove my eye patch."

"For once and for all?" Breanne asked, not daring to hope it was so.

"I suppose I must face the consequences of my Evil Eye as I must our destiny as man and wife."

As Breanne reached on tiptoe to pull off his eye patch, she smiled in joyous elation. Quickly tossing the patch aside, she smoothed his hair in a tender, possessive motion. "You look quite the same, you know," she teased, cocking her head to study him, "if not even more handsome."

His mouth quirked in amusement. "Indeed? I've never considered myself so, but if 'twill stir your desire for me and hasten you into bed . . ."

"Oh, 'twill do that and more, m'lord." Breanne giggled. "And, hopefully, very soon."

With that, Aidan swung her up into his arms in a shimmer of green silk and rustle of petticoats. "Have a care, lass. My control wears thin even now."

"And what of it, m'lord?"

His expression turned suddenly somber, serious. "I wouldn't want to hurt or frighten you with the intensity of my response. I've had to contain my natural desires for so long, I fear. . . ." He sighed. "Contrary to what you may have assumed back there in the 'Bed and

Brisket Inn,' there were few women, whores or no, who took me into their beds."

"Then we've a vast amount of time to make up," Breanne replied with an impish grin. "You'd better hurry. Though my experience is nonexistent, I, too, have natural desires that cry out for fulfillment."

He shook his head in wonderment. "You're a most remarkable woman—in every way."

"Aye, m'lord." She glanced pointedly at the bed.

Aidan noted the action. He wheeled about and strode to the bed in a few quick strides. Then, lowering Breanne to her feet, he turned her away from him.

Though his trembling fingers quickly divined the workings of the hooks and ties, it seemed to take an inordinate amount of time before the back of Breanne's gown was free. The soft, sweet undulation of flesh over bone, peeking above a thin, lacy chemise, at last lay exposed to him. His breath ragged in anticipation, Aidan turned Breanne around to face him.

He pulled the gown from her to let it fall in a silken puddle at her feet. Grasping the single braid that lay down her back, Aidan removed the fastener and deftly freed her hair, raking his fingers through the silken strands until they lay free in golden waves over Breanne's chest, shoulders, and back. "So beautiful," he murmured, fingering a long, curling lock. "So very beautiful."

Then, gathering her to him, he kissed her, long, deep, and hard. The sinewed length of his leg pressed intimately against her. His chest crushed the soft swell of her breasts.

But, no matter what Aidan did, Breanne responded just as ardently in turn. His blood surged hotly as he imagined her naked, her silken, long-limbed body beneath his, her hips rising to meet his thrusts. It only excited him the more.

His hand moved, capturing a full, jutting breast. Through the linen chemise, his fingers found her nipple, teasing it to pebble hardness between his thumb and forefinger. She gasped with startled pleasure.

At the small, feminine sound, Aidan went wild. He tore the shift open to expose her breast, then, with a quick movement, lowered his mouth to capture her nipple, drawing on it with hard, suckling motions.

Breanne thought she'd go mad from the exquisite sensations that began at her breast and shot clear through to the heart of her womanhood. Her body sprang to vibrant life in his arms. A thick, sensual haze engulfed her. Suddenly, she felt an overwhelming need to feel him, to press her hands, her body against his flesh as he now did hers.

Her hands moved to the loose tunic he wore over his breeches. She tugged at it with impatient fingers.

Aidan chuckled, though the sound was hoarse and unsteady. "Have a care, lass, or you'll tear my clothes."

"Then help me!" she cried. "I want to see and feel you."

He pushed her hands away and pulled the tunic over his head. Breanne inhaled an admiring breath. Her healing had indeed worked miracles. Not a wound marred his flesh, not a hint of redness or blistering remained.

Aidan was magnificent, from the impressively wide shoulders and solid swell of his powerful chest, to the flat, hard belly and tautly narrow hips. He stood there, an impossibly virile, devilishly attractive man. Breanne's heart filled with pride.

He was hers, her husband and soon-to-be mate. At long last she had won his trust and at least some small measure of his affection. 'Twas more than she'd ever dared hope for.

With a quick motion, Breanne slid the chemise from her shoulders and let it fall away, so that she stood naked before him. Her hands moved to the tie of Aidan's breeches. "If you'll allow me, m'lord, I'll take great care not to tear these."

"The breeches be damned!" Aidan snarled, and all but ripped them from him.

Her glance lowered, trailing down his rippling, hair-roughened abdomen to a tangled nest of dark curls and a thick, jutting organ. Her eyes widened at the size of him. She swallowed hard and lifted her gaze.

"Have I frightened you at last?" Aidan asked quietly.

His softly couched query jerked Breanne back to the reality of the situation. She loved Aidan, trusted him implicitly. There was nothing about him that frightened her, even the thick evidence of his arousal. Even that was hers, meant only for her.

321

She shook her head, the action fierce, denying. "Nay, Aidan. There is naught that frightens me about you." She lifted her arms. "Come, take me; hold me close. Only there am I certain of everything."

He pulled her to him. Crisp body hair pressed into her, rough, rasping, but deliciously stimulating all the same. His manhood throbbed against her belly, all stiffness and velvety smooth flesh. Breanne laid her head over Aidan's pounding heart and sighed in contentment.

The need, the hunger, the yearning building between them, however, could not be long contained. With a quick move, Aidan swept aside the comforter and lowered Breanne onto the bed. He knelt over her, nipping and licking her breasts until she moaned and writhed in total abandon. He threaded his fingers through the dense curls guarding her femininity, finding her secret core in her slick, damp folds. With a sure, knowing touch, he began to stroke her there.

Breanne had thought there was no greater excitement than the sight and feel of Aidan's body, of the sweet joy of his mouth upon her lips and breasts. But this newest of sensations . . . !

She felt herself grow wet where he touched her. She grasped at him, suddenly overcome with the need to feel his body pressed back against hers, to feel him inside her. The teasing play of his fingers between her legs suddenly wasn't enough. Not nearly enough.

"A-Aidan!" Breanne gasped out the strangled plea. "I-I need you. I can't bear to be separate from you! Please. Come to me!"

He moved then, kneeing her legs apart, slipping in between them. For an exquisite, agonizing instant, Aidan knelt poised above her, his manhood huge and thick, straining toward her. Then, with a guttural sound that was as primitive as his need, he grasped himself with one hand, slid the other beneath Breanne's hips to lift her, and thrust his shaft into her.

She arched upward with a tiny cry of pain as he penetrated her maidenhead. Aidan froze, his big body going rigid.

"Are you all right, little one? Shall I stop?"

From the swirling mists of her passion, Breanne heard the doubt, the tremor in his voice. Though he'd surrendered so much of his former restraint in joining with her this night, it had also opened his heart once more to rejection. And Breanne knew if she withdrew from him now, the damage might well be irreparable.

"Nay," she murmured, forcing her body back to the bed, willing her pain-tautened limbs to relax. "Please don't stop. 'Tis to be expected, is it not? My maidenhood was yours to take."

Her arms lifted, entwined about his neck. "And now 'tis your turn, my dearest love. What will you give me in return?"

Aidan's mouth lifted in the most heart-stopping of smiles. "All of me, and more, m'lady."

And, with that most ardent of threats, he proceeded to pull her hard up into the iron-thewed strength of his groin and thrust into her again and again as their excitement rose to dizzying, soul-searing heights. Breanne lost all ability to think as the delicious sensations built within her, spiraling to higher and higher realms of pleasure with each plunging movement of Aidan's body. Breaths rasped ragged, bodies sheened with sweat, and still he thrust on.

With a cry, Breanne shot over the edge and tumbled into an abyss of mind-numbing ecstasy. Her body shook with the pleasure of her release, her hands grasping blindly at the man who rocked himself endlessly, rhythmically into her.

Then, with a hoarse gasp and racking shudder of his own big body, Aidan felt his own release. His eyes clenched shut; his features strained with the majesty of his climax; his head arched back. With great, shivering bursts he spewed his seed, moaning her name over and over as he did.

"Breanne . . . Breanne . . . *ah, Breanne!*"

He watched them lying there in the aftermath of their loving, a tangle of arms, legs, and sweat-dampened flesh, the woman possessively clasped to Aidan. Their sleep was innocent as was their nakedness, the sated repose of two young, passionate animals.

As it had once been for him and Eislin, Morloch thought with a bitter pang. But now all he had to show for their brief moment of loving were the memories . . . and his son. A son who was slipping farther and farther away.

But no more, no farther. He needed Aidan, needed his abilities to join with and enhance his. 'Twas the plan from the beginning, and he'd brook no obstacles to its fulfillment—be they Aidan's or the woman's.

Rage transformed his features. Especially not the woman's!

With a vicious, enraged sweep of his hand, the necromancer knocked his enchanted mirror from the table. Swept it away to go crashing to the floor, shattering in hundreds of tiny shards. Then he rose, turned to the powerstone, and summoned his son with every bit of strength within him—calling Aidan with words no child could ignore.

Chapter Sixteen

Aidan woke in the middle of the night, his breathing labored, his body drenched in sweat. For a moment, he didn't know where he was. Then his vision cleared. Relief surged through him. He was in his bedchamber in Castle Haversin, the room still dimly lit by the red-hot embers of a dying fire.

Beside him, someone moved. Aidan froze, grasping over the side of the bed for his sword with a careful, stealthy motion before he remembered. Breanne.

With a soft groan, he turned, scooted close and pulled her pliant, sleeping body into his. He held her tightly, until the solace of her soft, woman's body gradually eased the terrors of his slumber.

The strange dreams had come again, and this time they were more horrible than before. The words, whispered before, were now clear and haunting. They called him to Morloch, pleading with him to hurry, warning it might yet be too late. Morloch—his father—was dying.

Stranger still was the confusing tumult of emotions the dream stirred. Could it be true? Was the necromancer really dying? If so, why should the news fill him with such a queer, gut-knotting pain and a renewed urgency to reach the magical fortress?

Mayhap, in some twisted way, Aidan mused, he wished to meet his real sire just once, even if that meeting ultimately resulted in a fight to the death. Wished to take the measure of a man even more feared and reviled than he and discern, if it were possible, whether he'd inherited his father's evil predilections.

Aidan's head lowered to nestle in the sweet valley between Breanne's neck and shoulder. He inhaled deeply of her woman's scent, musky now in the aftermath of their lovemaking. The unsettling dream notwithstanding, he felt unaccountably happy.

A sudden thought struck him. If Morloch truly were dying, mayhap their quest wouldn't be as difficult as first anticipated. The danger to Breanne, a consideration that constantly haunted him, might not be as acute.

'Twas the only comfort in the remainder of what promised to be a sleepless night. The restless, unnerving need to be on his way, stirred anew by his dreams, would permit little else.

Aidan slipped his high-collared black tunic over his chain mail shirt, added his thick belt, and cinched it closed. After pulling on his tall, black boots over his breeches, he strode to the full-length floor mirror, encased in an ornate brass frame. Critically, he surveyed himself, his gaze finally alighting on his hair. With a frown, Aidan grabbed up a hairbrush from the nearby table and began to stroke his locks back into their usual warrior's topknot.

"Aidan, nay," Breanne murmured in protest and hurried over. Her fingers closed over the hand that held his brush. "Leave it be, I beg you. You always look so fearsome, so unapproachable, when you wear your hair that way."

His mouth twisted wryly. "As I intend it to look. A mercenary with a kind, friendly appearance is soon either a starving mercenary or a dead one."

"But you're not a mercenary anymore and never will be again. When this is over . . ."

"There are no guarantees, lass. You must accept that if you're to remain with me."

Breanne smiled, took the brush away and placed it back on the table. "Oh, I accept it, m'lord. Have no doubt of that. But grant me this small boon. After all, I'm the one, besides Lucifer, who must look at you most of the time. 'Twould ease the strain on my eyes."

Aidan chuckled. " 'Tis that bad, is it? Have it your way, then."

"Thank you, m'lord." She planted a small kiss upon his lips, then stepped away to finish the braiding of her hair.

"A small boon, m'lady," Aidan's deep voice rumbled from behind her.

She smiled and continued to weave her hair, then tie it off. "Aye, m'lord?"

"On the road, during the day, I realize 'tis necessary to hide your hair. But at night, when we are alone together, will you promise to unbraid it and comb it out for me?" He stepped close to stroke the long, thick braid she'd just tossed over her shoulder. " 'Tis such glorious hair. Like spun gold, or the finest silk."

His voice lowered to a rich, sensuous timbre. "Last night, when you lay there beneath me, your hair fanned out about you, 'twas almost as if I lay in a bed of gold, with the most beauteous, desirable woman spread upon it. 'Twas like some dream."

Breanne turned, her sapphire blue eyes aglow. "A dream we'll share again and again, for the rest of our lives."

He impaled her with an amber stare. "Have a care, lady. I may well hold you to that."

Her whole heart was in her answering smile. "I expect you to, m'lord. 'Tis your husbandly duty." She gazed up at him for a fleeting moment more, then grasped him by the arm.

Aidan's brow arched in inquiry.

"Come, m'lord." Breanne began to tug at him. "If we stand here much longer, gazing at each other like this, 'twill be a late start for us this day."

He chuckled and allowed her to lead him over to where his sword hung. She released him then to take down the sheathed weapon and belt it about his trim waist. As Aidan wryly watched, she fastened the buckle closed, then settled the belt over his hips.

"There, m'lord," Breanne said, glancing up at last. "Baldor's sword and the soulstone are now safe, hanging at your side."

"No more safe than they would be with you," he drawled. "You never did tell me much about how you ran off the outlaws, you know."

"Ah, that. There isn't much to tell. 'Tis as I said before. Caerlin's powers aided me in frightening them away."

"So your own powers continue to grow."

She sighed and shook her head. "Not fast enough. I still cannot free the mage from the stone. And we are only three days' ride from Morloch's fortress."

"Time enough. Think how much your abilities have improved the past week."

"Aye, that is true." Breanne paused to eye him closely. "Have you a plan, once we arrive there?"

"At Morloch's fortress?" Aidan shrugged. " 'Tis difficult to make much of a plan, until I see how we're received. If the tale is true that I'm the necromancer's son, it could well be some form of twisted boon."

"How so?"

"We can claim entrance on kinship. Surely Morloch must be as interested in meeting me as I am him."

"Mayhap," Breanne admitted grudgingly, "but I wonder about the depth of his fatherly affection, if he truly was the one who sent those creatures to attack us."

"Aye," Aidan agreed, "but they were trying to capture us, not kill us, if you recall. Morloch may have sent them to bring us to him." He shoved his leather gauntlets into his belt, slung his cloak over his shoulder, and strode over to where their packs lay. He picked them both up, then glanced back at Breanne.

"Well, lady? Are you ready? We must still say our farewells to Dane." His eyes danced with mirth.

"And pray, what's so funny?" Breanne asked suspiciously.

"Oh, naught, save that I'd imagine the Lord of Haversin Castle will be sorely disappointed that I decided to take you along after all. I think he was fast developing an affection for you."

Breanne flushed. "Stop it, Aidan! We are friends, naught more."

"And that's exactly the way I intend to keep it." With a devilish grin, Aidan headed toward the door, opened it, and, with a grand flourish, motioned her through.

Dane eyed Breanne and Aidan as they strode across the outer bailey to where he awaited them at the stables. As they halted before him, he smiled in wry amusement. "So, the lovers have reconciled?"

Aidan shrugged. "'Tis evident, is it not?"

His friend laughed. "With you, naught is evident!" He held out his hand. "'Tis farewell, is it?"

"Aye. Morloch calls." Aidan clasped his arm, then released it.

Dane's expression sobered. "Have a care, Aidan."

"I will."

"There's a bridge in the mountains that spans a great chasm," Dane added. "'Tis the only way to Morloch's fortress and guarded by twin brothers." His mouth quirked in remembrance. "They are dwarves and quite eccentric at times. Especially when it comes to whom they choose to allow over their bridge, and the purchase price for the privilege."

"They'll let me across, one way or another," Aidan growled.

Dane shrugged. "I'd imagine so, if murder is a possible method to achieve that end. I suggest, though, a more friendly approach and a willingness to be creative in bartering with them."

"I go to rid the realm of Morloch," Aidan muttered, "and I have to beg these creatures to allow me across their precious bridge? I think not, Dane."

"Mayhap 'twould be wiser if I spoke with them first," Breanne hastened to offer.

Aidan scowled down at her. "Are you implying I lack the skills—"

"Aye, m'lord," she interjected smilingly. "At times you do indeed, but you are improving rapidly."

He gave a snort of disgust, then turned to where their horses waited. Without another word, Aidan strode over to Lucifer and mounted. He glanced down at Breanne. "Well, are you coming or not, lady? I'm certain the dwarf brothers would sorely regret not meeting you."

Breanne gave a small laugh, then turned back to Dane. "My thanks—for everything. You are a good and true friend."

A warm regard glowed in Dane's eyes. "And you are a good and true wife to Aidan. I'm happy for him and, I must admit, a little jealous."

Her expression sobered. "You'll find another love, Dane. A man as fine as you won't last long. Women know a good catch when they see one."

"Do they now? But I rarely get visitors in my mountain kingdom."

"Then when I return to Anacreon," Breanne countered with an impish grin, "I'll pick out a score of the finest ladies in the realm and send them to you for a visit."

He arched a dark brow. "All at once? That could get very sticky, not to mention dangerous."

She laughed. "We'll work out all the details later." Then, taking his face in her hands, she stood on tiptoe and kissed him on the cheek. "Farewell, my friend."

"Farewell," Dane said, touching her face in a tender parting gesture.

Breanne turned then and strode to her horse. She mounted with a quick, lithe motion. Glancing over at Aidan, she cocked her head in query. "Well, are we off or not?"

"Aye, that we are," he agreed sardonically, "before you and Dane make a scene right here in the bailey."

"Why, Aidan," Breanne laughed as they rode from the stable yard and toward the castle's main gates, "I do believe you're jealous."

"I'm not jealous!" he shouted. Then, as if to give lie to his words, he nudged Lucifer into a gallop, intent on putting as much distance between Castle Haversin and them as quickly as possible.

The trek upward into the Improbus Mountains began early in the first day of their journey. Almost as if influenced by the malignant presence of Morloch and his minions, the land quickly gave up much attempt at greenery or wildlife. As Breanne and Aidan climbed higher and higher, the trees thinned to sparse stands of scraggly pines, their needle-covered branches drooping dispiritedly in the thin, gray air.

The pull toward the necromancer's fortress only intensified as the days wore on. Winds churned and howled their frigid way through rocky crags and yawning chasms, the land now devoid of any plant life save a few scraggly bushes eking out their existence in the meager soil. Save for a few eagles soaring occasionally overhead, they were alone.

Aidan drew farther and farther into himself, all his energies devoted to a desperate battle with the incessant, mind- and body-draining call. And once again he found it difficult to sleep when they made camp at night, even held in the comforting haven of Breanne's arms. His lovemaking took on a savage intensity, as if he sought escape, if only for a brief time, in mindless, almost uncaring passion.

Breanne gave of herself to the utmost of her abilities, not expecting or demanding anything of Aidan, who seemed increasingly incapable of any consideration save his relentless need to reach Morloch. 'Twas enough they were together and she was there when he needed her most. Each night her loving ministrations appeared temporarily to ease the wild look in his eyes, the burgeoning madness in his mind. She shuddered to think what would have become of him if she hadn't been there.

The peaks wherein lay Morloch's fortress, shrouded in swirling gray clouds, came into view near sunset of the third day. Barren, windswept rock, they boded yet another painfully difficult journey. Cold, weary, and hungry, Breanne gazed up at them with despairing eyes, then nudged her mount after Aidan.

The chasm with its narrow bridge, the final barrier to the last of the mountains that separated them from Morloch, suddenly loomed before them less than an hour later. True to Dane's words, the bridge was guarded by two dwarves.

Aidan rode over to the nearby cave where they resided. "Come out," he called into them. "There are two of us who desire passage over your bridge."

"And do ye now?" a surly voice rasped from the pitch-blackness inside their stony shelter. "Well, ye'll just have to wait until twilight. We don't like the sun."

" 'Tis hardly the bright of day," Aidan growled, his irritation quickly rising. "The sun is already setting. And I'd think some consideration for paying customers would be adequate motivation to tolerate a little light."

"Ye'll not pass over our bridge afore we're ready to let ye, paying or not," the surly voice snapped. "Now, let us be. 'Twill be dark soon enough!"

"By the Holy Ones!" Aidan snarled and, wheeling Lucifer around, rode back to where Breanne awaited. "The arrogant little curs won't let us pass until—"

"I heard them," Breanne softly cut him off. " 'Tis only a quarter hour until twilight. We can wait."

"And I say, let them be damned. I'll not tolerate such rudeness, especially when I don't even require their permission—"

"Aidan, please." A gentle entreaty gleamed in Breanne's eyes. "We may need them later, if we're to have any hope of escape after we're done with Morloch. Let's not antagonize the dwarves without cause."

He shot her a disgruntled look, then lapsed into a grudging, if impatient silence. And, as the first shadows of darkness stole across the chasm, the dwarves bustled out of their cave, grumbling and mumbling to themselves as they lit great torches that they shoved into the ground on either side of the bridge.

"A fine thing," the slightly taller of the two powerfully built but squat, gray-bearded dwarves said. "In such a hurry that he couldn't wait until the sun went away. As if any man could pass across our bridge at his liberty. Would have fallen into the chasm for sure, that he would."

The other dwarf, finished with his torch more quickly than his muttering brother, ambled over to stand before Breanne and Aidan. He squinted up at them, his nearsighted gaze narrowing in intense scrutiny from above a long nose tipped with a red, bulbous end. His clothes were nondescript, consisting of a ragged, green tunic, belted at the waist, that hung to midshin. Beneath his tunic he wore moth-eaten brown hosen and oddly misshapen boots.

His glance caught Breanne staring at his boots. "Looking at my feet, are ye?" the dwarf demanded accusingly. "Haven't ye ever heard 'tisn't nice to so brazenly stare at another's misfortune? For shame! 'Twill cost ye extra because o' it!"

Breanne flushed, recalling tales of the famous dwarf thin skin when it came to their invariably deformed feet. "I-I beg pardon. I meant no offense, truly I didn't. I'm just tired and not thinking well—"

"Don't apologize, Breanne," Aidan cut her off in irritation. "His oversensitivity about his feet is his problem, not ours." He made a motion toward the bridge. "How much to cross? We've a need to get to the other side before we make camp for the night."

"How much? How much?" The dwarf's brother waddled over. Similarly garbed, his appearance varied only in the fact that he lacked two upper front teeth, a fact that was revealed when he grinned up at them in avaricious delight. Breanne immediately named them Red Nose and Gap Tooth.

Gap Tooth stroked his bearded chin with a thoughtful hand. "First things first. How much do ye have?"

"Aye," chimed in his brother. "Tell us all. We don't always take money, though we likes gold especially well."

"I've no intention of giving you everything we have," Aidan growled. "We've still a long journey before we can return home and will need money to get us back."

"Ye'll give us what we want or ye won't cross our bridge!" Red Nose cried.

"Mayhap if you tell us what you like besides gold," Breanne offered, trying to ease the rising tension, "we can work out some compromise."

Red Nose moved closer and squinted up at her. "Ye're a lass, aren't ye? Let me see yer hair."

Puzzlement clouded Breanne's eyes. "And why would you want to see my hair? It has naught to do with—"

"Yer hair, lass," Gap Tooth snapped. "Don't keep my brother waiting. He gets very nasty if he's made to wait."

Breanne glanced over at Aidan. He rolled his eyes in reply. With a shrug, she pulled off her cap.

Her thick braid fell free, tumbling down to her waist. In the flickering torchlight, her hair shimmered like molten gold. Both dwarves inhaled admiring breaths.

"Have ye seen such hair, brother?" Red Nose asked.

"Nay, never." Gap Tooth made a motion toward Breanne's braid. "Unbind it. I want to see if 'tis as beautiful when it lies free and flowing."

338

"Enough!" Aidan's sharp command pierced the air. "She's shown you her hair and that's quite enough. The longer we stand here talking, the later—and darker—it grows. Tell me your price so we can be on our way."

"A haughty young human, wouldn't ye say, brother?" Red Nose exchanged a look with his twin. "If only he knew all he stands to lose . . ."

Red Nose eyed Breanne's braid once more. "Her hair. 'Tis as fine as any sack o' gold coins. Give us her hair in payment."

Breanne gasped.

Aidan roared. "Not if it were the last thing I possessed! You'll not lay one hand on her hair!"

The two dwarves exchanged glances, then shrugged. "That's our price. Either give it to us, or find some other way across the chasm."

"The hell you say!" Aidan signaled Lucifer forward. "Come on, Breanne. I've had enough of their games. We'll ride across the bridge with or without their permission!"

She nudged her gelding forward after the big black war-horse, uneasiness twining about her heart. Surely it couldn't be as simple as riding past the two dwarves and across the bridge. True, they were bigger and better armed, but these brothers wouldn't own a bridge they had no way of protecting. It only remained to be seen what surprises they still had hiding up their sleeves.

The surprise wasn't long in coming. As Aidan approached, the bridge suddenly disappeared. Lucifer immediately halted.

I think you've a slight problem, my friend.

And whatever would make you think that?
Aidan asked, his words dripping with sarcasm.
His gaze narrowed as he scanned the spot where
the bridge had been to ascertain if magic hid its
existence.

There was no spell masking the crossing's
presence. The bridge was truly gone. Anger
filled him.

"By the Mother!" Aidan wheeled Lucifer
around. "What did you do with the bridge?
If you think to play games with me, you've
chosen the wrong man!"

The two dwarves looked at each other. Then
Red Nose walked up to stand before Aidan.
" 'Tis our bridge. We made it and can destroy
it anytime we please. Ye'll pay us, or it stays
gone."

"Mayhap you need a lesson on what my eye
can do," Aidan threatened.

"Nay!" Breanne urged her mount alongside
Aidan's. "Nay, Aidan. My hair isn't worth that."
She pulled her dagger from its sheath. " 'Tis
only hair, after all. 'Twill grow back."

His expression went bleak. "Nay, Breanne.
'Tis so beautiful. . . ."

"Aidan, please."

His jaw hardened. "Do it then. 'Tis your
choice, your life. Why should what I want
matter?"

A hurt confusion swelled in her breast, but
Breanne choked back further protest. Turning
from him, she locked glances with Red Nose.
"You're quite certain my hair will fully pay the
price? If you intend further tricks after I cut off
my braid, let me warn you now that I might

not be able to restrain my husband."

Red Nose arched a shaggy brow. "Yer husband, is he? Poor lass. A more foul-tempered, evil-tongued—"

"Er, mayhap ye should be getting on with it, brother," Gap Tooth said, shooting Aidan an apprehensive glance.

"What?" Red Nose followed his twin's line of vision, and swallowed hard. "Aye, that we should." He gestured up at Breanne. "Let's have it, lass. There'll be no tricks. Ye have my word on it."

Breanne nodded. Then, before she had a chance to ponder the act and most likely regret it, she grasped her hair with one hand and proceeded to saw off her braid. When it was free, she tossed it down without hesitation and resheathed her dagger. "The bridge, if you please," she commanded tightly. "The payment has been made."

Red Nose grinned. " 'Tis already restored, lass." He cocked his head speculatively. "Where are ye bound? There's naught that lies across the chasm but barren mountains—and the necromancer's fortress. The way—"

"We owe you no answer," Aidan intruded harshly. "Just move out of our path and—"

"The way to the necromancer's is hard to follow," Red Nose reiterated doggedly. "Ye'll need a guide, unless ye've a wish to wander these mountains for the next week or two."

Aidan glared down at the dwarf. "And you're the one to lead us, is that it?"

Red Nose nodded. "Aye."

"How much will *that* cost us?"

The dwarf's gaze lifted to Breanne, sitting white-faced and rigid on her horse. "The lass has paid for that service as well. There's no extra charge."

"Well, I don't want—"

"Accept his offer, Aidan," Breanne interrupted softly. "We need all the help we can get."

He swung around, his steely glance locking with hers. "Fine," he said. "Then let's get on with it."

With that, Aidan nudged Lucifer forward. Breanne shot the dwarf a quick look. "Do you have some sort of a mount?"

He nodded vigorously. "Aye. Grant me a moment to gather supplies and saddle my pony, and I'll be ready to go." Then, with a sheepish grin at his twin, Red Nose hurried off.

Aidan awaited them on the far side of the bridge. He took one look at Breanne's hair when she and Red Nose drew up, then grimaced and shook his head. "You'll have no difficulty passing for a lad now."

For some reason she couldn't quite fathom, the simple statement sent an unexpectedly savage pain slashing through her. Tears, so firmly held in check along with any regret she'd felt at mutilating her hair, flooded her eyes. Fiercely, Breanne blinked them back, angry at her own weakness as much as at Aidan's cruel words.

"I'm sorry if my appearance offends you, m'lord," she muttered tightly. "I had no idea that my only value lay in my hair."

Her barb shot home. The taut expression of Breanne's face and the subtle quaver to her words dispelled the last of Aidan's frustration and anger. Remorse surged through him.

"I'm sorry, lass." He shoved a hand through his hair, suddenly at a loss as to what to say next. Too many emotions roiled within and coupled with his exhaustion and the incessant, distracting call to Morloch's fortress. Thus, he had little energy left to deal with much else. But, for Breanne's sake, he'd try.

"You don't offend me." Aidan sighed. "Far from it. 'Twas unfair of me to take my anger out on you." He managed an apologetic twist of his mouth. "I'm not the most pleasant of company of late."

"Nay, you're not," Breanne agreed stiffly, but even as she spoke, he knew she understood.

Somehow, the knowledge eased his guilt, stimulating a most disturbing swell of tenderness and gratitude in its place. That realization, however, was even more unsettling. It was becoming increasingly difficult to accept the fact that he more than wanted Breanne—he needed her.

He jerked his gaze away, lifting it to the top of the first rise in the land. "Come on," he growled. "The ground seems stable enough and I see no reason not to ride on for a few more hours. My night vision will carry us safely along, at least until the trail becomes too rocky and narrow."

"That will occur sooner than ye think," the dwarf volunteered cheerfully. "These mountains are most unfriendly."

"Then come up and ride by my side." Aidan motioned for him to move forward, thankful

Kathleen Morgan

for anything that would distract him from further consideration of Breanne, even if it meant having to deal with the irritating little dwarf. "You *are* the guide, aren't you?"

"Aye," Red Nose grumbled, as he reached Aidan's side. "But I never agreed to risk my neck riding out in the dark."

A feral smile lifted Aidan's mouth. "That's the least of your worries, my friend. The very least."

They made camp after about two hours' ride into the mountains, when the way finally became too treacherous for further travel. The next morning, just after sunrise, Aidan was up and breaking camp. His urgency to be on the road was evident even to the dwarf, who soon fell behind to remark on it to Breanne.

"Yer man," he began, after a prolonged bout of throat clearing. "What's his problem? Does he mayhap possess a death wish, to seek out the necromancer? And to take his lady wife along!"

Breanne's lips tightened. "You only agreed to guide us. An explanation of our motives was never part of the bargain."

"Well, I don't favor riding with mad people!"

She wheeled about in her saddle. "Then don't! Just tell us the way and you can head back to that precious bridge of yours!"

Red Nose held up his hands, his eyes wide. "Now don't get yer kirtle in a flap, lass. 'Twas but an honest question. A man has a right to know where he's headed—and why."

Breanne inhaled a steadying breath. The dwarf was right. But dared they trust anyone, so close to Morloch's fortress? "Are you friend of the necromancer?"

"Morloch?" Red Nose laughed wryly. "Yer joshing, aren't ye? Who would dare make friend o' a man who cavorts with the undead?" He shuddered. "Why, the very thought makes my skin crawl!"

"As it does me. We go on a mission of greatest import to Anacreon. That's all I can tell you."

Red Nose arched a shaggy brow. "A mission of greatest import, do ye? And who sent ye out on such a ludicrous task?"

Breanne said nothing, her only answer to turn her gaze back to the road ahead.

Red Nose, however, persisted in fretting to whoever cared to listen. "A fine thing. A body offers to help and all the thanks he gets is a haughty lift o' the nose and a refusal to speak. Well, see if I ask anything else, or offer anything more, for that matter!"

At his words, Breanne bit back a small grimace. In a different situation, Red Nose might have been an amusing companion, but not now. All her thoughts, all her support, had to be centered on Aidan. Aidan, and how to assure he survived his coming encounter with his father.

Something mysterious yet powerful drew him to the necromancer's fortress. Breanne suspected it was a spell cast by Morloch. The man, father or no, was crafty and possessed an underlying motive for calling his son to him. Breanne doubted it was because the sorcerer was dying or for any loving, paternalistic reasons.

As they climbed higher and higher, the land began to resemble Aidan's grim mood. Finally, they reached the summit of the next mountain range. As they paused there to briefly rest the horses, Breanne scanned the terrain.

Below them stretched a jagged mass of barren, lesser peaks and fog-shrouded gorges. The trails that traversed the mountainsides were narrow and rock-strewn, wending gradually downward until they joined into one road that led to a dark, imposing fortress. Sheer precipices fell off on one side of many of the trails, while steep, unstable gravel and rock slides bordered the other. Treacherous going, Breanne thought grimly, when combined with the unpredictable but powerful gusts of wind that frequently roared by.

As she gazed down at it, her heart began to pound. Despite the difficulty, excitement coursed through her. The danger be damned! They'd found Morloch at last!

"Ye see it, then?" Red Nose asked. "And the route that leads to the fortress?"

"Aye," Aidan grunted his reply. "And 'tis past time we were there." With that, he urged Lucifer forward.

Breanne glanced over at the dwarf. She managed a wry grin. "It seems our rest is over."

Red Nose shook his head. "Nay, lass. This is as far as I dare go. The necromancer has no use for the likes o' me."

"What will you do, then? Return to your brother?"

"Mayhap." The dwarf shrugged. "And mayhap I'll wait here awhile. See if ye come out alive."

She smiled. "Worried about us, are you?"

"What?" Red Nose flushed to the roots of his long, gray beard. "Ah, nay. Never for a human. I'm jest curious, that's all."

"Well, I'll be sure to look for you," Breanne said, nudging her horse forward, "when we return this way." She glanced back over her shoulder. "My thanks for all your help."

The dwarf nodded, then flushed again.

Breanne turned her attention to the rock-strewn slope that lay below her. Aidan had already reached its bottom and was again urging Lucifer onward. She wondered if he'd noticed, or even cared, that he'd left her behind.

The thought bothered her. 'Twasn't like Aidan to be so heedless of her safety. Always in the past he had insisted on remaining at her side.

She finally reached him about a mile down the trail, after having pushed her mount to a pace that could only be termed reckless, considering the rocky, crumbling terrain. "Aidan, don't ride away from me like that again!" Breanne cried. " 'Tisn't safe for either of us!"

He turned to her then and the look he shot her made Breanne gasp. From the depth of shadowed sockets, Aidan's eyes burned with a feverish light. His skin was flushed, his breathing ragged.

"Aidan!" Breanne reached out to grab his arm. "What's the matter? Have you taken ill?"

"Nay," he rasped, fiercely shaking his head. " 'Tis th-the call. I must get to Morloch. The need . . . 'tis eating me alive!"

She forced an encouraging smile and squeezed his arm. "And we will, my love, just as fast as 'tis safely possible. But from now on, you must follow me and heed my words. Can you do that?"

Uncertainty gleamed in his eyes. "I-I think so. Only hurry, Breanne."

"Aye." She released his arm and signaled her horse to take the lead. "I'll hurry."

Despite the assurance of her words, the trail precluded haste. It was two hours later before they finally reined in before the huge stone edifice that seemed suddenly to rise from the substance of the mountain itself. There were few windows and those were but eerie black slits perched high above ground in a structure that was little more than a span of walls interrupted frequently by narrow towers with crenelated tops.

Gazing up at the fortress, Breanne was engulfed by a sensation of oppressive malevolence—and of being watched. She repressed a shudder and turned to Aidan. "Well, what now?"

He gestured toward the tall, arched opening that shimmered opaquely before them. "Ride up and see what comes of it. Either 'tis guarded or 'tis not."

Breanne inhaled a steadying breath, then once more urged her horse forward. "As you say. 'Tis more than evident Morloch knows we're here."

He shot her a haunted look. "You've felt it, too, then?"

"Aye."

The sense of oppression crushed down on Breanne the closer they drew to the strange gate until she thought she might scream from the tension. Sounds rose in her mind, assuming the clarity of voices, moaning, crying out for her to turn back, to flee. The air around her became hot. Each breath Breanne drew seared her lungs. Her heart pounded so hard in her chest, she thought it might burst.

Panic rising, Breanne glanced over at Aidan. Though his features were strained, his skin still flushed, he appeared no different than before. The change, she realized, was in her.

Something, or someone, was trying to frighten her away. But to what purpose? To lure Aidan alone into Morloch's lair?

The consideration angered her. It also sent a surge of white-hot determination coursing through her, banishing the oppressive sensations. Suddenly, everything was clear. She was here to support Aidan through this, and no one would stand in the way of that resolve.

A man, dressed in plain brown robes, stepped suddenly through the gate, halting before them. He peered up, his gray eyes curious, but benign. "And how may I serve you, m'lord? M'lady?"

Aidan halted Lucifer. "Is this the fortress of the necromancer, Morloch?"

The man smiled thinly. "Aye, 'tis Morloch's fortress. He prefers not to be called a necromancer in his own home, however, no matter what the rest of the world may think of him."

Aidan shrugged. "As you wish. Pray, tell your master I've a wish to meet with him."

A thin, grizzled brow arched in query. "And who may I say is here to see him?"

Aidan glanced over at Breanne. "His son, Aidan, Prince of Anacreon, and his son's wife, the Lady Breanne."

The man's expression remained an inscrutable mask. "Indeed? My master should find that news most interesting." He gestured toward the gate with a wave of his hand.

The shimmering barrier dissolved to reveal an outer bailey bustling with activity. Servants hurried to and fro, carrying foodstuffs, loads of bedclothes to wash, or buckets of water from the well. Soldiers shouted messages from high up on the parapets. Sheep bleated, cows bawled, geese honked. It was all quite a normal castle scene—and totally unexpected.

Once more Aidan's gaze met Breanne's and she saw her own confusion mirrored what she saw in his eyes. Then, with a shrug, Aidan turned and signaled Lucifer forward.

Chapter Seventeen

This doesn't feel right, Lucifer grumbled. *I see the people, the animals, but it still doesn't feel right.*

'Tis no magic, Aidan replied warily. *I would know if it were.*

Aye, but the place is too clean, the servants too happy, too eager. Almost as if this scene, real as it now might be, was created but a few moments ago.

Aidan shrugged. *Well, be that as it may, there's naught we can do about it save keep our guard up. Though we don't know what Morloch plans for us, let us hope he's just as ignorant of our motives in coming here.*

And if he isn't?

A dark look shuttered Aidan's features. *Then we call upon all our powers to defeat him.*

With that, he turned his attention away from

his horse to the man who led them toward the great stone keep. As their guide paused at the broad expanse of steps that led up to a huge oaken door, he glanced back at Breanne and Aidan and gestured.

"Enter, if you will." As he spoke, the doors swung open. "My master awaits in his bedchamber. He is too ill to receive guests save from his bed."

Aidan dismounted. A stableman ran forward to take Lucifer from him, as did another when Breanne swung down from her horse. She strode over to Aidan.

The sun caught her short tumble of hair, glinting off strands that gleamed gold and silver in the bright light. With her boyish cap of hair and piquant little face lifted to his, she was the picture of endearing loveliness. Aidan's heart twisted in his breast. She had sacrificed so much for him and now risked the most horrible danger of all, yet Breanne only smiled, a trusting look shining in her striking, sapphire blue eyes.

He would protect her, Aidan vowed, see her safely from this fortress if he accomplished nothing else. 'Twas his duty, no matter how insistent the call, no matter what he ultimately learned of the man Morloch was.

His duty was clear, his commitment strong, yet why did his anxiety continue to grow? Aidan shook the uneasy feelings aside with the greatest of difficulty. By the Mother, but he was weary, drained of all energy until he felt little more than a dry husk of a man. And the greatest trial of all lay just ahead.

With a superhuman effort, he indicated the door. "Come, lady. Our host awaits."

Together, they climbed the stairs and entered the keep. Its interior was unremarkable from others of its kind. After a large entry area, they crossed to another door that opened into a great hall with a lofty ceiling. High up on the stone walls were windows secured by wooden shutters locked shut with iron bars. Though the hall was dark, the stray beams of sunlight filtering through the slats in the shutters revealed several long trestle tables, each with its attending set of benches.

The floor was of inlaid stone of various hues, strewn with rushes and dried rose and lavender flowers. Their fragrant scents wafted to Aidan's nostrils. Freshly laid, he thought, if the intensity of their aroma and brightness of their colors were any indication. He lifted his gaze to scan the rest of the room.

On the distant wall stood a massive fireplace, blackened with smoke, its intricately beveled wooden mantel set with a selection of silver plates and mugs. A heraldic crest of two rampant dragons, a human skull gripped in each of their claws, crowned the smoothly whitewashed wall above. All quite normal, almost homey, Aidan mused once more, and totally unexpected in a necromancer's fortress.

"M'lord?" a low voice intruded into Aidan's thoughts. He wheeled around.

A rotund little man stood behind him, dressed in a simple, long-sleeved dark blue robe that hung open to reveal gray breeches, boots, and tunic. He rendered Aidan a bow. "I am Astorath, the Lord Morloch's physician. He asked that I greet you and bring you to him."

"His illness isn't life-threatening, I hope?" Aidan asked.

Astorath cocked his head in a speculative gesture. "You sound almost as if you care."

Aidan returned his intent scrutiny with an unwavering look. "He is my host. 'Tis common courtesy to inquire as to his health."

The physician sighed. "Aye, that 'tis. But I'd hoped . . ." He paused. "It doesn't matter. And, in answer to your question, aye, Morloch's illness is indeed life-threatening. 'Tis an old wound that never healed, and 'tis finally killing him. He hasn't long to live."

"Then all the better to take us to him immediately," Aidan said. "I've much to speak with him about."

A thin smile quirked Astorath's mouth. "Aye, I'd imagine you have." He indicated the flight of stairs a short distance from the hearth that wound upward to the second floor. "If you'd follow me."

Their journey led down dark, torchlit corridors that twisted and turned into a confusing labyrinth of hallways until their guide finally halted at one particularly large, arched door. He knocked and yet another servant quickly appeared.

Astorath turned to Aidan. "I'll leave you now. You'll want some time to yourselves, I'm sure."

Before Aidan could reply, the man turned and disappeared back into the maze of hallways. Aidan grimaced wryly. 'Twould be next to impossible to find one's way back to the Great

Hall without the aid of someone who knew the building. Briefly, he wondered if there were some special purpose served in constructing the keep that way.

Then the servant was stepping aside, revealing a large, opulently furnished bedchamber and a curtained bed set close to the room's only window. Someone moved within the bed. Aidan's attention riveted immediately on it.

Beside him, Breanne felt Aidan's big body tense, grow rigid. Out of the corner of her eye, she saw his hand snake to the dagger that hung at his side. "Easy, m'lord," she murmured softly. "Man-made weapons will do no good here, and an aggressive stance might only anger our host."

His eyes slashed to her, then back to the bed. Aidan exhaled a deep breath. "I thank you for the reminder."

"Yet there is a threat here," Breanne muttered. "Can you not feel it in the air?"

Strangely, Aidan's oppressive, incessant sense of urgency had evaporated as soon as he'd entered Morloch's bedchamber. Its departure was a welcome relief. Mayhap the call had been but one of a dying father to his son, he thought. Mayhap, even far away, he'd known his father needed him.

With an inward jerk, Aidan recalled himself from the surprisingly tender consideration. To linger on such maudlin thoughts was ridiculous, not to mention distracting and potentially dangerous. All that mattered was confronting Morloch, then determining the next course of action.

He strode across the room, Breanne at his side. The figure buried in comforter and pillows shifted as they approached, lifting himself to a sitting position. He was a middle-aged man, his shoulder-length, wavy black hair streaked with gray, his strong, square-jawed face lined, his firm, sensual mouth taut with pain. He turned in bed to face them and, as he did, Breanne's throat tightened in a spasm of surprise.

Amber eyes, piercing to the depths of her soul, locked with hers. Amber eyes in a face that, though years older, so strongly resembled Aidan's as to leave no doubt as to his parentage. If there had been any question before, there was none left now. None in Breanne's mind nor, she realized as she shot Aidan a quick glance, in his, either.

Morloch held out a hand as Aidan drew up at his bedside. "Welcome, my son. It has been a long time since I last saw you."

Aidan ignored the sorcerer's hand. "A very long time indeed," he growled. "Mayhap since I was a babe and you visited long enough to lay the curse of the Evil Eye upon me?"

"I laid no curse upon you." A brittle wariness flickered in the necromancer's eyes. "Your abilities were your birthright as my son. Even before I chose to become a mage, I, too, bore the powers of the Evil Eye. I was but following my destiny to answer the call of magic. A destiny that I'd wager you share as well."

Aidan laughed, but the sound was hollow, devoid of emotion. "You'd like that, wouldn't you? 'Twould justify all you've sacrificed—and become."

Morloch arched a brow in quiet challenge. "And pray, what exactly have I become?"

His son glared down at him. "You play some game, to ask that. Everyone knows you for a soul-rotted fiend who associates with the undead and demons. And yet you dare look up at me and claim innocence of such—"

Breanne's hand settled on his arm. "Aidan, this is no way to speak to your host. To insult him in his own domain—"

"Is at best discourteous," Morloch finished for her, casting Breanne a shrewd glance, "and, at worst, foolhardy." He waved her closer. "And who are you, lady? For all your simple garb and close-cropped hair, I'd wager you're no peasant lass?"

"She's my wife, the Lady Breanne," Aidan snapped.

"Indeed?" Morloch smiled. "So, I'm doubly blessed this day, in meeting my daughter-in-law as well as reconciling with my long-lost son."

"I said naught about any reconciliation!"

The mage turned back to Aidan. "Nay, I suppose you didn't, but I hope for it, nonetheless. There is much that has passed between us in the past years, outright lies about me as well as half-truths and rumors until my reputation scarce resembles who I really am. All I ask is that you and your lady agree to remain here a short while and grant me the chance to share my story. 'Tis only fair, is it not, that I be given the opportunity to vindicate myself?"

"Nay." Aidan shook his head. "Do you think me such a fool to believe anything a necromancer would say?" He took a step back and withdrew the sword slung across his back. "I've seen more than enough to satisfy my curiosity. Now I'll finish what I came to do."

With that, Aidan lowered his sword to press the tip against Morloch's throat. The older man simply sat there, his glance locking with that of his son. Aidan angled the blade until the metal pricked the sorcerer's throat. Blood welled and a thin stream of crimson trickled down to stain Morloch's white linen nightshirt. He flinched but neither moved nor said a word.

Breanne's heart lurched beneath her breast, then began a wild pounding. Why was the necromancer permitting such an attack upon his person? Why hadn't he summoned his powers to protect him, to at least fling Aidan's sword aside? Was this another game, or was the man truly debilitated and perhaps not as evil a being as the tales would have him be?

An impulse to cry out to Aidan to stop filled her. Then she looked into Morloch's eyes. Something glinted there, something hard, malevolent, and edged with triumph. The realization startled her. Morloch knew Aidan better than Aidan knew himself—and knew that his son wouldn't kill an unarmed man.

Even as the thought streaked through her mind, Aidan lowered his sword. "Use your powers!" he rasped. "Fight me!"

Morloch smiled. "And what would that accomplish? My wish is not to see us both destroyed, but finally to come to know each other—as father and son. To discover if there's some common ground left between us in which to forge a bond—or if too many years have passed and 'tis now too late. I am dying. Can't you spare me a few days before you journey on? Just a few days to try to ease the regrets, the mistakes of a misspent, misunderstood life?"

Aidan hesitated, overcome suddenly with indecision and a strange yearning. He'd been so lonely for so long, his heart a wasteland of isolation, unable to call anyplace home or any man truly father. Marus had never been a father to him, and now Aidan finally understood the reason. He had never been Marus's son. Only Dragan. Only Dragan.

He locked gazes with Morloch. Amber eyes met amber eyes. He saw himself in his father's firmly chiseled lips, in the stubborn, almost arrogant set of his jaw, in the broad forehead and arch of cheekbone. He saw the torment that burned in his eyes from the years of similar rejection and revulsion. Here was a man who understood what Aidan had gone through and suffered. Dared he risk losing the only opportunity he might ever have to know his real father, no matter what he'd become?

And who was to say the vile tales about Morloch the necromancer were any more accurate or fair than the tales told about him? The common people were, by and large, an ignorant, superstitious lot. Frequently, what they didn't understand they chose to disparage and fear. And rumors rapidly grew far out of proportion to the actual deeds.

He would be careful, Aidan vowed. He would grant Morloch his request and remain a few days in his fortress. The concession would lose him naught and would most likely lull the necromancer into imagining he'd won his son over. If all went well, Aidan could pierce his father's veil of secrecy and discern the true man within—and his weaknesses. If all went well, he had nothing to lose and everything to gain.

"We'll accept your offer of hospitality." Aidan resheathed his sword. " 'Tis the least I could do. I, too, have a need to know you better. No matter who you may truly be, you are my father. I owe it not only to myself, but to those I may leave behind to learn more of you."

Morloch nodded, smiling. "Good. Good. You'll not regret it, I swear." He motioned over the servant who stood by the door. "Show my son and his lady to the guest quarters."

He turned back to Aidan. "They are quite well-appointed rooms, but if there's aught else you may desire, don't hesitate to ask. What little luxury and wealth I possess is yours. You are, after all, my only child. Someday soon, if you care to accept it, this fortress and its lands will be yours."

Aidan frowned. "I didn't come here to claim title to anything you own—"

"Aye," his father interrupted him, "but I can still hope that someday we will be as one, can't I? 'Tis all I've left in the waning of my life."

"We can talk of it later," Aidan muttered.

"Aye, that we can. At the supper meal, may-hap?"

Aidan glanced over at Breanne. She struggled to contain her rising unease, as his gaze returned to his father.

"Aye," he slowly agreed. "At supper."

*   *   *

As the door closed behind them in the privacy of their own bedchamber, Breanne wheeled about to confront Aidan. " 'Tisn't wise, your decision to remain in Morloch's fortress. 'Tis too dangerous."

"Is it?" Aidan strode over and began to shed his sword belt and scabbard, then sat down on a nearby chair. "Come, lass. Help me with my boots."

Breanne frowned, then walked over. "Are your wits finally addled, to act so relaxed in a necromancer's abode? Why, if I didn't know better, I'd imagine you'd decided to accept Morloch as your long-lost father."

"Accept him, nay," Aidan corrected her calmly. "Acknowledge him, aye. You saw him, Breanne. He *is* my father."

"But—"

"We're safe enough," he interrupted her protest. "He wants something from us, just as we do from him. Until he gets it, we're in no danger."

Breanne knelt before Aidan, her hands settling on his knees. "He wants *you*, Aidan. He wants your heart, your mind, your soul. Can't you see that?"

"You exaggerate, lass." Aidan chuckled softly. "And even if it were so, do you doubt me equal to the challenge?"

A loving exasperation softened her features. "Truly, you are equal to anything a normal man could confront you with. But a necromancer has all the forces of evil on his side."

He reached down and pulled Breanne up to

him, cradling her in the warm haven of his arms. "And I have you, little one, and the powers of a mage within my sword. Is that not sufficient to the task?"

"Aye," Breanne murmured, her arms encircling his trim waist. "What other recourse do we have, save to believe that?"

Aidan's head lowered. Firm, masculine lips moved to nuzzle the silky column of her neck. "'Tis several hours 'til suppertime," he suggested huskily, "and the bed, after the past days on the trail, looks most inviting."

She glanced up at him. "Is it safe to lower our guards for even a moment in such a place?"

"There's no magic here, within this room, if that's what you're asking. None," he growled as his warm breath rasped across the sensitive skin of Breanne's neck, sending a rippling current of excitement coursing through her, "save the magic your woman's enchantment works upon me."

She shouldn't let him distract her so, Breanne thought, but the heady, masculine scent of him, the heat emanating from his big body, the feel of his hard-muscled frame, drove the lingering doubts away. Aidan's powers were sufficient to sense danger, be it from humans or magic. And, in the meanwhile, she needed all the comfort he could give.

Her hand slipped down to cup his thickly swollen shaft. "Magic, is it?" she purred. "And I thought 'twas you who wrought the spells, not I."

At her touch, he drew in a ragged breath. His

hand captured a soft breast and he squeezed gently. "I need you, lass. 'Tis all that I know. Be it magic or not, you are more woman than I ever hoped to have. And now that I have you, I intend never to let you go. Never."

She was losing him.

As Breanne stood before the mirror brushing out her cap of golden curls into some semblance of order, her anguished gaze sought out Aidan in the glass's reflection. He dressed nearby, apparently oblivious to her worried perusal.

In but a half hour they would once again join Morloch in his bedchamber for the evening meal, a routine they'd followed now for the past three days. Three days spent increasingly in the necromancer's company as father and son slowly lowered their guards and came to know each other. From Aidan's point of view, at least, the knowing was but strengthening his filial attachment—an attachment Breanne watched grow with a sense of rising dread.

As tactfully as she could in the past several days, Breanne had tried to urge caution, advising Aidan to exercise some restraint in his dealings with Morloch. Urged it to the point of irritating Aidan. Yet despite his rising anger, she refused to stop trying to warn him. There was no other choice. She would fight for Aidan until there was naught left to fight for.

"Our visit," she began carefully, setting aside the gilded silver hairbrush, "how much longer do you plan to extend it? You originally intended on making it just a few days—"

"I know what I intended," Aidan growled, turning to face her as he fastened his belt over his black tunic. "It should be evident even to you that my plans have changed. My father is dying. He weakens more with each passing day. I intend to stay with him until the end comes."

Without the added thickness of a leather under tunic and chain mail, he presented a trim, if powerful appearance. The absence of the protective garb that, in the past, he had habitually worn was but another worrisome testimony to the insidious influence of Morloch over his son. Though they'd originally come to kill the necromancer, Aidan was instead gradually being won over to his father's side.

His words, spoken with a wearily patient tone, cut Breanne to the quick. Not only was Aidan turning to the necromancer; at the same time, he was turning away from her. In many carefully phrased statements in the past days, Morloch had sought to put Breanne in her place—the place of an obedient, docile wife who said little and accepted much. And, though she had yet openly to defy him in Aidan's presence, Breanne would spare no words when she was alone with her husband.

"Then you are a fool." She turned to face him, her chin lifting a defiant notch.

Aidan's features tightened with disapproval. A dark brow arched over glittering amber eyes. "Indeed? Truly, lady, you are fast becoming a sharp-tongued shrew."

Breanne's eyes narrowed. Her hands fisted at her sides. "A shrew, am I? Just because you don't care to hear what I have to say? Morloch has surely enchanted you, for you so suddenly to have lost your wits. He is a necromancer, Aidan! He is evil personified! Father or no, he wishes naught good for you!"

"And how can you be so certain?" Aidan's bejeweled left eye glinted dangerously. "From the start, though you've heard Morloch's story just as fully as I, you've refused to cast aside your prejudices and hear him out. He is no different from me, though even my treatment at the hands of others pales in comparison to what he has suffered."

"And you have refused to see past the outward man and his false tales to the being who lies beneath!" Breanne strode over to stand before Aidan. "Have you once truly looked into his eyes, seen the foul, corrupt, evil soul that governs him? He is lost, was so years ago, even before he became your father." Her hands lifted to touch him on the arm. "Listen to me, Aidan. Hear me now—before 'tis too late."

At her movement toward him, Aidan stepped back, his hand rising in warning. "I've heard you for a long while now. I've tried as well to listen. But you refuse to hear me or respect what I tell you I want."

"And what is that?" Breanne demanded.

He eyed her for a long, tension-laden moment, then sighed. "You know it. I want time to be with my father, be there for him at his deathbed. I want time to decide what I must do next."

Aidan grabbed her by the arms. "Think about it, Breanne. Morloch will die soon. Whatever he was or did, 'twill die with him. But this fortress, this land, will be mine. We can change things to suit us then."

"So, you intend to stay. And what of Anacreon?"

He laughed bitterly. "What of it? I'm accepted here. Anacreon will have to survive without me, which I'm certain they'll be more than happy to do."

"And if I refuse to stay? What then?"

Aidan opened his mouth, then clamped it shut and averted his gaze. "I-I don't know. If you persist in making me choose between you and my father . . ."

Tears filled Breanne's eyes, but she glared past them. "He has done naught for you, save lay a curse upon you that all have held against you for your entire life. I, on the other hand, have saved your life time and again, have steadfastly remained at your side no matter the circumstances, have given you my heart and soul and body. And still you persist in placing me on equal footing with a necromancer?"

"Not a necromancer, lass," Aidan corrected her softly. "My father." He took her hands in his, fingering the runic bracelets that encircled her wrists. "You have never given him a chance, not even ever daring to remove these. And what have they done for you since we've been here, save turn your skin green from prolonged contact?"

"I-I do what I must," Breanne said, fighting the tremor that threatened to rack her voice and body. "I am your wife. I love you."

He cradled her chin in his large, callused

hand with a tender but regretful smile. "And I never asked for your love. In fact, I warned you 'twould be a painful, even futile thing to waste on my behalf."

"Nay." Breanne shook her head in vehement denial, spilling tears down her cheeks. "Nay, Aidan, 'tisn't the truth of it. You simply value your father's regard more than mine."

He released her and turned away then, shrugging his broad shoulders. "Call it what you will. I'd prefer to enjoy the regard of you both, but if you persist in your selfish, jealous demands . . ."

"Selfish? Jealous?" Breanne couldn't believe her ears. "Why you arrogant, pigheaded, stupid man!"

She lost control then, strode over, and, with a tightly fisted hand, struck Aidan on the back. With panther quickness, he wheeled around, captured her wrist in an iron clasp, and twisted her arm behind her back. Jerking Breanne back roughly to him, Aidan glared down at her.

"Never do that again! Never, do you hear me? I have killed men for less. If you weren't a woman and my wife—"

His words cracked about her like a whiplash. Breanne recoiled momentarily, then gathered her courage and forged on. He'd not intimidate her. She had naught to lose.

"Aye, what would you do, Aidan?" Breanne taunted. "Use your eye upon me? Or merely throw me down and beat me into a senseless pulp? Or is that mercy saved for men, and do you mayhap instead rape any woman who dares defy you?"

"I've never raped a woman—" He paused and inhaled a shuddering breath. "Curse you. Haven't I enough to think about without you goading me like this? By the Holy Ones, but you're fast becoming more trouble than any one man should have to bear!"

"Then mayhap I should go, leave you here to wither into some twisted, evil, lonely sorcerer, muttering incantations over a pot of boiling herbs. Mayhap that would suit you better!"

"Aye, mayhap 'twould!" Aidan released her with a jerk. He strode over to a small serving table and poured himself a goblet of ale, sloshing some of the spicy brew over the sides of his cup in his anger. Setting down the flagon, Aidan grabbed up the goblet and drained its contents. Then he turned, his expression set in stone.

" 'Tisn't the time to decide what we should do about us. Neither of us is in the most impartial frame of mind." He indicated the door. "Come with me to supper. We can talk more later, when we've both had time to calm."

Breanne briefly considered his offer, then shook her head. She couldn't bear to sit near Morloch tonight and pretend to a civility she didn't feel. She'd choke on her food. "Nay, I'd prefer to stay here. I'm not hungry, at any rate."

Aidan frowned. "You know I can't leave you alone—"

"And why not? Surely I'm in no danger, with such a good, kind man as your father as host? And who else would dare attempt to harm me within a necromancer's fortress?"

"Have it your way, then," Aidan muttered. "As you say, you're in no danger here."

He strode over to the door, grasped the handle, then paused. His glance met hers. The steely, implacable look Breanne shot him must have sealed his decision. He opened the door and walked out of the room.

Breanne sank down in the huge metal tub with a blissful sigh. The water, warm from the kitchen fire, lapped over her, soothing her frazzled nerves, muting the tension of the recent encounter with Aidan. Nothing, however, could ease the pang in her heart over his blunt words.

"You're fast becoming more trouble than any one man should have to bear!"

Did he truly believe that? Mayhap had secretly believed it all along? Or was it just another misconception Morloch had planted in Aidan's mind? The water's heat ebbed into Breanne, seeping down to her very bones. Bit by bit the doubts, the pain, the fears about Aidan dissipated, and the sensual feel of her bath turned her thoughts to other times.

Times in Aidan's strong arms, cradled against his hard-muscled body, listening to his words of need, of passion, aye, even of affection. He'd cared for her then, though he'd never mentioned love, yet Breanne knew he wasn't a man who spoke lightly or felt superficially about anything. For all the vigilance he kept about his heart, Aidan had never been a man of lukewarm emotions or actions.

'Twas hard, though, to stand there and watch Morloch seduce him away from her. She felt so helpless, so much at a loss as to how to vanquish a necromancer. If he had attacked them as warrior to warrior, Breanne would have known how to fight him. As Aidan would have as well.

Instead, Morloch had quickly discerned Aidan's blind side, his son's need to be loved and accepted. And, just as Breanne saw that quality in Aidan as a potential strength to be nurtured, the necromancer viewed it instead as a weakness to be exploited. Weakness versus strength. Breanne only wondered which of them was right.

She sank yet lower in the bath. Her runic bracelets clanked on the sides of the metal tub. Breanne lifted her arms. The firelight glinted off the beaten copper and shadowed, feathery script of ancient protection. She frowned, recalling Aidan's disparaging remarks about the marks they had left on her skin. Until now, she had never considered removing them, recalling Olenus's caution about doing so. But what would it matter if she set them aside for a short time to cleanse herself?

Aidan was with Morloch and would remain with him until he returned to their room. Surely she was safe enough with Morloch occupied. And if the act would prove Aidan wrong in his insistence that she refused to give the necromancer a chance . . .

Her fingers closed about one bracelet, hesitated, then twisted the metal band free. Setting it on the bathing table beside her soap and scrubbing sponge, Breanne quickly removed the other. Then, grabbing up the bar of fragrantly scented soap, redolent of a meadow of springtide flowers, she lathered the sponge and began to wash her arms.

The sweet scents encompassed her, the water caressed her. Breanne surrendered to the luxury of her bath. Time passed, the tormenting dilemma of Aidan and his father dulled. All she remembered was her love for him. A love that, no matter the obstacles or pain, refused to be discounted or defeated.

Renewed determination filled Breanne. Though she'd threatened to leave Aidan to Morloch, they were words spoken in the heat of her anger. She'd stay, fight with him and for him until she finally made him see the true reality. Morloch would never win. Never.

Behind her the door to the bedchamber opened. A draft of air surged through, sending chill fingers rippling over her water-cooled skin. Breanne turned. Aidan stood in the doorway. She smiled and, in one fluid, graceful motion, rose from her bath. Beside her on the table the runic bracelets sat, forgotten, glinting dully in the firelight.

Chapter Eighteen

Aidan traveled the labyrinthine corridors back to his bedchamber, relaxed and sated after a sumptuous meal, several cups of a finely brewed ale, and yet another warm, enlightening conversation with his father. As ill as Morloch was, the depth and myriad facets of the man never ceased to amaze him. His compassion for others, in spite of the cruel rumors and revulsion repeatedly heaped on him, was a neverending source of inspiration. In comparison, his own life had been so empty, so meaningless, so embittered.

But never again, Aidan vowed. Anacreon was in no danger from Morloch. Whatever was slowly destroying the kingdom came from within, from the realm's own internal corruption. They must deal with it on their own. He owed Anacreon naught.

'Twas past time to see to his own needs, needs best served in alliance with Morloch. He had all he could ever require right here—a father who truly wanted and understood him, the future of a kingdom to rule as he saw fit, and subjects who would accept him. And then, there was also the love of a wonderful woman.

Aye, a wonderful woman, Aidan thought, the memory of Breanne flooding back to fill him with a warm sense of contentment. He must find some way to change her opinion of Morloch, to make her see him as he truly was and learn to accept him. Though, in the heat of anger, they had both threatened to sever the marriage, the actuality of such an undertaking sickened Aidan. After the long years of denial and loneliness, he now found he wanted it all— and that all included Breanne.

No matter what she said or threatened, he'd never let her go. She was as necessary to him as breathing, sleeping, and eating—an integral part of his life. To lose her now would irreparably tear a part of him away, never to be healed.

A sudden thought assailed Aidan. Was this what love was? If Breanne abandoned him, would it leave a wound that would pain him the rest of his days? Even as he fought to deny it, Aidan knew it to be true. Breanne had crept into his heart through some secret portal he'd not thought to guard, and now, once in, he could never send her away. As frustrating and frightening as it was to admit, he did indeed love her.

His strides quickened, his long, strong legs rapping out the steps in an ever increasing tempo of booted feet upon stone floor. He must get back to Breanne, tell her of his love. Surely that would convince her, once and for all, to stay.

One dimly lit corridor opened onto another, then another. All began to look the same. Aidan frowned. Had he, distracted by his thoughts, taken a wrong turn? By now, he should have reached their bedchamber door.

Aidan halted, then turned slowly to survey the hallway. Hadn't he already passed this same way just a few minutes ago? He shrugged and strode on. If so, the corridor he now approached would lead directly down to their bedchamber. The next hallway, however, was one he didn't recall ever seeing before, and didn't open onto another corridor.

A dead end. Once more, Aidan halted. The first tendrils of unease coiled within him.

Something was amiss. He doubted it was due to a mistaken sense of direction. In the past three days he'd traversed the fortress to and from his room often enough to ingrain the way in his memory. His warrior's acute skills of observation had always stood him in good stead, whether outside or within the confines of a building. As confusing a maze as the fortress was, Aidan knew his abilities served him just as aptly now.

Had someone—and it could only be Morloch—cast a spell upon the corridors so they changed each time he drew near his bedchamber? If so, why? There was only one logical reason, Aidan realized. Morloch wished to keep him from his room.

Wished to keep him from Breanne . . . who was alone for the first time since they'd left Anacreon.

Fear surged through Aidan, then a blazing anger. Curse Morloch! If anything happened to Breanne . . .

He closed his eyes, summoning his powers, envisioning her. She was still in her room but another was there, too. 'Twas a man, tall and broad-shouldered, who carried her, naked, in his arms. Carried her over to their bed.

Aidan wheeled around and ran, the certainty of her peril growing with each pounding stride. At the memory of the man's face, turned briefly to his magic-summoned view, Aidan's heart twisted in his chest. The man had been himself or, rather, one garbed in the illusion of his form. And garbed skillfully enough to fool Breanne, whose wrists, entwined about the impostor's neck, had been free of her protective bracelets.

His pace quickened into a dead run. Once more he'd been a fool, to leave her unattended, to allow himself to be lulled into a false sense of security by Morloch's skillful lies. And it had to be Morloch with Breanne. Who else possessed such powers? But his motive? What, by all the Holy Ones, was his possible intent?

The answer, immediately put to question, crystallized in Aidan's mind. He loved his wife. She held his heart in a loving, if gentle, bondage, and would always exert an influence upon him to be reckoned with. If Morloch had truly intended to possess his soul and bend him to his evil plans, Breanne was the one and only obstacle.

Savagely, Aidan cursed himself, cursed his blind, foolish gullibility. How could he have been so stupid, so easily led? Had the lessons of all those years of hardship and danger been squandered? Had he learned naught?

It didn't matter now. Nothing mattered but reaching Breanne. Powerful legs pounded down one stone hall, then another, but this time Aidan relied on his own magic rather than normal human abilities to guide him. And they guided him true.

Chest heaving, he finally slid to a halt before his bedchamber door, paused to regain his composure, then opened it and stealthily crept in. The scene that greeted him across the room froze his heart into a block of ice.

A naked man, his back turned, straddled Breanne upon the bed. Caught up in the throes of passion for one she imagined to be her husband, she lay pliant and receptive beneath him.

Rage exploded within Aidan. A primal impulse to protect what was his filled him. With a growl as animalistic as his response, he slammed shut the door and flung himself across the room.

Morloch heard him. In an instant he was off the bed and facing Aidan, clothed in his long black robes, back in his own form. Calmly, he awaited his enraged son.

With a gasp of horror, Breanne sat up and pulled the comforter around her as Aidan drew to a halt before his father. "You appear . . . quite recovered . . . from your fatal illness," he bit out between ragged breaths.

" 'Twas necessary. First, I needed to win your trust."

"My trust?" Aidan's features hardened into a mask of incredulity. "For what purpose? So you could eventually seduce my wife?"

"Her seduction was merely a means to an end." The necromancer snickered. "Isn't that obvious? My powers are now such that when I entered her body, I'd have also entered her mind. When she yielded in her passion, she'd have yielded her will to me as well. I needed that. She stood between us, threatened our affection and bonding."

"And you couldn't permit that, could you?"

"Nay. You are mine. 'Twas meant that way from the beginning. It has always been your destiny."

Rage flared anew in Aidan's eyes. "Nay, *Father*. My destiny has always been to destroy you!"

With that, Aidan leaped at Morloch. An evil grin on his face, the necromancer flung up a magical barrier. Aidan slammed into it and was thrown to the floor. His eyes glinting amber fire, he climbed slowly to his feet.

"Yield, son," Morloch urged, his voice tinged with a mocking pity. "Your powers are as naught against mine. You'll only harm yourself if you persist."

"Never," Aidan snarled. " 'Twon't be over until one of us is dead." He summoned the fullest powers of his eye and directed it at Morloch.

The necromancer threw up his arms to increase the strength of his enchanted shield, well aware of the deadly prowess of his son's eye. He diverted the searing blast, then, with a motion of his head, set the bed curtains ablaze.

With a small cry, Breanne flung herself out of the bed, dragging a sheet about her to cover her nudity.

Aidan shot her a quick glance, ascertained she was unharmed, then turned back to Morloch. "Your bracelets," he tersely tossed over his shoulder at her, "find them and put them on. Now!"

As she scrabbled across the room to where she'd left the runic bracelets by the bathing tub, the door to the room swung open. A powerful gust of wind coursed in, nearly knocking Breanne over. 'Twas Morloch's doing, she knew, intent as he was on keeping her from the bracelets.

Breanne dropped to her knees, lowered her head, and doggedly crawled on. Thunder boomed, shaking the fortress; lightning flashed outside, so close she thought at any moment the stones would come tumbling down about them. And still the wind came, howling, turbulent, and rife with horrible, fetid odors. Somehow, though, she reached the tub, found the bracelets, and slipped them on.

Instantly the wind died, the smells subsided. Grasping the bed sheet about her, Breanne staggered to her feet and stumbled over to the door. She shoved it closed and bolted it shut. The battle was Aidan and Morloch's. She intended to keep it that way. Then, though terrified at what she might find, she turned to the two men.

Again and again Aidan flung the full force of his eye against his father. Though Morloch deflected each attack, it was evident he was weakening. Aidan sensed the wavering in his father's defenses and seized the opportunity. He leaped forward, his hands, then arms, then body at last piercing the magical barrier. His fingers found Morloch's neck, encircled it, and began to throttle the life from him.

The necromancer fought wildly. Before Aidan's eyes, he changed to a slavering tiger, then a demon, then to an increasingly more horrible creature as each attempt to frighten his son failed. The efforts only angered Aidan further, until he was consumed by a single-minded, murderous bloodlust.

Breanne watched in terror as the two men grappled on the floor. Nausea churned in the pit of her stomach at the realization of how close she'd come to losing her body—and soul—to Morloch. If Aidan hadn't reached her when he had . . .

With a superhuman effort, she flung the consideration aside. What mattered now was Aidan and that he survive the death battle with his father. If there were but some way to help him . . .

As if drawn to it, her gaze found Aidan's sword across the room, its sheath and sword belt slung over the top of a high-backed chair. Caerlin. Could she at last free him to join Aidan in the fight against Morloch? She must. There might never be another chance.

Breanne shot the men fighting on the floor one quick glance. Aidan still had his hands about Morloch's neck and was choking the life from him. Oddly, though, no sign of fear twisted the necromancer's face.

Then she was racing across the room. Her hands settled about the bejeweled hilt, calling to the imprisoned mage even as she pulled the weapon from its sheath. *Caerlin,* Breanne cried. *Help us; help Aidan! Come out of the sword, I beg of you!*

Nay, child, he whispered instead. *My time has yet to come. This battle is Aidan's and yours.*

A horrified disbelief filled her. *What? You promised you'd aid us when we reached Morloch. We cannot battle him alone!*

This battle you can and must fight alone. 'Tis the battle for Aidan's soul. I can do naught.

Confusion welled to mix with Breanne's growing sense of betrayal. *I don't understand. Caerlin, don't do this to us!*

Look at him, child, the mage urged softly. *See his soul-stealing rage. Morloch fosters it. 'Tis his last trap, the final ploy to win his son to him. You must stop it.*

But how? Breanne's heart twisted within her. *I have no skills to stop Morloch. He is too powerful for me.*

Go to Aidan, child. Call him back from the savagery that will tear out his heart and soul. 'Tis why you've always been destined for him. If the love you share is strong enough, you will prevail.

She wheeled around, her heart hammering beneath her breast, her hands clammy, her breath coming in great gulps. Terror pounded through her—a mind- and body-numbing fear that now, in the moment when Aidan needed her most, she'd be unequal to the task. Wide, frightened eyes took in the scene before her, of two men battling to the death, locked in a combat of souls as much as bodies.

Breanne forced herself to run back across the room and kneel beside them, Morloch flat on the floor, pinned beneath Aidan's greater weight and strength. She extended a hand toward Aidan, grasping him by the shoulder.

"Stop it!" she cried, giving him a small shake. "You're killing him, Aidan. Stop it before 'tis too late!"

His muscles flexed and bunched beneath her hand, his face contorted in a rage both focused and uncaring. He didn't appear to hear her. Breanne felt the power, the strength, the essence that was Aidan flow out of him into Morloch. And still he battled on.

She dared a quick glance down at the necromancer. Though his face was mottled a deep red, he fought only to prevent his air from completely being cut off. Instead, his efforts seemed directed to urging his son on in his murderous attack while a triumphant light gleamed in his eyes.

He wants Aidan to attempt to kill him, and will goad him on until Aidan goes mad with the effort.

At the realization, a white-hot rage filled Breanne. "Nay!" she screamed. "You won't win. I won't let you have him!"

She flung her arms about Aidan and pulled with all her might. "Stop it! Listen to me, Aidan. 'Tis Breanne. Let . . . go . . . of Morloch!"

He was a man made of stone, immovable, implacable, intent on his mission—the murder of his father. Panic surged through her. If she didn't reach him, and soon . . .

Behind her, a pounding began on the door. Horrendous snarls, earsplitting shrieks interspersed with a scrabbling, clawing of nails upon wood and incessant, eerie chittering sounds. The hair rose on the back of Breanne's neck. Morloch had summoned his horrible creatures. If they should get in before she could stop Aidan . . .

They'd come right for her, that she well knew. 'Twould be what Morloch intended, to draw her away, to silence her before she ruined everything. She must reach Aidan now . . . while there was still time.

"Aidan," Breanne sobbed, her words pouring forth in anguished little gasps. "Don't . . . do . . . this! Come back to me. Come back. I love you. Don't leave me." She hugged him tightly, attempting to draw the madness from him. "You promised always to be with me, take care of me. Would you break that vow?"

A violent shudder coursed through him, then another and another, until he was racked with the fierce spasms. His grip about Morloch's throat loosened slightly, enough for the necromancer to catch his breath and speak.

"Fool! Coward!" he taunted. "Are you so weak that you permit a woman to lead you? Even I wouldn't allow your mother to change my destiny. I, instead, changed *her* destiny—and shall to her dying day. As I soon will yours, and that of the slut you call a wife."

Morloch saw the rage flare anew in his son's eyes and pressed his advantage. "Aye, a slut she is. Do you truly imagine she didn't know who I was? That she didn't willingly, nay, eagerly, spread her legs to one who possessed the true power? The bitch is like all the rest. Like all women, even your beloved mother! Heartless, selfish, deceiving."

"Liar!" Aidan snarled. His grip tightened once more about Morloch's throat. Relentlessly, he choked the air from his opponent's body. " 'Tis you who are the deceiver. There's naught else left you. Not a shred of human decency or affection remains in that twisted piece of flesh you call a heart!"

The necromancer only smirked and, with a toss of his head, magically flung Breanne off Aidan. She slid across the floor to slam into the wall, the force of impact knocking the wind from her. Everything grayed; bright lights whirled before her eyes.

With a desperate shake of her head, Breanne tossed aside the dizzying fog that threatened to engulf her. She saw Aidan, livid with rage, throttling and pounding his father's skull into the stone floor. She saw Morloch turn red, then purple. His eyes bulged, then rolled back in his head. And still Aidan persisted, grinding his hands into the column of flesh and blood vessels and windpipe. Grinding, twisting, choking, until the man beneath him finally went limp.

"Aidan! Nay!" Summoning all her strength, Breanne climbed to her feet and staggered back over to the two men.

From a distance, her panicked cry pierced the heated mists of Aidan's fury. With a reluctance that was all but a physical pain, he turned toward Breanne, bewilderment wreathing his features. Tear-filled blue eyes gazed back at him.

"Nay," Breanne whispered. "Don't let him do it, Aidan. Don't surrender your soul. 'Tis the last and greatest advantage he needs." Her fingers entwined in his, and she gently pried his hands free of Morloch's neck. The necromancer lay there, all but unconscious, but still quite alive.

Breanne sighed in relief. Climbing to her feet, she pulled Aidan up with her. He blanched, swayed, and if not for her quick support, would have fallen. His head lowered to rest upon her shoulder.

"B-by the Holy Ones!" he groaned. "Why did you stop me, lass? A moment more and I'd have killed him. 'Twould have all been over."

"Aye," she murmured, stroking his hair to soothe him. " 'Twould have been over, but only for you. He'd have had your soul, my love. He could only win it from you in your loss of control and mindless rage. Even the death of Morloch isn't worth that, as if," she muttered bitterly, "you could've ever killed him. Once he'd won your soul you'd have lost your power over him."

Aidan inhaled a shuddering breath. "Aye, you're most likely right. I was mistaken to have thought I could vanquish him as easily as I did. 'Twas but a trap and, fool that I was, I fell right into it."

"You weren't a fool, my love. He betrayed you." She cupped his face between her hands and lifted his head. "Now, no more of it. 'Tis time to use Caerlin to destroy Morloch once and for all. Now, while he is still weakened."

Breanne released him and ran for the sword. The fortress was suddenly strangely quiet, the cacophony outside the door stilled, the sounds of battle within now over. She grasped the sword and turned, just in time to see Morloch rising to his feet in an effortless flow of magical powers.

"Aidan!" she screamed and lifted the sword.

Aidan saw the direction of her gaze and wheeled around. Like some huge, black bird of prey, Morloch loomed over him, a strange, mesmerizing light glittering in his amber eyes. Aidan stared up at him.

"Never," the necromancer snarled. "Never will I let you best me. You are mine, have always been. Your heart, your soul, your body— all have been promised to the Demon. And what you will not give willingly, I will take!"

As he finished speaking, the room was encompassed by a shrieking and howling like none heard before. The shutters banged, the door was struck so hard from without it began to groan and shake. A bright, blinding light exploded around them.

Aidan staggered backward until he reached Breanne. "The sword!" he cried. "Call forth the powers of the sword before 'tis too late!"

They stood, arm to arm, leg to leg, against the onslaught of Morloch's mind-numbing, soul-searing powers. Yet even their love, combined with runic bracelets and Evil Eye, could barely withstand the horrible intensity of Demon-strengthened magic. Panic spiraled within Breanne, snatched hold of her heart, and squeezed the blood from it.

Caerlin, she called, nearly choking on her terror. *'tis time now, or 'twill never be again!*

Aye, 'tis indeed time, the mage replied. *Stand fast, don't let go of the sword no matter what happens, and let my power flow through you.*

A whirling maelstrom engulfed them. Blackness enshrouded Breanne and the breath was sucked from her lungs. She couldn't breathe, she couldn't think, she wanted to turn and run. Only the pressure of Aidan's strong body, touching hers, and the solid grip of the sword in her hands kept her linked to reality. Aidan. Caerlin. The quest.

She repeated the words over and over in her mind, until they became a litany, a fervent entreaty for succor, for sanity in a world gone insane. The darkness began to surge erratically, falter. A light pierced the blackness, and Breanne saw it came from the tip of her sword. Morloch saw it as well. With a bellow of rage, he flung it aside, but it returned time and again. He took a step back and, for the first time, Breanne saw his fear.

"We have won, Aidan," she shouted above the din. "With Caerlin, we are strong enough to—"

The necromancer's face contorted in malevolent fury and, with a snarl, he made a sharp, slashing movement with his hand. In the next moment, Breanne found herself standing outside the fortress, sword in hand and bed sheet still wrapped around her. She glanced around wildly to find Aidan, equally confused, beside her.

He swallowed a savage curse and strode up to pound upon the now closed fortress gate. "By the Mother!" he roared. "Spineless coward, let us in!"

Breanne hurried over. "Aidan, stop it. Morloch's no fool. He's cast us out because he knew we would've soon vanquished him. He'll not let us near him again until he's ready."

Aidan turned to her, anguish twisting his features. "And by then we may have lost our advantage. This might have been the only chance we will ever have to defeat him!" He glanced down at Baldor's sword. "Call on your mage. Demand he help get us back into the fortress. We must attack Morloch now!"

She shook her head. "Aidan, I don't think—"

"Do it, Breanne!" He grabbed her by the arm. "I fear for Anacreon, for us, if we don't see this through here and now. Though, united, we may be too strong to conquer, Morloch knows there are always other ways to undermine us. Anacreon, the queen, your family . . . all are prey to his evil plans. And if he destroys our land and people, what victory is left, though we still ultimately vanquish him?"

She stared up at him, wonder setting her eyes aglow. "You truly do care about Anacreon, don't you? You have reclaimed your birthright at last."

"Mayhap." Aidan's mouth quirked wryly. "And mayhap I just prefer not to give it up to Morloch." Once more, he motioned toward the sword. "Will you try now, or not?"

'Twill do no good, Caerlin's voice immediately filled Breanne's mind when she nodded and

closed her eyes. *My strength is gone and 'twon't return for some time to come. Leave now, before Morloch finds some way to detain us. His powers are even now being restored by the Demon, and when he's strong again, he'll come after you.*

Then we must await him, fight him again.

Nay, all of us are too weak from the recent battle. We need time to rest, to plan our attack anew.

And in the meanwhile, Breanne bitterly replied, *Morloch will turn his anger on Anacreon.*

Not if we reach it first. 'Tis only fitting that Morloch follow us to Anacreon. 'Tis where he first surrendered his soul to the Demon. 'Tis fitting, as well, that he lose his life there.

He'll not allow us to get to Anacreon, she protested as the frustration welled within. *We're on foot. He'll easily hunt us down on the way and attack us when we're most vulnerable.*

Aidan has other powers, though he has yet to recognize them, one of which is sufficient to cloak our presence from the necromancer. And, though my powers are greatly weakened, they are still sufficient to retrieve your mounts. Come. Point the sword at the fortress.

Skeptically Breanne did as told. Once more Baldor's sword began to vibrate; then a flash of light emanated from its tip. It pierced the fortress's shimmering door, forcing an opening in it. With a pounding of hooves and cloud of dust, Lucifer and Breanne's gelding galloped through.

As the gate resealed itself behind them, she walked over and resheathed the sword in the scabbard that hung from Lucifer's saddle. Then

Breanne turned to Aidan. "Caerlin's too weak to go against Morloch just now. He has done all he can in freeing our horses. 'Tis best we set out for Anacreon."

"And leave Morloch alive, with another chance at us when he chooses the time and place?" Aidan shook his head. "Nay. If you and the mage wish to turn and run, do so. But I can't leave until I've finished what I came to do."

"Whether you fight him here or elsewhere is no longer the issue," Breanne cried. "What matters is that we win! And, as hard as it still may be for you to accept, you need me and Caerlin to do that. 'Tisn't just your pride at stake here, Aidan. 'Tis the welfare of your land and people."

His eyes narrowed and he regarded her with a hard, angry gaze. "Once again, you ask me to believe totally in someone I cannot see."

"Rather, I ask you to believe and trust in me," Breanne softly corrected him. "Is it that hard, Aidan? Even now, after all we've been through, meant to each other?"

For a moment longer he regarded her in thoughtful, poignant silence. Then he sighed. "Come, lass," Aidan said, as he walked over to grab Lucifer's reins and swing up into the saddle. "We waste valuable time standing here arguing. Once again, you have given me no alternative but to do as you bid. And, as far as the depth of my trust in you goes, I'd wager what lies ahead will amply prove the truth of that, whether we win or lose."

Chapter Nineteen

Though Aidan willed a spell of unseeing, neither he nor Breanne had any indication that his powers were effective until they rode up the next morning on Red Nose. True to his word, the dwarf had waited for them, his small camp hidden from view beneath a low overhang of rock that was bordered on three sides by huge boulders.

"What are you still doing here?" Aidan demanded irritably as he drew Lucifer to a halt to avoid trampling the unsuspecting dwarf.

Red Nose, his eyes still sleep-weighted, a pot in his hands, tumbled over backward in his surprise. Water sloshed over him, drenching his face and upper torso. He glanced around, terror wreathing his features.

"Wh-who goes there?" he squeaked. "Are ye hidden somewhere, or is this magic?"

" 'Tis magic," Aidan drawled. He released his hold on the spell. They flashed back into view.

The dwarf's eyes widened and he swallowed convulsively. "I-I had no idea ye could do that. Why didn't ye just cross our bridge that way? We would've never known."

"Because I didn't know I could do it then," Aidan growled. His gaze scanned the rocky terrain that jutted up all around them. "Speaking of your bridge, I doubt 'twill be safe to attempt a crossing of it. Morloch will soon be hot on our trail, and in a rather unfriendly mood. Is there another way through these mountains that bypasses the bridge?"

Red Nose gazed up at Breanne and Aidan and saw the truth written in their grim expressions. He climbed to his feet. "Yer mission wasn't successful, was it? Well, I'd wager ye were lucky enough just to get out alive." He paused to stroke his long beard thoughtfully. "Aye, there is another way, but the path leads *under* the mountains, and 'tis quite dangerous. The tunnels are ancient, carved out of the mountains' very substance. None but the dwarves know o' them."

"Then we are most fortunate that you chose to wait for us," Breanne said, smiling down at him.

At the warm look she sent him, Red Nose's heart swelled within his breast. By the ax of the dwarf god Thoran, she was the most kind and beautiful lady he'd ever known!

He managed a lopsided smile of his own. "Aye, lady. Something told me ye'd need me again."

Aidan gave a snort of disgust. "Believe that if you want. In the meanwhile, I'd suggest you lead us to these tunnels forthwith. The more distance we put between us and Morloch, the better. The shelter of the mountains might lessen his chances of finding us too quickly."

"As ye wish." The dwarf ambled over to his little cave and quickly stuffed his belongings into his pack. Then he mounted his sturdy little pony. "Follow me."

The going was arduous to the entrance of the ancient tunnels. Red Nose pointed it out from its camouflage of shadows between a stand of monolithic stones, high up near the summit of one of the tallest mountains. The wind blew down in powerful, howling bursts, impeding their progress up an already difficult incline. The trail was of unstable shale and the horses frequently slid or stumbled as they picked their careful way. At last the party reached the tunnels.

Red Nose gestured to the cave's opening. "There are three routes within. One leads through the mountains to the northern lands, little inhabited and long uncharted. Another takes ye to the sea."

"And the other?" Aidan prodded. "Where will that one take us?"

" 'Twill lead to Anacreon."

Breanne shifted in her saddle, glancing back at Aidan. "That's the one we want, isn't it?"

A dark, shuttered expression settled over his features. "Do I have much choice? You and Caerlin seem to have made all the decisions for me."

"And 'tis a good thing for you that we have!" Breanne snapped, her patience at an end with his sullen, tight-lipped attitude since they'd left Morloch's fortress. "You're in no condition to make any kind of reasonable decision. Look at yourself, Aidan. You're still under his influence, whether you care to admit it or not. And I demand an equal chance—and the necessary time—to turn you back to a better way."

Aidan shot her a startled glance and his lips twitched with the faintest hint of laughter. Breanne breathed a silent prayer of thanks. She was beginning to win him over.

"You're an impertinent little wench," he chuckled, the dark look fading from his eyes. "I vow I've never been so frequently or thoroughly insulted until I met you. Is this what fate has in store for me, being married to you?"

"Aye," she replied stoutly, "but only when you insist on making pigheaded decisions. 'Tis my duty as your wife to apprise you of your errors."

He cocked his head in mock speculation, a devilish look gleaming in his amber eyes. "Strange, but I don't recall such wording in our wedding—"

"Er, pardon, if ye will."

A harsh throat-clearing accompanied the dwarf's interruption. Two pairs of eyes turned to Red Nose.

"Am I correct in assuming ye'll both be taking the path to Anacreon?"

"Aye." Aidan eyed Breanne a moment more, then motioned him forward. "Lead on, dwarf."

The clouds overhead, churning ominously, went suddenly black. As the masses of moisture-laden air slammed together, lightning flashed from one cloud to another. Thunder exploded. The newborn day grew dark and strangely foreboding.

Breanne and Aidan exchanged glances, their thoughts identical. Morloch's powers had been restored.

"Now, dwarf," Aidan rasped. "Cloaking powers or no, if we linger here much longer 'twill be over for all of us."

Red Nose spared one look at the lowering sky and spurred his pony forward. Down the steep grade he went, Aidan and Breanne following closely in his wake, straight for the gaping mouth of the cave. Behind them the weather, whipped to a frenzy, released a torrent of sleet and hail. Frigid blasts of rain and a barrage of painful ice balls pelted the earth. Then they were inside the mountain, drawing sharply to a halt in the pitch-blackness that loomed ahead.

The dwarf pulled a small brand from his pack, then his tinderbox. In but a few moments he had a torch flaming brightly in his hand. He lifted it high overhead, glanced back at his two compatriots, and grinned. "Are ye ready for the wildest ride o' yer life?"

Aidan shot a quick look over his shoulder. The storm was gaining in ferocity—and heading straight toward them. "Naught you have in mind can match what is coming for us. Let's go—and now!"

Red Nose's gaze caught what loomed behind

Aidan. He blanched. Without another word, the dwarf signaled his pony forward.

They rode as if all the legions of the damned were behind them. A crazed howling filled the tunnel. Wind shuddered past, gaining in strength with each terror-struck moment, encompassing them in a foul, choking stench. The horses snorted, shook their heads, and began to fight the bit. Only determined hands and relentless legs kept the animals galloping forward.

Suddenly, Red Nose swung his pony over to the far side of the tunnel and waved them ahead with his torch. Breanne drew even with him.

"Go on!" he shouted. "I must close the tunnel against Morloch!"

"But how?" Breanne cried. "You've no powers—"

"I created the tunnels." The dwarf's voice rose above the shrill cacophony rearward. "They are known only to dwarves—not because we hewed them from the mountain many centuries ago, but because we possess the power to create and destroy them at will. Just like my brother and I created and destroyed the bridge."

Sudden realization filled her. "Then you meant to help us all along . . ."

"Aye." He flashed her a quick grin. "Yer hair bought more then ye thought, didn't it?"

Breanne nodded, blinking back a hot rush of tears. Before she could say more, Red Nose shoved the torch at her, then used his leather whip across her mount's flanks to send the animal leaping ahead. He glanced back at Aidan.

The two men's gazes locked for a fleeting instant. "Go," the dwarf cried. " 'Tis yer destiny not to meet yer father here!"

With a great lunge forward, Lucifer passed the pony and barreled down the narrow, twisting tunnel. Behind them the shrieking wind grew to a deafening roar. Then, with a violent burst of sound, the tunnel vibrated and shook. Rocks fell around them.

Breanne shot Aidan an anxious glance.

"Ride on!" he shouted. "Ride on, and don't look back!"

The ground beneath them heaved. A cloud of dust exploded, then surged forward to engulf them in a choking, blinding maelstrom. Breanne bent low on her horse, closed her eyes, and pressed her mouth to the animal's sweating, heaving neck—and rode on.

Then they were outside, the air suddenly fresh and sweet. Warmth and sunlight bathed them once more. Breanne straightened in the saddle, reined in her mare, and turned. Aidan drew up at her side.

Behind them, where once the mouth of a tunnel had been, the face of the mountain was now unblemished and whole. They exchanged an anguished glance, then nudged their horses on. The dwarf, an unexpected ally in the battle against Morloch, had met his own destiny— battling to save them.

"They won't want me," Aidan observed grimly as he and Breanne reined in their horses at the forest's edge. Below them the pastoral view of Anacreon's farmlands, undulating in gentle dips and swells, was washed in gilded splendor by the fading light of the dying sun. The river wound its quiet way through the sleepy countryside, its shimmering water glinting like molten gold.

The scene reminded Aidan of that day, now seemingly so long ago, when he'd last returned. The day he'd first met Breanne. The day he'd begun to discern his true destiny, so carefully orchestrated by others, each for their own motives. Aye, it seemed so long ago, and much had happened, much had changed, and yet, oddly enough, much still remained the same.

"They won't want me, no matter how badly Morloch threatens them," he repeated, turning to Breanne. "In their mind, accepting me is but trading one evil for another."

"You can't be sure of that. Desperate times force people to examine things in different ways." Breanne forced a wan little smile. "And sometimes they discover treasures they would have never found otherwise."

Aidan reached over and squeezed her hand. " 'Tis enough if Morloch is defeated. Anacreon can choose to accept me or not. I've all the treasure I could ever hope for in you."

Fresh color bloomed in her cheeks, and her eyes glowed with joy. "As I have found in you, my love." Breanne's gaze turned back to scan the summer-sleepy land. " 'Tis so quiet, so peaceful. 'Tis hard to believe Morloch's hand lies heavy here."

"But you have seen the undead creatures roaming the land. You can feel Morloch's presence as strongly as I, can't you, lass?"

"Aye," Breanne muttered, her voice taking on a tight edge, "that I can. He is here, somewhere, awaiting us."

"But awaiting what?" Aidan's brow furrowed in puzzlement. "For me to call upon him?"

"Aidan—" Breanne jerked back, fear, stark and vivid, glittering in her eyes.

"Whether I choose to fight him in his own lands or in mine, it cannot be over until one or both of us is dead." His keen eyes knifed into hers. "You know that as well as I."

"When the time comes, I must be there. I won't let you face him alone."

His firm lips twitched in amusement. "Could I stop you, even if I wished it otherwise?"

"No, m'lord. You couldn't."

Grim determination darkened his features and he turned his gaze back to the land. "Then let us be gone from here. Anacreon languishes the longer we tarry. Before we turn to the necromancer, we must first strengthen the people and aid them in the fight against Morloch's creatures."

Breanne nudged her mare forward. "Aye," she muttered, "that we must, m'lord. But if Morloch wins in the end, 'twon't matter how well they've learned to battle the undead."

A monumental task, Lucifer added as he stepped out alongside the gelding. *As monumental as the defeat of a necromancer.*

Aidan tensed. *Indeed? And do you seriously imagine I've any hope of prevailing against Morloch?*

Then why go against him? Why not turn tail and ride away?

Amber eyes swung to the woman who rode beside him. *You know the answer as well as I, Lucifer. 'Tis all I've left to give her.*

"He is dead, Aidan." Queen Eislin's clear, strong voice cut through the muffled sobbing from her maidservants across the room. "Your father is dead."

Anger tautened Aidan's features, hardened his powerful body. "He was never my father. You know that as well as I."

"Aidan, don't," Breanne pleaded.

He shot her an anguished glance, inhaled a ragged breath, then willed himself to relax. "Marus," he said in a more neutral tone. "How did he die?"

A haunted look crept into his mother's eyes. " 'Twas but a night ago. Marus couldn't sleep, so he left our bed and went to stand on the balcony. He must have remained there for a long while, as I finally drifted back off to sleep. Then a terrible cry woke me. I heard the sounds of struggle, dreadful animal snarls, and then one final cry."

Eislin paused, blinking back fresh tears, her features stretched tight with her horror. "I forced myself from my bed, made my way across the room, my fear giving me strength. I found Marus lying there on the balcony, his face . . ." Her voice faded at the memory of what she'd seen. "His face had been clawed into raw meat; his throat had been ripped out!"

The queen buried her face in her hands. "And the blood! Ah, Aidan, there was blood everywhere!"

"And you think Morloch was responsible?" her son demanded.

" 'Twas the work of some undead creature. Who else could have sent him?"

"Few others," he muttered grimly. "Well, as hard as it may be to hear, I cannot say I mourn his passing. He never treated me as his son, or showed much kindness or caring."

"Aidan," Breanne protested, glancing up at him from her seat beside the queen's bed. " 'Tisn't necessary to be so harsh. No matter how you felt about the prince consort, he was your mother's husband." She patted Eislin's hand comfortingly.

The queen smiled wanly at Breanne, then turned her gaze back up to her son. Her eyes, red-rimmed and swollen, widened. "I . . ." She sighed. " 'Tis true enough, your relationship with Marus, but he did try to love you. He did try to accept you as his."

"But he never could."

The queen's head lowered, her gaze moving to stare down at the slender hands clenched in her lap. "Nay, he never could. He imagined I never stopped loving Morloch, always suspected I'd gone to him willingly that night he fathered you."

"And did you?"

At the flat, hard edge to her son's voice, Eislin's eyes lifted. "I never realized, until your birthing day, that the dream I'd had the night before Marus and I wed had been more than just that. I imagined 'twas but the excitement of my impending marriage that had stimulated the dream of my making love to him." Her brow furrowed. "But even then, each time I recalled it, there had always been something strange about Marus, something different. And when you were born, and I looked upon your black hair and amber eyes, I finally knew. Knew even before Morloch returned to claim you as his own."

"Why didn't you tell me?" Aidan's eyes burned clear to his mother's soul. "Why did you let me grow up thinking Marus was my father, a father who could barely hide his disgust for me? Do you know how it made me feel? I'd already been cursed by Morloch, and then to have the man I thought my father reject me!"

Something flared in Eislin's eyes, a surge of regret, of shame, yet love flickered there as well. "I thought it best. I thought Marus would eventually come to accept you. And what would it have done to you then, to know you were the spawn of a necromancer? I did the best I could, Aidan, and awaited the day when there'd be other choices."

The expression in Aidan's eyes went bleak. The rigid tautness ebbed from his big body. "Morloch, it seems, permitted few of us choices." He shoved an unsteady hand through his hair. "By the Holy Ones, how can one man hate so deeply and for so long?"

"He loved his magic and the power it gave him too much," Eislin replied softly. "He loved it more than life and honor, and sold his soul to the Demon to gain even more. I mourn the man he used to be, but 'twas his choice." Her gaze locked with Aidan's. "Just as 'tis your choice. Never forget that, my son."

His mouth twitched in annoyance. "And how

would that be possible? Both you and Breanne never spare an opportunity to remind me of it." He shook his head and sighed. "'Tisn't as easy as you make it out to be. Choice there always is, but 'tis hard to ignore the calling of one's blood."

"Your blood is as much the queen's as Morloch's!" Breanne interjected hotly.

Aidan wheeled around. "You tell me naught I don't already know!"

Breanne flinched at the savagery in his words and demeanor, though she knew it was nothing more than the draw of Morloch's enchantments once more weighing on Aidan's heart and mind. The taut look, the fever burning in his eyes that had begun again as soon as they were free of Morloch's fortress had only grown as the days passed. And would continue to grow and eat at Aidan until he once more faced the necromancer.

She summoned all her courage and determination, wrapping it about her like a cloak. "These are hard times, Aidan. Much is required of you, more than any one man should have to bear. I'd fail you if I wasn't there when you needed me most."

His mouth tilted upward in rueful acknowledgment as the tension once more eased from his body. "I know that, lass. And you are right to remind me. Sometimes it gets so very hard to battle on. 'Twould be simpler to acquiesce to Morloch's desires."

"Aye, m'lord. Simpler, easier, but wrong."

He turned back to his mother. "Whatever has happened in the past, has happened and cannot be called back. We must now look to the future—and the defeat of Morloch."

The haunted expression returned to Eislin's face. "Does that mean you forgive what happened as well? Though Marus cannot benefit from that forgiveness, your brother still can."

Aidan gave a disparaging laugh. "Dragan? I hardly think he'd care. I'm still a threat to him and his ambition to gain the throne."

"I fear for Dragan's life, Aidan," the queen hastened to say. "Morloch means to destroy him just as surely as he did Marus." She reached out to him. "I beg of you. Don't let Morloch kill your brother!"

He stepped close and took her hand, engulfing the pale, translucent flesh within the sun-bronzed expanse of his own hand. "And since when does my brother admit need for my aid?"

"Marus's death unnerved even him. He cowers in his bedchamber, hiding in the comfort of Sirilla's arms, and refuses to leave. I have no man left to gather the people, to lead them in these most difficult of times." The queen gazed up at her son. "You are our last hope."

Aidan gave a snort of derision. "The Demon Prince is now the last hope of Anacreon? How ironic! The man all despised and reviled, the one they tried to kill, is now their only hope. 'Twould serve them justly if I turned my back and rode away."

Delicate auburn brows lifted in challenge. "But you won't. You are still too much my son to repudiate your people's need."

His mouth twisted in a bitter grimace. "Aye, for what 'tis worth, I am." He released his mother's hand and stepped back. "But if I'm to win the people to me, I'll need my family's help."

She smiled up through a haze of tears. "You have it."

"Aye, yours," Aidan agreed grimly, "but I need Dragan's as well." He glanced down at Breanne. "Come, lady. We've work to do."

"What first, m'lord?" she said, rising to her feet.

"We go to my brother's bedchamber. He'll rise above his fears and selfish needs and aid us, or he won't need to wait for Morloch's wrath to descend on him. I'll personally see to it that he suffers a quicker and far more painful end."

The maidservant peered timidly around the door. At sight of Aidan, she blanched. "A-aye, m'lord?"

"Is my brother within?" Aidan demanded without preamble.

"A-aye, m'lord, but he doesn't wish to be disturbed."

"And I'd suggest you open the door or I'll break it down," Aidan growled. "He *will* see me."

"But, m'lord—"

"Who is it, Mara?" a soft voice came from behind the frightened maid.

The woman turned from the door. " 'Tis your husband's brother, m'lady. He wishes to speak with—"

The door opened fully and Sirilla stood there, delight shining in her eyes. "Welcome, m'lord." She rendered him a deep curtsy. "It has been so long, and you couldn't have come at a more propitious time."

Her glance strayed to Breanne. "Ah, Bree, thank the Holy Ones you've returned! I've thought about and prayed for you many times in the past weeks." Sirilla grabbed her hand and pulled her into the room. "Come. Come. Don't stand out there like two strangers."

She waved Aidan in and shut the door.

"Where's Dragan?"

Sirilla shot him a sharp, anguished glance. "You've heard it all, have you? About Marus and what it did to Dragan?"

Aidan nodded. "Aye. But he can cower in here no longer. If we're to prevail against Morloch and his minions, I'll need use of Dragan's influence over the people." His mouth twisted wryly. "They'll hardly listen to me."

For a long moment more, Sirilla eyed him, then sighed. "What can I do to help?"

"Send your maid away. What I have to say and do may not be fit for a servant's notice. Then give me time alone with Dragan."

Sirilla hesitated. "He doesn't allow me out of his sight."

"Then stay, but across the room, with Breanne."

"As you wish, m'lord." She motioned her maid out of the room, then gathered her skirts and headed across her bedchamber.

They followed her over to a dimly lit alcove. It was furnished with two comfortable chairs and a small, round table set with a silver flask and several cups. A man sat curled up in one of the chairs, his head tucked into the cushioned backrest, dozing. Sirilla moved quietly over and laid a gentle hand on his shoulder.

"Dragan? Wake up, beloved. Your brother is here and wishes to speak with you."

Dragan woke with a start, his eyes as bloodshot and swollen as the queen's had been. "Whwhat? Aidan's here, you say?"

"Aye, beloved."

Wildly, her husband glanced around and found his brother. His eyes widened. "P-pour me a cup of wine," he cried, his voice hoarse and strained.

Sirilla did as requested, then set the cup in Dragan's hand and curled his fingers around it. "Drink, beloved."

Dragan emptied his cup in one gulp, wiping away the excess that escaped to trickle down his chin. Then, squaring his shoulders, he met his brother's steely gaze.

"So, you're back again, are you? Heard about the latest visit of Morloch's henchmen and come to gloat? Or mayhap you've returned to finish the deed yourself?" Dragan indicated himself with a defiant flourish. "Have at it, then. Get it over with."

Aidan's lip curled in disgust. Morloch's spell, so easily recognized now that Aidan's powers were enhanced, still sat heavily on his brother. This time, however, with the recognition, came the ability to eradicate the effects of the spell. Aidan quickly did so.

"And what manner of man are you, brother," he challenged then, his words harsh in light of his new knowledge of what had happened to Dragan, but necessary, nonetheless, "to so meekly sit here and await your death? I'd thought better of your courage, no matter how arrogant and self-serving you'd become."

Tears filled Dragan's eyes, eyes that now saw things in a strangely different light. "There's naught that can be done against a necromancer. You are cruel to mock my courage!"

"And have you forgotten that I'm the Demon's spawn?" Aidan extended his hand. "Rise, if you can, before you surrender our family and kingdom. Help me, brother. I can't do it without you."

The years of jealousy, of determined intent to see his uncommonly gifted brother destroyed, flashed before Dragan. To now accept his aid, restore him to his rightful position so long and avidly coveted, demanded more than he was capable of giving. His eyes narrowed and his chin rose in defiant dismissal.

Then his glance met that of Sirilla, full of entreaty and love—a love that had always been there for him in spite of the man he'd become. His former existence, filled with years of deepening corruption and despair, faded in light of the enormity of their peril. Dragan knew, in that instant of soul-shattering clarity, that he must fight—for himself, for his wife, for his lands and family. The past, and its consequences, could be dealt with later.

Later, if they survived.

He clasped Aidan's hand and climbed to his feet. "What do you need of me?"

Chapter Twenty

"M'lord?"

Aidan looked up from the plans he and Dragan were studying. They'd pored over them long and hard for the past several hours since the supper meal, meticulously eliminating every possible source of entry by Morloch's summoned creatures. His glance met that of the servant. "Aye?"

"The monk wishes for you to join him and the Lady Breanne in the solar."

Aidan sighed and rolled up the parchment scroll. Olenus had suddenly appeared a day after his and Breanne's arrival, claiming he was but awaiting their return to Anacreon to join forces. With his help, they'd devised several schemes to help fortify the castle.

The guards were increased and each supplied with a set of runic bracelets to warn against the enemies' magical assault. Then Olenus had cast a mystic circle about the fortress's outer perimeter to keep out Morloch's minions. Yet there now seemed even more left to do.

Aidan handed Dragan the scroll. "Can you see to the safeguarding of the well and food supplies to prevent their being tampered with? Though it grows late and I know you must be as weary as I, it appears the last of the necessary precautions we must make. Soon, the only being left who'll possess sufficient power to torment us will be the necromancer himself."

Dragan grimaced. "A small consolation, to be sure."

"Nay, brother, 'tis no consolation at all," Aidan corrected him grimly. "Morloch will have to be faced sooner or later. But I'd prefer to do it on friendly grounds."

"Aye, friendly at last." Dragan grinned. " 'Tis amazing how quickly the people accepted you, once they realized you were the only one with sufficient power to withstand the necromancer."

Amusement tugged the corner of Aidan's mouth. "Indeed? And did that revelation strike them before or after you stood up for me, defying any to utter one word of dissent?"

Dragan shrugged. "I merely pointed out the obvious. They understood."

Aidan turned to go, when a hand stayed him. His brow cocked in inquiry, he glanced back at his brother.

"At first, I didn't agree to aid you because of any brotherly feelings," Dragan said. "I did it for Sirilla and Anacreon, and because there was no other choice. I liked it not, nonetheless. Your return threatened my ascent to the throne, and I knew, as well, you might never forgive me for my active participation in the past in seeking out your death."

"And Breanne's, when you summoned your witch lover to kill her?"

Dragan flushed. "Aye. I don't know why I listened to her . . . but I did."

"I'd wager she was an underling of Morloch. I'd wager he knew, even then, the threat Breanne posed to his plans for me."

"Mayhap. Do you think you, or she, can ever forgive me?"

Momentarily, Aidan considered his brother's question. " 'Tis possible. 'Twill all depend on your future treatment of us—and Sirilla."

"Sirilla? What has she to do . . . ?" Dragan's voice faded. Once more, he flushed. "Ah, aye, I've much mending to do there, too." He lowered his head and massaged his temples. "By the Holy Ones, Aidan, what happened to me? Why did I treat those who loved me most so abominably?"

" 'Twas a spell. Morloch meant to have his revenge against the entire family. We were all pawns of some sort."

Dragan glanced up. "Yet the one he meant to win over to his side, by turning his family and people against him, is now the only one who can save us from him."

"Aye, so 'twould seem, if such a feat is even possible."

His brother clasped him on the shoulder. "It has to be. There's no other hope."

A haunted look slashed across Aidan's face, then was gone. "I must be going. Olenus awaits."

"Ah, aye, so he does." Dragan released him and stepped back. He waved the scroll in the air. "And I have my own duties to attend to."

Aidan turned once more and exited the room. *No other hope.* Dragan's words echoed repeatedly in his mind as he made his way through the castle to meet with the monk. 'Twas a sad day indeed when the lives and welfare of an entire kingdom rested on his inadequate shoulders. Though the responsibility was a sacred calling of his royal house, Aidan had never envisioned he'd be asked to fight a necromancer, and with only the uncertain powers of his own, poorly understood magic.

Ah, if only it had been a battle to the death with sword and shield, he on Lucifer's broad back, his opponent equally matched! That he'd face eagerly, without qualm or trepidation. But to go up against Morloch again . . .

For the first time in his life, Aidan knew real fear. It pounded through his veins, turning his blood to ice. It emanated from the very sweat that suddenly sheened his forehead and dampened his palms, engulfing him in a rank odor of barely contained terror. His throat constricted, his breath became ragged.

Aidan wheeled around, striding back the way he'd come before halting, then turning again to the hallway that led to the solar. His fists clenched at his sides. He threw his head back, the muscles and tendons of his neck bulging with the effort not to roar out his fear and frustration.

They didn't understand. None of them did. All, even Breanne, saw him with such trusting, shining eyes of confidence—a confidence he had never, ever, felt when it came to his ability to overcome the seething core of evil within his heart. Too long had he faced it to imagine it something easily vanquished. 'Twas as much a part of him as 'twas of his father.

And Morloch knew him better than anyone—knew how to stir the evil within. Even Breanne's love might not be enough to save him this time.

Yet what else was there to do but face his father? He couldn't run from it the rest of his life, though he fled the fortress, fled Anacreon, and left them all to Morloch. He was trapped, as much by his destiny as by the responsibility he felt to his land and people.

By his love for them.

The realization, when it had first struck him as he stood on the castle parapets a few days ago, had startled Aidan. He gazed down at the people crowded in the outer bailey—the mothers clutching their children to their breasts, the soldiers working bravely to fortify the castle against attack, the farmers and shepherds and village laborers huddled together discussing how they'd fight to the death rather than surrender to Morloch. Aidan felt a strange, most foreign swell of emotions within his breast. A sense of kinship with his people, a fierce commitment to their welfare, and a pride that they now depended on him.

Breanne. He had her to thank for it all. She had wrought more than one miracle in the time since they'd first met. Not only had she taught him to trust again, to need and love her, but she'd opened him to others as well. To lose them all now, to be engulfed in the burgeoning morass of Morloch's powers, was the most exquisite of torments. He couldn't go back to the empty, bitter man he'd been before, yet that was exactly what his father wanted and needed.

A grim determination filled Aidan. He might ultimately lose to a necromancer's far stronger powers, but not without great cost. He had too much—everything—to lose. And Morloch, though he might win, would still have naught.

Once more Aidan's strong steps rang out on solid, stone floors. Once more his resolve grew. He had Breanne's love and, he fervently prayed, a mage in the stone to aid him. With their help, he could do naught else but the very best he could. Naught else, and hope, *pray,* 'twould be enough.

"Caerlin is all but impotent?" Aidan's initial surprise quickly turned to outrage. "Are you telling me, after all this time, that he has never possessed the power to leave the stone?"

Olenus scowled. "Nay, I didn't say quite that." He shot Breanne a look of entreaty. "Calm him, child. He is close to losing control."

She glared back at the monk with frigid wrath. "And why ask me for help? I've been as sorely used as Aidan."

Olenus pursed his lips in annoyance, then turned back to Aidan. "All I said," he began again with exaggerated patience, "was that Caerlin's powers have been severely weakened, drained bit by bit by the years of entrapment within the soulstone. He has barely enough strength to escape, if and when the opportunity arises. That is all I meant to say, that you cannot depend on him to defeat Morloch alone."

Aidan whirled to confront Breanne. "Is this true? Did the mage tell you this?"

Breanne nodded. "I wondered at his surprising weakness after Morloch expelled us from his fortress. So I finally asked him, just a short time ago."

"And he admitted to this? That he is too weak to ever leave the stone?"

"Aye."

"Then what good will he be when we battle Morloch again?" Aidan demanded. "What if he is unable to kill the necromancer?"

Olenus calmly returned his challenging stare. "Then he won't, will he?"

"I think," Aidan gritted, turning on him, "that this has all been a farce, a means to trick us into going up against hopeless odds."

The monk shrugged. "We all do what we can with what we have. Some have just been gifted with greater powers than others." His expression turned solemn. "But I swear to you, everything I've worked in your behalf has been done in good faith. I have as much to lose as you, m'lord. As does your mother, your brother, your people. As did that dwarf, who sacrificed his life to buy you time to escape Morloch's wrath."

Breanne stepped forward. "How did you know—?"

"It doesn't matter, lass." Aidan grasped her arm and pulled her gently back to his side. "Olenus has always known more than he cared to share with us. And 'tis hardly the true issue here, at any rate."

His expression sharpened to glittering awareness. "We've done everything we can to fortify the castle's defenses against Morloch's magic. But, with or without the mage's help, the issue of Morloch still remains."

A penetrating pair of dark eyes leveled on him. "He must die. There is no other option."

Aidan's jaw clenched. "You are but stating the obvious. Tell me, wise monk who holds the answers to everything. How do you plan to go about killing Morloch?"

Olenus's gaze never left Aidan's. " 'Tis your destiny, not mine, to find that answer."

Aidan went rigid. He studied Olenus for a long moment, then gave a bitter laugh. "Indeed? And have you any idea what happened the last time I fought Morloch? Is that what you see as my destiny, the loss of my life and soul in destroying the necromancer?"

"Nay," the monk stated flatly. "I see instead the *redemption* of your soul. I see the final liberation of your bitterness-fettered life. I see," he proclaimed, his glance briefly meeting Breanne's, " 'the House Laena rising from the ashes to free the heart of the one-eyed son.' "

"Yet you offer no help but brave words and a weakened, near useless old man trapped in a stone," Aidan snarled. "I see it now as it has always been. Ultimately Breanne and I are alone in this, to be sacrificed on the altar of Morloch's insatiable greed for power, and the cowardice of others."

He made a dismissing motion with his hand, his lip curled in contempt. "You may go, Olenus. We have no further need of you or your meaningless prophecies."

"And what will you do? How will you battle Morloch?"

Aidan's mouth went grim, his eyes deep pockets of shadow in the flickering firelight. "I don't know. Without the mage's powers to aid us, I honestly don't know."

She watched him undress for bed, the red-gold glow cast by the hearth fire dancing across the broad expanse of sinew-threaded shoulders and the whipcord muscles of his back. She watched Aidan lean over to lay his under tunic beside his thick warrior's belt, chain mail, and over tunic upon the intricately carved oaken chest. Already his tall black boots stood propped against the chest.

He straightened then and turned, his eyes lifting to meet Breanne's as his hands found the fastening of his breeches. An unexpectedly savage pain slashed through her. By the Mother, but he was so beautiful, so overpoweringly virile, so . . . magnificently male!

How she loved him. And she knew, whether he uttered the words or not, that he loved her, too. The miracle had happened. She had freed his heart from its fiercely guarded prison, had opened his eyes to the emptiness of a life not lived with and for others. Though Morloch's powers might ultimately be too great for any of them to overcome, he would never take that knowledge, that happiness—however fleeting it might have to be—from Aidan.

She stepped off the thick fur rug and padded over to him, her bare feet beneath the diaphanous swirl of her lacy bed gown suddenly cold on the stone floor. He watched her approach, his gaze narrowing, his eyes gleaming like some predatory animal. Even the smile that lifted his lips was feral . . . anticipatory.

Breanne felt no hesitation or fear, however. Aidan was hers this night, and she meant to ravish his body as avidly, as ardently, as he would hers.

Halting before him, she cocked her head, a smile on her lips. "You look all the fierce animal." Her hand lifted to smooth the furrows from his forehead, the careworn lines that feathered out from his eyes and carved deep grooves alongside his mouth.

Aidan caught her hand, stilling her ministrations. "I want you so badly that I ache with it. The blood pounds in my skull, courses through my body, when I look at you. So late have I come to know a woman such as you, and now there seems so little time left."

"We have this night, my love," she murmured. "And however many more Morloch deigns to give us."

"Nay, only tonight." He lifted her hand to his lips and softly, tenderly, kissed each fingertip. "On the morrow, I seek him out. I must. He is near and the waiting is grinding me down. And I must do it alone."

"Nay, Aidan!"

"You must stay here, lass." He captured her hand within the huge expanse of his own. "Without the mage's help, 'tis doubtful I'll win. And, whether I defeat Morloch or fail in the attempt, I'll not return. At best, in my dying, I'll take him with me. At worst, I'll lose my soul to him. Either way, I don't want you there to see it."

"But you need me—"

Aidan silenced her protest with a gently placed finger. "Do this for me. I can't bear the thought of you watching what will happen to me. Prove your love. Grant me this one boon."

Panic surged through Breanne. 'Twas too soon, his decision to fight Morloch on the morrow. She needed more time to convince him otherwise, to strengthen him against his father's evil onslaught, and to gather her own courage as well. She needed more time just to be with him. Mayhap 'twas greedy, but a few more days might be all she'd ever have of him.

He lowered her hand to rest upon the hair-whorled expanse of his chest. Beneath her fingers, Breanne felt his heart, thudding rhythmically, reassuringly strong and alive. Her fingers curled, clutching at hair and the smooth, bronzed flesh that lay beneath. By the Mother, did he seriously think she'd let him face Morloch alone?

"And what of your love for me?" He didn't understand that she needed to be there, to fight at his side. That there was always hope that together they might prevail. But if he went up against Morloch alone, there was no hope whatsoever.

"Aye," Breanne persisted, her ire rising the longer she thought about it. "What of your love for me? Is it so small, so suddenly possessive and narrow-minded that you now think to make decisions for me? Think again, m'lord. You forget all too easily what manner of woman you wed."

He arched a dark brow. "Do I now? And how is that possible, with a sharp-tongued wench like you constantly harping at me?"

"One can only wonder," Breanne muttered sarcastically. "Now, on the topic of your love for me . . ."

"Aye?"

Her lips pursed in annoyance. "Aye. Are you ever going to admit it, or not?"

"Is there need?" Aidan grinned. "You seem to have already decided that for me, too."

"Aidan, stop playing games! This is serious!"

He instantly sobered. "Aye, you're right, lass. 'Tis." His arm slipped around Breanne's waist and he drew her close. "Aye, I love you. For what value there may be in my loving you, I do."

Joy flared in Breanne's eyes. "Truly, Aidan? Truly?"

"Truly."

She smiled up at him, and then her gaze altered slightly, as if something had just struck her. She giggled.

"What, pray tell, is so amusing?" Aidan attempted a dark scowl, but failed miserably.

"Oh, naught, m'lord," Breanne said, but a teasing light still gleamed in her eyes. "I was but imagining Lucifer's reaction when I tell him I've finally won your heart."

Puzzlement creased his brow. "Lucifer? Can you now commune with him as well?"

"Like you do?" Breanne laughed. "Oh, nay, but he understands me, nonetheless. And I'd wager he'll find this recent bit of news most amusing."

"Will he now?"

Aidan's head lowered to brush his lips down the side of her face. Shivers of sheer delight rippled through Breanne.

"And what makes you think he hasn't known for a time now?" His voice lowered until it was little more than a deep rumble emanating from his chest. "Lucifer and I are very close, you know."

Outrage momentarily stole the breath from Breanne's lungs. "Y-you told y-your *horse* before you told me?" She twisted in his arms, but his suddenly iron clasp held her fast. "Why, you despicable, craven—"

"Pigheaded knave?" Aidan innocently supplied. Then, before she could gather her wits for another barrage, he swung Breanne up into his arms and strode to the bed. Only there, Aidan knew, locked in a passionate, loving embrace, would he soothe her ruffled, and most delightfully feminine, feathers. Aye, he'd kiss her anger away as he savored the pleasures of her delectable body—and bury the subject of his plans for the morrow, at least for a time longer, in the heated embrace of their young, ardent bodies.

*   *   *

Aidan awoke with a start. The room was black save for the glowing embers of a dying fire. He glanced around him, willing his pounding heart to still, his breathing to even. What had awakened him—and why?

He glanced around, recalling his old bedchamber in the royal castle, the white plastered walls lavishly covered with brilliant tapestries, the tall, dark chairs that stood before the hearth, the clothes chests, the lavishly strewn fur rugs that warmed the bitter feel of stone floors. And his bed, big, warm, and filled with a softly rounded, sleeping woman.

Breanne. Aidan turned, relieved that nothing was amiss with her. It hadn't been any danger to Breanne that had awakened him. But if not her, who?

He sat up and summoned his powers, searching the palace for anything that might be amiss. Through the darkened corridors his magic scanned, finding everyone sleeping soundly in their beds—everyone, that was, but the queen. Her fur coverlet was thrown aside, half on, half off the bed as if someone had left, or been pulled from it, in a hurry.

An uneasy premonition settled over Aidan. He viewed the entire room, sweeping it for sign of his mother. Only an aura of lingering magic pervaded her bedchamber, a magic laced with evil intent. He widened his own magic to encompass the entire castle. She was nowhere to be found.

With a savage curse, Aidan swung out of bed, strode over to where his clothes lay, and began to dress. His sudden movement woke Breanne. She levered to one elbow, blinking drowsily.

"Aidan. What's wrong?"

He shot her a quick glance, then resumed his hurried dressing. "The queen. She's gone and Morloch has taken her."

"Queen Eislin?" Breanne paused a moment to clear the last remnants of sleep from her mind. "But why? What would he now want with her?"

Aidan fastened his breeches, slipped his leather under tunic and chain mail over his head, then sat down on the chest to pull on his boots. "To bring the battle to a head on his own terms," he replied harshly. "Outside the castle, with my mother as the pawn between us. He knows I'll do anything to save her, even . . ."

At the bleak tone of defeat in his voice, Breanne sprang out of bed and ran to his side. "Nay!" she cried, kneeling before him, her hands curling about his wrists to stay his efforts with his boots. "Nay, Aidan. Not for her or me, or any single person, should you willingly surrender your soul to Morloch. The welfare of the realm depends on your defeat of him. No one person is worth more than the many!"

He met her gaze, his face a tortured mask. "Not even the queen, my own mother?"

"Nay, not even her."

With a low growl, he shook her hands away and rose. Aidan gazed down at Breanne, his eyes burning pools of agony. "And I say you are wrong. I will not desert her. I will not hide away within this castle while she remains out there somewhere, terrified and helpless, in Morloch's

422

evil clutches. I am weary of this battle between us. I will see it over and done with this very night!"

There was no stopping him, Breanne realized. She climbed to her feet. "Then give me a moment and I will go, too."

Aidan shook his head, a hard, set look to his features. "Nay. I told you last night, Breanne—"

"And how will you stop me? I can follow just as easily as go with you."

He grabbed her arm and jerked her to him. She slammed up against chain mail, which clinked faintly, then stilled.

"I haven't the time to waste on argument," Aidan warned. "You will obey me in this!"

"Will I now, husband?" A fierce defiance gleamed in Breanne's eyes. "Obey and watch you ride out alone, when I possess the ability to draw the mage from your sword? When I possess powers to influence you that even Morloch fears? When my fate—and my life—are as tightly entwined with Morloch's destruction as is yours?" She shook her head slowly. "I think not, Aidan."

He eyed her, frustration welling within. Curse her. Despite his wishes to the contrary, Breanne was determined to die at his side. And die she would, unless something miraculous happened. That much he was certain of.

But there was no time left to spare in argument. And Breanne was right. If he lost the battle against Morloch, there wasn't much left for her at any rate. The necromancer would turn on her instantly.

"Do as you wish," he muttered. "You will, despite anything I can say or do to prevent you. Just make it quick. I leave in five minutes' time."

Breanne lost not a moment more in comment. Swiftly, she stripped off her bed gown, donned her tunic and breeches, then dragged on her own boots. Aidan handed her her cloak, then swung his own black one over his dark clothing and grabbed up her sword.

"I doubt 'twill do much good against Morloch's magic, but if I can manage to weaken him enough, mayhap he'd be at least temporarily vulnerable to a judiciously placed sword thrust. And 'twill at least offer you some defense if his undead servants lurk about."

"Aye," she agreed, buckling the scabbard belt about her waist. "But I think the real weapon will be the sword of Baldor."

Aidan fastened his own sword in place, his mouth twisting in bitter irony. "Ah, yes, most certainly. If the mage ever deigns to leave his little sanctuary, and possesses any remaining power against Morloch." He strode over to the door and opened it, motioning her out. "I, however, doubt that will ever come to pass. I think 'tis wiser to rely on what we can be certain of."

Breanne paused in the open doorway and glanced back at him. "And that is?"

He smiled down at her, an expression of bleak, bitter resignation burning in his eyes. "Each other."

Chapter Twenty-One

"He'll be here soon, you know."

Eislin shifted restlessly atop the massive gray charger Morloch rode, a small tremor of anticipation rippling through her at the words he whispered so close to her ear. Fearfully, her glance scanned the trees that surrounded the small glen. Eerily glowing eyes, low, guttural mutterings, and the minute rustling of underbrush all assured her they weren't alone. Morloch had summoned his hideous underlings to wait nearby.

To wait for Aidan . . . just as she was forced to do.

Anger surged through her. Eislin turned to meet Morloch's gaze. "Haven't you done enough to him? He's your son. Set him free once and for all. Allow him a chance at happiness!"

"Happiness?" Morloch's even, white teeth

gleamed in the moonlight. "And who's to say that I *don't* offer him happiness? He can't make an informed decision until he knows all choices, can he? I but offer Aidan that—something you never cared to do."

"He already knows the evil of demon-led magic!" Eislin turned away, her mouth twisting in disgust. "You have effectively pointed it out, time and again, in your unrelenting cruelty to Anacreon."

" 'Twas no less than you and your kingdom deserved!" the necromancer snarled. He grasped her chin and jaw in one hand and jerked her head back around to face him. "You made your choice years ago, when you picked that weakling over me. *You* are responsible for his death, as well as for what has become of me."

"Am I now? So, you would have forsaken your magic then?"

His amber glance met hers. "Nay, I know now I wouldn't have, but at least I'd not have had to turn to the Demon to possess your body before you wed. To possess what was rightfully mine."

"No one is worth the selling of your soul, Morloch," Eislin replied softly. "Not for wealth, not for power, and certainly not for me."

Anguish flared in his eyes. "You don't understand; you never have! You never loved me, either!"

"I wanted to mean more to you than your magic. You wouldn't let me." Her gaze lowered. " 'Twas always you, Morloch, though I ultimately wed another. Why do you think I cherished Aidan as much as I did, knowing

426

he was no offspring of my lawfully wedded
husband? Why do you think I strove so hard
to help him overcome his Evil Eye when he
was young, to protect him from your vengeful
curse? Why do you think—"

Eislin paused to inhale a shuddering breath.
" 'Twas because I never stopped loving you,
though I knew our love could never be. All
these years I tried to understand, to forgive
you, and then y-you killed Marus. . . ." She
lifted her eyes, a resolute light gleaming there.
"I swear to you, Morloch. If you harm our son
this night, or fail to set him free of you, you
will have destroyed whatever hope there ever
was for your immortal soul."

"Will I now?" Morloch chuckled grimly. "And
what is that to me? I ceased to care about that
long ago."

She flinched, swallowed hard, and stared up
at him. "So be it then. And Aidan? What of
your son?"

"He has always been a means to an end.
I've always twisted his life to suit my needs,
to achieve the ultimate revenge—total power."

"How?" Eislin demanded hoarsely. "Why?"

Morloch shrugged. "The Demon has need of
him. Who am I to question his desires?"

"You inhuman devil!" she choked. "To sell
your own son—"

"Enough." He silenced her with a hand over
her mouth. "You prattle on like any other
female. I made the correct decision all those
years ago. 'Twould have never worked between
us." His head lifted and he searched the night.
"Aidan draws near even now."

The necromancer motioned to one of his vile creatures. He lumbered over, hulking, hairy, with a pair of tiny eyes that gleamed in the darkness and a set of lethally sharp fangs. Morloch handed Eislin down to him.

"Take the queen and hold her tightly," he commanded his henchman. "I've a far more important task to attend to. A task long overdue and not to be thwarted again."

He smiled. "The Demon grows impatient for his newest servant."

They rode hard, the army following close behind, out of the castle, across the wooden drawbridge, and down the mountain to the farmlands. Aidan led the way, his night vision guiding them even as his magic traced the trail of Morloch and the queen.

He would have considered Morloch's conventional mode of travel on horseback strange, Aidan thought as they galloped along, if he wasn't convinced his father meant to bring their battle to a final and decisive head. The realization that this would be the last time they'd meet sent a spasm of fear spiraling through him. He was riding to his doom, a fate he knew would someday be his, but no longer considered inevitable or desirable—not since he'd met and come to love Breanne.

With a superhuman effort, Aidan shoved the thought aside. There was no time left for doubts as to the wisdom or folly of his action. He must be decisive, clearheaded, and coldly calculating. 'Twas the only way. The way of battle.

Aidan glanced over at Breanne as the road

widened and she pulled up to ride beside him. Behind him the clang of weapons and clink of chain mail melded with the squeak of leather horse trappings and pounding of hooves. What were her thoughts as the moment of confrontation grew near? She looked unperturbed, her dainty little chin jutting out mayhap a bit more than usual, but her features were smooth, unfurrowed.

Despair filled him. Breanne's trust in him, like that of the men who followed them, was implicit. Because of that, she had no doubt as to the outcome. He, it seemed, was the only one who doubted . . . feared.

Let me be worthy of her, Aidan prayed, as he guided Lucifer down the road that would skirt Breanne's village. *Let me not fail her.*

I never thought I'd hear you say that about anyone, much less a woman, Lucifer said, his thoughts rising out of the darkness.

I'm not in the mood for your gibes this night, Lucifer, Aidan mentally snapped back. *I need your support, not ridicule.*

And have I not always been there when you needed me?

Guilt flooded Aidan. *Aye, that you have. I am but a little short of temper and patience, considering . . .*

Considering the battle to come? his horse supplied. *'Tis understandable. You always get this way.*

But 'tis far worse tonight. Tonight I fight a necromancer.

Aye, and you risk everything you've come to cherish—and love.

429

Aidan paused, taken aback at his mount's blunt insight. Then he smiled. *Aye, that I do.*

Then what is the problem? Will not a man fight all the harder to defend what is his?

Aye.

Which brings me back to my original statement. I never thought you'd say or feel that way about anyone, much less a woman.

Breanne isn't an ordinary woman, is she?

Lucifer snorted and tossed his head. *Nay, my friend, she isn't.*

Aidan opened his mouth to reply, when a sense of danger struck him. He tensed.

The necromancer is near, his horse silently observed.

Aye, as are his minions. Aidan slowed Lucifer to a trot, signaling for Breanne and the soldiers to do the same.

"What is it, Aidan?" she asked. "Is . . . is it Morloch?"

He reined to a halt. "Aye. And he's not alone."

"Eislin is with him?"

"Aye, but also a legion of undead creatures, hiding in the woods before them."

Breanne smiled. "Not the sign of a man confident of his powers."

He shot her a quick glance, a grudging respect gleaming in his eyes. "An astute observation, lass. We'll make a warrior of you yet."

Aidan withdrew his sword and glanced over his shoulder at his captain of the guard. "Light the torches."

In silent, preordained accord, torchlight flared and spread down the line. The flickering flames lit the faces of the men in stark relief. Shadows played about tightly clamped mouths, apprehensively darting eyes, and tautly strung bodies.

They were all afraid, Aidan well knew, but the grim resolve burning in their eyes heartened him nonetheless. They fought for home and land. They fought for him.

For him.

In a breath-grabbing rush of insight, Aidan finally saw true basis for Breanne's confidence in him. He possessed the same power, the same potential to be as lethal, as evil as his father. All that had ever stood between him and the dark side of his soul had been the strength of his will. And yet not once had he purposely chosen to use his fearsome abilities for a wicked cause. Breanne had seen that in him from the beginning, that the powers he possessed and feared for their potential for harm were the same powers to do good. All it had ever required was a conscious decision and the courage to abide by it.

That was the difference, and would always be, between him and his father. He had made the choice to use his abilities for the good of all. And would die before ever placing the seductive pull of magic above the call of his heart. Joy surged through Aidan, as wild, exultant, and liberating as the long-sought self-knowledge.

He was free at last, no matter what Morloch tried to or succeeded in doing to him. Free, to be his own man, choose his own path, and seek out the happiness he deserved as equally as anyone. Free, and 'twas all because of Breanne.

Breanne.

Aidan turned to her. "I ask you one last time. Leave Morloch to me. Go to the back of the army where you'll be safe. To ride beside me will only put you in the thick of the battle—and worse, when and if we reach the necromancer."

She returned his gaze, a fierce determination blazing in her eyes. "And you knew my answer before you even spoke the words. I am with you to the end, whatever that may be."

His mouth lifted in a soft, tender smile. " 'Tis as I suspected. Draw your sword then, and follow me."

With that, Aidan gave a harsh battle cry and urged Lucifer out. The big black war-horse sprang forward, his great hooves throwing clods of earth into the air as he thundered down the road. The soldiers, three hundred strong, echoed their prince's battle cry and followed, surging behind in a deafening clamor of hoofbeats and clanging weaponry. Toward the forest they rode, piercing its deep, dark depths to meet the hordes of unearthly beings.

Shrieks mingled with screams, cries of pain with raw shouts, as steel clashed against steel. Lunging horses and flashing swords fought for dominance in the morass of struggling bodies. Breanne was encompassed by the sheer numbers and overwhelming noise and scents and jostling forms, uncertain as to who was friend and who foe. If not for Aidan and Lucifer before her to guide them through the chaos, she knew she'd have been lost from the start.

But, miraculously, they passed through the attack unscathed and rode on, leaving the fighting behind. Their followers would have to deal with Morloch's creatures as best they could. They had a far more horrible opponent awaiting them ahead.

The sounds of battle gradually muted, until the softly blowing wind covered them completely. The woods thinned, fading into a small glen of gently undulating grass. Across one corner of the open area a stream coursed by, the tumult of water splashing over earth and stone the only sound to pierce the ominously heavy silence. Moonlight gently sheened the land.

'Twas the same as any other summer's night, Aidan thought. Save that this piece of land might be his final battlefield, this eve the last moment of his life. He glanced around. Recognition stirred, a bitter irony at the location filling him. 'Twas the same glen where he'd slain Rangor in, those many years ago.

He had used his powers for the first time then to kill. It seemed only fitting that he do so here again. Here he would fight the last battle and put to rest his terrible curse.

The necromancer awaits in yon trees, Lucifer said, indicating the spot with a toss of his head.

Does he now? Aidan thought grimly. *Then we must go forth to meet him.*

They reached the middle of the glen before Morloch stepped from the trees, dragging Eislin with him. Moonlight glinted off his face, casting bone and shadowed sockets into stark, skeletal relief.

Aidan dismounted. Breanne followed suit. Together, they met and strode over to stand before Morloch and the queen. For a long, tension-laden moment, no one spoke.

Magic rose, surrounding the necromancer in a shimmering aura, then arced across to Aidan. He blocked it before the enchantment could reach him, flinging it back to his father. Again, Morloch tried. Again Aidan repelled it.

A startled respect gleamed in the necromancer's eyes. "Untutored as you are, your powers grow stronger each day. Do you have any concept of how high you could rise if you'd but allow me to teach you?"

"And for what end?" Aidan snarled. "To become a soul-rotted fiend, a man who now stoops to endangering the life of the woman he once loved?" He shook his head in bitter negation. "Nay, *Father*. I'd rather die than ever be that kind of man. The greatest of magic is for naught, if it buys only power, and that at the expense of others."

"Yet you will bow to me, one way or another." Morloch's mouth curled in an evil travesty of a smile. "You'll accede to my desires in this, or your mother will die."

Aidan smiled. "If you'd truly wished to kill her, you'd have been wise to have done so before I arrived. 'Tis too late for that now. Your magic is strong, mayhap stronger than mine, but you can't kill her as long as I live."

Anger flared in the necromancer's eyes. "Can't I now?"

His son shrugged. "Try it, then, if you dare. But the moment you lower your guard against me to turn your powers on the queen, I'll take you on your weak side."

"You'd sacrifice Eislin to have a chance at me?"

"Aye." Aidan's eyes, eyes that burned with a fierce, resolute fire, locked with his. "Am I not your son?"

Morloch nodded his approbation. "Aye, that you are. And, because of it, my victory over you will be all the sweeter." With a disparaging motion, he flung Eislin aside.

Breanne immediately ran to the queen and helped her stand. Morloch spared them both a fleeting, contemptuous glance. "The women mean naught to me. Neither of them is of any value, save what pleasure you and I found between their legs. I will make you see that very soon."

With that, the necromancer gathered his powers and flung the first of his most lethal weapons at his son. An aura of fear, stark, breath-grabbing, and heart-stopping, encompassed Aidan. A black, stinking morass engulfed him. He couldn't see. He couldn't breathe. He couldn't even think as a shrieking cacophony howled in his skull.

Aidan gave a strangled cry, grabbed at his head, and sank to his knees. For an instant he was totally overcome, immersed in the horror, helpless, confused. Then reason returned. 'Twas naught but an illusion.

He summoned all his strength and fought past it, clawing his way up through the sticky, soul-sucking terror. His mind cleared. His gaze refocused, back to a moonlit glen and the man who stood before him.

"You bore that well," Morloch observed approvingly. "Your will is strong. But even a man's will can be bent to another's, if the coercion is right." He held up a small wooden doll, dressed like Aidan, inscribed with runic symbols and Aidan's name. "I will turn you to me, whether you wish it or not."

A flame appeared in his other hand. "You will obey me. You will relinquish your heart and mind to me," Morloch intoned as he held the doll over the flame. "There is no other choice."

Excrutiating pain engulfed Aidan. As he watched the doll go up in a red-gold ball of fire, he felt his whole body burn as well. He felt his will slip away, flow out of him with each fiery lick of the flames. Suddenly, he had no ability to resist Morloch's demands.

By the Holy Ones, but the necromancer was too powerful for him! He must find some way to defend himself or 'twould soon be too late. Too late . . . for himself . . . for Breanne and his mother . . . for them all.

Anger. That was all he had left. Anger would strengthen him, would fuel his will to resist long enough to summon his own powers. It had worked well enough before.

Yet a small voice warned that 'twas a dangerous power to use against the necromancer. A power that could easily be turned against him. For a fleeting moment, Aidan quailed before the decision. And, for a fleeting moment, the barely contained emotion surged past the fragile barriers of reason and restraint. Surged past and totally consumed him.

Then his anger cooled, hardened into a grim resolve. Whether he ultimately succumbed to Morloch's greater powers or not, never again would he let his emotions gain control.

Aidan leaned back, then shoved to his feet before the stunned necromancer. "I'll not let you control me, not through fear or anger," he rasped. "You are done, finished."

"Am I now?" Morloch snarled. "And you're a fool to believe that!"

A bolt of light shot from the hand he pointed at Aidan. Aidan parried it with a quick, psychic shield, but the strength of the necromancer's power was now incredibly strong. He realized, with a sickening inkling of what was to come, that Morloch had restrained himself before, using his earlier attacks to lull Aidan into a false sense of security, to goad and anger, but not harm. But now the assaults were vicious and death-dealing.

Over and over, the necromancer flung one killing spell, then another at him. Aidan repulsed them repeatedly, but each one weakened him. Soon, Morloch's magic was making inroads, slicing and slashing at him, sending torturous jolts of pain spiraling through his body.

Aidan fell, knocked to the ground by a particularly brutal assault. He rolled, struggled to his knees, then was struck again. His head jerked back, his body arched in a spasm of overstimulated muscles, his mouth opened in soundless agony.

Again and again Morloch attacked, until his son convulsed helplessly before him. And Breanne watched, her heart ripped asunder with each vicious onslaught. Watched and could do nothing. Nothing.

Breanne. Child.

Through the chaotic tumult of horror and frustration, Breanne heard Caerlin's voice.

Come, child. Aidan has won his battle. 'Tis now time to win mine.

She turned to where Baldor's sword lay. The soulstone glowed brightly in its hilt, calling to her. Breanne ran over and grabbed up the sword. *What must I do? Tell me, though it demands even the sacrifice of my life.*

Hold the sword tightly, Caerlin commanded, his voice growing louder, stronger. *Channel all your strength, all your love for Aidan into me. 'Tis his only hope!*

"Aye," she whispered. " 'Twill be as you ask."

With that, Breanne willed everything she possessed into the mage. Baldor's sword, the sword Aidan cherished and revered, grew warm, then hot, until it threatened to set her hands afire. She ignored the pain. It didn't matter. All that mattered was Aidan, and that he lived.

Suddenly, light exploded around her. The sword was torn from her grasp, arcing through the air. Arcing, tumbling, sailing straight toward Morloch.

He saw it too late; the movement of his arm, upraised to deflect the weapon, was far too slow and ineffectual. The sword shot past, its tip plunging deep into the necromancer's heart. With a shriek of rage, Morloch staggered back from Aidan, his hands clawing at the sword.

A blinding aura of light engulfed him. As it grew in power and intensity, his screams rose in an excrutiating crescendo. Then, with one last, earsplitting shriek, he and the sword were gone.

For a stunned moment Breanne stood there, her mind struggling frantically to fathom the significance of what had occurred. Morloch, Caerlin, the sword of Baldor. All gone . . . forever. Caerlin, with the last bit of strength left him, had killed Morloch and sent him back to his evil master. 'Twas over at last.

A low groan pierced the haze surrounding her. Aidan. Breanne turned back to the man who had become her whole life, a man who needed her, who now lay in a twisted, agonized heap on the ground. With a small cry, she ran to him.

"So, you are not only my sister-in-law but my long-lost cousin as well," Dragan chuckled, as he sat between Breanne and Sirilla in the palace gardens. "I should have known that a lass of your spirit had royal blood in her veins."

Breanne arched an amused brow. "Indeed? And what first led you to that conclusion? My rescue of Aidan, or my defiance of you?"

Sirilla laughed at the look of discomfiture that passed across her husband's face. "Aye, Dragan. Pray, share the answer with both Breanne and me."

" 'Twas a mixture of many things," he mumbled, shame flushing his cheeks. "And the less said about my past misadventures, the better."

"Ah, husband," Sirilla chided, patting his hand. "You are forgiven, but must learn to accept a bit of good-natured teasing nonetheless."

He shot her an appraising look. "Aye, that I must. It just comes strangely from you, my gentle, submissive little wife."

"But gentle and submissive no more, Dragan," Breanne interjected, an impish light glinting in her striking blue eyes. "We have all changed."

"Aye," Dragan muttered glumly, "and I'd wager I've you to thank for the bulk of Sirilla's 'changing', haven't I?"

"And if you have, what of it, brother?"

At the sound of Aidan's deep voice, all turned. He'd made his approach from around the garden's water fountain and the merry spill of water, splashing down into the large stone basin, had covered the sound of his footsteps.

He stood before them now, a proud, dark warrior, and Breanne's heart swelled with pride. Though he still wore black tunic, breeches, and boots, his amber gaze, now permanently free of his eye patch, was relaxed and mildly amused. His black, unruly hair, curling onto his high, intelligent forehead and tumbling down the back of his neck, was unrestrained by the severe warrior's topknot. To Breanne's thinking, in shedding the topknot and eye patch, Aidan had shed at least 15 years of his life and looked once more the lad he must have been that fateful day that had irretrievably changed everything.

Yet, though so much was indeed irretrievable, so much more still lay ahead. So much, she thought in dreamy contentment, her hand sliding down to rest upon her belly. And their babe was but the first of many surprises that lay in store for her proud, dark husband.

Dragan rose, drawing Breanne's attention from Aidan. "I owe your lady much, including Sirilla's awakening into a woman of spirit in her own right. I wasn't complaining, I assure you, brother. Nay, far from it."

"Good," Aidan said. "I'd dearly wish for you and Breanne to become friends."

Dragan laughed. "That's a far easier task than being the lady's husband, I'd wager. I only hope you're man enough for her."

Breanne pulled Aidan down to sit beside her. "He's certainly been so far. I can only hope, with further training, he'll improve even more."

Aidan shot her a skeptical look. "Indeed? We'll just have to see who trains whom, won't we, lass?"

"Aye, m'lord." Her lashes lowered in demure obeisance.

"Ah, I see how 'tis to be now!" Dragan cried. He rose, and offered Sirilla his hand. "Come, m'lady. I sense our presence is no longer desired here."

Breanne made a motion of protest, but Sirilla quickly silenced her. "Nay, Bree. Dragan speaks true. You two need some time together." She graced her husband with a sly smile. "As do we, for I find the idea of this training very intriguing."

She began to lead her husband out of the garden. "Very intriguing indeed."

Breanne and Aidan watched until the couple disappeared into the keep, then turned to each other. "Well, lady," Aidan then inquired. "What have you to say for yourself? You border perilously close to disrespect for the soon-to-be crowned king of Anacreon."

A joyful surprise flared in her eyes. " 'Tis decided then? Your mother will abdicate in your favor?"

"Aye, on the morrow. Now that her firstborn has returned for good . . ."

Breanne smiled. "So, you've made your decision, then. I am happy for you."

He lifted a hand to stroke a flawlessly feminine cheek. "You'll be queen soon as well. How do you feel about that?"

She considered his question briefly. " 'Tis an awesome responsibility. As awesome as the thought of becoming a mother." She lowered her gaze to some imaginary wrinkle in her gown and carefully smoothed it away. "But at least I'll have adequate time to adjust to that. A good eight months or more, at any rate."

Dead silence settled between them. Breanne awaited Aidan's reaction with bated breath. Finally, he spoke.

"What are you saying, lass? Have I somehow managed to get you with child?"

She lifted her eyes. "Aye, m'lord. That you have."

He frowned. "If I recall, I stated most emphatically that I didn't want—"

A slender finger urged him to silence. "And does not a king need heirs, m'lord?"

"Aye," Aidan admitted slowly, speaking a-round her finger. "But the spawn of the Demon Prince . . ." He inhaled a ragged breath. "I'd not want any child of mine to suffer what I did."

"And what would our child suffer? His father

the king, the son of the man who saved Anacreon from the evil clutches of Morloch and—"

"And what if our child is a daughter instead?" Aidan demanded. "What then?"

"'Twouldn't matter what 'twas. Any child would be fortunate to have a father such as you."

Aidan turned more fully to face her, then pulled Breanne into his arms. "Nay, lass. 'Tis I who'd be the fortunate one. To have a wife such as you, and a family . . ." He sighed. "You have saved me, heart and body and soul. I love you, Breanne, so much so that I fear I'll keep you busy for a long time to come, producing heirs for the kingdom."

She hugged him tightly to her. "Aye, m'lord. But in between time, shouldn't we see to the commencement of your training? I mean, you *are* a very pigheaded man, and I anticipate the lessons will go very slowly. . . ."

He gave a great shout of laughter. "Do you now?" Aidan stood and, pulling Breanne to her feet, swept her up into his arms. "Do you indeed? And I thought you had great hopes for me?"

"Oh, I do, m'lord. But a wild demon like you will require even extra effort." She leaned up and kissed him full upon the lips. "But then, I've never been afraid of demons—have I, m'lord?"

Dear Reader,

I hope you enjoyed *Demon Prince*. It was a very special book for me. Although it was first conceived all the way back in 1986, *Demon Prince* didn't find a home until 1991. Still, just as I always had faith in my futuristic romances, I truly believed in this book as well. Sometimes, there's just something special about a certain story. . . .

My next Love Spell venture will be a futuristic short story in the *Enchanted Crossings* anthology, due for release in September 1994. "The Last Gatekeeper" is the tale of Thorn Marwyn and Karin de Cedrus. Karin is the last Orcadian capable of opening the interplanetary gates between her planet and Voltaran, the home of the fabled beastslayers. When Orcades is beset once again by a fearsome monster that wreaks death and destruction, Karin is called upon to seek out one of the beastslayers and bring him back. But the last beastslayer to kill one of the monsters has died, and his son Thorn has no intention of carrying on his father's proud, if highly risky, vocation.

Possessing mental ability that compel others to follow her wishes, Karin has no choice but to force Thorn through the gates and back to Orcades. Thorn, needless to say, is not happy with his new place of residence or his new mission, but he cannot return to Voltaran without Karin's help. Even as Karin battles her guilt over the forcible abduction of the handsome off-worlder and her confusion over her growing attraction to him, the monster's vicious rampage worsens, setting both her and Thorn on a course that only courage and love can ever hope to traverse.

I truly enjoy hearing from my readers about any and all of my books. Feel free to write me anytime at P.O. Box 62365, Colorado Springs, CO 80962. For a reply and excerpted flyer of my next release, please include a self-addressed, long or legal-sized envelope. In the meanwhile—happy reading!

Kathleen Morgan

HISTORICAL ROMANCE
BITTERSWEET PROMISES
By Trana Mae Simmons

Cody Garret likes everything in its place: his horse in its stable, his six-gun in its holster, his money in the bank. But the rugged cowpoke's life is turned head over heels when a robbery throws Shanna Van Alystyne into his arms. With a spirit as fiery as the blazing sun, and a temper to match, Shanna is the most downright thrilling woman ever to set foot in Liberty, Missouri. No matter what it takes, Cody will besiege Shanna's hesitant heart and claim her heavenly love.

_51934-8 $4.99 US/$5.99 CAN

CONTEMPORARY ROMANCE
SNOWBOUND WEEKEND/GAMBLER'S LOVE
By Amii Lorin

In *Snowbound Weekend,* romance is the last thing on Jennifer Lengle's mind when she sets off for a ski trip. But trapped by a blizzard in a roadside inn, Jen finds herself drawn to sophisticated Adam Banner, with his seductive words and his outrageous promises...promises that can be broken as easily as her innocent heart.

And in *Gambler's Love,* Vichy Sweigart's heart soars when she meets handsome Ben Larkin in Atlantic City. But Ben is a gambler, and Vichy knows from experience that such a man can hurt her badly. She is willing to risk everything she has for love, but the odds are high—and her heart is at stake.

_51935-6   (two unforgettable romances in one volume) Only $4.99

TIMESWEPT ROMANCE
TEARS OF FIRE
By Nelle McFather

Swept into the tumultuous life and times of her ancestor Deirdre O'Shea, Fable relives a night of sweet ecstasy with Andre Devereux, never guessing that their delicious passion will have the power to cross the ages. Caught between swirling visions of a distant desire and a troubled reality filled with betrayal, Fable seeks the answers that will set her free—answers that can only be found in the tender embrace of two men who live a century apart.

_51932-1 $4.99 US/$5.99 CAN

FUTURISTIC ROMANCE
ASCENT TO THE STARS
By Christine Michels

For Trace, the assignment should be simple. Any Thadonian warrior can take a helpless female to safety in exchange for valuable information against his diabolical enemies. But as fiery as a supernova, as radiant as a sun, Coventry Pearce is no mere woman. Even as he races across the galaxy to save his doomed world, Trace battles to deny a burning desire that will take him to the heavens and beyond.

_51933-X $4.99 US/$5.99 CAN

TIMESWEPT ROMANCE

TIME OF THE ROSE
By Bonita Clifton

When the silver-haired cowboy brings Madison Calloway to his run-down ranch, she thinks for sure he is senile. Certain he'll bring harm to himself, Madison follows the man into a thunderstorm and back to the wild days of his youth in the Old West.

The dread of all his enemies and the desire of all the ladies, Colton Chase does not stand a chance against the spunky beauty who has tracked him through time. And after one passion-drenched night, Colt is ready to surrender his heart to the most tempting spitfire anywhere in time.

_51922-4 $4.99 US/$5.99 CAN

A FUTURISTIC ROMANCE

AWAKENINGS
By Saranne Dawson

Fearless and bold, Justan rules his domain with an iron hand, but nothing short of the Dammai's magic will bring his warring people peace. He claims he needs Rozlynd—a bewitching beauty and the last of the Dammai—for her sorcery alone, yet inside him stirs an unexpected yearning to savor the temptress's charms, to sample her sweet innocence. And as her silken spell ensnares him, Justan battles to vanquish a power whose like he has never encountered—the power of Rozlynd's love.

_51921-6 $4.99 US/$5.99 CAN